This is an Advance Reading Copy

Dear Reader/Reviewer,

We appreciate you taking the time to read this advance copy of *Mortal Weather* and give us your feedback or an honest review.

Please respect the author's intellectual property and do not sell this copy. It is an uncorrected galley, so please do not quote for publication until you check your copy against the finished book.

Also, please do us a considerable favor and once the book is available for sale, write a review on Amazon, Goodreads, or your preferred bookseller's website. You have the power to influence others to share your journey through the books you read. In fact, most readers pick their next book because of a review or on the advice of a friend. So, please share!

Please follow the author and publisher on social media and sign up for updates so you know when *Mortal Weather* will be available.

Thanks again for spending your valuable time with the colorful characters of *Mortal Weather*.

Author

www.kpmccarthy18.com
18kpmc@gmail.com
facebook.com/KPMcMW/
instagram.com/mortalweatherguy/
kpmccarthy.substack.com

Publisher

topreadspublishing.com
teri@topreadspublishing.com
fb @topreadspublishing
ig @topreadspublishing

MORTAL WEATHER

a novel

KP McCARTHY

TOP READS PUBLISHING, LLC

VISTA, CALIFORNIA

ISBN: 978-1-970107-37-1 (hardcover)
ISBN: 978-1-970107-36-4 (paperback)
ISBN: 978-1-970107-48-8 (ebook)

Library of Congress Control Number: 2023907997

Mortal Weather is published by: Top Reads Publishing, LLC, USA

For information about special discounts for bulk purchases, please direct emails to: publisher@topreadspublishing.com

Cover design, interior illustrations: Katarina Prenda
Book layout and typography: Teri Rider & Associates

Printed in the United States of America

For Patricia Elizabeth Porter McCarthy

Enough Sky

Not getting enough sky now that
it's pindrop dusk and Venus
flirts with a slabby moon

Spalls of silver flush livid —
I cannot flank desire
and all this reaching

for what must be, this needing
to cultivate the verge,
always it must be

as lewd as breathing, must be
looking for this and finding that
shadow, you must be

not getting enough light for
jade pockets of faith,
volunteers for tenderness

closeted to compensate
the urge; so still I
saw you kneeling

for poppies that burst
though the sidewalk, urging
tangerine starward,

pausing as we do in
vesper half-light, waiting
for more, knowing

only else, abiding shyly to
be known and not heard, still
ever and not ever

brawling as we do
in trajectory, arcing
for the cobalt edge

Not getting enough mauve, you
there by the view, seeking
gauze to pull away, find

only me watching, warmly
embracing else, when
it is enough sky

just then, enough answering
glances in deep focus
for mortal weather

Foreword

To my mind, the best moments in reading come when a reader sees facets of their own behaviour, which they thought unique to them, represented on the page, helping them view their own lives and the world anew. This is what Kevin Patrick McCarthy achieves in *Mortal Weather* —an emotionally honest, boldly rendered, and often hilarious novel that left me feeling fundamentally changed.

Tolkien said that "not all those who wander are lost," and while this aphorism has come to feel a little trite, it's perfectly fitting for the hero of McCarthy's novel—the story of a complicated individual coming to terms with catastrophic events, while trying to find a place for himself in a changing world. A character "bracketed by wonder," Stanhope Ellis is a protagonist to cherish as he shambles through what has come to be an unfulfilling existence, learning to live alone following the death of his wife, Eva.

McCarthy writes in an aphoristic style, managing to find truth and meaning, page after page, in the seemingly mundane. As the narrative progresses, Stan is also saddled with another, more astonishing dilemma—a superpower that completely upends the bland comfort of his former existence, and forces him to confront mortality itself. McCarthy, a writer capable of surprising readers out of their own complacency, explores this element with characteristic empathy and humor, putting us in Stan's shoes as he probes the parameters of this extraordinary endowment.

The author refuses to let "Stan the unmanned" drift—he might not quite know what he's looking for, or how to find it (who among us does?), but that doesn't mean he closes himself off from new experiences, or gives up on real happiness. McCarthy, a born storyteller, captures this journey in a confident, effortlessly funny way. He is a skillful conjurer of memorable, cinematic images that stay in the reader's mind long after the final page is turned.

Eventually, Stan is "tractor-beamed" into a new relationship with a nurse, Gayathri, which changes his perspective on life and love, and speaks to his willingness to take lessons wherever he can find them. These lessons might come from his travels, his fellow man, or Greek and Hindu mythology, but all help shape his consciousness in a way that propels him through a satisfying emotional journey. Without being in any way didactic, McCarthy—with a musician's ear for rhythmic, stylish prose—teaches us to see things through a different lens, and as a contemporary writer his insights into the inherent complexity (and absurdity!) of the human condition are nonpareil.

We might all do well to emulate Stanhope's ultimately exhilarating approach to life, even if we don't possess the superpower with which he has been mysteriously gifted. After what has been an abjectly miserable few years, it is a genuine pleasure to immerse oneself in the expansive, prismatic world of *Mortal Weather*. I hope you find yourself as thoroughly transported as I was. Though its protagonists undoubtedly wander—and wonder—they are anything but lost.

Dominic Wakeford
Margate, Kent, UK
August 2022

Preface

I'VE WRITTEN SOME USEFUL THINGS OVER THE LAST 30 YEARS, BUT HERE, at long last, is a story that might make a difference in the world. Its genesis is compelling. Early in this perplexing century, I wrote a critique of modern storytelling that suggested a way through artistic chaos:

> *Each of us is a story without an ending. Collectively we are a story without an ending. But we can start living as if we have some idea where we want to go and as if we are capable of getting there. Of the stories we use to suggest possibilities, true mythology is the organic archetype for living as if in the boldest way. It assumes a future and provides a framework of healing symbols. Heroic stories— beyond ego, beyond motionless yearning—fuel the quantum leaps required of our culture and species. Hopeful, imaginative myths rise above grotesque posturing to explore exhilarating and familiar new landscapes. They set us dreaming the dreams of all that may be, and we can't get enough of that.*

Many years later, *Mortal Weather* emerged, organically. I trusted the process, despite myriad distractions. Only after many drafts did I realize that I had unconsciously followed my own storytelling advice. The novel might be criticized in various ways—mostly for being unexpected, I suppose—but it would be hard to make the case that it is not hopeful and imaginative. However it is received, I am pleased with that result.

Because I was experimenting with style and stalking a big theme, the novel required many rewrites. The work overlapped long-planned travels, so I have fond memories of jotting notes and typing all over the world—at the Duns Castle gatehouse in Scotland, in the Vaxholm, Sweden Library (occasionally interrupted by shrieking towheads), on Majorca after touring the home of Robert Graves, while listening to roaring lions in South Africa, on our boat in Marlborough Sounds, Aotearoa (and in the excellent Picton Library), and on the beaches of Hawaii and the Cook Islands. My laptop is beat to hell, with sticky keys and a peeling screen gasket. I think a bug just crawled across the *inside* of the screen. But the experiences were epic. The people and places Tricia and I met thoroughly reshaped the story—and our pilgrim souls, as Yeats would say. Along the way, I never hesitated to tell the tale to anyone interested. It always kindled a light in the eyes of the listener, and that kept me going.

This is a different sort of novel. The large theme required poetic perspective. The mortal premise required a story of stories. I want to say that Mortal Weather is comprised of small stories that interlock as the minerals in granite interlock. But it's messier than that. Some stories could not be fully integrated without contrivance. These testify to the intrinsic value of story.

Every day, we exchange stories, vignettes, and tableaus on the fly, with beings we hardly know. For, within the elemental parameters of evolution, we know each other well. With its focus on story in all its forms, *Mortal Weather* is stuffed with characters. The Character Guide on the following pages will help you manage who's who.

Three characters were fashioned from living people. Keiko the dog walker's story of being struck dumb I received nearly verbatim from a dog walker in Boulder, Colorado. I used it when I realized that few would probably hear or share my modest friend's tale. Like Keiko, she is smiley and spiritual, with flowing hair. The Spuds were largely drawn from two neighbor boys who often dropped by with their huge, boisterous hound, who also left her mark on the novel. The mayhem was energizing. In writing this, I realize that the scene in which the brothers help their mother operate a treadle sewing machine came from a couple of other bright boys in the same neighborhood, years earlier. Bless them all.

The story predates the coronavirus, which clocked in one year after the first draft. Adding its weighty set of complications to a complete story seemed like rolling bowling balls onto a trampoline: an interesting effect that renders the apparatus useless. Other changes naturally occurred during the rewrites. The main one is that the replica of the brig *Pilgrim*, upon which Richard Henry Dana sailed, sank in its slip at Dana Point in March 2020. It's still afloat in this story.

The seed of *Mortal Weather*—Sadie by the sea, telling a wanderer of her cottage burning down—came to me in a dream. As the story grew, well-meaning colleagues called Sadie a trope. Well, I wasn't about to trick out my charming provocateur. Stories and dreams are full of tropes. Others suggested that a hands-on guy like Stanhope Ellis is inherently less interesting than, say, an Ivy League professor. I disagree. If you have not met a hardworking lunch-bucket toter who is inquisitive, largely self-educated, and seeking spiritual expansion, then you'd best crawl out from under your rock. I've also been told that a relatively vanilla person like me cannot or should not try to convey the points of view of diverse characters. Again, I disagree. Our differences pale in comparison with all that makes us human. Imagination, dreaming the dreams of all that may be, binds us together.

Kevin Patrick McCarthy
Aitutaki, Cook Islands
2 December 2021

Character Guide

Admiral Spencer	A flinty veteran in Dana Point (DP). AKA Spence.
Anshu Das	Stanhope's friend and neighbor in Park Hill (Denver). Eva's guru. Gayathri's brother.
Arwen Ellis	Stanhope's sister in Maine. Daughter of Justin. Younger sister of Elanor.
Astra	Border collie with a comet blaze–a new friend of Stanhope and Gaya's.
Bard	Eldest son of Halle. Brother of Randy. Age 8. AKA Spud.
Ben Morris	San Diego Police detective.
Beth Morris	Ben Morris's deceased wife. Professor of Philosophy.
Bianca	White tiger at Parnassus Wildlife Sanctuary.
Billy Mills	Street tough that Ben Morris once knew.
Bix	Window washer. History buff. Runner. Community college student. AKA Zen Obama.
Brian	Owner of Brian's Window Wizards. USC fan. AKA Iron Man.
Bus Bredda	Rasta who rides buses with Stanhope.
Caprice	Mark's English Lab. Playmate of Kevin. AKA Dharma Dog.
Captain Carrot	Natural food grocer in Ocean Beach (OB). Also an imaginary character to Stan and the Spuds. Also Stan's nickname for Pigeon.
Champion	Stanhope's 1951 Studebaker Champion Starlight Coupe. AKA the Studie, bullet nose.
Chanda	Lioness at the Colorado Wildlife Sanctuary.
Chet	Shelvador. Guitarist. Vocalist. Friend and roommate of Cub Crosley.
Chuck Duran	Stanhope's work partner in Colorado. Husband of Kitty. Father of Donna.
Cinder	Sadie's Scottish terrier.
Clayton	Dennis and Irene Murphy's brother. Founder of the Apostles of Calvary.

Connie	Owner of the Pilgrim Grill in Dana Point (DP). Girlfriend of Cub Crosley. Guardian of Kevin. AKA Connemara.
Cub Crosley	Leader of Cub Crosley and the Shelvadors. Fiddler. Vocalist. Boyfriend of Connie. Son of Jake.
Dariana	Gemma and Tom's adult granddaughter.
Della	Sadie's daughter-in-law. Mother of Theo. Owner of the Jazz Café. Girl-friend of Howard.
Dennis Murphy	Aging athlete with failing kidneys. Sportsman. Partner of Pigeon.
Donna Duran	Deaf young woman obsessed with classic literature and animals. Daughter of Chuck and Kitty.
Dr. Bronner	(Fact, not fiction.) Legendary soap maker who covered his products with altruistic slogans and philosophy. The family company still makes the eco-friendly soap and uses the same historic packaging, donating much of the profit to charities.
Drow	Window washer. Weightlifter. USC fan. AKA Batman.
Duncan	Flame-haired sailing instructor in Dana Point (DP). Boyfriend of Skye.
Elanor	Stanhope Ellis's older sister in Maine. Daughter of Justin. Older sister of Arwen.
Emily Gray	Bristol shipping engineer. Sister of Harvey Gray.
Erin	Bix's globe-trotting girlfriend. Waitress.
Eva Ellis	Stanhope's former wife. Curator. Florist and chocolatier. Voice of Yota.
Eva	Waitress at the Jazz Café.
Fred and Ginger	Donkeys at the Parnassus Wildlife Sanctuary.
Gayathri Das	Sister of Anshu Das. Nurse at Blessings Hospital. AKA Gaya.
Gemma	Old friend of Sadie. Widow of Tom. Guardian of Pax. AKA Gremma Gemma.
Greta	Tiger at the Parnassus Wildlife Sanctuary.
Grindel	Female wolf at the Colorado Wildlife Sanctuary.
Haley	A veteran keeper at the Colorado Wildlife Sanctuary.

Halle	Stanhope's Ocean Beach (OB) neighbor. Mother of Bard and Randy. Employee and friend of Rick. AKA Viking.
Harold	Beaver. Drinking buddy of Jake Crosley.
Harvey Gray	Expressionist artist. Gayathri's patient. Brother of Emily Gray.
Hazel	Black bear at the Parnassus Wildlife Sanctuary.
Hector	Young mountain lion at the Parnassus Wildlife Sanctuary.
Henry	Previous owner of Stanhope's Champion.
Howard	Jack-of-all-trades. Boyfriend of Della.
Irene Murphy	Dennis's sister. On disability. Fundamentalist Christian. Guardian of Lester.
Jack	Jack Kerouac (usually). Jack London (rarely). Jack-of-all-trades.
Jackie	Executive. Friend of Dennis and Pigeon.
Jake Crosley	Cub's father. Handyman-ranger. Drinking buddy of Harold.
Jill Simmons	Retired schoolteacher in Stanhope's Park Hill neighborhood (Denver). Guardian of Molly.
Juniper	Tom's ailing hound, back in the day. Friend of Gemma.
Jupiter	Grizzly at the Parnassus Wildlife Sanctuary.
Justin Ellis	Stanhope's father in Maine. Retired forester and professor. Father of Elanor and Arwen. Widower. AKA Pop, Poppy, Popcorn.
Katy Sue	Dennis's high school girlfriend. Also his boat.
Keiko	Dog walker in San Diego.
Kevin	Connie's Rhodesian ridgeback. Playmate of Caprice.
Kitty Duran	Generous baker. Wife of Chuck. Mother of Donna.
Lester	Irene's Weimaraner. Playmate of Popeye.
Mahir	Gayathri's first love in Kolkata. Spice merchant. Son of Saan.
Mark	Volunteer at San Capistrano Mission. Surfer. Guardian of Caprice.
Mo	Georgia blues man in the early 1940s. Sadie's crush.

Molly	Jill's smiley collie in Stanhope's Park Hill (Denver) neighborhood. AKA Molly the collie.
Nichols	San Diego Police detective.
Nick	Stan's geologist bandmate back in the day.
Nina	Window washer. AKA Wonder Woman, Woman, den mother.
Pax	Retired greyhound. Couch potato. Friend of Gemma.
Pigeon	Produce manager at Captain Carrot. Runner. Partner of Dennis. AKA Pidge, Walter Collins, Captain Carrot.
Popeye	Dennis and Pigeon's cat. Playmate of Lester.
Randy	Youngest son of Halle. Brother of Bard. Age 6. AKA Spud, Ran, Captain Carrot.
Rafer Morris	Autistic college football player (safety). Son of Ben Morris.
Rick	Halle's friend and employer. AKA Unsulky Achilles.
Roger	An alcohol intervention psychologist.
Ruby Watson	Former bandmate of Stanhope's (Ruby Raven). Vocalist. Ruby went on to fame with an all-female band, Ruby Rocket.
Saan	Spice merchant in Kolkata. Father of Mahir.
Sadie Colter	Blues musician. Retired coffee factory worker. Once smitten with Mo. Guardian of Cinder. Old friend of Gemma. Mother-in-law of Della. Grandmother of Theo.
Sam	Black bear at the Colorado Wildlife Sanctuary.
Shelvadors	Cub Crosley's band (Cub Crosley and the Shelvadors). Chet, Taz, and Wendy.
Shiva	A principal Hindu diety—known as the destroyer in the Hindu Trinity.
Silk Crosley	Cub Crosley's young adult daughter.
Sir Walter Raleigh	Pipe tobacco favored by Justin and Stanhope Ellis. Sometimes referred to as a person.
Skitch	Ball-obsessed golden retriever in Stanhope's Park Hill (Denver) neighborhood.

Skye	Duncan's girlfriend with short, dark hair. Seamstress and sailor.
Spence	See Admiral Spencer.
Spuds	The Ocean Beach (OB) Elementary Spuds, especially Bard and Randy.
Stanhope Ellis	Window washer. Widower (Eva). AKA Stan, Sir Stanhope, Hoppy, Stevie, Death Man, the Boy Wonder.
Studie	Stanhope's 1951 Studebaker Champion Starlight Coupe. AKA Champion, bullet-nose.
Taz	Shelvador. Drummer. Vocalist.
Theo	Sadie's grandson. Della's son. Athlete. Musician. Animal advocate.
Thor	Male wolf at the wildlife sanctuary in Colorado.
Tom	Gemma's late husband. Guardian of Juniper.
Trudy	Teenage Stanhope's collie mutt in Maine.
Usher	Stanhope and Halle's Ocean Beach (OB) landlord.
Walter Collins	See Pigeon.
Wendy	Shelvador. Keyboardist. Bassist. Vocalist. Old girlfriend of Cub.
Yama	Hindu God of Death.
Yota	Stanhope's old pickup in Colorado. Voice supplied by Eva.
Zan	Associate of Anshu's (Citizen Jewelry). Athlete.

THE WORLD WHISPERS
(FALL, WINTER)

YES. I'M SIXTEEN FEET UP ON THE SCISSOR LIFT. THE HAZE IS THICK FROM fires in Utah, though it is October, and dawn. Even the snowy peaks of the Front Range, tipped with rose, are dull in the mirrored skyscrapers of Denver. The dark translucence unfastens my mind, which reminds me of Shiva, the destroyer, which reminds me of Eva. I stand, like some rookie, on a toolbox to reach a brush I'd left on a ledge, but I'm so into Eva and her quality and her absence that I forget I'm on this box, forget I'm not clipped in. I step back to take in the wall, and nothing is there. A power line catches me, but it snaps and spews blinding light across my thigh. The charge blows my hat off, and I'm out before my smoking back hits the asphalt. I can't see, but smell and hear everything: my smoldering overalls, rasping shouts, Chuck's burrito breath. The danceable absurdities pouring out of his phone. Dad's pipe-smoke safety. Eva's chiming laugh. Her rose bouquet.

Illumination. The transformations of sound to color, to klaxons of red, to matter-of-factness of death, form a pulsing release. Blue life peels and skitters red. No more Eva. No more breathing and touching and knowing. Fine. I don't want to breathe and touch and know. The merge, the unbeing, goes on, and I luxuriate in nothingness. I'd never realized the triumph of not having to care. I will not care again. I ride uncaring into rose fragrance and song.

Whoa there, big fella. Smoke and roses loop me back to the beginning. Why? Chuck wants his partner back: Stan the Man, who slathers tall mirrors. And Eva wants me doing. She was a strong swimmer. Her long strokes in the pool are pulling me home. Vision returns, but something is wrong. It takes me a sweet eternity to figure it out: this is not eye vision. I watch a crumpled Stan far below, as if I'm a puppeteer returning for this abandoned marionette. Where have I been? This guy has more story in him. Is he up for it?

Eye vision returns gradually, annoyingly. I want the other vision. I want Eva's eyes. She wore glasses. Built dioramas. Died on an ordinary Wednesday. A sad man asleep at the wheel and two lives gone. Something to do with overwork. Her glasses, her telescopes, shattered.

❈ ❈ ❈

Eva stands in the sea of rosebushes she crammed into our postage-stamp yard. Closes her eyes and breathes deep. "All these ego-tripping trivia tests! I want to know what I *don't* know. Impossible, I guess. It's too big. Immeasurable."

"Hey, space telescopes are out there measuring the whole universe."

She laughs and bends to her pruning. "That's what I need. A pocket Hubble. Maybe Hubble sunglasses. I always want to know what's beyond—what's left to do, you know? The future calculation, not the rearview."

I'm on shovel duty. I should defend Beloved History, so I bounce a clod off her earnest ass. "I like the rearview. But I get it. The expansion, rather than the bang."

Eva beams at me as if just realizing how useful her garden gnome can be. "Well, you can't have one without the other."

A space telescope actually looks deep into the past. I realize that now.

It sees the expansion *and* the bang. Our future calculations turn on what has ever been. Possibilities require absolutes.

No diamond for Eva. She wanted a star sapphire ring: gold rays embedded in deep blue. From Thailand. It wasn't expensive, and she didn't show it around. She said it helped her focus. It matched the sky and sun of our outdoor wedding in Estes Park—a crystal Colorado day when Long's Peak crowded the altar: Best Mountain.

She had insisted we live in Park Hill, near Denver's City Park. So we found an old bungalow with room, barely, for roses. Walked to the park and museum every day. Some of the dioramas at the natural history museum date back a century or more. Most museums are replacing them with virtual-reality whiz-bang, but Denver preserves them: arctic wolves watching caribou, polar bears on ice, grizzlies on tundra, sandhill cranes in prairie grasses. Wolverines, pronghorns, geese. A Jabba-the-Hutt elephant seal. Eva took classes on sprucing up the old classics. Said she saw the future in them. I didn't get it.

Two years ago, my wife was a florist who longed to be a curator: one who selects, organizes, presents. But she was already doing that— choosing roses for fragrance, books for power, friends for gratitude. Every window or display or diorama she worked on seemed more hopeful afterward. More an expression of what *should* be.

After the glasses shattered, I kept dreaming that Eva was building a diorama of our lives together: we're deep in the garden, between the pinwheels she had sown, huffing the sweetness like college kids bonging their brains out. I'm all about her, but Eva is turned outward from two steps up a ladder, peering through her thick Hubble glasses at the twilight horizon. A raven watches from the blooms. A black dog runs into the yard behind us. Swallows dart overhead. The Eva piecing the diorama together is ten times our size. The crystal glasses she wears are shattered, but she is precise. Then I see through fractured glass what both Evas are watching—a knowing something in the distance. A chestnut foal trying to stand.

✳ ✳ ✳

We breathe from bloom to bloom. Eva pauses to deadhead. The air is smoky, but she takes comfort in Hindu mythology. "The three aspects of Krishna are Brahma, the creator; Vishnu, the maintainer; and Shiva, the destroyer."

"What a show-off."

"I think Shiva is the spirit of our age."

"You still want to try for a kid?"

"Yup."

"You want to bring new life into a world of destruction."

She smiles tolerantly and disappears into the bushes. "Shiva clears the way for Brahma. Maybe a creative Brahma time is on the way."

"She says from her rose-colored world."

She laughs, but stays hidden. "Shiva is a big deal! He-she also creates. Seeing the creation is key."

It all seemed dicey to me, but I've read enough history to know that things are always dicey. In the end, it didn't influence our decision. Nothing could have stopped us from trying for a child. We were full of creative impulse—until Shiva destroyed. Now every loss, every car accident, every smoky day during fire season reminds me of Shiva. I understand that creation comes out of destruction, can be part of destruction, but, you know—it's hard to spot. Sometimes I'm too small to try.

✳ ✳ ✳

Christmas is coming, but there's no comfort or joy. It's stupidly hot. The back of my head is still sore from the concussion. The docs look at me like I'm a freak, but don't say much. I'm sure I died on the asphalt that October dawn, but can't talk about it, and no one asks. Who needs that can of worms? Sometimes the secret keeps me going. I'm afraid to give it away.

The current left a source wound in the thigh and a ground wound in the shoulder. Electrocution is like being microwaved: you're cooked from the inside out. The flesh burns are tricky but treatable. The internal kabob is harder to deal with—organ damage, mostly. My heart fibrillated, but they teased it back into rhythm the first day. Alkalizing my urine somehow helps the kidneys mend. I drink strange concoctions, to no effect that I can tell—just endless trips to the small room.

Chuck and Kitty Duran bring a basket of holiday nonsense to my hospital room. I mime gratitude. After Eva died, these two had harassed me daily—tromping across the porch with casseroles, coffee table books, and assorted football crapola. Big smiles and bad jokes—then and now.

I have the attention span of a puppy. Try to read but cannot care. All the old interests are gone. History died with Eva. Even the Greeks lost their allure. The blot in the personal story made the species story reek. I'd always been fascinated with origins, with causes and effects, but suddenly it all seemed pointless. Why had I bothered? Human history amounts to a litany of ambitious thugs clawing their way to the top and ruining everything for everybody. Once in a blue moon, a Buddha-like creature breaks through, and we have a little evolutionary burst. But the in-betweening kills the soul.

I have this idea that those who die early feel it coming. It shows up in their work and moods. Amy Winehouse, for instance—the casual references to death, the annoyance at being in the crosshairs, the waves of depression. Eva fought the foreshadowing blues by scanning for dogs. If you're feeling thin, find a familiar mutt and allow yourself to be thoroughly greeted. You'll know your place in the world. So we'd walk the neighborhood, looking for connection. Skitch, a big golden, always carried a tennis ball. Molly, a collie mix, stuck with her person, a retired schoolteacher. But if Molly saw Eva and me, she'd run half a block to leap and sing. After the glasses shattered, my solo act was less popular. Molly's gallop devolved to a saunter as she scanned the street. At least she kept up the collie smile, as if apologizing. Skitch still showed me his ball but always saved it for Eva. *Where is she?* These mugs provided comfort, but the searching was contagious.

I never understood why Eva wouldn't keep a dog. It must have been the mortal knowing—a subconscious unwillingness to leave another relationship unfinished. A child would have been something else: an evolving expression of what we were together. Consolation for Shiva.

January. Anshu Das drops by my hospital room on a too-warm day, looking dapper in butter yellow with his salt-and-pepper beard and ready smile. He lives down the street, near the park, in a compact Edwardian place with a carriage house converted to a one-car garage. In the cool garage, he keeps two things pristine: a red Vespa, which he rides to work eight months of the year, and an AWD Union-Jack Mini Cooper. "I always want to know I can escape." Eva and I would talk with him in his driveway. I usually bailed early, but Eva always stayed to sop up Anshu's stories from the *Gita* and Hindu mythology.

Anshu owns Citizen Jewelers on Capitol Hill. Our first conversation, years ago, was about Eva's sapphire, which he had scored for us. "A seed truth," he said, turning to me. "Precious." He told us he admires the gold on the Capitol dome as he Vespas and Minis to work. We learned that his appreciation has a broader scope. He sees all that is precious. "Bijou" is how he describes his cottage, which is artfully framed within a manicured garden. Anshu lives in a world of setting, luster, chroma. You can see it in his walk, in the way he swings a cricket bat.

Today he looks thinner, radiant. He asks personal questions, but I can't say much. I tell him about the toolbox dive, then run out of things to say. He ascribes my escapade to dharma. "Eva's universal answer," I say as if I know enough about it to call anyone's bluff. He beams and says the word isn't entirely translatable, but he thinks it means something like "duty that sustains cosmic order, that makes all possible." I can't dismiss this because his *Bhagavad Gita* had saved me two years ago. He had been so attentive after Eva died that I gave him her too-thick *Gita*. It was far more commentary than source, and I hadn't seen the point. But Anshu promptly returned with a simple version of the sacred text. Small. Not scary. Not so much swami 'splaining. So I finally read it, as Eva had always wanted. Tried to honor it, for her. *Set thy heart upon thy work.*

Anshu carries a worn cricket bag—the keeper of relics. When I ask about it, he ignores me and points to the ragged horizon framed in the hospital window. "Do you see Mount Evans? Once I climbed a ridge up there and peeped over the top. I was face-to-face with a mountain goat! A magnificent old billy with big shoulders, one foot away. I froze. So did he. But I was ready to retreat. He was not. He just stared at me, saying, 'Give way, or I will butt you all the way back to Kolkata.' I gave way. The strength in those black eyes!"

His eyes are black and shining. "I've hiked about half the Continental Divide Trail. The highest part. I climbed the fourteeners until they were overrun with tourists. Then I climbed unnamed mountains, which have no registries to sign. The best thing I have found is to be a nameless man on a nameless mountain!"

"Do you always hike alone?"

He collapses into a chair. "Sometimes my sister, Gayathri, comes up from San Diego."

"What's the next adventure?"

He kneels and organizes the cricket bag until I stop expecting a reply. He smiles up at me. "I have been thinking about moving to San Diego. Gayathri is a nurse at Blessings Hospital, and sometimes she has several days off at a time. I've had a glorious mountain life. If I am permitted, I will have a glorious ocean life. I might learn to sail. I can see Gaya and me skimming along the coast through sunlight and sea spray. I dreamt of it. Precious!"

He smiles into the middle distance. "*Gaya* is precious; the most adaptable person I know. You can see her changing her mind—changing the course of her whole life—as she receives new information. When she was nine, she fell from a banyan and broke her right arm, which was dominant. She would not rest until she could do everything left-handed. Even her penmanship became fluid. When her arm healed, she would not go back. Then she learned to write Hindi for our grandmother. She's ..."

"Protean."

"That sounds impressive."

I wave a weary arm. "Proteus was a shape-shifter. He could tell the future but would rather escape—change into a lion or boar—than spill prophecy. Finding and holding him was the trick."

"That sounds like Gaya."

Anshu stands and stretches. I wish he'd leave so I can get after the Sandman, but he needs to talk. "Darwin said that it's not the strongest or most intelligent who will survive, but those who can best manage change. Adaptation is a kind of superpower, I think."

I only have energy for nodding. Anshu laughs childishly. "Gayathri is every day, all the time, adapting. She is a protean ideal, my friend!"

Beaming like the sun, framed against Mount Evans and a spotless sky, Anshu looks *through* me. I want to give everything to those eyes. He waits patiently for me to form the words. "I—*died*."

The eyes give everything back. "Yes. I know."

"Anshu, what the *fuck*? Why am I here? Where am I going?"

My face throbs. Anshu represses a laugh. "There is only one reliable kind of prophecy, Stanhope: the self-fulfilling kind. Who do you *think* you are? That's you. The world whispers, so *listen*. Imagine the dharma that approaches and prepare a welcome."

His charity unclenches my heart. A nurse stops at the open door and stares. He glances at her sheepishly. She's not amused. "Anshu Das?"

He laughs as he makes for the door. "They have my cricket bat downstairs."

"You tried to bring a cricket bat into a hospital?"

"That is a story for next time. The healing of Stanhope Ellis must proceed apace!"

I'm presented with an aluminum cane, with which I lurch through bustling halls. I drift for days, dreaming of sea spray, keeping an eye out for Anshu. But he never returns. Instead, Chuck appears on a grey afternoon, looking eager in a pumpkin-orange Broncos cap with blue trim. He fumbles with the bed controls. Cranks me vertical. Wonders about the fried Stanhope Ellis. The replacement stiff is squirrelly, he says. Will his anchor, the straight man, the unclipped-in, toolbox-diving rook, rejoin the circus?

UpChuck has been a patient, skyward partner. We've worked hard, scrubbing hot, wobbling landscapes. For two years, the flexing, tweaking labor, the prospects, the jokey work talk kept me going. On big jobs, we'd plant our feet wide and wave long, water-fed poles in slo-mo, like raggedy-ass Kabuki warriors. I razzed Chuck relentlessly about his Broncos gear. "Chuckles!" I'd shout, poling sloppy lather. He would lean into whatever I called him, vamping and drenching my bib overalls. We lived for afternoon breezes off the foothills.

After the glasses shattered, I couldn't face the book and flower shop. It had been a comfort, but now it was the opposite—a pit of memory so deep that I could only go there to die. I considered that. But I was chickenshit in the end. Once I started staying away, I couldn't stop. All the time Eva and I had logged there now repelled me. The teamwork was everything. I couldn't be worthy by myself. Good people wanted to lease the space, but my heart wasn't in it. I sold the building and stock for a song, as is, to the good people. Then I needed work—not distraction, but immersion. I stashed Eva's sapphire in my bibs and took the window-washing job Chuck dangled. Bless Chuck for that. He pulled me up-up-up. Every day.

Evenings and weekends, I'd walk the neighborhood, fix up the house, binge on *Star Trek*. Eva was a serious Trekker. *Voyager* was her favorite. She loved the idea of being distantly flung across the galaxy and working her way home. Always the future, even when pretzeled, and home. The thought of her back-trekking fueled long to-do lists. I remodeled compulsively, remembering every detail of her arm-waving plans. No additions, just upgrades of existing space. All the things she wanted. As if a new bathroom or granite countertop would tractor-beam Eva back to me. I finished the basement, replaced the floors, installed efficient windows. Set toilets, tiled walls, hung doors. But I couldn't face the rose garden. Refused to learn what Eva knew. Needed to leave that hole in my understanding so she'd come back to fill it. I hired a kid to water, and the bushes grew wild until a few of Eva's friends quietly trespassed, restoring order. But as all was completed, the property became more echo than substance. It was all for Eva. Too flanged out for me. Too empty.

Anshu's father died just before Eva. Then, a few months later, his mom. So we haunted the park and museum, talking about death and life. I stopped myself from asking about reincarnation. It would have sounded hollow, as if I was grasping at straws—which I was. But Anshu understood. He smiled and said beautiful things about the rhythm of time. It was pure poetry. I was so shell-shocked that I retained nothing of it, but I'll never forget how it made me feel. It was as comforting as a rose bouquet.

Chuck waits expectantly at my bedside. Am I up for more up-up-up? I can feel Anshu's idea of cosmic duty inflating into a life preserver. Meaning is everywhere implied in Eva's rose dharma. Okay. I survived for a reason. *Set thy heart upon thy work.* What work? I don't know what, but I know where. The white peaks are majestic, but dulling, flattened by dark translucence. I've been lost—no, found—in Anshu's sailing dream. The song is there.

I tell my partner that I can't wait for Strike Three. "I'll try the coast." He grabs my shoulders and slams my bullet head into his chest. This surprises us both, and we blink a lot. A week later, he brings a realtor by. A month later, he helps me pack.

- II -

Perfect Strangers
(Spring)

Eva had killed the mortgage—by dying. A sucker bet. With the improvements, our dressy pillbox finances a good launch. It's March: a blustery, unpredictable month in Denver. We'll be clobbered by a wet snowstorm any minute. On closing day, I walk to the park, stopping at Anshu's cottage. Bijou, as ever, but no signs of life. At home, I finally manage to walk through the place without looking for something. Eva's pinwheels draw me to the garden, where bulbs bulge hopefully. Skitch's bark reminds me to move on.

The flight to the coast aches. Hope for hope trickles in, but still no sleeping. Fucking Sandman. Here comes the nightmare shadow. Leaping is a good dream.

"You come too."

Eva runs along a sandstone ledge, then turns back, peering warily from beneath a purple cap. A fall hike in slick-rock country, and she's

11

tentative. She saw something she didn't understand—or something she understands too well. She rarely uses those three words together, and I remember each instance. They're code for *help!* Words for me only. Words she knows I can't refuse.

San Diego is warm and blooming. I find a cheesy studio near Dog Beach and eat chips. Everything tastes like nothing. Strip-mall neon buzzes listlessly: art-echo flashbacks of falling. My apartment is full of weird odds and ends: a cat clock with shifty, tick-tock eyes, a blue toaster, four Elvis bobblehead dolls (*Theng yew. Theng yew, vurrah much*). The place smells like the alley behind a fast-food restaurant, which reminds me of long-ago gigs with the band. We spent a lot of time hauling gear through stinking alleyways. But it was worth it for the precious *listening*—to song stories and getting-laid stories and drunken stories of poverty and regret. Stories were shelter.

I pore over the *Gita* for comfort. For Eva. *We are kept from a goal not by obstacles, but by a clear path to a lesser goal.* Okay, what the fuck is my greater goal? What is my story? What is my work? I'm freaked about climbing again, about hanging my ass on a monolith. Vertigo is too easy a word for this box I live in. I pass days and weeks without looking up. I remember several times trying to make a dog look to the sky. That's hard to do. It's not something that occurs to them. That's me: downward dog.

I'm not interactive, but the prompts are here. The pups at Dog Beach cavort ecstatically—picking up partners in crime and tearing across adjacent Ocean Beach, where they're not supposed to be. The funky Ocean Beach—OB—neighborhood is a world of its own, with a good library and other old-fashioned comforts.

Fucking Sandman. I ditch the cane and stalk the beaches at night. Blackness and breezes and rushing tides. Smells like salty sex, but futureless. The scars throb. I speak to no one, thinking I might go on in silence, as Maya Angelou did for a time. This either forges her beautiful soul or insanity. Suddenly, for me, I know it will be the latter: Stan the raggedy-ass kabuki, chittering in the sad cafeteria of the sad home for workless fucks.

Sometimes I thread through downtown as far as Sunset Cliffs. There, pelicans form in squadrons of up to a dozen. Over the ocean, they look like Spitfires on patrol. As they circle back along the cliffs, you catch the head-back nonchalance. Piece of cake. No one can out-cool them.

I'm out early tonight. The cliffs look high enough. *You come too.* I pick up the pace. But, no. Anshu's eyes say no. Eva's long strokes say no. I'm here for work. So I slow and scan for opportunities to engage, to elude being warehoused. A bony woman on a bench watches the sun flatten, her white curls streaming landward. Her polished mahogany skin is creased around the mouth and eyes. Lurching up a sandstone slab, stopping at a respectful distance, I speak to the sea. "I'm a child here."

She pulls a worn, pink robe tight and smiles, blinking in the breeze. "I'm out here 'most every night."

"Yeah. Me too."

"I've seen you—marching, marching. The drum major."

I resist the urge to scoot. Her smile penetrates, but I can't face it. Make a lame drum-major move with an imaginary baton.

"Can't sleep, huh?"

"How'd you know?"

Her laugh is an ancient bell. "You really should look in a mirror once in a while. One sorry drum major."

I smooth stubby side hair, as if this makes a difference. My feet are amazingly filthy, and my pants are shredded. I check the fly. The stubble on my face flutters as I turn into the breeze. "Nice robe."

She delights in her tatters. "I'm an old woman. You're too young to stop caring."

"Wanna bet?"

She locks onto me like moonlight. "Yes, I do. I'll bet your life."

"Penny ante. How about yours?"

She shakes her head and waves me over. "You come here."

As I approach, stupidly grateful, she turns and gestures to a hodgepodge of manors on the hillside. "See that little cottage up there, tucked between the big houses?"

I gape. Did I let the stink out? What shirt is this? Did I brush my teeth? I have no idea. She wags a long finger. "It's pink."

"Oh, yeah. I see it."

"Well, it burned down a while back."

"Two years ago."

"How'd you know?"

I know because that's when the Hubble glasses shattered. I know because this woman is nothing like Eva, but Eva is here. This woman has to do with my work. But I need a short answer. "Have you looked in a mirror lately?"

"You've been saving that up. Couldn't wait to get me back."

"Yeah."

"One time when I was a toddler, my mother pulled me out of a sandbox. 'Oh, Sadie!' she says. 'You're a mess.' So I look at her and say, 'You don't look so hot *yourself!*'"

Her joy is a refuge. "So, you and me, that's what we'll say to get some back from each other. We'll say, 'You don't look so hot yourself.'"

"Perfecto. I'm Stanhope, Sadie."

Here comes a sickle moon. She cocks her head at it. "I don't know. I think you lost the hope. You're Stan, until I say different."

"You don't look so hot *yourself.*"

"You should've seen me fifty years ago, *Stan.*"

"Uncle!"

She unfurls the finger again. "You better say uncle, 'cause I will *teach* you."

"Yes, ma'am."

She purses her lips. "That pink bungalow burned like a Roman candle. Into the night. The wiring, I guess. Burned right to the ground."

Sadie stands and wraps the robe tighter. "Anyway, I wasn't there. My little dog and I came home to a smoking mess. To a bunch of sad firemen cleaning up. Those guys were as sorry as I was."

She sits again and I join her on the bench, leaving a stink buffer.

She smiles. "My little Scottie's name was Cinder, do you believe it? Just because she was black. Now I had a cinder house!"

She leans back, cackling. Turns to me with motherly regard. Turns outward again, addressing the sea. "I had it rebuilt just the same."

"But it hasn't been the same."

The moonlight gaze. "How'd you know?"

"You're out here every night, Sadie. Like me."

She nods thoughtfully. "Yeah. It hasn't been the same. Especially since Cinder died in October. I never put much stock in material things. Or so I thought. But I lost some trifles in that fire that I mourn to this day. A box of pictures. A sweet old dobro."

Sadie peers into the past. "I did find the metal resonator. Hm. When I think of the *blues* that *oozed* outta *there!*"

We track the final parade review of pelicans. Sadie speaks as if in a trance. "Dobro means 'goodness' in Slovak. A friend told me that when he gave it to me. He said he would teach me how to play it. I couldn't wait for him to come home from the war and keep his promise. I had some goodness for *him!*"

"Did you love him?"

"I was just fourteen when he left. But I made honey in my heart just the same. He had soft eyes. Could he make that old guitar sing? Slow Georgia blues. Syncopated, like Willie McTell. But he was a baritone and played slower than we were used to. He was never afraid to slow down. We called him Mo, for his voice like molasses. I fell in love with Mo. Now, I don't mean that he was improper with a young teenager. But she thought of being improper with *him!* I thought I might eat him up. He was kind. I think he meant the dobro as a substitute for a man, which I was *not* ready for—I was ready for something, though. I didn't know what. I imagined my life would be some kind of screwball comedy, with adventure and music. *Lots* of music."

She gives me a sheepish smile. "You better get along before I bore you to death."

No chance. I tune out selling or preaching or complaining, but I'll listen to a good story for as long as it takes. If I'm home when a repair guy comes, I know all about the wife, kids, and dog before he leaves. Sometimes it makes my day. Sometimes it makes the repair guy's day. Or the wife's day. Or the kid's. Or the dog's. Will I find a use for this listening need? "I'm not going anywhere, Sadie."

She looks at me uncertainly and starts again, reading the sky. "We girls would sneak into those smoky jazz clubs on Decatur Street in Atlanta and dance to Count Basie or the barrelhouse blues. At first, we'd just dance with other girls. We must've looked like a bunch of scrawny chickens, we were so small and scared. If a man tried to dance with us, we'd just run. That was too much. We were afraid of our own bodies, you know?"

Sadie leans back, self-consciously. She's no longer age and defiance, but youth, vulnerability. Eagerness. "I wanted to stick to the screwball script, just runnin' and laughin' with my gaggle. My friend Gemma used to say, 'If I'm somebody's fuss, that's *all* I'll be.' We still wanted to *be* heroes, not marry them. I wanted to be Jesse Owens. Douglas Fairbanks in a sweet dress. If a man started touching me, I wouldn't want it to stop, and then all the fun would be over.

"It all changed with Mo. I wanted to be *his* fuss. He would come in late to the Gatto and sit in an old back room that smelled like a stable. Folks would shuffle back there to mellow before going home. My friends started talking about this bluesman with a voice like a dream, but I never could stay up late to see him. Finally, I snuck out when my parents were at a wedding. I was thinking about weddings and wedding nights when I put on my sister's coral dress and ran with Gemma down to the Gatto. We snuck into the back room without looking at anybody."

Sadie stands and steps toward the cliff. I realize now her robe is coral. I see the richness of her young limbs. The girl plunges her hands deep into embroidered pockets and beams back at me. She must be ninety-five. "It was one of those warm Georgia evenings when every fragrance and color is alive. The reek of sweat and leather in that old backroom gave us goosebumps. The whiskey smelled clean and sweet. The blue overalls of the sharecroppers looked royal, you know?"

I know. I miss my bibs. Sadie pulls up her robe collar, conferring a fragile majesty. "I couldn't think how I might look. Couldn't stand the thought of anyone's eyes on me. That coral dress burned. I *wanted* it to burn."

The robe ripples in the moonlight. "Anyone could see we were trouble. We were too young. But they let us stay. Gemma was pretty in blue, even scared half to death. Her crooked smile could melt your heart a block away. She would tear up when she was nervous, and that would make her blink. So there she was, batting her eyes nineteen to the dozen, looking down so no one would take it the wrong way. I just wanted to bundle her up and rock her to sleep. Oh, I love my Gemma dear!"

The Pacific is a starlit immensity. I track the lithe form as if watching a play. If I move, Sadie might end her story. She looks hard and soft in the breeze—angular and sweeping, like a hood ornament for a frumpy, celestial chariot. Suddenly, she's shy. "I don't know why I'm going on like this to a perfect stranger."

"Because of the strange perfection."

She snorts. "Oh, listen to you."

But we think about it. There's something in my smart-ass comeback. Something in the idea that every stranger carries the possibility of perfection as a story receptacle: no negotiation, no ego. Just a vessel arriving empty, right on time, and leaving fully loaded. That's me: Supertanker Stan. I make myself still, unwilling to break the spell, and slip into a reverie of story time with my parents. Children are perfect little strangers, after all. Mom was the best loader of stories. She had taken acting classes and used a dozen different voices. Dad was a monotone. Every character had his husky voice. But I didn't mind because he always checked in with me, asking how I liked this or that. It was like talking to the characters as I pulled them into my dreams. I wish I could tell Sadie all this. But it's nothing to do with me. I'm the vessel. "It's a good story, Sadie."

She looks askance. It's a pity how unaccustomed people are to being heard. Running fingers through rebellious hair, she speaks softly. "Mo walks in, holding that shiny guitar by the neck. White shirt, red bandana. A beautiful, real man. Sits on a stool, plinks and plunks and *winks* at me! The dress was good for that, I guess. He starts in on McTell's 'Death Room Blues' like he has all night to play it."

Sadie swings her hips and shuffles in ragged corduroy slippers, singing the song: a haunting meditation on bedding down with tombstones, cold earth, and moonlight. I'm watching an old woman sing a death song on a cliff under a cradle moon, and it's wondrous. Chilling. The world whispers, and I listen. Sadie turns, shoves her hands in the pockets, and speaks outward again. "Gemma and me—we'd never thought about big things like that. That smelly back room turned soft and bright, like we were in a painting or something. We needed to hold and *be* held. Men were starting to notice."

She faces me again. "We made it through another song, then the owner—a big, soft Creole—came for us. She took Gemma and me behind the bar to a little coal door, hugged us, and shoved us through. We crawled out to an empty alley. The breezes were delicious after that smoky room. We chattered all the way home, feeling womanly. Victorious."

She studies a slipper. "I jumped at every chance to see Mo, with or without Gemma. Stopped wearing church clothes, though. It just embarrassed me to do that, and my sister wouldn't loan me her dresses anyway. Now I didn't have to be pretty; I could just be curious. So I asked about his guitar. I'd never heard anything like those clean, wandering tones. It sounded like what the soul wanted to say. Like heaven built out of pain."

She hums an eerie progression. "We sat close, and he taught me the twelve-bar blues. Showed me how to bend a note. How to tell a sad story. I can still smell the tobacco in his clothes. His voice was the most reassuring sound I'd ever heard."

"Did you get to be his fuss?"

Sadie grabs the lapels of her robe and bends forward, confiding. "I did get him to kiss me. Just because I wore that flamingo-colored dress again, and he was off to war."

"Sweet."

She sits and sighs. "You know, it was *very* sweet. Mo said, 'I shouldn't have kissed you, Sadie. You're just a child. But I'm glad I did.'"

We hold the rest note. I stand and bow, but it doesn't seem enough, so I kneel. She extends a playful hand, which I kiss. She touches my brow. We disengage carefully, amazed, unsure of the barter but feeling a limitless verity. I'm a historian. Is this history? Tonight, Sadie was the Greek triple-goddess: maiden, mother, crone. A crone reliving maidenhood and mothering me along the way. She takes a few proud steps homeward, then turns and waves theatrically, as a child.

I quickstep home, thinking I'll take one of the green pills that makes me sleep on and off for days. Instead, I grab chips and beer and sit at the wobbly kitchen table with a pad and pencil. Sadie remade the world with her story. I have to do something with it. It pours through my pencil: maiden, mother, crone. A diorama takes shape—Sadie, an endangered species, dancing in Pacific starlight. A smudge of a man in the foreground, listening. I don't know if it's the trek, or Sadie, or the beer, or history, but I forget the pill, fall into bed, and sleep like a mountain. Like I haven't slept since the toolbox dive. No—since Eva.

WONDER LOOKS UPON YOU
(SPRING)

OBSESSIVE DOORBELLING PULLS ME OUT OF DREAMLESS BLISS. MUST BE children. Yup, Bard and Randy from next door: eight and six. Bard is a brainiac angel, a broadcaster of fun facts to know and tell. Randy is a micro Pale Rider, defined by his stubborn jaw. We talk every day, but it looks like they're ready for more. For one thing, their purple towel-capes must be admired. "A dartboard!" crows Bard, peering into my threadbare living room. Randy smirks at my boxers and tee. I wave them in while I grab a robe.

Randy points to my thigh scar, just above the knee. "What's that?"

"It's a source wound."

"What's that?"

"It's where an electrical current went in."

"Whoa! Did it hurt?"

"I don't know. I wasn't there."

"What?"

"Never mind. Yeah, it still hurts sometimes. And guess what?"

"What?"

"I have another one. A ground—or exit—wound. Where the current came out."

I kneel and show them. They probe and squeeze my shoulder until I yell. Bard hops around. "Oh! Did you get superpowers?"

It's not possible to answer that question in the negative. "Damn betcha."

They flourish the capes. "What are they?"

Must play for time. "Umm. There are three."

Randy sticks his chin out and blocks my way. I bend forward, wave Sadie's no-bullshit finger. "My farts smell like cherry blossoms."

The boys giggle and goof. Bard does most of the talking.

"Whaaat?"

"You smell cherry blossoms, it's me."

"That's not a superpower!"

"Can you do it? Do you know anyone else who can do it?"

Wheels spin in their little heads. "What are the others?"

What will I say next? "The second superpower is that I can fly anywhere."

The wheels tach out. "The third superpower is that I can travel in time."

"Let's see!"

"To fly or travel in time, I have to clear my mind and focus. So I sit quiet and pretend I'm a precious stone, like a diamond or a sapphire."

"Whaaat?"

"Yeah. Things never work like you think they should. Remember that."

"Whaaat?"

"Don't you have school?"

"Teachers' meeting."

Randy's a counterpuncher. "Don't you have a job?"

"Not just now, no."

Wrong answer. I'll be seeing a lot more of Bard and Randy. They fly with their capes across the room to the dartboard. I try to think of something to say that doesn't sound like "you could put an eye out." Slide a worn coffee table around and make them stand behind it as they launch darts. Then step stools are necessary.

"Where do you go to school?"

"OB Elementary."

Randy shoots a look of pride over his shoulder. "We're the Spuds."

"Solid. The OB Elementary Spuds."

My place is a new rec center for the Spuds. They love the cat clock's shifty eyes, but darts are the main attraction. Sure enough, Randy can't stay behind the coffee table. A dart ricochets and stabs his bare foot. He yipes and stands still for a brave minute, fighting tears. "If anyone cries, we have to go home," Bard explains.

"Good rule."

I whip up a cure-all: cinnamon toast with real butter on brown bread from Captain Carrot, the local grocer. This sends us into prancing ecstasies. Then they're all over the apartment, demanding the history of everything, treating junk as treasure. I'd forgotten about boys in cahoots. I have to gulp coffee to keep up. At least I'm able to unload the cane and other clutter. We make a pile by the door. As they inspect a whale calendar, I notice I have something to do today: one scribbled appointment in a sea of empty squares. My doc had made a follow-up appointment at Blessings Hospital. Why should I go? Because in-betweening kills the soul. I'm meant to breathe and touch and know. Eva and Anshu would insist on my being clipped in. But there's another reason to keep the appointment. Something about Blessings Hospital. Right—Anshu's sister works there. Gayathri.

Bard and Randy come to me with several of Eva's emery boards. It's easy to explain what they are, but I'd have to recite the full history to explain why I still have them. Never mind. The Spuds need more to do, so I line up the Elvis bobbleheads for sacrifice. Stoking boyhood mayhem allows me to clean up and shave. I step from the bathroom to find Voldemort Presleys leering. The Spuds had put the emery boards to work, sanding away Elvis noses (D*eg yew. Deg yew, burrah buch.*).

We organize the booty and drag it to their place. Mother Halle is a formidable Viking, a head taller than me, with a mobile mouth and broad shoulders. She sits at an old treadle sewing machine. The boys dive under it to work the foot pedal. "There's my help!"

The three work together as a unit, Halle instructing: "Slow, slower." "Quick, quick!" It's mesmerizing. Living history. "Great-granny's treadle?"

"Yeah! Isn't it great?" Without missing a stitch, she issues a well-practiced apology for the Spud raid.

"They're always welcome."

She shakes her head at me and speaks to Bard and Randy. "You ring the doorbell and ask politely if you can interrupt."

Halle releases the Spuds and they roar off with their treasures, capes flying. She stands and makes eye contact. "They always take you at your word, you know."

"I'll try to remember."

"They'll help. If anyone cries—"

"It's time to go home."

She smiles and squints *through* me.

At the hospital, a bleary nurse points to an empty waiting room. A guy who looks like a constipated Chuck tries to beam from a blaring TV: "Side effects include headache, memory loss, neuralgia …" No shit. Sticky gloom, stubble, down-dogging …

No brick handy, but I find the off switch. Gossip magazines repel. I sit and watch a couple of strangers down the hallway—an old lunch-bucket guy and a coed. They had hardly exchanged nods a minute earlier, but now they're diving deep. It's not flirtation. Not sex. It's humanity. They have nothing to lose. She reminds him of his daughter; he reminds her of a kindly actor. They have a disease or patient in common. They'll either never see each other again or see each other every day for weeks. There's no ulterior motive, no wheedling. The presence of death, the chance of it, draws them together. There's no possibility of bullshit. Hospitals are crucibles.

Diorama Mode again. Dioramas everywhere: At a coffee kiosk, a father consoles a gangly boy who streams tears without a sound. In the hallway, a kneeling woman peers over a stroller at the hazy sea. I might shake Diorama Mode if I tried, but it's a comfort—snapshots of a helter-skelter world through Eva's eyes.

The night's rest was so good, I want to do it again. Want to catch up on missed sleep, which I hear isn't possible. Chuck would disagree. He always fantasized about taking a sleeping vacation—not getting out of bed for a week. I understand that now. I'd sleep a year if I could. But the Sandman had mercy last night. Maybe he's got another ten minutes: chump change.

Eleven minutes later, my eyes pop open. I'm being examined by a small, bald guy in the adjacent chair. He squats, facing me, in worn jeans, running shoes, and a silk aloha shirt. A frayed day pack is splayed on the floor.

"Sorry," he says, rotating forward in his squat. Here comes weird. "You were twitching. Good dream?"

"Something about coyotes."

"Saweet!" He holds out a hard, white hand. "I'm Pigeon."

"Stan."

"Going to the Kidney Center, Stan?"

"Internal medicine. You?"

"My partner's in dialysis."

Pigeon hops up and strides to the window. Presses himself against it, peering. "A wren. Not sure which."

"So, you *are* a bird guy."

"I'm learning."

He kneels on the floor, opens the pack, and fusses with pill bottles and heavy oxygen canisters. "Everything's in here. Dennis is prone to pneumonia, among other things."

"You're the medic."

He rocks back and studies me. "He's been on the transplant list for eight years."

I look for the wren.

"They won't let me donate. Dennis comes from a big family, but no luck."

"Must've pissed somebody off."

"Yeah." He circles back to the window, tracking birds. "He turned out to be gay."

Do I need this? No. "You sure that's the problem?"

Pigeon turns and leans against the sill. "Well, the sisters say all the right things, but they have all these convenient surgeries and illnesses. The brothers don't make excuses: 'No kidneys for queers! God's punishment.'"

Awkward. "How do you know I'm not—"

"I have a sense about people."

Steady gaze. I smile toothlessly and nod. He picks up the bag and squats in a chair facing me. "Sorry. It just—*bothers* me how we talk about nothing day after day. I might lose my life partner. I might be cut in half. I can't just talk about the weather."

Shit, yes. I could riff on this. I could talk about losing Eva. But I won't. Where's the goddamn wren? Pigeon's jaw sets, and he's the spitting image of Randy. Okay, I should do my part. "Have they *said* it's God's punishment?"

"No. They just go all Old Testament and talk in parables when we mention Dennis's walnut-size kidneys."

Pigeon stretches aggressively, as runners do. Paces, swinging long arms. "You can't prove a negative. They just say the schedule doesn't work, or they have Mad Cow Disease, or you smell funny or something." He pantomimes. "'And, by the way—here, read this *Book. Of. Shame.*'"

I consider escape routes as Pigeon picks up steam. "They talk about redneck television and cheesy appliances like that's all there is. As if there's no ticking clock. I could scream."

"Don't!" An unshaven athlete gone to seed stands in the hallway, holding a grocery bag. He wears a Padres cap and an unbuttoned denim shirt over a white tee. "You can't hate people for not donating a kidney, Pidge."

"Can too."

Dennis grimaces. "A kidney's a lot to ask."

Pigeon juts his jaw again. "*Death* is a lot to ask. Kidneys come in pairs! Donors outlive the hell out of everyone."

Dennis gives me an evil grin. "Pidge wants your organ, buddy."

I can't think of a thing to say. Pidge gathers his pack and forces a smile. "Sorry. I always try too hard."

Dennis stands erect, soldierly. "Thing is, I'm getting a transplant next month."

His protector snorts, rounding into form. "A *deceased* donor. An *expanded criteria* donor. Hard-used. Riskier than anyone will admit. Show him your fistula, Dennis."

"No."

In desperation, I introduce myself to Dennis. Catch a glimpse of ropy veins as we shake. He pulls cans of cat food out of the bag with ceremony and shows them to his partner. "Doc's cat died."

Pigeon grabs one. "Saweet! Popeye *loves* these."

He juggles and drops the can. As he bends for it, Dennis boots it down the hall, grinning like Bard. Pidge shags the cat food and executes a perfect turnaround jump shot, dropping it into Dennis's bag from twenty feet. Dennis shoots me a proud look and follows. Stoked, Pidge runs back and gives me a card.

WALTER COLLINS - DENNIS MURPHY
SUNDRY ENDEAVORS
Now accepting kidneys!

Contact info crowds the back of the card. Pidge sniggers and runs to harry Dennis, who marches on, stiff-arming. They spar down the hall. Is that my work? Letting Dennis and Pigeon have a piece of me? Maybe Anshu's sister, Gayathri, knows. Why would she know? Because she's a nurse? Because I like her brother? Because Anshu told me a story about her? *Get a grip, Stan.* The bleary nurse appears with a clipboard, and we head down the opposite hall. I'm poked and prodded for a while before I think to ask about Gayathri. The nurse frowns. "I don't know," she says. "I'm new. There are a couple of Indian women in the Kidney Center."

Okay. If Gayathri is in the Kidney Center, she'll know whether I can donate. I could ask the doc about it, but I think Gayathri is the one to give me the word. She's a California Anshu. We can talk about the work I might set my heart upon. About the *Gita*.

The doc examines the source wound at the thigh and the ground wound at the shoulder. *Upsy-daisy.* He asks about sleeping habits, attention span. Neither is great. Mood? I can't begin to describe the nightmare shadow. Sadie and the Spuds perked me up, so maybe I don't have to. He draws blood and pronounces me recovering. Reminds me that I'm lucky to be alive. It's lame not to ask about donating. Maybe I'm not serious about it. At the Kidney Center, a receptionist says a Gayathri works there but is taking time off.

At home, I clean up and trek back to the cliffs. Imagine Sadie looking for me. Tell myself that she needs my ears, just as I need her voice. But her bench is forlorn. I scan the cliffs and turn landward. Here I am, all dressed up with no story. No yarn to play with. Sadie's cottage glows on the hillside. I'm halfway there before veering back to the ocean. If you don't fit anywhere, they put you someplace special. How is it suddenly hard to avoid being warehoused? I flash on a TV bulletin: *San Diego Police are looking for a stalker who claims he just wants to be told a story. Why? So he can sleep. Yes, this sad man just needs a bedtime story …* Well, I'm not there yet. I don't even wear pajamas anymore.

My story obsession paid off all through childhood. I'd jump into my pajamas early and pick out a book, but I couldn't go to my room because I'd fall asleep before anyone would look for me. So I'd charge around, bothering everyone. I often had something to answer to, but all was forgiven when I held up my book-shield. PJs—even the too-large Disney ensemble with a torn pocket—were armor.

Fuck the pills. I try warm milk and sleep in ragged intervals. Keep thinking I'm late for work—late for Eva—late for falling. But I don't even own an alarm clock. Just the cat clock with the eyes in sync with the buzzy neon of the art-echo strip mall. Klaxons. Too much current and not enough.

Every few days, I pull out Sadie's story and rewrite it, adding things I'd forgotten. *I imagined my life would be some kind of screwball comedy, with adventure and music. Lots of music.* When her absence goes on, I move on to other histories—mostly Eva's.

After high school in Maine, I picked up a history degree from Denver University. *When in doubt, go higher.* I couldn't talk myself into grad school. My excuses were many and lame. I think I was spooked by teaching. Listening and reading were great; droning from a lectern was too much. I'd never been a frontman. I liked playing the drums—keeping time from a hiding place. Anyway, I'd acquired Mom's books and found myself collecting more from cohorts and profs. I stored them for a few years while touring with a band, then opened a bookstore in a funky storefront near the DU campus. The best way to make it as a bookseller is to own the real estate, so I shoehorned myself into a mortgage, using a small inheritance from Mom. Dad hated that. He was for grad school. The streamlined building—living history—seemed so obviously the better investment that I was blunt about it. He hated that, too.

I had only a single story to work with—one story to hold thousands— but the ceilings were high. I tore out a loft in the back and built high bookcases. Restored antique rolling ladders and built new ones. Showcased gilded old tomes in the storefront windows with loving care. Opened in August and was sinking fast by Christmas. I moved more books to the back and advertised the storefront area for lease, trying not to sound desperate. Nada. In the middle of a bleak January, here comes Eva with a yellow rose and a bag of chocolate-covered macadamia nuts. The flower symbolizes friendship, she said, and the simple sentiment hit me amidships. Yes—friendship with this beaming artist. She'd never owned a business but had managed a greenhouse and spoke passionately of her vision: a flower and chocolate shop.

She opened on Valentine's Day. It was bitter cold, but people flocked to her free peppermint hot chocolate and stayed for the warmth. It became a tradition. Eva's energy was high, but she could never be over the top. The glasses made her seem more serious than she usually was, but also emphasized her consideration. The shopper was always the star because she liked every sort of person. I was the straight man, "Stanner," from day one—sometimes even "The Gold Stanner."

Together, we made it all happen. Navoti Bookshop and Flowers— *navoti*, a Hopi word for wisdom—showcased Eva's arrangements, and her arrangements saved the bookshop. Once you have your flowers and chocolate, you're ready to drop into an overstuffed chair and think about books. It wasn't always smooth sailing, but once we combined forces—offering themed package deals, we stopped sweating the overhead.

There wasn't much she didn't know about flowers and their fragrances and meanings. When I filleted my forearm with a box knife, she healed it with rose oil. She named everything—stools and vases and registers and children's drawings and every single bouquet. "Chloe," she'd say, presenting flowers—or "Beatrice" or "Merlin" or another obscure name. She was naming her children, each a work of art. I realized that stories begin with names, and we talked about that for hours. What are the best names in literature? Surely Douglas Adams's Wowbagger the Infinitely Prolonged and Melville's Ishmael. She countered with P. G. Wodehouse's Pongo Twistleton and Hardy's Bathsheba Everdene. What's the best sentence in a novel? Dear Douglas again: "He died, testily." I can still hear Eva laughing about that. She added it to her self-effacing repertoire. Every day, she warned of her fastidiousness, which she ascribed to "rigid potty training." It was an all-purpose excuse.

I could tell she couldn't wait to get her hands on my books. Once I gave the green light, the shop was transformed, and it improved continually ever after. For one thing, she freed up the high windows I'd blocked in the back. She loved the rolling ladders and made them centerpieces of the organic decor. We had to put signs up, telling patrons to move potted plants as needed. I built bookcases, ladders, and plant stands to her specifications.

She organized the books around our tastes. Half the store was history, of course, thanks largely to my cohorts from DU. Mom was proud of having a Cherokee ancestor, and she had a lot of the beautiful books on native cultures that came out in the '80s and '90s—*Touch the Earth* by T.C. McLuhan, *Seven Arrows* by Hyemeyohsts Storm, *House Made of Dawn* by N. Scott Momaday, *Ceremony* by Leslie Marmon Silko, *In The Spirit of Crazy Horse* by Peter Matthiessen. She had everything by Frank Waters and Sherman Alexie. Several early editions of *Black Elk Speaks* by John G. Neihardt. Inspired, I'd added a lot to the collection.

We had a long shelf of breathless Victorian narratives about exploring the West—books like *In the Rocky Mountains: A Tale of Adventure* by W.

H. G. Kingston, *Knocking Round the Rockies* by Ernest Ingersoll, *Travels West* by William Minturn. They're full of good humor and unspoiled landscapes. The covers are baroque, so we often put them in the windows. I flanged out this sub-genre with hefty old treatises by the likes of Ferdinand Vandeveer Hayden and John Wesley Powell. Those graded into high-minded American Transcendentalism. Eva's favorite books were the children's anthologies. We were impressed by the illustrated sets produced back in the day to acquaint kids with the great stories of the world—*My Book House*, for example. These were the heart of the shop. I could hardly keep them on the shelves after Eva loved them up.

Most of the books were ordinary, but stout—ready for another fifty years. I figured hardbacks were due for the resurgence that vinyl records had experienced. Modest sales increases kept my hopes up, anyway. In the wintertime, we emphasized the insulating value of a good library. But the mixed vibe, the neat integration of the shops, really made the place. We built a new loft and enlarged the windows up there, which faced the mountains to the west. The loft's four easy chairs were seldom empty, thanks to the views and Eva's flowering plants.

We couldn't *help* but collaborate. Providing a literary backdrop for Eva's sorcery was a boon in every way. My tomes looked fresh in her splashy storefront. She'd come in early to dress the windows, and I found excuses to be there. I'd chosen the building, in part, because it faced east. Mom was big on that. She'd always insisted that the doorways of our homes opened into the sunrise—as do Navajo hogans. Like Mom, Eva and I picnicked on our front stoop, in morning light. *Seeing the creation is key.* Friends and customers would join us as opening time approached. Whenever I can't take another step, I play the loop of our door swinging open, eager faces following us in.

One day I wandered in through the back, climbed a ladder, and found myself watching Eva and a young deaf girl—Donna, a part-time employee—dancing to Earth, Wind & Fire. Eva had placed the stereo speakers face-down and turned up the bass for Donna. The artless abandon, the honest connection, were too much. I couldn't wait to descend the ladder. "Marry me!" I shouted from above.

＊ ＊ ＊

All this history, which I try to write plainly, activates Eva's dioramas, which invade my sleeping and waking dreams. All history is personal now, so I sift memories. I should contact my sisters and dad in Maine, but I have too much and not enough to tell. We can't talk about Eva—too painful for everyone—and I have no routine to describe. If I get into the twilight rambles, I'm advertising my crazy. They'll worry or try to manage me. So I put off the family correspondence. Instead, I buy a postcard with a skimming sailboat on it and write to Anshu. "Wish you were here."

When I'm tired of walking, I ride the bus. Just beach to beach or downtown. Soon I'm riding every day. My favorite driver is a smiling hippopotamus who plays doo-wop. I sit in the wayback and dream through "The Great Pretender," "Since I Don't Have You," "Earth Angel," "Come and Go With Me." The hippo attributes every song with pride, even when I'm the only passenger: "The Platters!" "The Skyliners!" "The Penguins!" "The Del-Vikings!"

Between dozes, I read Kerouac and the *Gita*. Jack Kerouac makes some famous-people-who-were-evil lists, but I wonder how many professional dissers have read his beautiful pages? Jack was inspired and insane, like van Gogh. *I had nothing to offer anybody except my own confusion.* You and me, buddy. We are *dream beings. Dreaming ties all mankind together.*

I live a bus dreamer life—watching palms glide by, catching snatches of conversation, bailing now and then to find a nothing sandwich. What am I looking for? *Work.* What a concept. When tackling a critical job, my father, Justin Ellis, would make a show of pulling on his overalls—his monkey suit. This gave notice that he meant business—monkey business. Every tool and process was goofed out. A chalk line kit was a *chocolat box*, pronounced in the funniest French way. He'd riff on Inspector Clouseau—*Do you have a lisawnze for ze minkee?*—the pronunciation ever more ridiculous. I could tell when he was about to do it but laughed every time. I loved the jokey work talk—the idea that work is so special that it requires play. My hippo bus driver knows it well. Dad and I had plenty of trouble later on, but Justin Ellis made work fun. Made sure I would never be afraid of it. And *Eva* made work fun. So what is my work? Driving a bus? Cotton candy tunes and familiar faces. Body memory. But I have a vision of wearing a groove into the street. I can't climb yet, but I'd better not sink.

A gaunt Rasta with a white beard and tattered tam rides as much as I do. When the bus is filling up one morning, I move next to him. He acknowledges me with rheumy eyes, and we watch a load of high school kids troop on. Tender faces, full of empathy, wonder, determination. Caricatures of what they will become. When half of them gape at their phones, my seatmate gives me a sad look. Leans forward and opens up. "Long time ago now, geeks give us a window on de world, see? Computers, den de web. Okay. You can sit—and here's de *wonda* world! *Catches* me. I sit in de library every day, watchin' de wonda. One day my *son* comes, and I don't know him! I was too much away. Didn't know my neighborhood. My city. It is the *mocker*. So I stop. *Cold*. It was hard, mon. Had a long thinking dream. I see screens become *screams*. Too flat."

He shakes his head as if to shame the world. "When I stop thinking, I had not sat at de *witchin'* window for a year. All right. Now I sit twice a week. But—*careful*."

He scans the kids. "Now come—keyholes. *Portable*. You can watch de world all de time, everywhere. From bedroom or mountaintop. *To* bedroom or mountaintop. Keyholes on an' on. *But*—you don't know something: de world watches *you*. Coo 'pon.

"A keyhole keeps you on your *knees*, yah? Squinting, squinting. You see only pieces. Random or *very* too-much. Fuckery. You learn just so to be dangerous. Just so to be a *slave*. You're part of the whole Babylon Shitstem. All de keyhole peepsters come dung to fuck up de world."

I pull out my phone. The Rasta points at it accusingly. "Okay—but does *not* stop. Goes too on. Cannot bring well conscious. Will use you hard, 'less you're maye-wizard. One in a thousand, mon. A million. Stop."

The *Lord of the Rings* is part of my DNA. My parents read those books to us six times. And everyone saw the movies—maybe even this Bus

Bredda. So I say, "It's like the Palantir in the *Lord of the Rings*. Remember when Pippin got ahold of that crystal ball? Whoa!"

"Yuh *seet!* All de Pippins out deh."

I offer him the phone. He recoils like Gandalf refusing the One Ring. "Coo yah! I have only—a *little* time yet to be. To walk and see. I hear de *echo* of de last breath. Want to look my bredren in de *eye*. Make my fullness. Creation stepper, me."

He stands abruptly and makes for the door, nodding. "Bless."

I dick with the phone. If I cared about the news, if I wanted to check in with friends and family, I'd keep pushing buttons. I'd rather look out the window. How do you bring "well conscious?" Maybe I need a thinking dream. Sure enough, I nod off and twitch through an intense tracking shot of a bear limping through a mountain forest with a dead swan tied around its neck. Just as terror closes in, a pine breeze makes everything tolerable. The bear drinks from a stream.

When I come to, the kids are gone. Time to wake up and drive my destiny. I need a car. Freedom. In Denver, I had an old pickup, Yota. Eva supplied its voice. *Let parking find YOU, Luke. Suck, you must not.* Miss them, I do.

Finding and buying a car takes a week. I look at everything—even these new jobs that drive themselves. They conjure Bus Bredda in my head: *No, dat. Stop.* When I see an ad for an old Studebaker, I have to look. My grandfather's first car was a Studie, and he spoke of it with reverence. This one's a 1951 Studebaker Champion Starlight Coupe. Wrap-around rear window. Bullet nose. A Pacific-blue cartoon. Its beefy owner, Henry, says that it's hard to get parts, but the trunk is full of extras, and everything has already been rebuilt anyway.

Henry sits next to me, fussing mournfully with a pipe, as I give it a spin. He's told me everything, so now he spouts Studie slogans: "Different by design!" "The thrifty one for Fifty-One." It handles fine. Not much power, but I don't care. Glasses shatter when you drive fast. As we head back in the slow lane, Henry's pipe smoke launches daydreams. As he puffs away dejectedly, all I can think of is Justin Ellis. Dad always smoked a pipe when working around the house. My sisters and I still love the aroma. It always meant the car had been fixed, the walk had been shoveled, or something had been made right. We were *safe*.

I curb the Studie. Henry stares at the winged hood ornament. Breaking up is hard to do. We get out and admire the Champion together. The sofa seats are a star attraction. It's a stylish snooze-mobile for the king of catnaps. Something to love. Henry looks ready to cry. This will ding my savings, but I pull out the checkbook without a tremor. "Sweet and low—a melody in metal," Henry says. He boggles at the check as I pull away.

Next day, I pilot the Champion out to the hospital. Gayathri is still gone and somehow this is a relief. What would I say to her? *How is your brother? Do you want my kidney?* I ask a nurse about donating. He thinks I should ask my doctor. No shit. I need Gayathri. First Sadie, now Gayathri, whom I haven't even met. I want to see if she still writes left-handed. Will that do it? Will I then be able to leave her alone? No. Because I want to know about her and Anshu and Kolkata. I want to *listen*. All that electrical current tweaked me. Too much and not enough. I'm forever outward, seeking connection. Stuck on characters. Narrators.

Maybe I'm just trying to fill an old need. Mom died when I was thirteen and Dad took comfort in field work. We lived too far from town to see my friends regularly, and my sisters had friends nearby. So I'd head out along the shore with our border collie, Trudy. I'd always take the pellet gun for random target shooting. Sometimes I'd take an old rowboat out and track the coastline. Trudy made a fine figurehead as she scanned for gulls. Sometimes, listening to a song about loneliness, I'd try to feel sorry for myself. But walking—or rowing—was always the cure. Like listening, it turned me outward. Once, because guys my age had talked of shooting birds, I emptied my pellet gun into a songbird—thinking after each shot that I had missed. Eventually, the bird tumbled sickeningly through a larch, trailing yellow plumes. It had been wounded or dead through most of the shots but had hung on. As I counted the holes in its beautiful breast, I was knocked out by the tenacity of the thing—its grip on life a stark contrast to my careless, relentless murder. I saw myself as I was: a disciple of reach, incapable of reverence. Suddenly, I understood what the sad songs were about; I knew the depths of loneliness. When Eva died, that nightmare shadow came back in a rush.

Trundling through the parking lot, I stop to watch superhero window washers scattered across the children's wing of the hospital. Something about the dumb spectacle wakes me up. Back at the apartment, I drag a sixteen-foot ladder from the common shed, brace it against the two-story building, and climb halfway up—a little shaky, but not bad. I come down, drink a beer, think about it. Then I climb up and down, gradually higher, until I'm walking around on the roof. The sun flares and dissolves into the sea. I take a pill.

I leave the ladder up all the next day. Between reading Kerouac and tinkering with the histories, I scale the ladder a dozen times. I'm getting comfortable with vertical again. This opens up possibilities. The Eastern expression, *yab-yum,* the primal union of wisdom and compassion, lodges in my sticky brain. Jack used it to mean mindful sex. Yow. It's been more than two years. Mind*less* would do. The writer's dharma-bum brilliance runs through my head in endless loops. *My witness is the empty sky.*

On a yab-yum hunch, I drive back out to the hospital. *Nowhere to go but everywhere.* The superheroes are just knocking off. I present myself to a bearded giant in a too-small Iron Man suit: Brian.

"We're shorthanded. You got references?"

I show him a letter from my old partner and a guild card. He's alarmingly impressed. I need to manage that. "It's been a while. I'm kind of rusty."

Batman descends clumsily, arcing sheets of water on everyone. Brian winces. "Who you wanna be?"

"Who you got?"

"Green Lantern, Spidey, Wonder Woman—"

"Must be hot as hell."

"Wonder Woman's smokin'. Kids'll love a whiskery Amazon."

"I mean the suits. In the sun."

"Yeah. They're hot. We'll be off the children's wing next week. Then you can wear a bikini for all I care."

"Smokin'."

"No doubt." Brian rummages through miscellaneous gear in the bed of his old (*Yota!*) pickup. He tosses me a bundle. "Okay, you're Robin, the Boy Wonder. Lightweight uni. See you in the morning, six sharp." It's a hazing, of course—give the new guy the stupid suit. But I don't mind. I'm pumped from the jokey work talk. Walking back, I break into a run, circling the building before jumping into the Studie. *Home, bullet nose.*

The Spuds invade as I'm trying on the outfit back at the apartment. They're always primed for a pounce, but my costume is license for real violence. They're on me before I can set my feet, and down I go. I'll have to remember that on the job: kids attack superheroes. As well they should. The roughhousing is noisy and prolonged. This draws Halle, who demands that I identify myself while the Spuds snap my mask and twist my rubber muscles. She gives me the squint. "Kind of a wimpy cape."

She's right. The canary color is okay, but the cape is too small. She shifts it to the front and tisks at it. "It's like a lobster bib."

At least it's not likely to get caught and drag me to my doom. Don't need any more help with that, thanks. Halle frowns at my pate. "You'll need a hat, or you'll get fried."

We troop back to their place, where Halle digs a square of yellow silk out of a mountain of scrap material and sits at the treadle. Within minutes, exaggerating a Bard template, she has improvised a billed cap. Perfecto.

I'm at the job site early, amped and ready to go. Stride purposefully here and there until Brian shows up and shows me all the gear. Almost everything has been repurposed. The buckets once held drywall mud. The tool belts look pre-war. Brian is proud of this but also likes cutting-edge. "Make do on the small stuff, and don't hold back on whatever might save your life."

Brian offers a fancy boom, but I don't want anybody next to me for a while. I clip into a bosun's chair and ascend with hardly a flutter. Maybe I'll take up pipe smoking. The kids seem confused about my Super ID until I scrawl a "Robin, the Boy Wonder" sign. That draws them in—probably because of the "Boy." I wonder about all the meanings of wonder: Being awestruck. Something fantastic, like the Grand Canyon. A questioning. Being curious. If you wonder enough, do you *become* a wonder? Like Eva? Anshu? Sadie? Gayathri? What did Bus Bredda say about that? *De wonda watch you. Coo 'pon*: look upon. I looked it up. Wonder *looks upon* you.

I overthink everything, particularly shattered glass. Touch Eva's sapphire every few minutes. She builds the dioramas in which I wonder. The kids are wonders. They gape from everywhere. One sharp-eyed boy on a bed-mobile follows me from room to room, floor to floor. Gives me a flipper wave. I waggle the squeegee. This idea of revealing in order to bootstrap pulls me upward and outward—as Chucky once did, bless his pigskin heart. They don't call it opening *down*, after all. *Open up, Stan. Upupup*. Anti-downward dog. How do you crack open? What's the opposite of armor? Membrane. Breathing the right things in and out.

Someday the Thought Police will quick march old Stan to the warehouse for dithering daydreamers. I'll plead profession. Roofers and window washers can hardly stem the flow of *de dreams dat whiz*. Possibilities fly from deep landscapes—reflected or real. Maybe we crow's nesters are maye-wizards—however Bus Bredda defines those. *Dis make my fullness*. Melville nailed it in the mast-head chapter of *Moby Dick*: night-watch on a mast—an ancient occupation, stripped of desire. You dangle in time and space. Arrested. Hurtling. *Creation stepper, me*.

- IV -

THE REVEAL
(SPRING)

IN THE MORNING, I CHOOSE A BOOM. WONDER WOMAN CLOSES FAST ON a boom to my right. She zips by, beating me to the top. Nina has had to pin her oversize togs, but she looks great and outworks us all. She shows off for the kids, posing theatrically. This exasperates Brian. Watching Iron Man splutter and split his suit makes my morning.

Most of the day, I'm bracketed by wonder—showy Nina and the bed-mobile kid inside. The exercise kickstarts my imagination, and I find ways to make kids laugh. You have to exaggerate the visual, like a silent movie actor. I start with precious poses and devolve to fake electrocution and a stuck-in-a-bucket routine. At night, as I stalk the Sandman, dioramas come. There's the Bus Bredda diorama, the bullet-nose diorama, and now this vertical superhero thing. Big dimensions. Birds and kids and bright, bulging suits. *Nowhere to go but everywhere.*

By day three, I'm dedicated to the sweat, the smell, the exhibitionism. The warm and wobbly familiarity. By quitting time, I'm so fried as I descend that I'm slow to track a familiar patch of coral moving across the parking lot. It's Sadie, in a wheelchair, wearing hot-pink sweats. Same sharp eyes, but the face is slack. She clutches a carpetbag. A small woman in blue pushes the chair. Back on the ground, I run hard, micro-cape flapping, to catch them at the hospital door. They're freaked by the outfit and urgency, so I pull off the cap and catch my breath, trying to explain. Sadie nods and pats my arm. She clearly can't speak, so I introduce myself to her helper. This is Gemma, Sadie's oldest friend, the one with the crooked smile. She's dark, attentive, and surprisingly agile. As we enter the hospital, she confirms that Sadie has had a stroke.

While Gemma checks Sadie in, I go back to the children's wing to stow my gear and change. The crew was impressed with my super-sprint. Batman says I looked like Ronald Acuna rounding second. Brian says more like Ronald MacDonald. I can work with these guys. Back at the hospital, the nurse is tending to Sadie, so Gemma and I sit in a waiting room that smells of bacon. Gemma flutters shyly, just as Sadie had described. *Oh, I love my Gemma dear.*

She says that Sadie might still have speech, but she won't try. "Theo would get her talking—trying, anyway."

She pulls a puzzle book out of her purse, but I need to know about Theo. In her confidential voice, she explains that Theo is Sadie's only grandchild.

"Mo's grandchild?"

Gemma shakes her head. She stands and walks to the window and back, wringing her hands. "Mo never came back. An ammunition ship they were loading blew up—near Oakland. Three hundred sailors died."

The Port Chicago Disaster. History-buff Stan read all about it. The compensation to most families was cut because the victims were black. When the working conditions didn't improve after the explosion, some men refused to load ammunition without more training. For which they were fucking crucified. The brass called them mutineers, forgodsake, so they could throw the book at them.

Gemma sits, closes her eyes. Dioramas pop: a dark boy with a mylar balloon peers into an infinite hallway, a mummy on a paused gurney sits up to catch sunlight, a brusque businesswoman collapses in a chair.

When we enter Sadie's room, she looks flat, detached. I miss the superhero getup. Pat clumsily, as a child.

Three days later, I ask my doc about donating an organ. He smiles tolerantly. "You're still recovering from organ damage yourself, Stan. Wait a year, at least. Let's get your rest cycle back to normal." Well, WTF is normal? It's a shock, somehow, that I can't help Dennis and Pigeon. I couldn't save Mom or Eva or myself, but I wanted to save *somebody*. Shiteroo—the nightmare shadow goes on.

I'm saved by a call from Anshu. It's surprising how the connection has grown. When we first met, Anshu and Eva did all the talking. But after Eva died, he offered me hope. Now here we are, a thousand miles apart, talking easily for more than an hour. He's happy I landed in Ocean Beach and promises to come out. I tell him about the beaches—their calm busyness. This reminds him of Kolkata, of bathing in the Hooghly River on clear mornings. The peace in the bustle. The nine-day Durga Puja Festival, with its explosions of color. The kindly professors and earnest students at the institute where he studied gemology.

Traveling and trading precious stones, he had eventually saved enough to emigrate to the US. He smuggled sapphires and pigeon blood rubies out of India, because, he says with a laugh, that it was easy to do. In the US, he drove higher and higher, seeking the freshest air. He appraised and sold wholesale gems for five years in Denver before opening his shop on the day he was granted citizenship. Then he started saving to bring Gayathri to the US. She worked at the university hospital in Denver before finding better pay in San Diego. I stifle the urge to ask Anshu about her, and he volunteers nothing. Maybe he's protecting her. Maybe it doesn't occur to him. I tell him about Brian and the crew. He knows they're not the real story, but that's all I have. I can't get around to Sadie or Pigeon. He says he'll call back.

We finish the children's wing and move to the main building. I stop in to see Sadie almost every day. Sometimes I see Gemma, usually with one of her daughters and grandkids. They call her Gremma Gemma. Sadie smiles weakly at the kids but won't speak. She doesn't eat much. Thrives on touch. I have nowhere to go, so we sit for hours, holding hands. Eventually, I tell her all about storytime at the Ellis household—my mom's theatrical dialog, my dad's checking in, the pipe-smoke safety, my sisters, the book-shields, the baggy Disney pajamas. I'm not sure Sadie tracks it all, but she listens well, as I had listened to her.

As I leave late one night, Pigeon darts across a distant hall. I find him slumped in a corner, his pack on the floor before him.

"How's Dennis?"

He tucks his legs and blinks. I recognize the insomniac blear. "Coffee on me."

It takes him a minute, then he grabs the pack and follows me to the garden-level café. He won't say what he wants, so I set coffee before him. He lurches to his feet, but only to fetch cream.

"Did Dennis get a kidney?"

"Uh. Expanded Criteria. *Deceased*. Motherfucker won't wake up."

I wait for the caffeine to kick in. Pidge's eyes brighten and he begins his fidgeting. "The docs are great, but—EC kidneys are a bitch. They lowered the standard because so many are needed. Part of the problem is the dead donor rule. It says that procuring organs can never be a *cause* of death. Sounds reasonable, right? Except that, once a body is taken off life support, it *lingers* for hours. Sometimes it makes the organs practically unusable."

Pidge drains the cup, stands, and stretches. "We need a live donor rule. They call it *imminent death*. It would allow people to donate under general anesthesia. Beat death to the punch."

"Makes sense."

"It won't happen. Someday, I'm gonna create a cartoon character named Political Will. Completely—hapless. *Never* where he needs to be. Always AWOL. Always a little sick. A hypochondriac, probably."

The smell of grease fills the room. They're cleaning the fryers. Pidge looks up sharply and paces. "It shouldn't be hard to rewrite the rules. It's just a matter of allowing someone to say, 'Bye-bye. I'm gonna die now, instead of two hours from now, so *you* can live.'"

"I had no idea, Pidge."

"You and every single person in the world. But it would …"

"Shrink the list."

"Yeah. Shrink the—damn list."

The words are defiant but he speaks softly. Absorbs himself in rearranging chairs in neat rows. "I had this weird dream about a bear with a big, white bird on his neck."

Shit. My nightmares are contagious. I grope for coffee. Speak without thinking. "A swan. It's a swan."

Pidge gives me a wild look. "Uh. Yeah. A swan."

As if suddenly unplugged, he drops to a knee. What will he say? We freak quietly together. *Breathe, Stan. Just sit quiet and listen. That's all you ever have to do. Listen, and everything will be all right.* Tick. Tock. A door opens down the hall. It's raining. Pigeon twists into the freshness and takes a deep breath. I walk to the counter, buy a glass bottle of quality water, and hand it to him. He drains it. Stands and resumes the runner's prowl. He's letting the dream connection go—it's a spiritual can of worms. But he looks at me as if I've validated his trust.

"Dennis's brother, Clayton, has started asking about Dennis's guns."

"Harsh."

A stiff smile. "Yeah. I'm the executor."

"Of the will."

Pigeon nods.

"How many guns?"

"Lots." He misfires on another smile. "Creepier by the dozen."

Now I say something stupid. "What will you do with them?"

Pigeon stops and looks resolute. "Believe Dennis will live."

Shit, Stan. "How's your health?"

He turns toward the open door. The rain has stopped. "I had testicular cancer. Chemo disqualifies you from donating an organ."

The temperature drops. Pidge shudders. Stares out the door into the night. "Dennis dragged me through it like a crusty old coach. Then his kidneys failed, so I moved in. A couple of years ago, my cancer came back and Dennis saved me again."

I need to honor Pidge's trust, his trouble. "You can't return the favor."

I take a step toward him, but he shakes himself, yawns, and checks a turquoise watch. "Last bus in ten minutes."

"No problemo. You're with me."

 "You'll give me a ride?"

"Sure."

"It's far."

"I like to drive."

The wet Studie shining under a streetlight animates Pigeon, just as I'd figured. "Saweeeet!"

"It's a Studebaker Champion. Starlight."

Fist pump. He jumps in the back, seduced by the sofa seat and wrap-around glass. "Like Studebaker Champion isn't cool enough. It's a damn Studebaker Champion *Starlight*."

"Starlight *Coupe*." I get in and adjust the mirror around his beaming face. But he's too burned out to last. Flops over after a couple of blocks, barking the address. He reminds me of Spud Randy again: the burst of hectic energy, then collapse. Forty minutes later, I pull up to a run-down apartment building. Listen to Pigeon's steady breathing for a minute before tapping a knee. "Hey, dreamer."

"Coming, Mommy."

But he just lies there. I slip him into a fireman's carry before he can squawk. "Uh," he says again, in his expressive way, and cackles as we bounce up the stairs. He jingles the keys in my face, and I grab them, popping open a warped metal door. Smells like sandalwood. As we enter, a calico cat darts down a hallway.

"Popeye, girl! Come to Daddy."

Pigeon points to a back bedroom. I dump him on the bed. By the time I retrieve his threadbare pack, still heavy with oxygen canisters, he's under the covers. Popeye watches from the next pillow. When I drop the kit, Pigeon's head pops up. "We are the *champions*."

I pull the door shut and launch myself down the stairs. Later, I try to dream about the bear and swan again, but it turns into something else: Anshu and I are at a huge movie theater with thousands of people. Crass ads and subliminal messages are part of the film, but everyone loves them. The audience goes crazy for every come-on. Anshu's smile is gone, as if for good. Young Sadie walks in, wearing the coral dress. Sits by Anshu and takes his hand.

I lie low over the weekend, telling myself that a healthy man shouldn't hang out at a hospital. Sure, this is different. But, Christ, everything is different since Eva, since my dipshit dismount from the scissor-lift. Halfway through a rough Sunday night, I drop a pill, but it makes me late for a long, hot Monday. Brian is grim, but we push through it together. Then I wash up for Sadie. Why this connection? Because she made me human again by showing her essence. I dream of a stupid ceremony in which she restores my name.

Sadie is a minimalist expression of strength. Razor-thin. A Lennon sketch with hawk eyes. She might slip away without ever seeming frail. As she rolls an ice cube around her mouth, Gemma takes her hand and tells me there's a new diagnosis: cancer of the esophagus. She says this right out, but Sadie registers nothing. The doctor recommends a feeding tube, but she won't have it. Her eyes search continually. Gemma knows what's up. "I don't know where Theo is, dear. Nobody knows."

Sadie turns the searchlights on me, as if I have answers. I want to say that her grandson is coming, but there's no bullshit here. She tracks my walk to the window, where I take in the blue Pacific. Where are my superpowers? "I'll—try to find Theo, Sadie."

Gemma looks at me like I'm crazy. Sadie drops Gemma's hand and reaches out to me. The searchlights rest. As Gemma and I walk down the hall, she tries to let me off the hook. "Stan, you *don't* have to find Theo. It's not your problem. Not your family."

"You and the kids have your own lives, your own work. I'm just a ringer. An outsider on some weird trajectory. I should try, for Sadie."

Gemma slows, gathering courage. "They say she won't last long."

Bringing Theo to Sadie is probably hopeless, but I might track him down eventually. It feels like an important thing to do. "I won't stop trying."

She radiates motherly wisdom. "There was trouble, you know. Theo is *hiding*."

"Maybe he's seeking."

The old woman stops and peers up at me. "His father wrapped a car around a tree. The insurance money wasn't much, but Theo's mom, Della, was able to open the Jazz Café in Oakland. The last time I saw her, she said someone had paid off her mortgage. Must've been Theo. Such a man he must be! My son saw him at a wildlife sanctuary in Colorado about fifteen years ago. We tried to follow up, but he was gone."

Now we're in the cavernous hospital lobby. Gemma pulls me into a chair and extracts four puzzle books from her purse, looking for something. Finally, she produces a phone, which she swipes and hands to me. It plays an old video of Sadie playing her dobro on a kitchen table while a powerfully built boy strums a guitar behind her. Sadie stops and looks into the camera. "This is a song Theo and I made: 'Upholstery Blues.'"

There are no words, just the blues chugging along at "Key to the Highway" pace. Sadie hammers a slow rhythm and bends notes like a skilled blacksmith. The kid is camera shy, so I stop watching and listen as the vaulted room echoes with distant greetings and goodbyes. These blues are the perfect soundtrack for all this anguish and joy. Wheelchairs whiz and creep. The ladies at the information desk relentlessly dispense cheer. For a long while, Gemma and I track these skirmishes and negotiations with mortality. The tune fades and I hand the phone back to her. She touches my head maternally and leaves me in the lobby. I sit quiet, watching surrenders and departures. Dioramas.

In the evening, I make an effort. Searching for "Theo" at wildlife orgs is kind of hopeless, but necessary for due diligence. In the end, all I can do is scan the websites of wildlife sanctuaries and scroll through the faces. After a while, it becomes surreal—I want to know these people. Find myself embellishing their stories. I make notes for the calling and emailing I must eventually try. The hardest part of the whole business is trying not to lose myself in the animal stories. This will take time.

I hit the Kidney Center the next day and ask about Gayathri again. She's still out, but there's another stop I can make. I fish Pigeon's card out of my wallet. Murphy. Pidge's partner is Dennis Murphy. The nurse checks with a doctor and gives me the room number. It's random to drop in on a guy I hardly know, but all bets are off at Blessings. Hell, I was ready to give him a kidney, after all, without even knowing his politics. I like this new standard: awareness of need.

Dennis is white as his bedsheets but nods as I enter and tries to smile. The alteration is stunning. To help me out, he says Pidge told him about the Studie. In a halting, determined voice, he tells me about his old '55 Ford pickup. "Caribbean blue. Bench seats. A dog will lie there. Scoop, the bird dog. Rest his head on your lap. I think a lot about ridin' out early for pheasants. The flush. Routine—until you can't do it anymore."

"Did you ever take Pigeon hunting?"

"Pigeon won't hunt."

Dennis takes a pull of water and coughs out a dry laugh. "Thing is, he's a good shot. Better than me or anyone I know. I guess he and his dad would go out there—blaze away at beer cans. The old man was tryin' to—make a man of him."

He chortles as I take his cup and set it back on the nightstand. "His dad had this antelope mounted on a wall. Pidge fell in love with that thing—just like him, by the way, to go for a moldy old trophy. Anyway, he can shoot like Annie Oakley, but never would hunt."

"You're the one."

"Oh, I—had to be doin' all the time. Playin' ball, mostly. Batted four-fifty in high school."

I nod reverently. He squints into the past. "I remember some of the home runs and—big wins—but mostly I think about sittin' in the bleachers on a hot day, holdin' hands with my girlfriend. She was sweet. Thought I was special because I wasn't always tryin' to get her bra off. I still think of Katy Sue every day."

Dennis is fading fast. I see it all from above—too crisp, too weirdly somber. Ordinary would be a thrill about now. I make ready to leave, but Dennis perks up. "Pidge'll be here soon."

"Guess your family has a hard time with Pigeon."

"He has a hard time with *them*. They're good people if you give 'em a chance."

"Have they come to see you?"

"Most of 'em are in Kansas. My sister Irene'll—come by."

Pigeon appears, jovial, with a shopping bag. He's stoked that I came to see Dennis and goes on about it until Dennis and I heckle him about his garish turtle shirt. He theatrically pulls a big pill carousel out of the bag. Crouches comically, like a discus thrower, with the disk in one hand. "Did I tell you guys about the statue I posed for?" I leave them with the new toy.

In the evenings, I write the histories, trying not to embellish, and assemble pages of notes about wildlife sanctuaries and other possible haunts for Theo. I'm ready to flee, to get out, to drive horizon to horizon and scour the world. But Sadie holds me here—and work, the anchor I was missing. The Window Wizards are solid. We finish the hospital windows and move to a couple of condo complexes downtown. It's easy—minimal danger, shade from other buildings, and primo lunch options. Besides Brian and Nina, there's Bix, a Zen Obama, and ruddy Drow, who works out a lot and always has a new tat. Drow and Brian are USC football fans, so they have deep conversations about somebody's knee. It's hard to care. When we were still on the children's wing, Brian tried to insist that Bix be Black Panther, but that costume is way too hot for twenty-first-century San Diego. Bix held out for Captain America and nailed it, out-cooling us all. The kid knows what he's about. He likes to run but refuses to compete. When Nina draws him out, he says he'll take up community college again, when he can. His doughy girlfriend sometimes brings him lunch. I let them have the Studie for privacy. In the time-warp car, they look like a vintage advertisement for racial harmony.

Without the Wonder Woman suit, Nina retreats into shyness. But she doesn't miss a thing. Asks about the Studie. Tags me as the designated driver. I don't mind. With the five of us packed into the retro-droplet, we feel stupidly invincible. There's power in the clown-car pageantry. Now and then, I glimpse Pigeon running—loose-limbed and focused and chewing up the miles.

Here comes skinny Pidge one afternoon, wobbling across a parking lot. A stocky woman in a business suit holds him up. I hesitate, then intercept. Pigeon is hollow. *I might be cut in half.* He tries to compose himself when he sees me. His friend fixes me with a steady gaze and introduces herself as Jackie. I reciprocate and focus on Pidge.

"Is Dennis …?"

Pigeon nods.

"Sorry, buddy."

Pigeon waves dismissively. "Doesn't—Doesn't—"

Jackie pulls a cream hanky from a breast pocket and dabs her eyes. "Shut *up*, Pidge! It—most *certainly* does matter."

Dark hair falls into her face. She shakes it back and manages a smile. "We're after some blueberry waffles. This man runs too much and doesn't eat enough."

Pidge blinks and works his jaw. "Waffles. Doesn't that sound awful? Actually, it sounds …"

Saweet. I want him to say it sounds *saweet.* But he can't get there. He's a rag doll with bulging eyes. The big chin quivers. I supply the trademark word and Pigeon smiles gratefully. Nods and wags a finger at me. Jackie invites me to join them for brunch, but I plead work: the universal excuse.

I felt Dennis's death coming. We were frozen in a diorama—a terminus. Waiting for the Reaper. The scene feeds into my expanding collection of late-night dioramas: Eva in the roses. Sadie on the cliffs. Bredda on the bus. The superheroes going vertical. Dennis in the old Ford with Scoop. Stanhope and Pidge goofing with Dennis in an antiseptic room. The dioramas blend, blotting the sun. I need Anshu.

The Wizards are working hard, but I make time for Sadie. The doctors talk about scraping her esophagus, but they're afraid she's too weak. They need to build her up, but she won't have a feeding tube. Gemma and I toss out haphazard phrases, thinking we might hit on something that will get her moving or eating or something. I finally bring in the several pages of Sadie history I've composed. I've surely got some of the story wrong and hope she'll correct me. But it's just as before—she likes listening but won't engage, even in her own story. Still, I read it over and over. I have the time, and she likes the sound of my voice—as she once liked the sound of Mo's. I elaborate more every day, sometimes ranging far afield, and ask questions about life after the war. Gemma responds, explaining that she and Sadie had jumped at a chance to play clubs in the Carolinas. Then Sadie talked Gemma into joining her for the long train ride out to the Bay Area—where Mo had been. But Sadie never adds to the story. She never says anything, except for one day, after my blather, when I'm coaxing her to eat. "You're a scarecrow," I say. Sadie glares and sits upright. Her breathing picks up, and she works her mouth. Here it comes: "Don' look so hot. *Yursef!*" I pantomime a shot to the heart. Her lips twist into a dry smile. Her head falls back, and she waves me out.

I can't tell the Wizards about Sadie or the dearly departed. My life is too strange to relate, and I'm not up for anything comparably weird that my cohorts might be inspired to share. Everyone seems comfortable with this. So we talk about stupid things and laugh a lot. We eat out on Mondays and Fridays—styling around in the Champion. The rest of the time, we mix and match lunch-bucket treasures, picnicking in the shade. I bum so many tamales from Nina that she hooks me up with her grandmother. I want to ask about granny but don't. All I need to know is that the woman's cilantro tamales are better than sex. I say this, trying to be funny, and Brian says my sex life must be pathetic. Drow says, "Yeah, it must not suck at all." "No," says Nina, "It doesn't blow." She flushes, having embarrassed herself, and this strikes me as charming. She's a single mom dreaming of an art career. A wonder. She could reel me in without half trying. But I keep my distance. I don't understand my work yet. She needs a rock—Drow, maybe. I'm a juggler on roller skates.

As I turn into Sadie's hallway on a rainy afternoon, Gemma slams into my chest. Steps back and tries the crooked smile, but it sags. Blinks nineteen to the dozen. Sadie is dead. Suddenly, the hallway is full of Gemma's children and grandchildren. A whirl of compassion. Blessings. We're in Blessings Hospital.

When Gemma calls to invite me to the funeral a few days later, I plead work. I'm a doer. I'll remember Sadie while moving—climbing and opening up views. Not everyone would get this, but Gemma does. She says Sadie made a gift of the cottage to her. *Oh, I love my Gemma dear.* I tell Gemma I'll meet her there after the funeral. That evening, exhausted, I trek back to Sunset Cliffs—where I'd thought of jumping. Where Sadie happened instead: Coral innocence, hands deep in pockets. The soft-shoe in slippers. The child-crone gestures. Her escape from the Gatto into the thick Georgia night. *Feeling womanly. Victorious.*

Sadie's—Gemma's—bungalow is nested in a clean and bright landscape. Bijou, Anshu would say. I see myself from above again. The vision shakes me out, makes me feel positively dharmic. There's Stan climbing starward, up Sadie's flagstone walk. Gemma greets me in a white dress with a navy belt and scarf. The place is angular redwood with cream accents—the richness soothing after the bright coastal sun. Mystery novels bracket the couch. Here and there, worthless treasures wait in boxes for the trip to the thrift store. I don't pity them. I hadn't kept much of Eva either. Somewhere in Colorado, an eager woman wears Eva's favorite sweater, warm in future-seeking.

As we look out the upstairs dormer, Gemma's daughters arrive with six kids and a few grandkids. They greet me as kin—not because of who I am, but because of who *they* are. They scatter through the house they know well and return noisily with boxes and a few sticks of furniture. The old woman comes alive amongst her brood. We end up in the kitchen, which smells of roasting almonds. Over iced tea and snacks, theatrical discoveries are made. An ancient, electric scalp stimulator is a big hit. The kids plug in the glass wand and shriek as blue lightning moves along the curved tube. They take turns rubbing it on their heads until breakage is imminent and Gemma restores order. She runs the electric tube over her short gray hair and laughs. "Look out! I feel too wonderful!"

But she checks herself and coils the antique appliance back into its box. A serene granddaughter, Dariana, envelopes her. Gemma flutters. "It's too much. Sadie didn't have all of this. All of *you*. She didn't have Theo—or anyone."

No one tries to fill the silence. With children on every counter, the adults leaning into one another, the restored 1960s kitchen is church. Dariana looks fresh in a baby-blue hoodie. She runs out and returns with a square something that she hangs on a nail over the stove. It's the metal resonator from the dobro set in a frame made from Sadie's coral robe—a funky old heart for this home. Gemma weeps freely on her granddaughter's shoulder. After an unhurried, tender interval, we're shooed through the living room and out. There's a slow leave-taking in the yard. Two hatchbacks and a pickup fill up with arms and legs and bits and pieces of Sadie.

I should've left long ago, but Gemma asks me to stay. Grabs a bottle of chianti and directs me to two lawn chairs on a small patio overlooking the sea. Slips off her shoes and holds up her feet. "Sadie and I would sit here in the evenings and drink a glass of wine. Cinder would lie at Sadie's feet and worry a bone. About every ten minutes, the dog would look up and stare at Sadie in adoration. For a long while. Like Sadie was about to sprout wings. We decided that Cinder had learned to do that while Sadie was watching TV. At every commercial break, Sadie would do something interesting, so Cinder came to look for that. She never stopped checking in like that, even though we spent most evenings out here. Old Cinder! It's funny, the things you remember."

The night is still. The wine goes, and I get chatty, telling Gemma about aromas and dioramas and how Eva died. "She had weak fingernails. Always worked on them while we talked about the future. I can still see her filing away, talking about having a kid. I found emery boards everywhere for months after she died."

Gemma nods reverently, stands, and tops up my glass. I can't shut up. "I never wanted a son. I wanted a little Eva. Wanted to love her all over again from the beginning."

The old woman walks around and hugs me from behind. *Roses.* "She was happy, Stan."

After a Cinder interval, I blabber on. "Dying happy: Herodotus had a good story about that."

Gemma settles back into her chair. "Do tell."

My brain is oatmeal but Gemma is patient. Finally, the story emerges. "When the Athenians made a hash of things, they asked Solon to come up with a new legal framework to put them back on track. He agreed, on condition that they could not repeal the new laws without his approval. Then he took off for ten years."

Gemma nods. "He didn't want to be around when they started hating him."

"So Solon's out traveling the world. Meets Croesus, a fabulously wealthy king."

"Rich as *Croesus*."

"That's the guy."

I slow down so my tongue can catch up. "Croesus gives Solon a tour of his palace and landholdings and treasury. He needs Solon to acknowledge his plenitude.

"'Solon,' he says, 'Who's the happiest man in the world?' Solon doesn't hesitate. 'Tellus of Athens,' he says. Tellus was healthy, his household flourishing, his children abundant, beautiful, and responsible. When war came, he came to the aid of his countrymen, defended his city, and died gloriously on the battlefield. The Athenians honored him with a lavish funeral.

"Croesus keeps trying. 'Okay,' he says. 'Who is the second happiest?' 'Two brothers,' replies Solon. 'Cleobis and Bito.' They were great athletes of good fortune. When their mother needed to attend a festival and oxen couldn't be found to pull her cart, these heroes yoked themselves and delivered her in style. Everyone was impressed by the show of honor, and Mom was exalted at the party. So, she asked the gods to bestow on her sons the highest blessing of mortals. That turned out to be death that very night, at the peak of their power and honor. Statues of Cleobis and Bito were sent to the shrine at Delphi.

"So—you can't measure true happiness or worth until the race is run. The Greeks weren't talking about a sweet hereafter. They didn't believe in that. It's about making a good end. Adding the exclamation point to your life."

I refuse more wine and try to focus. "The main Greek word for happiness—*eudaimonia*—meant something like 'good spirit' or 'expressing your genius.' They thought of themselves as embedded in a tapestry of family and community. Sophocles said, '*Wisdom* is the supreme part of happiness.' You couldn't be selfish and happy at the same time. You had to be useful."

Gemma is up and moving. She sweeps across the grass, shuffling her bare feet. Walks to the edge of the patio and hugs herself. "Did Sadie make a good end?"

I pick out the bench in the hazy distance where Sadie and I met. "I don't know. She left this place for you and the kids. You told me that her daughter-in-law, Della, opened the Jazz Café in Oakland. Her grandson, Theo, is probably doing something meaningful in the world."

She hums softly. "This is how I felt when my Tom died. It's hard to know what you're left with."

The contours of the cliffs blur. "We can't know—not right away."

Gemma perches on the edge of her chair and speaks to the sea. "Yes, sir. It's a hard puzzle. You might never figure it out. But it's good to try. Good to gather the pieces and work on the pattern."

"Yeah. Roses. Dioramas. Emery boards."

The old woman swirls her wine and sighs. "I think I want a *scout*. A sweet old dog."

"Like Cinder."

"Well—I don't need worship. I don't need Cinder praising me every ten minutes. I'm grateful every day. My thing is, I want to *give* praise."

"Then you need a cat."

She laughs, stands, and shuffles around the grass again, beaming. "Thank you, Lord, for cool grass on bare feet!"

I slip off my shoes and socks, and we shuffle across the lawn together, like choo-chooing children. "Tell me about Tom, Gemma. Tell me about all those kids."

She turns and glides by. "I'm writing it out for my kin. A chapter for each child. I'm doing all my talking on those pages. I am not going to *talk* about a thing until talking *becomes* the thing. Not me. I'm writing it all out."

She chugs toward me and gestures with maidenly sincerity. "But I want to hear about you and Eva and whoever else you might fall in love with and where you go and how you remember Sadie. I'm all ears. I'm a *grandmother!*"

Stopping suddenly, she claps her hand to her mouth, and runs into the house. A few minutes later, she emerges with a fat folder. "I found Sadie's file on Theo."

Gemma picks through it, handing me things. "This envelope is for him—a long letter from Sadie and some sheet music they wrote together."

Flipping through a sheaf of heavy paper, she shakes her head, then presents the pages with reverence. It's Theo's artwork. Each page is a sketch or watercolor of an animal: Lions, tigers, bears, elephants, giraffes. Each creature looks directly, penetratingly, at the artist.

"Theo is the most talented person I've ever known. Sadie taught him to play guitar, and even gave him Mo, her dobro—but he left it when he took off."

Gemma wrings her hands and blinks at the stars. "He could never leave things alone. Sometimes, all he could see was—how things *should* be. He was mellow, anyone would say. But when he'd had enough, he had had *enough!* I hope he's learned to be easier with the way things are. I hope he's learned to warn people when he's getting full up."

The pictures tell a story: Shy boy looking over a shoulder. Defiant teen in shadow. Missing man. She hands me the folder. "You'll meet Theo someday, but don't you worry about it. He's a man in full, and Sadie is gone. I know you want some purpose to hold on to. You want to be *useful*, like some kind of Greek. But your business is here right now. We'll put you to work."

Relief surges and I can't feel guilty about it. Laughter bubbles up. Maybe it's the wine. Maybe it's the humbling Pacific. Maybe it's Gemma's crooked smile, lit from within. She takes my hand, and we shuffle shoulder-to-shoulder toward the yellow windows of the cottage. The inviting glow reminds me of Eva filing her nails, thinking of the future. A fundamentalist neighbor always called us unbelievers. We never knew what to say to that. There was so *much* we believed in. It all rushes back and I trust everything: Gemma, the not knowing, Anshu. The reveal.

There's the little bungalow, far below. Gemma stands in a circle of light in the kitchen, pondering a puzzle. Stan floats down the walkway, carrying in a folder the essence of a man. He doesn't know where to go. He never knows.

- V -

WHEN TO SOAR
(SUMMER)

I'm a Window Wizard and that's all. We use our super nicknames. Nina's morphs from Wonder Woman to Woman. She's the only one, after all. Bix is mostly just Bix, because it's easy, like the man, but Brian takes care to call him Captain America—compensating for his early insistence on Black Panther. Every time I decide Brian's a hopeless redneck, he does something cool like that. My tag devolves from Boy Wonder to Wonder to Stevie. So I get some wicked shades and goof to "I Wish." The easiest impression in the world: Dark specs. Eyes to the sky. Soulful bob and weave. Beam like the sun. So simple to pretend. Hard to *be*, no doubt. Everyone loves the Wonder of Stevie.

Turns out Nina is a bowler, of all things. I'd have taken her for the queen of an adrenaline sport like parkour or BMX. She's dabbled in those, she says, but there's no conversation in them. Bowling is drinking beer and shooting the breeze. So she signs us up in a sort of numbnuts C League. We're all slack about it until she shows up one day with silk, sapphire-blue shirts with our names embroidered over the pocket. "Wizards" stitched across the back. They ripple shamelessly. Must've cost

Brian a ton. This is serious, C League or not. Now, all of a sudden, we're punctual about bowling night. We generally get our asses kicked, but we try to get better. We don't want to embarrass Nina. We want to live up to our shirts.

I find myself grandstanding in my Stevie shirt. Stevie's a lot more fun than Stan. Sometimes Bix cranks up his little speakers in our corner of the bowling alley, and we goof to "Don't You Worry 'bout a Thing." Sometimes other teams join in.

Nina insists that I drive on bowling night, so we cram ourselves into the Studie. As the weeks roll by, the rides turn surreal. "We're cartoons," I announce, as if it's fixable. "All we need is a talking dog and some mysteries to solve." But it's unanimous: cartoonification is a *good* thing. The process accelerates. At least we're clear on the objective. Everything's a joke, but I suggest privacy rules. This is tough because I need stories. But I have to protect my emotional self, such as it is and will be. I'm still working on Eva. Sadie. Bus Bredda. Dennis and Pigeon. I don't juggle stories well. Eva and I once went to a film festival, but it was a waste of money because we couldn't handle more than one or two movies a day. We needed brooding time. And I've always been a slow reader. I take stories as they come but digest them like a snake with a bellyful of rodent. A story is a load of protein.

Everyone is chill with the privacy rules, which confer a crazy freedom. We're always in the moment. I don't know how these people vote or with whom they sleep, and don't care. We don't want to know about anyone's relatives. And no shop talk. A nutshelled personal memory is okay if it sets up a parody of culture or bowling. But that's it. Here's how it goes: Nina comes spinning out with wet hair on a warm night. Says she loves a cool shower. She gets caught up in some reverie and says, "Remember when you're a kid, and your mom takes your underwear out of the freezer—"

Well, we can't leave *that* alone. "Your mother kept your underwear in the freezer?"

"Yeah. Didn't—"

Drow shakes his square head. "I've *never* heard of a mom doing that."

We murmur agreement. "Where did you grow up?"

"Phoenix. At first, she just did it in the summer, but it kept getting hotter. We wanted to wear them every day."

That makes sense, but we're not about to let it go. It's a gift. For days, we make droll observations about frozen panties. Nina finally makes the excellent point that you can't knock it until you've tried it. After we're smoked by a platoon of blotto plumbers, Bix says he thinks frozen underwear might help our game. We agree to try it the following week. Brian seals it with a threat. "Anyone who chickens out loses his shirt."

He says "his" because Nina will absolutely do it. She's probably been doing it all along. Anyway, no one will risk losing the sapphire shirt. Next week, we win our first game. Now iced skivvies are ritual. Mine hang out with frozen waffles. Drow keeps his tighty-whities pressed between ice packs in a cooler, and pulls them on, screaming, in the bathroom. The ceremonies become more elaborate as we continue to win. Bix experiments with dry ice. Brian freezes his socks too. We keep winning. Monkish embellishments goose the work chatter.

So that's how we shuck and jive within the rules. You might let a personal tidbit slip, like what your mom did with your underwear. You might tell us *why* she did it. But that's all we need to know about you or your mom. How much you can get away with depends on the entertainment value. Riffability is key. The cartoon ethic prevails. This is how you end up flirting with frostbite in the nether regions while rolling a leaden ball down a polished lane toward a row of prigs. We call it fun. Sure, it's stupid. You just have to flip the right switch and believe. There's beer, after all. Snazzy blue shirts. We're not always a riot. Sometimes we take our underwear too seriously. But everyone peaks on bowling night. Wednesdays. Intermission.

Sometimes I leave the shades on to admire our den mother on the sly. Nina moves with grace—a picture of health and awareness, subtly managing us all. When her boy ran a high fever, she wasn't so jokey for a few days, and I regretted the privacy rules. But she refused to break them and we loved her for it. The kid has some health issues, but we don't ask. She has a sitter every week; that's the main thing. I see possibilities in Wonder Woman. She loves my Stevie vibe. The flirting is overt, but I know it's the last tug of gravity as I arc into deep space. I make room for Drow. He's thick as a brick sometimes, but finally starts coming around. The Nina flower bends toward his sun.

Every week, we close ranks. When Bix, our incognito Captain America, steps up to bowl, we whisper, "Oh, Captain, My Captain"—and he delivers. On the job, shoulder-to-shoulder teamwork paves the way for shoulder-to-shoulder goofing. Once you've nailed some mondo objectives—cantilevered office complexes scrubbed clean—clockwork companionship fills the holes in your life. Bounded, boundless frolics elongate the summer. I'll hang on to this shimmery shirt.

One winless Wednesday, the stars are just winking in a stonewashed sky when we walk out of the bowling alley. Pigeon lies dozing against a wheel of the Champion, squiffed. He wakes with a sneeze and grunts to standing. Shoulders the clunky pack. "Sorry, Stan. I saw the Champion. Can I have a ride? I'll pay for gas."

I missed Dennis's funeral. Pidge had left an invitation on the windscreen, but I had opted for vertical perspective with the Wizards. Dennis had told me about his life, his dog, and his girlfriend—Katy Sue—and I hadn't paid my respects. What a rook I still am. I give Pidge a smirk. "I don't need no stinking gas money. Can you wait until I get back? I'm the chauffeur tonight. The grill is still open."

Pigeon gives us all a little-boy smile and shuffles toward the bowling alley. I stifle the urge to introduce him. No one asks. But by the time we're packed in the Studie, there's a unanimous change of plans. A clown car *must* be overloaded, after all. We intercept Pidge at the entrance. He's thrilled but dubious. "Thanks, but I don't think—"

"I don't think either."

My compadres back me up. "We stopped thinking at five o'clock."

The back door swings open, and Bix waves to Pigeon, who grins tipsily and tumbles in. In the front seat, Nina turns around and takes his pack. After much shoving and cajoling, Pidge ends up draped across the backseat laps. Bix holds Pidge's feet daintily before him, admiring the running shoes. We shout and laugh and hang out the open windows, but everyone is on good behavior. Pidge riffs as if he's been the heart of the crew all along. "Who do I kill for one of those shirts?"

Nina promises him a shirt and even a place on the team. Stoked, he asks for his knapsack back and hands out cards. Nina gets it immediately. "Are those oxygen canisters in your pack? You could go lighter. I carry the small cans."

Pidge sobers. "I'm sentimental about the old heavies. They fill 'em for free at the hospital."

He redirects deftly, asking about Nina's need for oxygen. Turns out her boy has cystic fibrosis. Pidge could not have known how fraught her answer would be—considering the fact that none of us knew—but he compensates well, leaning forward to give her both arms. We all respond to Nina's glistening eyes. I curb the Studie while she speaks of the kid's bluff trudge through huffing exercises and shaking machines and soul-thinning drugs. She keeps it short and recovers quickly, but the atmosphere is suddenly crisp and deliberate.

Drow speaks slowly. "I just read a long article about that, and I thought, *Why am I reading this? I don't know anyone with cystic fibrosis.*"

No one knows what else to say until Pidge works his beautiful jaw in mock seriousness. "Is he a lumper or a splitter?"

Nina smiles and shrugs in bewilderment. Pidge explains that Dennis is a splitter because he doesn't let any type of food touch any other type of food in the pot or on the plate. It drives a lumper like him crazy. Everyone weighs in on lumping and splitting. Nina and Drow are the splitters. "Where does that come from?"

I channel Eva without thinking. "Rigid potty training."

My mates know instantly that this authoritative bullshit is not original and pump me until I say too much about Eva. In the rush of sympathy that follows, I watch Pigeon. He's hugely empathetic but drawing inward, probably knowing he's the reagent in our overstuffed crucible. Missing Dennis, anyway—always, but especially now.

We roll on with our gentle inquisitor, through a surreal night of confessions. Bix's girlfriend's parents keep introducing her to white guys. Drow can't find his father. Brian and his wife can't take another miscarriage. The bond is stronger now, and I'm grateful. It's this warm and breezy night. It's Pidge. He gave Stan's stupid rules the night off.

Bix is the last bowler we drop off. He and Pigeon run in place by the fender, going on about running shoes. Suddenly, Pidge pitches forward, but Bix catches him playfully, and we all feel better. Bix turns and trots into the night. Affirmed, sated with our secrets, Pidge slides smoothly into the front seat. "You should be a cab driver, Stan."

"You should be a—what are you, anyway? Do you have a job?"

"I'm produce manager at Captain Carrot."

Of course. I've seen Pidge darting through the aisles there. I can see him having some attitude as a checker, but fussing with bok choy suits him to a tee. It's therapeutic, probably. We tick along for some time before he blows his nose and opens up. "Dennis gave me the sailboat. *Katy Sue.* I took her out last week."

"You must be a pro."

"Dennis taught me. Do you sail, Stan?"

"Not yet."

"Yet! What a hopeful word."

Pigeon rolls down the window and sticks his head out. He looks wild and wistful when he pulls it back in. "I spread Dennis's ashes in the harbor."

We stop for gas in thick, salt air. Pidge comes out of the convenience store with a couple of ice cream cones, which remind me of the Spuds. We lean against the fender and try to stay ahead of the melting.

"What about the guns?"

"Clayton really wanted them."

"But you're keeping them."

"I'm a good shot, Stan."

"Who you gonna shoot?"

He smirks. "You know me so well already!"

"You insisted! What about the guns?"

"I took 'em for a boat ride!"

"Uh, oh."

He shoots me a conspiratorial look. "They wanted to go swimming. But, you know, they're not good swimmers."

I know, as if he had said so, that he dumped the guns so he couldn't use them. It's in his hunted look, in how desperately he needs me to laugh. I manage a weak smile. "Plop, plop."

Pidge turns solemn. "It was dreamy out there, Stan. Letting all those—*life extinguishers* go. *Katy Sue* picking up speed. *Saweet!* We were cooking with gas when I laid Dennis out under the moon and stars."

He's quiet the rest of the way. When we arrive, he doesn't move. I don't know what to say. "How's Popeye?"

"Pissed."

"What will you do now?"

He pauses for a minute, trembling, but sounds centered when he speaks. "I just wanted to run and run. But I have all these meetings with psychologists and lawyers. Turns out it's kind of cool. I get to make sure everyone is taken care of."

"Including you?"

"I—just don't know where to run."

"Yet!"

Pigeon stumbles out of the car and trudges up the front steps. Turns and waves, tracking my slow departure. "Yet!" I yell again, but it's useless.

Here comes the nightmare shadow. A load of it. Eva taught me how to meditate, but I haven't done much out here yet. As with sleep, it's probably not possible to catch up. But that's what I want to do—not just check in with the cosmos but rent a condo there and have a look around. Ask some questions. So I sit motionless on beaches and cliffs every day. I'm terrible at first. Waiting impatiently for a quiet mind, I play with Eva's ring. That does it. I'm still small, but anchored.

Sheltered in the bay, the beaches of Coronado Island are low and mellow. The classic old hotel sets the tone. It's easy here. Luxurious. The beaches of Maine, where I grew up, were different. Windswept and cold, usually. I must've logged hundreds of miles there as a teenager. Dad was stoic after Mom died. He just worked a lot—as a forester for the state forest service and an adjunct biology professor at small colleges. Anyone who thinks government employees lack motivation should've met my dad then. Even at home, he would go on about using Scandinavian forest management methods in North America. He was a true believer. It's why he kept teaching when the pay dwindled to nothing.

My sisters, Elanor and Arwen, filled in for Mom and chipped away at Dad's façade. They still fought when he was at work or traveling, but when he was home, they harmonized in the key of Mom. When Dad was gone and they started in on each other, Trudy the collie and I would head out the back door. Sometimes I tried not to come back. But by the time we turned homeward, I was over it. Trudy and I would linger as we dried off on the back porch, breathing pine and listening to laughter—wavering between wilderness and community. In the living room, the girls would be cutting Dad's hair, reading to him, or railing against school hierarchies. Diverting him, always.

The girls were named for characters in *The Lord of the Rings*. As a teenager, Arwen would say, "My parents were sooo stoned when they named me." But it wasn't like that, and she stopped saying it when she dropped theater. Our parents weren't stoners. Mom, an English major, just loved Tolkien. She named me for her favorite professor. Sometimes she called me Hope or Hoppy. When I started reading history as a kid, she was sure I was headed for an academic career, like Professor Stanhope. I don't know how I'd have liked that. I made a good start at DU, but discovered I'd much rather listen—and read—than lecture.

Bix and I often work together. He's a history guy, jonesing for a full-bore degree. "I was into World War Two, but I'm kind of done with that."

"Why?"

He moves close, speaks low. "I like horses. Never owned one or even ridden one, but I like horses. Their heart, man. The way they run."

I figure Bix has forgotten my question. Just as well, because I had flat-out asked him for a war story. I must be slipping. I don't want to know why he lost interest in World War Two. But later, shoulder-to-shoulder, he delivers. "One day, I'm watching footage from P-47 Thunderbolts at the end of the war. I always liked that rugged airplane. But I have to bail on the video when I find myself watching draft horses spooking, running, getting strafed. All of a sudden, war isn't a video game anymore—it's horses dying."

He wipes his face and hands me a water bottle. "Did you read *Hiroshima* by John Hersey?"

"No."

He slows, as if wishing he hadn't opened this pit of sorrow. "There's a horse in that book; its skin burnt away by the atomic blast. Yeah, I know that a quarter million beautiful humans were smoked and tortured by those bombs. But none of it was real until that one helpless animal put me on my knees."

Right. The screaming horse in Picasso's *Guernica*. Robert the Second of Artois begging for his horse's life after the Battle of the Golden Spurs. Bix doesn't need those stories. Probably knows them. He's a solid history guy, with most of his own history unwritten. I'd like to read his books in twenty years. I wonder if I should bail on window wizarding? It's getting harder to stick to Stan's Rules of Non-Engagement.

We return to the hospital to finish a section that was under construction. I'm alone on a boom, about forty feet up on the east side, when I spot Pigeon perched in a chair, asleep in a large waiting room. Why is he here? It can't be for organ donation—the chemo he went through for testicular cancer had bumped him from the donor list. He's here for counseling, I guess. Head forward, lip protruding, he's just like Randy at naptime. He blinks awake and locks onto me. It's like our first meeting, but this time he's the snoozer. I hang outside the building, forty feet away. He gives me a sleepy smile and I waggle my squeegee. He stands deliberately, showing off pressed jeans and that bright green turtle shirt. His fire-engine-red shoes are right out of the box. He points at them, beaming. I nod, relieved by the hope of new clothes. The tattered rucksack lies on the floor, still weighed down by oxygen tanks. Why are they still necessary?

Pigeon grabs the pack and moves away from me, parallel to the window. Stops in front of a big TV. With the concentration of an athlete, he swings the pack by its straps a couple of times. Then he plants his feet wide and spins entirely around like a discus thrower, whipping the pack with accelerating speed, feeding a surprising heat. He puts everything into three rotations. Now Pidge is the center of attention. A nurse and a big cop move toward him as he launches the pack toward a damaged window three panes from me. It flies with a flat trajectory and shatters the tempered glass. Ten thousand micro-cubes arc over the sidewalk to the lawn below. The few people on the sidewalk run for cover.

Triumphant, Pigeon makes eye contact. This pulls me out of a trance, and I jump to the edge of the boom. "Don't do it, buddy!"

He flashes a Randy smile and turns away. The cop lunges with surprising agility, but Pigeon dips neatly under his arm and lopes to an inner desk. He taps it and turns, as if taking a victory lap, and accelerates past the flailing nurse toward the window. The cop lays out, but Pidge stiff-arms him. I wave my arms. "No!"

One, two, three long strides, and out. Windmilling his arms sickeningly, Pigeon clears the sidewalk and plows into the soft grass with knees tucked, in perch position. "Uh!" The head lolls. The deeply sunken torso rocks backward, rebounding, getting comfortable with eternity. Witnesses run to the bloodless body. A hubbub builds. Klaxons bleat. Are those necessary? Where should the body be rushed?

I can't account for the next few hours. When Pidge was asleep in the lobby, what was he dreaming? Of bears and swans? Guns? Dennis? *Katy Sue*? Beautiful, wasted organs? It's all I can think about. We bystanders move slowly to the cavernous lobby, where police organize interviews. I'm a star witness, so don't have long to wait. Yeah, I knew Pigeon. And Dennis. I can't say why Pigeon seemed to be performing. Some people testify that he did it for me. Why? I was a prop, I guess, a stage assistant exaggerating the drama. The one who shouts, "Stop!" when there's no stopping.

Was Pigeon happy? Sometimes. He was happy on *Katy Sue* with Dennis. He was happy sparring down the hallway of the hospital. He was happy in the Studie with the Wizards, telling stories, sleeping hard. He was happy drowning the guns. Skirmishing with anybody. He was happy as caregiver, three-point drainer, discus thrower, runner. Leaper.

After the interview, someone gives me soup and I sit in the lobby. Maybe I don't want to be alone, or maybe I'm too tired to move. More of Pigeon's friends arrive. No one sits. Dressy executives, sloppy nerds, flamboyant artists pace, cluster, hug. Jackie doesn't recognize me and that's fine. I don't want to talk. I might say too much. I might say that Pigeon's cannonball was the bravest thing I've ever seen. I might even say that he made a good end. Its consequences will be far-reaching, after all. It will probably make a dent in that fucking list by inspiring LGBTQ activists to fight the discrimination and donate in greater numbers themselves. It will save lives. But suggesting that Pidge's death was justified to anyone who knew him would be twisting the knife. Everyone knows or suspects the truth anyway. We just can't talk about it. Some sacrifices are so deliberate and profound that they shouldn't be discussed, lest they be imitated—messily.

The tears and rage weigh against speech anyway. Even Jackie breaks down, slapping a wall. I imagine Pigeon in the middle of the group, sparking: spinning stories for media consumption. *Saweet.*

As the soup congeals, my fevered brain distills a vision: I'm in a ghost Studie, careening stupidly across a shadow landscape, with Dennis and Pigeon and Jack Kerouac navigating. We roll along piers and beaches, pointing at the sea. I have to believe the ride is a gas—that we're bound for glory. Was this Pidge's dream? *Shut up, Stan.* I lurch to my feet, three hours from eye contact with Pigeon, not knowing if I'd touched the soup to my lips.

I write out my contact information and press it in Jackie's hand, asking to be notified of Pigeon's memorial. I won't miss this one. I skipped Dennis's, letting Pigeon and myself down. Would that have made a difference? Would Pidge still be alive if I had paid my respects? Jackie's face shows recognition, and she promises to keep in touch. On the way home, the quirks and mannerisms of lost friends crowd my mind—the detailed, shared memories I had avoided by working. Hi ho: off to work I'd gone.

Brian gives me the week off. I write out what I know of Pidge and Dennis—Pidge looking for trouble and Dennis the model of restraint. When I receive a card from Jackie about the memorial, I call her, asking about Pigeon's family. She says there are no blood relatives. *Blood relatives*: a narrow meaning for a vital idea. I spend a lot of time on the beach, organize the apartment, think about moving. Try to meditate, but am dragged down by the iron in my soul. The feeling of loss is too familiar. I've made friends in California without trying, and one badass enemy: death. I think I want a normal life, but what the hell is that? Too much to hope for.

The bright Colorado weekends with Eva are a fading dream. It all informs, but I don't know how. The Greeks cared enough about a couple of ideas that they etched them on the walls at Delphi. The first is to know thyself. Turns out, that's harder than it seems. A few years ago, I was sure I knew who I was. But I didn't understand where listening was taking me. I didn't understand the obsession with history. It wasn't just background recreation. It was turning me away, separating me from every life I knew, making me incompatible with lunch-bucket coasting. Trying to understand this tops the to-do list every day. The changes keep coming.

The other Greek idea, all things in moderation, was a favorite of Eva's. Maybe it will keep me from being warehoused. One of the ways I was changed or am changing is in a tendency toward obsession. Need to watch that. I almost stalked Sadie. I might yet stalk Gayathri. It's just a matter of interest. I become locked onto, fascinated by, sources of story. Dharma Bum Jack, for instance, whose dreams I devoured on my aimless bus rides. Part of my obsession was his obsession. Am I obsessed with obsessives? No. It all comes from me.

I'm a beacon: sweeping, fastening on unlikely people and things. I could blame this on the wounding, but that's not right. I've always tended to fixate. But everything is exaggerated now. I'm ballooning into caricature. I drive the Studie with stately deliberation—as if the act is sacred, as if I'm Shiva the Destroyer, creative seed and all. I have a lot to say but don't want to speak. I just want to be. I want to *be* the car, the landscape, the sky, the Earth. "I always want to know I can escape," said Anshu. Proteus: lost and profound. Someone said that we all become caricatures of ourselves eventually. The cartoonification of Stanhope Ellis is proceeding apace. I'll be very strange very soon. Is it injury? Insanity? Whatever is driving it, moderation has to be the anchor. I need to moderate the seeking and processing. But also trust it. I have this idea that movement itself—turning outward, moving on—is key. No wearing of grooves.

I will never forget Pigeon. Neither will the Window Wizards, it turns out. Nina organizes us for the drive to his memorial. The Champion feels weirdly spacious, though it holds the whole crew. The event is held at the San Diego High School gymnasium. Pidge was a scrappy point guard back in the day, of course. His former teammates tell animated stories of him stealing balls and fouling out. I can't tell the story of him juking the cop. The place is overflowing with fans, but not everyone knew him well. By now, most of the city has heard of Pigeon's big exit. His celebrity status has drawn some lookie-loos. But honor is manifest, even from them. A dozen speakers lay out the soul of the little man. Jackie tells everyone that Dennis gave Walter the "Pigeon" nickname after watching him perch in his odd way in the bleachers during a pick-up basketball game. Pidge had become so obnoxious that they sometimes made him sit, just to take the edge off. But there was no dulling the lightning-quick reflexes; they just had to deal with his aggressive ball-hawking. "He was a perpendicular little guy," Jackie said. "If you agreed with him about anything, he'd start changing his mind just to make sure he had his daily donnybrook. And this started early. Pidge was living large in elementary school."

A big, blowsy drag queen gets down to it: "Pigeon was always asking me to stay over, but I never did. I was afraid I'd wake up in a bathtub full of ice while Pigeon rushed my kidney to the hospital. But seriously: No greater love, right? Pidge was *the* helicopter hubby. He'd have fought Imperial Storm Troopers for Dennis. Come to think of it, in the end, he did."

Jackie returns to the podium to announce Pidge's Pledge, a new organization that will specialize in procuring organs for LGBTQ patients. A murmur in the crowd builds to a roar. It continues for so long that Jackie steps back and stops trying to speak. She just laughs and points to a signup table in the back, which is quickly mobbed. That's it. There's nothing more to say—just that one trademark word, and everyone is saying it.

At the after-party, Dennis's sister Irene approaches tentatively and introduces herself. She must've asked around a lot to find me, of all people. She's a solid soul with sparkly glasses, poorly hennaed hair, and an air of resignation. She says that Pigeon—Walter, she calls him—made her the executor of his will. This is so surprising that I can hardly understand what else she says. Eventually, I make out that she's inviting me to come to her place the next day. I reach for the old excuse, start to say I have to work—but find myself accepting, for Dennis and Pidge.

We Wizards talk quietly on the way home. Nina expounds on her philosophy of splitting—that you can't know or appreciate a thing until you separate it out. Brian makes the equally strong case for lumping. Bix applies each to the study of history. We hardly know how to be serious together, yet spool out a bright, loose conversation about when to come together, when to pull apart, when to fight on, and when to soar.

- VI -

Wanting to Smash the World
(Summer)

Irene's brick cottage is a tumbledown version of Eva's pillbox in Denver, with sand and weeds instead of a lawn and flowers. She leads me to a kitchen festooned with knick-knacks. We sit at a funky pine table next to a window that overlooks a bleak backyard and watch a Weimaraner mope around the chain-link perimeter. Irene seems distracted and moves with difficulty, but tries to be gracious, pouring out terrible coffee. "I never could do much with the yard. I can barely manage the housework."

I don't know what to say, and she takes this for skepticism. "Arthritis is the family curse. It caught up with all of us. Except Dennis—such a jock! We couldn't believe it when he suddenly took to bed."

"What about Clayton?"

"Have you ever heard of the Apostles of Calvary?"

"No."

"It's the fastest growing evangelical organization in the country. Clayton founded it. They're offering him a TV show."

It's hard not to imagine Pigeon's response. Irene stands and grabs a hip with a grimace. "Jeez-o-Pete!"

I move to help, but she holds up a hand. Leans on the table as the pain subsides. "I'll just tell you what you want to know. Clayton's church doesn't condone modern medicine. No transplants, for sure. They say we must all get along with what God gave us. The rest of us in the family are too diabetic to donate. Dot went through all the tests, but in the end, she said her doctor wouldn't allow it. Now, how do you argue with that?"

"I'm sure Pigeon found a way."

"Yes, he did."

She sits down and frowns, sipping coffee. "When Dennis received his scholarship, I think he was overwhelmed by the competition. Everybody was as big and strong and fast as he was. So he started taking things."

"Steroids?"

"I don't know. He took handfuls of pills."

Why can't I think of anything to say? Irene's eyes glisten. "Clayton said it was God's punishment." She wipes her face violently with a dishtowel. "For the—abomination."

She stands again and limps to the window, dabbing her eyes. "Dennis was the sweetest boy. You should've seen him with Scoop. And with his girlfriend, Katy Sue."

I sip the bitter brew to prevent myself from hugging Irene. Don't want her to think she's about to be molested after all she's been through. We're quiet for a while. She tracks the dog's movements. Sits with a wince, patting a pile of papers on the corner of the table. "Walter's will. I had my lawyer look at it. It's all tidy."

"Was a will necessary? All Pigeon and Dennis really had was each other."

"Well, there's the boat. *Katy Sue*. Walter wanted you to have her."

"But—he hardly knew me."

"He says here that you wanted to learn to sail."

"But it was Dennis's boat."

"He gave it to Walter."

"You take it. I'll sign it over."

Irene is suddenly prim. "None of us want it. I've talked to Dot and the boys." She looks down and blanches. "They—you know. Played games on that boat."

It takes me a minute to understand. "You could sell it."

"No. Walter spelled it out. It's in his will." She adjusts her glasses and fusses with the tablecloth. Her face is strained but firm. "I know you must not think much of our family because you've heard the gospel according to Saint Walter. But I am determined to do what's right. This is what he wanted."

She gets up and busies herself around the kitchen. "Dennis would expect us to listen to—the man he loved."

She's shaken by the admission. Steels herself. "Do you have a— boyfriend, Mister Ellis?"

"Stan. No. My wife died a couple years ago."

Irene touches her hair—surprisingly coquettish. I want to hug away the vulnerability. Instead, we busy ourselves with the arrangements for transferring *Katy Sue*. Irene has no interest in seeing the boat again. She pulls a packet of papers and keys out of a drawer and shoves it across the table. *Katy Sue* is a twenty-two-footer, berthed at a marina up the coast. Irene rubs the name on the folder. "We all just loved Katy Sue. I—*prayed* she would become my sister."

She pushes her awful hair back and watches the despairing Weimaraner. "She cried so hard when they broke up! Poor kid. Dennis cried too. He always talked about Katy Sue after that. I think she would've married Dennis no matter what."

I stand and step to the window. Irene clumsily moves the dishes to the sink. Gives me a soggy smile. "I'm glad I went out to Walter's—*Pigeon's*— memorial. I always thought Dennis deserved another Katy Sue. Looks like he found one. I should've known. We should've been friends."

"You *were* friends. He made you the executor of his will."

She looks down, blinking, and moves shyly next to me. Maybe a side hug would be okay. Yeah, that works. We stand like siblings, comforting cautiously.

"Who's taking Popeye?"

A sweet smile lights up her face. "I am!"

The doorbell rings, setting off the Weimaraner. Irene trots to the door. "And here she is!"

I trail along, carrying the papers so I can make my escape. Jackie stands on the porch with the calico cat. Irene waves joyfully. "Come in! Come in!" Jackie enters, and we stand in the living room, grinning at the cat, who peers over Jackie's shoulder with interest. Irene looks at me and nods toward the window. "Old Lester's lonely since his buddy died, and he likes cats. Popeye tolerates him fine."

Lester confirms this with steady barking from the backyard. Jackie and Irene begin complimenting each other, but Popeye has no patience for that. She leaps to the floor and makes for the back door. Irene admits Lester, who runs goofy circles on the rug, languidly pursued by Popeye. He eventually settles down on his haunches. Popeye flops in front of him, exposing her belly and pawing the air. As I leave, the women are perched Pidge-like on the sofa, sharing animal stories as if they've known each other for years.

On the way home, I imagine describing all this to Eva. She would nod gravely and file her weak fingernails, dispensing wisdom about the relationships that I'd overlooked. Eva had conversation. She knew how to listen—responding not to clumsy words, but to honest intentions. I touch her sapphire.

I generally avoid people on my walks, but now I track scattered crowds on Ocean and Dog Beach. Here and there, I kneel and close my eyes, listening for snatches of story: "—geek of the week." "I couldn't understand a word, but I was ready to take him home." "I mean, aren't those people grateful?" "Bailey! Back to me!" "It was worth your whole wardrobe, bitch!" "I'm not your boyfriend or your boss or your dad. I'm just—" "Hey, chorizo boy—" "Zoe! Where's your squidgy?" "Who votes for these guys?" Sometimes at house parties with the band, I'd dial up a buzz, find an empty room, and listen like this. The swirls of bragging and threatening and wheedling and flirting were a trip. I was addicted to these aural hallucinations and could drift for hours. But someone would always find me. Sometimes that was the best part.

Back at the apartment, I climb to the roof again. This new habit looks to be worrying some of the residents, so I'm careful to stay over my apartment, facing seaward, away from nearby windows. When Anshu calls, I try to open up for a change. Find myself going on about Sadie, Gemma, Pigeon, Dennis, Eva—the lives I've been drawn into, the patient duty that drives it. The doom that follows. He's quiet for a long while, then speaks slowly. "This listening of yours has elements of all yoga paths. All ways of connection. Just a moment."

He does some beeping task on his phone, then doles the familiar sagacity. "*All* yoga paths. You know, there's Jnana Yoga, the path of knowledge. Bhakti Yoga, the path of divine love and devotion. Karma Yoga, the path of non-attachment, of neutrality, of selfless action—not feeding the cycle of karma. Raja Yoga is the royal road of meditation, of becoming one with Brahma, the ultimate reality. Your dharma seems to involve weaving these yogas. You are *learning* by trying to understand the wisdom of the speaker. You are *serving God* by recognizing the divine in the speaker. You are *detached* by serving as a vessel for the speaker. You are *meditating* by listening with awareness—by merging into the reality of the speaker's story."

There's comfort there, but I can't hold up my end of a yoga conversation. I thank Anshu for the insight and retreat to the commonplace. He laughs about bowling night and the Stevie shirt. Asks about San Diego. Says nothing about Gaya.

"I have more for you, Stanhope, but it's late. Tomorrow."

Right. Tomorrow and tomorrow. Shock after shock. Whether my dharma involves the braided yoga paths Anshu described, I don't know. It sounds grand because it gives purpose to my Mister Chipmunk Ride. But that doesn't make it true. I *want* it to be true. Maybe that's enough.

Late the next afternoon, after walking and listening the shit out of the coast, I impulsively pull on the Boy Wonder uni. It's a sad attempt to buck up, but I do it anyway. What are the Spuds up to? I stride heroically through the apartment, packing for a trip to inspect the sailboat, *Katy Sue*. Dennis's sailboat. Christ. I didn't even go to the guy's funeral. Couldn't save his partner. Some hero.

Bing!—a text from Anshu:

> You want to hide away, but engage, my
> friend. The cycles of creation and destruction go
> on forever, yet every eyeblink counts. Everyone
> wants to stop making a bed that will only be
> unmade. But temporal concerns are muddles.
> Make your bed carefully so you may dream
> carelessly. Burnish every instant. If you do not
> engage in small things, soon you cannot engage
> in anything. Hope dies.

I climb to the roof, where the evening breeze is picking up. Oops—I'm still in costume. Another diorama, this one a hoot: Boy Wonder stalking around in the sky, worrying Anshu's words, muttering to the sea. Every day I shoot for moderation, but my aim is middling. I'd better get off the roof before someone really calls for help. Too late: here comes Halle, carrying a bag, with the Spuds, ready to kick my costumed ass. Round Two. I keep the combat close and safe, kneeling in the center, flipping the giggling forms across my knees and shoulders. Halle bounces around, giving everyone advice, whacking us with the bag. When we're worn out, she opens it and theatrically pulls out a silk, canary-yellow cape. It's much bigger than my lobster-bib pretender. I'm so knocked out by the gesture that I stay on my knees, as if following a chivalric script.

When I was Spud-size, my father made a knight's helmet out of an octagonal boot box. It was surprisingly creative, with a plume and hinged visor. Deep blue, with "Sir Stanhope" in red script across the brow. Dad was shy about his handiwork and just left the helmet in my room. I was stunned by its magnificence but didn't know what to do with it. No one else I knew had a helmet or even a sword. So I made a towel cape, found a broom-handle staff, pulled on the helmet, and stood, ramrod-stiff, as a sentinel by the front door. But motionless vigilance is boring. I began to worry about looking ridiculous and slunk inside. That was it for the helmet. Occasionally I'd put it on and charge around, but mostly I just admired it in my room. Looking back, I wish Dad had gone big with it, presenting it with reverence and knighting me. We might have crossed swords. Spun stories for years.

Halle and the Spuds remove the wuss cape and reverently install Cape 2.0. A breeze catches it, unfurling other-worldly splendor. I'm on one knee, still unable to stand. The wind drops. I rise, finally, as Sir Stanhope, Captain Carrot, the Boy Wonder, and a hundred other heroes. The outfit requires striding and flexing and underwear-model poses. Halle and the boys laugh themselves loopy. The upside-down, backward salute wins me a group hug. Halle and I kneel with Bard and Randy before us and imagine a shipwreck in the sunset. I commence babbling—future talk, thankfully. The brothers are jazzed to learn about the boat, *Katy Sue*. I'll introduce them someday. I promise.

Now I dream of sailing every night with my sister, Gaya. I wonder if it will come to pass? When I am too tired for rational thought, I think of it as a reward. This is the wrong attitude, of course, but my dreams are so exhilarating that the possibility is irrelevant. Stanhope's sailboat postcard feeds them. Before launching our dream this evening, I will send him one more text:

> The *Gita* teaches us to let go of any imagined reward—to remain unattached to results. I once heard a great actress say, "Love the sweat." That stays in the mind. Hardworking people understand. What do you call them? Lunch-bucket. Lunch-bucket people love the sweat.

Dana Point is one of those mash-ups of pricey and quaint that pepper the California coast. The village is scattered along a cliff that trails east and south from the jutting point. A small island shelters the harbor. I can't find anyone official at the marina, but the access card works. I'm standing on *Katy Sue* at dusk.

Dennis Murphy was more interested in his ride than his living space. The stowed blue sails look brand new. The deck is spotless. The outboard is old but well-maintained. The cabin is tidy, with a toolbox, fishing tackle, blankets, and a stove. The game stash—chess, Clue, Scrabble, cards, cribbage—makes me laugh. These are the games Pigeon and Dennis played on *Katy Sue*. I fidget in the bunk like a child on the cusp of adventure, and consider Irene's good, small heart. When the bobbing and lapping finally knock me out, I dream of falling with Pidge. Waking at dusk, I rummage through the galley with a flashlight. No food aboard. As I wander the length of the boardwalk, a neon sign beckons: PILGRIM GRILL.

The place is deserted, but it's late on a weekday night. A middle-aged redhead in glasses—name-tagged "Connie"—appears with a neat smile and points to a booth. I sit and tap out paradiddles with my fingertips. Should I put a band together? No. The best incarnation of our band had been Ruby Raven—mostly because we were fronted by Ruby Watson, a bundle of charisma with Aretha pipes. We did a version of Pink Floyd's "The Great Gig in the Sky" so she could wail like Clare Torry. But the song always did her in. We had to make it a finale so she could crash afterward. I loved Ruby's always-changing versions of the song—in part because I had a crush on her, as we all did—but hated seeing her flameout night after night. The passion devoured her. One night she collapsed, and I carried her to her room. We never did the number again. She moved on. Hooked up with some female musicians and called themselves Ruby Rocket. Last I heard, they were still kicking it.

Connie delivers fish tacos with a local lager and surprises me by sitting across the table. Makes bluff and dramatic conversation. She apparently feels obliged to entertain and is good at it. She fiddles with a swallow necklace. "Gorgeous here, innit? I came for the swallows out at Capistrano. Stayed for the sea lions and—*magnificent* whales. Bought this place for the *relationships*."

The tacos are fresh, seasoned to perfection. Connie assures me the place is crowded on weekends. She couldn't ask for a better little business. They even have a regatta in the fall. I tell her about *Katy Sue*, and she asks about Dennis and Pigeon. Their boisterous banter was famous in the bar. When I tell her they've both passed, she jumps up and tidies the condiments at every table. Comes back with passion. "Please! Don't tell me how."

She paces, touching the swallow necklace as if to ward off evil. "At least they had each other. Anyone could see that."

"Most people would want to know how they died."

She sighs. "Not me. Several years ago, I decided I just couldn't take any more bad news that I couldn't do anything about. If you tell me how Pigeon and Dennis came to leave this Earth, I won't be able to stop thinking about it."

She pulls off her eyeglasses and cleans them. "I don't read the news anymore. Or watch it."

Ah—a fellow traveler. "No news is good news."

"That's it! I remember when I stopped. A young family was killed out there on the overpass. I had to drive by it twice a day. I'd arrive at work in a funk and come home even worse. That was enough for me. If the post-office flag is at half-mast, I don't even ask who's been shot anymore."

"What about sports news?"

Connie jabs a short finger at me. "Now you're talking. The TV's dead, thank God, but I have some sports sections here from all the papers."

"Thanks."

She walks behind the counter and returns with coffee-stained sheaves. Disappears in the back. I'm soon absorbed in a story about an autistic football player at San Diego State who might have a shot as a pro. He's a safety—my favorite position. What a gig: badass protector. You can be a strong safety, regularly popping running backs—or a free safety, irregularly swatting away passes. Good service, either way. Strong safety is Dad's brand. I can still see him marching between house and yard and garage in his worn overalls, trailing pipe smoke, tweaking things. Everyone sleeps on his watch. Free safety is Anshu's brand—coming out of nowhere with the perfect angle on life. Just when you figure you're

cooked, bam!—over the top. Salvation. You want both of those guys on
your team.

I once loved the spectacle and disciplined gallantry of college football.
The old crowd energy provides strange comfort on the walk back to *Katy
Sue*. I detour to the nearby beach and pick planets out of the sky. Take
off my shoes and track the shifting waterline. Sadie's cradle moon breaks
free from simmering clouds. I don't know how it is that I became stuck
like family to an odd group of people, only to lose each of them. Was I
some sort of lens? No. I'm not glass. I'm a membrane, altered by every
passage. More is coming.

Sleeping on the boat is a childish thrill. The rocking, the rattle and
moan of rigging, the lapping of water feed my anticipation. I dream
through Eva's winking sapphire. Wake with a headful of gratitude—for
Eva, for Sadie, for Gemma and her kids, for Dennis and old Pidge. For
Halle and the Spuds. For Anshu. For Bix, Nina, and the rest of the crew.
For Dad and my dutiful sisters. For the Boy Wonder on his bed-mobile,
whatever his fate. For the Champion. For bobbing *Katy Sue* and the fuss
she will demand. I should remember this trick of extracting gratitude
from grief. It deserves a title: The Immaculate Rebound. Pidge would
love it.

In the morning, mist catches and burns. Sipping coffee with my feet
dangling off the bow, I wonder. The insistence of worship in religion has
always mystified me. Surely gods aren't ego furnaces that require stoking.
Devotion is a deeper idea, I think. Gratitude plus habit equals devotion. In
my Native American period, I dug *Black Elk Speaks*. Black Elk was Oglala
Lakota in the days of Custer. A total visionary. He and his biographer,
John Neihardt, spoke of walking in a sacred manner. The idea surfaces at
times like these. Worship feels servile—implies hierarchy. But this sacred
walking—gratitude—turns me outward, opens me up. Gemma knows
all about it.

Once in a great while, Dad would take Trudy and me on a field trip
and teach me about trees. One fall, when I was Bard's age, he jollied
me along a trail for a few hours. I complained the whole way but shut
up when we stepped into a holy glade. White pine walled the clearing,

setting off granite and stair-step brush of red and gold. One of the better lunches of my life, though peanut butter and jelly was the main course. A rich aroma fixed it in my mind. Pipe smoke—Dad's Sir Walter Raleigh blend, in particular—can conjure these precise memories. The gratitude and safety I feel now are just what I felt then.

Well, I've put it off long enough. I start the engine and putt *Katy Sue* into the harbor. When I'm far enough out to be safe, I cut the engine and drift about ridiculously, trying both sails, though I have no idea what the fuck. There's not much wind, but I still heel over alarmingly. After endless mucking, I manage one sporty turn with the wind. Now what? I quit while I'm ahead. A small but appreciative audience looks on as I motor sheepishly back to the marina. If you can't be cool, you can at least be entertaining. As I secure the boat, a gangly young man and his girlfriend offer a few tips. We joke about my ineptitude and the kid— Duncan—offers to give me lessons. He has the striking red-gold hair that the Scots claim as their own. He wears it long, so it whips and flames in the breeze like a banner. His girlfriend, Skye, strokes and adjusts it. She wears her dark hair short, in counterpoint. This accentuates her black eyes and cream complexion. They touch and play shamelessly—so obviously in love that I feel blessed. We agree to meet next week.

I should be working. I've always needed that anchor. But I can't go back to the city. Can't go back to death. Over stale sports and sinus-clearing rellenos, I convince myself that I need several days with *Katy Sue*. So I settle in. Stalk the cliffs and jetties, looking for—what? Someone to share this with.

Pigeon's last duty on *Katy Sue* was drowning the guns. "The weapon is the enemy," I once read. It makes sense. Pidge dug it, anyway. His dreamy cruise was a course correction away from the too-quick American fix. Emerson said it's often not what you do that makes a difference but what you refrain from doing. I expect Pigeon had grown to hate death— especially Dennis's but anyone's, even his own. He had to kill something and chose the instruments of death. He sought the death of death. In the end, all he was able to do, all we can ever do, is shift death toward meaning. Death is everywhere, will happen to everyone, but can't be commonplace. It should signify. If not loud and large, like old Pidge's, then it should, at least, *illuminate* something.

When Eva died, I hated death with blowtorch intensity. I wanted to fight it on land, sea, and air. The obsession probably kept me alive and persists to this day. Is that what's happening here? Do I hate death so much that I'm attracting it? Has the Reaper started the fight I was spoiling for? I'm on the ropes. How do I fight that supervillain? How do I save those who turn to me? Do they *want* to be saved?

Maybe this is all a tricked-out rehearsal for my own crash and burn, which is coming. Hope I don't die testily. But—I survived the fall. As a diligent dharma bum, I have to believe I was meant to live. Have I served my purpose? No. How do I know this? Because I'm so fucking brimful—full up with no place to unload. It *can't* be over. *Right, Stan. Probably half the victims of the Holocaust thought that as they were marched to those fucking "showers."*

On a boardwalk bench, I re-read Anshu's text: the paths of knowledge, devotion, non-attachment, meditation. Maybe that's the logical framework I need for understanding why friends are dying, one after another. Maybe those yogas are the yellow brick roads linking the stories that come to me. Maybe receiving and recording the stories is my work. What scares the shit out of me is the possibility that it's my work *forever*. I'll carry business cards: Death Magnet For Eternity.

Stop it. At the beach, I impulsively plunge into the waves. Thrash outward, without looking back, as hard as I can for half an hour. Forgetting that I haven't done this in years. Eva was a strong swimmer; sinking was my game. At least now that I have a little more body fat (tamales, beer), I'm more buoyant. I continue to pull mindlessly for the horizon, just because it's good to be physical again. The synchronization of mind and body arouses spirit. I order my thoughts for Anshu. We'll talk soon. He'll understand.

The beach is a hazy hairline when I turn reluctantly back and slip into a slow sidestroke. The temperature is dropping with the sun. My arms ache. Another half-hour and the beach is a hopeless smudge. Hey—I'm not going to make it. The absurdity strikes me amidships. I laugh at the bad end I've made for myself. After all my big thoughts. After convincing myself that I have some death-defying purpose. Ha! Life is a soap bubble in a windstorm. I wish some part of me would drown. Which? Hello, hypothermia.

I pick up the pace but then have to stop and catch my breath. Bob stupidly, trying to breathe deep without laughing. My arms are throbbing stumps. *Just another minute of rest.* But it's too cold. I squint shoreward. Something black is bobbing about halfway out. It's moving closer. A dog's head. Ha! The intensity on its face is too much. If this dog is coming to save me, I've crossed over: I'm in a cartoon. Then I see the fluorescent yellow tennis ball floating about eighty yards away. Right. It's not about me. Am I that close to shore? Must be. I can see the dog's owner on the distant beach—a huge guy with a ball flinger. The tennis ball gives me something to shoot for. I only make about half the distance when the dog scoops the ball with practiced nonchalance and makes for shore. That's okay. I have the bobbing head to follow. I keep checking it. Fall into the trance of the devoured. There's Anshu's smile. Must proceed apace.

I'm dog paddling when I reach the shallows, fixated on the now-prancing Labrador, and land on my knees, gasping. The giant wades out with his dog and waits until I'm breathing normally. Then he helps me to shore, ignoring my idiot 'splaining. The Lab is incredibly friendly, as if apologizing for the ball focus. And beautiful: black, well-muscled, about sixty pounds, with the sleekest, thickest coat I've seen. An English Lab, says the guy. He calls her Caprice. Okay. Maybe I'm in a cartoon after all. I watch the animal trot away. Caprice! Her shining flanks. Dharma dog.

I squish back to the Studie and pass out on the back seat. Dream of backseat sex and front-seat sex and future sex and sex as a general and particular concept. When it's all too much, when I know who's behind the shattered glasses, I drive to the small marina motel. Check in. Take the hottest shower I can stand. At the grill, I indulge in fajitas and two beers. Order a third but am getting my ass kicked so seriously at darts that I give the suds away to a deadeye blonde, just because. I don't know how to come on to her. *May I interest you in a death fetish?* The rowdy group that Dennis and Pidge hung with is a hoot, but I can't put myself out there. I just want to rejoice in my exhausted body and think about Caprice. I wake before dawn and hit the road, jump-starting the thrill of childhood adventure. When I was small, we always started vacations early in the day. Sunrise from a moving car means hope. Gratitude.

Back in Ocean Beach, I see I missed a call from the hospital. Yow—a voice message from Gayathri. Her voice is low, constrained by worry. Of course. She was gone so long that I must've asked five different nurses about her. She comes back to work after illness or accident to learn that a strange man has been asking about her. I'm sure I didn't leave my name with anyone. So Gayathri figures this guy is so whack that she takes the trouble—probably a lot of trouble—to track down his name and number. I'd like to know that story. I'd like to know how she turned the tables on an apparent stalker. Does she wear glasses? *Shut up, Stan.*

Gayathri asks me to meet her at the hospital. I flash on showing up as the Boy Wonder. Bad idea. How can I appear safe? I imagine geeking myself out in various ways. But I hate ties, don't wear glasses, and my overalls would be too obvious. A pipe would just be stupid. I wish I had a dog. Caprice. She'd be the perfect ambassador. But I wouldn't be able to get her into the building. She'd be barred, like Anshu's cricket bat. The weapon is the enemy. *Get a grip, Stan.*

Emptiness crowds my drive to Blessings Hospital. Alone and self-possessed is easy. Alone and nothing is a shell of a Stan. A hopeless poacher. A kid with a pellet gun erasing life and beauty just because he can—a stalker, thinks a protean woman.

Arriving early, I catch some knowing glances from hospital staff as I walk the long hallway to the conference room Gayathri has reserved. A few note-takers and gurney-pushers express outright hostility. I'm okay with their loyalty and protection—it reminds me of Anshu. I'd thought of calling him, but what would I say? He no longer mentions his sister now that I live near her. Must honor that. I like to think that he wants to introduce us in person. I like to hope.

I'm greeted in the conference room by a pale, dark-suited young man with a neck tattoo. He closes the door behind me and stands in front of it. Gayathri—it must be her—sits at the far end of a long, rosewood table.

I see Anshu in her right away—the squarish face, bemused expression. But the eyes are more liquid. Quicker. What's there? Intelligence, but also something larger. Something growing. They flash and sweep. She won't let them lock on. Good. Not ready for the tractor beam.

She's flanked by two men in shirtsleeves with guns on their belts. I'm still processing their attire when Gayathri rises soberly, shakes my hand, and introduces me to the detectives. Morris is burly, with an air of affable authority. Nichols is compact and intense. The pale kid remains standing. Their attempt to intimidate is probably more successful than they anticipated. Blood pools in my feet. Rational thought goes ta-ta. All I can think of is how Gayathri's jade Shiva necklace looks against her skin. She's smaller than I expected. Anshu is probably six feet. This woman is a rich abstraction of her brother. Less, but more. The eyes flare.

I sit hard, having lost the ballast of coherent thought. As if reading my mind, Gayathri supplies a glass of water, which I gulp. I must seem guilty as hell. I had expected a little mistrust, but not this. I stare stupidly at Morris's belt holster. Gayathri speaks first.

"We have a few questions."

Morris flips open a file folder. "How do you know Gayathri Das, Stan?"

I look directly at Gayathri. "I don't know her."

"But you asked for her by name."

"A mutual friend told me about her."

Gayathri won't be passive in this process. She leans forward. "None of my friends know you. I asked them all."

Nichols dicks with his phone. "How did you know Walter Collins?"

"Pigeon. I met him here at the hospital."

"When?"

"About two months ago."

"Did you know him well?"

"Yes. No. We had some conversations."

"Were you lovers?"

"No."

"Not your type?"

Fuck you. As if Pidge and Dennis's relationship could be casually violated. It's okay. These guys don't know. I watch Sphinx-like Gayathri. *Keep it simple, Stan.* "I like women."

That sounds cheesy, and I find myself blushing, in spite of it all.

"How well did you know Dennis Murphy?"

"We had a couple talks. And Pidge told me some things."

"People tell you things."

I wish I could put my head between my legs. "Aren't you supposed to read me my rights or something?"

Morris smiles. "You're not being held, Mister Ellis. You're not being charged. You're free to leave at any time."

We watch each other. Gayathri wants me to stay. If I leave now, there will be this between us. I sit up and take a deep breath. "I want to help," I croak, looking for jade approval.

The big man nods. "Mister Ellis, you were one of the last people to see Dennis Murphy alive. You were *the* last person to see Pigeon alive. In fact, Pigeon seemed to be waiting for you, so you could watch him jump. Can you tell us why?"

"I went to see Dennis because he was dying. I don't think many people knew."

"But *you* knew."

"Pigeon told me."

"Did Pigeon also tell you that he, Pigeon, was also preparing to die?"

"No."

Nichols smirks. "But people tell you things, Stan."

"They tell me their lives. Not their deaths."

"They just happen to die after these conversations."

This lands like a sucker punch. Stan the Death Man. I've been clinging to the possibility that it's all been a clusterfuck of coincidence. Yet here's proof that other people see the monkey on my back. Who's next? Gayathri? She must wonder why Death Man is stalking her.

Calm down. I need time to think. What about Brian's Window Wizards? They seem ready to live forever. But I don't know their lives.

I insisted on *not* knowing. Is that the key? Maybe I have to have the history first. *Time to die. Check your history with Stanhope at the door.*

Breathe. My eyes settle on Gayathri. Something about her is calming. Her jade. Her cool awareness. Her concealed contempt. I gulp water. "What was the question?"

Nichols thumbs his phone distractedly. "No question. Just facts."

"Sorry. I hadn't thought about—"

Gayathri looks incredulous. "Really?"

"That is, I thought it was—I *hoped* it was just …"

Jade. Breathe. Spilling my guts is a bad idea. These guys probably don't know everything.

Nichols glances up from the phone. "How did you meet Sadie Coulter?"

"On the cliffs. Sunset Cliffs."

"You sought her out?"

"No. I just needed—*she* needed to talk."

Morris stands. "What did *you* need, Stan?"

The holster is at eye level. "A story."

"What?"

Gayathri looks down and takes my part. "A story."

Nichols squints and types. "An alibi."

I can't justify that with a response. I'm in the middle of a heart-attack nightmare: having to explain myself to guys with guns. Hostile guys with guns. And a woman who wonders if I will kill her. Should I ask for an attorney? That would be telling. I'd seem desperate. It might focus these guys. Blood in the water. I won't place a lawyer between Gayathri and me. I'll never get her story that way. I may never get it anyway, but I should try to keep the possibility open. Why? Why do I need story? That's the question hanging in the air. And I can't answer it. But I have to say something. "A *story*. I just thought Sadie needed to talk."

Here comes Morris, trying, or seeming to try. "Are you a psychologist, Mister Ellis?"

"No."

"Do you play one on TV?"

I can't smile. There's not enough blood in my face. "I don't analyze or lecture. I just like to hear what people have to say."

Nichols nods. "You wash windows for a living."

"That's right."

"Do you *watch* people too, Stan?"

"No. Well, when I'm working—sometimes, yeah. You can't help it. But I'd rather listen."

"Doesn't that strike you as creepy, Stan?"

I try to focus on Gayathri. Our link is Anshu: my lifeline. This is just a conversation. I like conversations. "No. I think people are more creeped out by talkers. Listeners are okay."

"What about eavesdroppers?"

"That's something else. Not me."

"Why Sadie, Stan?"

"I'm new here. Sadie was friendly. Looked like she needed to talk."

"People tell you things."

"It seems that way."

"Why?"

"I don't know. Because I'm there. Because I'm not distracted. Because I ask. Because I don't—*talk*."

"Your wife's name was—Eva?"

They knew this would be a gut punch. Yes, Eva's accident is a matter of public record. But I don't want them speaking her name. "Yeah."

"She died—"

"In a car."

"Was there an investigation?"

"You tell me."

"And several months ago, you—"

"Fell. I fell."

"—were electrocuted. Have you recovered?"

"I don't know. That much current fuses some things, blows other things out. I don't think anyone completely understands what electricity does to the body."

"But you feel—"

"Different."

Nichols's turn. "Dangerous."

"*Different*. Inside-out. Aware. Is that a crime?"

We're quiet for so long that Gayathri blurts, "Who told you about me?"

"Your brother. Anshu."

Not what she expected. Not what she wanted me to say. She puts her hand to her mouth and blinks. We wait. "What do you know about him?"

I try and fail to make eye contact. "He lives in Denver. One of my Park Hill neighbors. I saw him two or three times a week for years. A jeweler from Kolkata. Loves cricket. Easy going. Likes to hike alone. And with you. He told me about San Diego. He's why I'm here."

Gayathri isn't capable of speech. Nichols picks up the thread. "When did you last see him?"

"January, I think. He came to see me in the hospital."

Gayathri gasps and spreads her hands on the table. "He was—checking in."

"The cricket bag."

She nods. Something's wrong, but I blunder on. "We talk on the phone sometimes."

Gayathri stares resolutely forward. I focus on breathing again. Have to ask about Anshu but choke on the words. "Your leave of absence. You were—visiting your brother."

"Yes."

"Is he—"

Gayathri exhales and bows her head. "Last week."

I lurch to my feet. *Anshu. My Friend. My lifeline.* The thought of him moving out here had kept me going. My hands move to cover my nose and mouth. Nichols addresses us all with authority. "Eva. Sadie. Dennis. Pigeon. Now Anshu. Can you see why we wanted to talk to you, Mister Ellis?"

Gayathri fishes a tissue from her huge purse. Shoots me a desperate look. "Do you know Sadie's friend, Gemma?"

I drop my hands. Try for eye contact again. "Yes."

Doubt and fear flicker across her face. Turning away, she studies a far window—the image of Anshu contemplating Mount Evans. She wants me to stay away from Gemma, of course. Nichols looks hard but says nothing. Morris leans on the table, but his words are neutral. "We know you were close to each of the deceased just before death. But without Pigeon and Ms. Das, we wouldn't have put it together. We have nothing to charge you with."

Everyone looks at me. My face pulses. I address Gayathri in an unsteady voice. "I'm sorry. Anshu was—why I'm here."

Gayathri must hate me, but she's always ready to change her mind. Anshu said so. She stands, shouldering the large purse. Nods. "Thank you, gentlemen."

The doorman performs his function, and she leaves quickly. Nichols gestures for me to follow. I can't trail after Gayathri, so I linger in the hallway, lean against the wall, slide to sitting, nod as the detectives file past. Morris stops and extends a card. "Anytime you want to talk."

Anshu is the hardest. I sit for ages, seeing his ready smile, wishing I had a cricket bat to swing. Wanting to smash the world.

I THINK OF YOUR MOTHER
(SUMMER)

HOW COULD I BE SO CRUEL? THIS STRANGE AND LONELY MAN—STAN—
needed help, and all I could feel was afraid. So I made *him* afraid. I called
the police—even though I knew he had seen Pigeon die. Even though I
knew he needed compassion above all. I received my karma, of course.
While punishing Stan, I learned that he was my only link to my dying
brother. I learned that he—I *think* this is really true—also loves Anshu.
Together we might have found comfort. But I insisted on fear.

Now I have had my kneeling meditation and begin to see again
with soft eyes. But something is in the way. I feel suddenly distant from
Anshu. I am too cruel. But I realize that he was distant too. I must think
about this.

※ ※ ※

It's time to leave the Window Wizards. Gandalf said it: "Do not meddle
in the affairs of wizards." Soon we'll know too much about each other.
Death will come. On Monday, I grit my teeth and trot out feeble excuses—

vertigo, the lure of the road, etc. I can't say that I fear for the safety of my cohorts. Brian is to the point, as always. "Candy-ass." The word is delivered without rancor, as if naming a color. I have to agree with him. I finish out the week so all can be said. We were becoming family, so I had to play candy-ass—had to watch the light fade in their eyes. A mournful mood settles in, but it's throttled by an epic bowling night. I lead the way with three punchy craft brews. Can't hold back tonight. Nina drops a ball on my foot, and I accuse her of being passive-aggressive. "Nope," she says with a shove. "Aggressive-aggressive." I could kiss her. Tipsy wrestling ensues, all parties devolved. We lose ridiculously, reveling in badness, despite flirtations with frostbite. But you'd think we won a championship. I drum the shit out of everything. Find Stevie's "Boogie On, Reggae Woman," and we make fools of ourselves.

Zen-Obama Bix drives us all home in the Champion. I ride in the back, committing the chatter to memory. I was determined to get drunk and be somebody tonight—not just to amuse my mates, but to forget the detectives. To forget that Anshu can no longer breathe and touch and know. I will remember it all in high definition, but not now. Am I really attracting death? Maybe death is attracting me, which is worse. Either way, it bothers me that Gayathri knows. At the apartment, I stagger up the outdoor steps, collapse to sitting, and blink at whirling stars. "Hey Jack Kerouac. I think of your mother," sings Natalie Merchant, far away.

In the morning, before I remember where the Champion is, Bix shows up to give me a ride. I hope he and his girlfriend made the most of the Studie after dropping me off last night. Bix and I sip coffee and grin at each other like geeky truants. Everyone's amped on the job. But even after the caffeine wears off, there's no carping or moping. We juked it. We'll remember the best of each other now. Nina flirts with Drow and the blockhead responds. I wish them beautiful babies.

The need for safety, for consolation, brings family to mind. Once Elanor and Arwen had Dad joking again, they orchestrated blind dates and chance encounters. Eventually, they couldn't agree on candidates and had to give it up. Dad hated that anyway. He was polite but had no romantic ambition after Mom died. Nothing gave him more pleasure than a healthy, mixed forest—Baxter State Forest was a favorite—and he didn't need to share it with anyone but us. Now, Dad's heart keeps him out of the hearts of forests. My sisters still bracket the old man like a couple of oaks—fulfilling their promise to Mom. What was my promise to her? Well, there were two: to obtain a bachelor's degree, at least, and to listen hard. "Pay *attention*, Hoppy! If you just listen, you always have a chance." *She* listened. Classic movies supplied her with quotes for every occasion. "The time to make up your mind about people," she'd say, quoting Phillip Barry's *The Philadelphia Story*, "is never."

I stop at a tobacco shop and come home with four billiard pipes and tins of Sir Walter tobacco. It's fiddly fun—satisfying, until I go green. Now I'm a yarking wonder, nobody's protector. Guess I need to ease into this. I'm recovering with deep breaths on the roof when Gayathri calls. Ouch. I have to kneel. Her voice is thinner, more distant.

"Did Anshu call you last week?"

"Yeah."

"What did he say?"

"A lot. I'll have to think about it."

"Can you meet me on Saturday?"

"With the nice policemen?"

"No. Just us."

She names a Thai café. I'm happy to have something to do. It'll offset my quitter's remorse. Already I miss the foolishness, the shoulder-to-shoulder work, but at least I have the Stevie shirt. After a short workday on Friday and heartfelt final toasts, I walk down to Ocean Beach, remembering Anshu. I find a quiet bench and meditate, with the help of Eva's ring. Manage a long sapphire burn. Fall asleep and dream of Anshu sailing. Wake and try to remember everything.

I've read a lot of high-flown things about friendship. When sulky Achilles won't fight, Patroclus is such a brick of a pal that he dons the hero's armor and leads the Greeks into battle. Chuck Duran was a brick of a pal. When Eva died, boom—there he was, keeping me sane. Chuck's wife and daughter had both been helping Eva with the flowers. We brought Chuck in to clean the high windows in the back of the shop that were thick with grime but promised mountain views. Chuck and I transformed the store in a single morning. Chuck's jokey work talk was right up there with the best of Justin Ellis. He punctuated everything with snatches of song—altering lyrics to suit every dropped tool or tweaky reach. "Isn't It Romantic?" became "Isn't It Pathetic?" He could break me up with subtle movements of lip and shoulder. He rang me up once in a while after that when he needed help. I think mostly he just needed a laugh track, but it worked out. I learned his business, and sometimes we took in a game together. After Eva, he didn't just offer a job; he offered a partnership, despite his senior status. I worked hard to ensure that decision never cost him a penny.

But Anshu and I were on the fast track to friendship with a capital F. UpChuck is my guy forever, and nobody can riff on my nonsense like him. But we never had much to talk about besides shop and football. Not his fault. Fatherhood was kicking his ass, and he didn't have time for books. Anshu encouraged my speculations on history and, in return, patiently explained his ideas on religion and philosophy. He was my spirit guide. I didn't fully realize it until he was dead. I feel the weight of all those years when I knew him only as Eva's friend. But maybe Friendship is always a long time dawning. Plutarch's advice was to judge first and love later. That takes time. My connection to Anshu was axed, so I choose to call it Friendship, whatever it was or might've been. I resent its slow start and quick end. He was a gift from Eva—one of her best—and I nearly missed it.

Saturday is rainy and fresh. I arrive early, but Gayathri is already waiting in a booth. Her jasmine tea smells sweet, so I order a pot. She wears a teal blouse and a ruby ring on her left hand. The ring finger. Why didn't I notice that before? Her smile is eager, but her eyes are wary. "Thank you for coming."

I can't suppress a gush. "I wouldn't miss the chance to know you."

Her eyes soften. "Even after I practically accused you of murder?"

Murdah. I wouldn't call the Indo-Brit clipped. She speaks low and slow.

I shrug. "You might've been right about that. Manslaughter, anyway. No premeditation."

"Certainly not. I was sure of it when you spoke—"

"Of Anshu."

We're bonded in sorrow. I can't help myself: I want to understand, to hear her careful words—her soft, formal voice telling me about Anshu, handedness, dharma. I want my tender listening to envelop her, pour her out, shield her. But I'd give it all up to lose the sadness that binds us. I flash on Anshu sitting next to his sister. Gayathri recovers herself, breathes deeply, sustains the smile. She tries hard, like her brother. She makes her bed every morning. Without thinking, I extend both hands across the table. "I'm sorry."

She won't give me the eyes. But she reaches out and makes contact with the now-dominant left hand. I enfold it in mine, and we have a nice few seconds. She pulls back as the waitress approaches, and we order haphazardly. Gayathri looks troubled. *Keep it simple, Stan.* "You're a lefty now."

She blanches. "Oh! I don't know why Anshu tells that story."

Present tense. "He tells it because it says a lot about Gayathri Das. He's proud of you."

This puts her over the top. But I'm glad I said it—and so is she. Sitting quiet, allowing her time to grieve, I savor the tea. It's hard. I'm blinking too much. She talks slowly and carefully about the loss—the surprise of it, the plans lain waste—until I realize she needs me to redirect. "Do you think you'll go back to being right-handed?"

She smiles. "About two years ago, I realized I cannot go back. I'm not even really ambidextrous. I'm left-dominant."

Like Eva. "Can you write script?"

"I don't know. For a few years, I wrote mostly Hindi—that is more like printing, you know?"

She pulls out a pad and a violet pen. With an old-world flourish, the ruby ring bobbing, she deliberately prints a line of rounded characters. Rotates the paper and pushes the neat calligraphy toward me.

"What does it mean?"

"One and one make eleven."

"What?"

"It's a proverb. For me, it's like a Buddhist *koan*, with its little surprise at the end. I think it means that two together can be more powerful than anyone knows."

She smiles and nods, as if reassuring the world. She talks on, pretending not to notice my blush. "Now I just use a keyboard all the time. So I don't know about script."

"Can you sign your name?"

She takes back the pad and slowly pushes the pen across the page, as lefties must. The letters are round, the lines straight. *Gayathri Das.* She turns it around for me to read again. I spin it back to her. "How about numbers? Can you write your phone number?"

She watches me, bemused, for so long that I have to speak. "You're still trying to decide how crazy I am."

"No! I—"

"It's okay. I'm trying to work it out myself."

"Then help me. What do you think?"

I gulp tea. "I don't know how to talk about myself."

"Then, you belong in a different century."

"Maybe we both do."

"We are talking about Stan right now."

Right. The dangerous one. I look for answers in the tea. "I'm just—a blur. Between Point A and Point B."

"Okay. Describe Point A."

"Happy idiot. Beer, football, history. A wife I didn't deserve."

"So she was taken from you."

"Yeah."

"You *think.* Point B?"

The food arrives and we work on our gingery mush. Gayathri smiles encouragement. "Well?"

"Well, I'm not there yet."

"Then what is this mid-point?" She interrogates like a detective. Like the health professional she is.

"Trying to figure out what my work is."

"But, you wash windows."

"Not anymore. Once I owned a bookstore. Once I played in a band. Not anymore."

"What do you do every day?"

"Walk. Read. Ask. Listen."

"What are your plans for the future?"

"Is there a future?"

Our waitress pours out the jasmine tea. The astringent aroma elongates the moment. Gayathri breathes deeply and frowns. "I wonder about that too."

I'm still surprised when she agrees with me. She doesn't oppose me on principle. She just wants the truth, like Anshu. "How do you cope, Gayathri?"

"I just—focus on my work."

Wish I could do that. "I try to keep moving."

"Why?"

I can't say why I'm avoiding connection. "I need to find my work."

"Perhaps it is right in front of you."

"Isn't that always the way?"

She smiles and writes her telephone number under her name, sliding the paper back to me. Her eyes are as soft as her mouth. Then she steels herself, and her speech slows further. "What did Anshu tell you—in your talk last week?"

I have to buy time. "How did you know we spoke?"

"It was a guess. I was trying to call him just then, I think."

"Sorry."

"What did you talk about?"

Aha! I *can* pass this test. I extract my phone with a flourish and dial up Anshu's texts. She brightens. I wait patiently while she reads his careful words about burnishing. Making the bed. Loving the sweat.

She holds my phone to her breast. "This is Anshu."

She wants more, so I fill the gaps. Describe how Anshu helped with good spirit and the small *Gita* after Eva died. How he helped with bootstrap dharma in the hospital. His generosity in crediting me for using all yoga paths. His gentle engagement. His trying to bring a cricket bat into the hospital. She laughs and spins out stories of Anshu's cricket obsession. As a teenager, he would spend entire weeks scouting other teams and players. He covered so much territory and lost so much gear that he took to carrying his cricket bag everywhere, all the time. As school and work duties took precedence, the contents of the bag became less useful. By the time he settled in Colorado, where cricket matches are scarce, the worn caps and balls were only tokens of a dreamy youth, of long afternoons on a green, green pitch. "He always carried at least one relic in his briefcase or backpack. For luck."

"He must've needed the whole bag in the hospital."

She looks away for a long while. "You know, Anshu came to Colorado for his lungs. He texted you because he could not speak for very long."

Recoiling from the thought of Anshu gasping for air, I focus on how Gayathri talks with her hands, like Eva. How her warmth keeps drawing me out. Too eager, I say too much. Go on about how I wouldn't be on the coast if not for Anshu's vision of sailing with her. The stitch reappears in her brow. Great—now she thinks I'm a stalker again. "I didn't come here for you, Gaya. I came for the sea. Anshu helped me understand that this is where I belong. Right now, anyway."

She closes up, sitting more erect. "Only Anshu calls me Gaya."

"Sorry. He—gave me the habit."

Her scrutiny is hard. "Anshu told you all about me. Why did he not tell me about you?"

I shake my head. She answers her own question in a small voice. "It is because you are—like Yama, god of death."

Ouch. I stare at the ruby ring. Her hands are curved around a cup, but the warming tea is gone. I address the hands. "Anshu was right to protect you."

Gayathri blinks hard and speaks with heat. "Why didn't he call me? Why were his last, *precious* breaths spent on you?"

I have no idea. The waitress brings me the check, but Gayathri snatches it. She digs cash out of her enormous purse and lays the full amount, plus tip, on the table while I thrust money at her uselessly. She stands, shoulders the massive bag in her military way, dabs her eyes, and looks down at me. She speaks softly, with an edge. "Because people tell you things, I suppose."

I'm blowing this. Stand, as if to hold her, but can't move or speak.

Fortunately, she's incapable of cruelty. She forces a toothless smile. "Thank you. I hope you find your work."

Eye contact, finally. "It's right in front of me."

Wrong again. I'm probably *her* work. But I can't ask for any part of all that I need. She pivots, brave and small, and walks to the door.

How could I be so cruel *again*? Stan helped me feel close to Anshu once more and I repaid him with childish temper. It was not his fault that Anshu chose to talk to him instead of me. I must try to resolve my anger with Anshu without resenting Stan. I must stop hurting this man who already feels a lot of pain.

Anshu was just trying to protect me, in his usual way. It *always* made me angry. Now he is gone, and I am just as mad at him as I was at twelve years old, when he refused to introduce me to his teammates. Perhaps there was more to Anshu's behavior in the end than just overprotectiveness. It feels as though something monstrous is coloring everything. That really is frightening. I must breathe through this and try to understand.

I hit Captain Carrot on the way home, though I don't need anything. There's peace in the bustle. I wander through every aisle, looking for what can't be there. Every shelf is expectant: practical and promising. I linger near huge heirloom tomatoes. What am I looking for? Pigeon. I finally walk out with a big bag of jasmine tea. In the parking lot, I pull out Gayathri's number and forward Anshu's texts to her. The response is immediate: *Thank you.* No exclamation point, no emoji, just the formality. I delete her text. I have to accept the way things are.

A package awaits me on the porch—a wheel bearing I'd ordered. Even the Champion is subject to the laws of physics. It's only human, after all, and not all spare parts are in the trunk, despite Henry's best efforts. Happy to have something to do, I roll the old coupe onto the lawn under a ficus tree. Jack up the left front wheel and throw myself onto the grass. Close my eyes and inhale the scent of mud and grease. Reminds me of working on my dad's old truck. I have to accept the way things are.

It goes well, with cursing, for a couple hours. I'm just putting it all back together when small shoes appear. Before I can react, Randy and Bard are on their hands and knees, poking things. Bard holds a couple of nuts out to me with black hands. Randy reaches up into the engine, knocking gradoo into my ear. I finish up in spite of their help. They talk me into a short spin. With Mom's permission, we cruise for ice cream. Henry had seatbelts installed in the Champion, which is good because Randy and Bard are ready to stand on the seat the whole way. Halle runs out with their car seats. Both boys insist they're too big, but Halle ignores the whining and straps them in. Randy gets the window seat and hangs out as far as he can. Bard sits in silence, humiliated. When we finally joke him out of it, he tries to be the adult in the car—grilling me on transmissions and manual shifting.

We find an old-fashioned drive-up and inhale ice cream. I lay out some rules: 1) Stan's bedroom is off-limits. 2) No family stuff. I don't want to know who Mom is dating or what happened to Dad. 3) If anyone cries—including me—it's time to go home. That's it for now. I'm sure we'll think of more. They're welcome to suggest rules, but I'm the majordomo. On the way back, Bard starts to tell me about the time he broke Randy's collarbone, so I come up with another rule: 4) No war stories. They're confused about this, so I say that reality bores me. I prefer made-up stories. "So if I tell you that an alligator lives under the bed, that's okay. And you can riff on that and say that the alligator lives on old socks and pizza bones. But you can't talk about the time you saw an alligator at the zoo."

"That's hard!"

"Nah. Pretend is always better."

"Yeah! Like Captain America!"

"And Captain Carrot."

"That's a store!"

"A store named for a hero. Heroes have the best *store*-ies."

Yes—heroes like Pidge. Randy finds a box of matches in the glove box. Treasure. Back at the apartment, Mom needs more alone time in the kitchen. Randy wants to light the matches, but I say the only safe place to do that is on the roof. They're all over that, so we get permission. My partners in crime tremble with excitement as we ascend the ladder. After ranging around and shouting, we huddle like a band of thieves over our booty. I say we can take turns lighting the matches. The one who strikes the match has to tell a Captain Carrot story before it burns down to his fingers. I start.

"Captain Carrot wrestles the sock alligator. The gator sings 'The Petulant Gerbil Song,' and Captain Carrot passes out from its bad breath." I blow out the match. Plenty of time.

Randy is amped. "What's 'The Peta—'"

"Petulant."

"—Gerbil Song?'"

"You tell me. It's your turn."

"Okay! Um …"

"No waiting. Make fire, Ran."

Randy strikes a match. "Um, gerbils like peanut butter and …"

He's mesmerized by the small flame. I give him a few seconds, then blow it out.

"My turn!" shouts Bard.

He strikes. "Captain Carrot makes a big pizza. Uh, with pepperoni and mushrooms."

Randy yelps. "And peanut butter."

"What kind of story is this?"

"We're hungry."

We contemplate the match's blue flicker. The micro-meditation is calming. Bard yips and drops the match.

Randy strikes the next one. "A monster eats Captain Carrot."

"Then what?"

"He yarks! And here comes Captain Carrot. He throws his shield and—gah! The monster bites his leg and—gah! Gah!"

Randy's action moves kill the flame. So much for micro-meditation calmness. But the spirit is good. We work out the captain's superpowers: he can fly, he shoots wicked carrot darts, and is a good cook. He smells like guano because guano is a funny word. Halle calls, and we troop back for Viking stew. After dinner, I splash around Fiesta Island. On the far side, Great Danes cavort with goofy dignity. The sun dissolves in silver blue. Everything—the dogs, the opal sky, my grubby feet—reminds me of Gayathri, whom I can't see again. Anshu was clear about that, by his silence. Even Gayathri sees the truth of it. Her anger as she left the restaurant served her well. She'll give Captain Cadaver a wide berth.

Back at the apartment, I write out everything I learned about Anshu. His cricket bag, mostly. I've seen the relics within—worn old caps and shin guards and gloves. He carried this happy childhood with him everywhere. With it, he sought out the freshest air. Found the glimmer in all—snowfields and facets and sea spray. Worked hard to bring Gaya to America. His history is deep, thanks to Eva—and Gayathri. Gayathri with the jade Shiva on her collarbone and the ruby on her small hand. Whom I must forget. It's like what Pigeon said about how you can't prove a negative. How do I think about not thinking about her? It drives me to serious, therapeutic meditation.

I look up Yama. Turns out he's not the wicked dude I'd feared. He's more like the naughty-or-nice god, doling out reward and punishment at the portal of death. I can't really be Yama because I'm no judge. Maybe I'm Chitragupta, his scribe. Nah—he judges too, sometimes overriding Yama. But I'm not just an innocent story junkie. Yama is there. Gayathri said so. At this rate, I'll Gayathri myself into doing something stupid. I have to distract myself enough to avoid calling her. So I place the scrap of paper with her neat name and number in the *Gita*, which I shelve with *The Dharma Bums* in my brick-and-lumber, dorm-style bookcase. I try not to do this reverently and fail, pissing myself off. I back out of the stashing and start again, trying to add nonchalance. Is this crazy? Damn betcha. The backside of the paper has a letterhead advertising my green pills. It's a sign. I haven't taken one of those in a week, but I need one now.

Saturday, the Spuds check in and drop big hints about tagging along to Dana Point. Sorry—I can't risk their perfect lives. I promise to take them sailing someday, wondering if I can follow through. Halle is warm and joyful as I depart. On the drive north, I think a lot about the little family. Kerouac's mom said that every man in America should get down on his knees and beg forgiveness from the women in his life. For shirking. For lacking wisdom and not seeking it. Only then can there be true salvation. *Hey, Jack. I think of your mother.*

THANK YOU FOR BEING
(SUMMER)

GULLS AND SEA LIONS EEP AND GURP AT DANA POINT. THE LIONS ARE A nuisance in the marina, where they flop onto and defend any platform that smells like fish. They have a slew of boats to work with. It's a pitched battle between pescadores and tuskadores. Today, blubber has the edge. The real estate scattered along the cliffs must be worth a fortune. At least I can sleep on *Katy Sue*. I don't know why Dennis stuck her up here, but I'm glad she's grandfathered into her berth. Both marinas are packed.

Richard Henry Dana knew his work, going off to sea at nineteen on the brig, *Pilgrim*, then turning his poetic soul toward improving conditions for seamen the world over. The museum on the waterfront is full of him. From there, I trail a classroom tour onto a replica of the brig anchored in the harbor. The kids swarm all over the ship as I make my way forward. Some mistake me for a teacher, so we discuss poop decks, poop sails, poop swabbies.

The grill is busy at lunchtime, but Connie waves and plants me on the deck with a crisp sports page. She chatters away about the Capistrano swallows and her grandkids, who are now in Singapore. "I needed a break from the kids anyway. I suppose it's a crime for a granny to admit that, but that's the way it is, pilgrim. They'll be back next year. The swallows won't. I miss 'em."

I'm not ready for the swallow story. I focus on Connie's Rhodesian ridgeback, Kevin, who hangs out on the deck with me. He's warm and drooly, resigned to waiting. But when he catches sight of sea lions across the harbor, every ridgeback molecule snaps to attention. Connie talks to Kevin incessantly as she delivers food. He listens hard. "We use a verbal leash. Kevin walks just ahead with his ears cocked back. We talk about everything—especially what we're hearing and seeing and smelling."

I imagine them walking along the cliffs, free from media hype, Connie chattering away, Kevin listening. She says her granddaughter named Kevin after a crush, and we agree that it suits the dog's humanity. Despite the media-shunning, Connie is a newshound—but her currency is personal. She's ditched the mass-produced suds in favor of local craft bulletins about people she knows. For example, she says the upright, white-haired man nursing an Arnold Palmer is a retired admiral. He always sits at the edge of the deck, facing the harbor. Once he was full of stories but doesn't have much to say since his wife died. Connie rubs his shoulder when she passes and ignores his request for a check. When I talk about learning to sail, she shifts to Duncan, my sailing instructor. His parents are sure the kid isn't going to make anything of himself. He just hangs around the harbor, picking up odd jobs, scanning the horizon. I like him already. So does Connie.

The kid gangles out to *Katy Sue* right on time, his flaming mop glowing in the afternoon sun. He teaches me how to dodge the boom and tosses out basic terminology. We stay in the harbor for most of the lesson, then take her out to sea. Head north to the point, where the winds get tricky. Duncan is fluid and efficient, tacking us around and back. We can see up and down the coast now—hazy both directions. We ride a jet of fresh air coming in from Japan. I'm starting to figure a few things out, so Duncan lets me take over. He leans out everywhere, looking out to sea as if finished with dry land.

Skye meets us back at the jetty and they spill their plans for sailing around the world. Reluctant to leave their bubble of inspiration, I offer to buy coffee. They lead me to a funky local place on the dock. There's something strange about the late-afternoon crowd that spills out of the shop onto the boardwalk. We're in line for ten minutes before I get it: everyone is under twenty-five or over sixty. Most of them know each other. They've bonded over sugar and caffeine. The admiral stands behind us— slight, but radiating competence. Duncan introduces Admiral Spencer. The old seaman waves a hand irritably. "Forget the rank." Fat chance.

Together we watch a fresh-faced girl top off coffees with easy precision. It's all in the bar-wrista. She's a willowy Gayathri. Every woman is a willowy Gayathri. The admiral gets it. "Call her," he whispers to me. I protest, but he insists. There's nothing to do but salute. His laugh is surprisingly warm as we go on watching the girl's dexterous display. Skye rests her head on Duncan's shoulder and closes her eyes, her jawline entirely Greek.

I line up lessons from Duncan for the next three afternoons. Walk the cliff in the early mornings and manage to avoid meeting anyone. Once in a while, the admiral appears—walking fast, probably meeting the tide. Our silence is a bond. On the last morning, he alters course to walk with me. If he has something to say, I'll listen. Connie says he's eighty-five, after all. But he looks as if he'll sail into a second century. He says nothing, seeming to require only my presence. It's probably natural for him to stride purposefully with another man, studying the weather and shoreline. We wind up on the beach, wading for an hour among the surfers. He looks on sharply, as if they're doing something wrong.

Duncan, Skye, and I sail *Katy Sue* progressively farther along the coast. Skye calls the dolphins that ride our bow wave "torpedoes of joy." On our last day, she shelters under Duncan's wing and goes on about their world tour. The future talk is easy listening. It occurs to me that I could move to Dana Point. Nothing holds me in the city anymore. I'm happy to flee the klaxons. Probably the best way to look out for the Spuds and Halle and Gemma is to remove Stanhope Ellis. Can I do it? I watch Duncan and Skye leap and spar on the dock, just like Dennis and Pidge. How might I warp these lives? Do I already know too much? The thing is, I don't know how to be a hermit. I still need to hear the stories we all need to tell. A move would be a fresh start. I might navigate the hazards here. I can always escape on *Katy Sue*.

The last afternoon, I return to the waterside museum and aquarium. Spend a lot on two toy sailboats at the gift shop. As I leave, I grab two kid-size life vests, making plans. The prospects of dreaming away in *Katy Sue* and hitting the road at dawn convince me to stay another night. I piece the little sloops together and lie on the jetty, launching and fetching. In bed, I compare Spud-size life preservers to dharma life preservers to life-preserving dioramas. Sleep like a brick. At dawn, I surf childish wonder the whole way home.

As I pull up to the apartment building, Halle trots down the stairs with sound-asleep Randy flung over a shoulder and Bard trailing behind, pale as his PJs. It's day four of the crud, and they're off to the doc. I help them load up, not knowing what to say. Halle's stoicism is starting to crack. The Spuds dropped right after I left. Yikes. Should I have taken them with me? Did I poison them with ice cream? They lie on the back seat, but Halle clips them into the car seats. They have rockets on their pajamas.

As she pulls away, Halle tosses me a key and asks me to make sure the stove is off. Inside, I take a knee. Find an overstuffed chair. Breathe. Meditation comes—not the half-assed variety this time, but a deep appeal to the universe: *not the Spuds*. The fitful peace morphs into action. I organize a mega-mess of blankets, medicine, half-eaten soup, toy trucks. Fix a bookshelf. Vacuum. I'm finishing the dishes when Halle and Bard return. Randy will be at the hospital for a while. Halle drops her purse and a bag of drugs coming in the door. She holds onto Bard, and I catch them both. Help her put the boy to bed. Try to insist that she stay quiet on the couch. She jumps to her feet, but I hold up a Sadie finger. That slows her a tick, for which she's grateful. She debriefs me, pacing and gesturing while I make tea. Randy still has the heaves, so they put him on an IV. Prognosis: the flu, with pneumonia coming on.

Halle seems younger than I remembered, probably because she's scared. She's been holding the fort for a long time. After tea, I talk her into asking her mom to come down from Long Beach. She calls, and

Mom promises to be on the road within the hour. Halle's anxiety abates. She leans back on the couch and notices things being in the wrong place. I check on Bard. He breathes like a water buffalo, but I shouldn't wake him. I leave Halle dozing on the couch.

The next evening, Halle and her mom knock on the door and present me with a cinder block of zucchini bread. Karen's also fit—slightly shorter than her shield-maiden daughter. Halle has a habit of squinting one eye in an appraising way, and I can see that it came from Karen, who radiates the confidence that has deserted her daughter. Halle and I should get away, she clucks, and go out to dinner. We protest—feebly. Trundle out to Old Town. After a few bad jokes, I realize Halle is more embarrassed about being tall than I am about being short. We're solid. She guides me to a bistro her boss once took her to. Over wine, she assures me that I didn't give the boys ice-cream poisoning. I can't say much. She delves into their quirks: Bard's hives—triggered by ethical dilemmas—and Randy's weak bladder. Her concern is charming. It's reeling me in. But I keep wondering how she'd react if she knew how dangerous I am. How dangerous the *police* think I am, forgodsake.

She smiles, waiting patiently, so I slip into Auto-Stan and drone on about beer, window washing, Colorado, and the Studie. I don't want her to ask questions. No worries. She's happy to listen. It beats worrying. On the way home, she suggests we go to the batting cages, of all things. Turns out she played first base on a championship fast-pitch softball team as a teenager. It's something I might've guessed from her directness, reliability, reach. And that gauging eye.

"Nickname, please."

"Stretch."

"Bet you could nail that throw to third."

"Yeah. I miss it."

At the cages, I buy a stack of tokens almost before she's out of the car. Rush to set her up in the last empty cage. When she trots toward me, laughing, I fluster and drop the coins. When I kneel to gather them up, I feel her cool hand on my head. Everything slows as she smiles down at me. It's all weirdly sacred, as if I'm being blessed. Her hand lingers. I wait. Pelicans wheel overhead. She bends slightly, protecting as usual. I embrace her exquisite knees. Gym rats troop by, taking it in. We don't care.

I might've snagged two cages if they were available, but sharing is better. Halle has a sweet swing. I admire her deep drives, and we talk about each. She places them surgically, over third base, mostly. Every once in a while, she steps back and plants one in deep center. Every connection is a release. After a kindly back-and-forth, she insists that I use the last third of the tokens. I revert to my usual MO: liners and grounders directly to the shortstop. Now and then, I go deep left. But the connections are solid, the shortstop is hypothetical, and Halle's creative excuses are a hoot. The shortstop she sees is about four-foot-six, with the motor skills of a frozen iguana. We arrive back at the apartment relaxed and grateful. Halle bends to kiss me on the cheek. There's nothing awkward about our embrace.

I stick close to home over the next several days to hear the news and help out. It's touch and go. Randy stays two nights in the hospital, then three, then seemingly forever. Halle talks about taking Bard in again, and I encourage that. It's hard to be a rock, but I'm between two Gibraltars. Halle has gained strength; she and Karen look ready to tag-team the hell out of whatever might be stalking the family.

Mostly, I'm standby. Karen has commandeered the kitchen, but sometimes I bring soup from Captain Carrot or escapist fare from the library. I move Bard's bed into Halle's room. Every day, I take someone or something to Blessings Hospital. But I wonder if I'm making things worse. *The Death Man Cometh*. I can tell Bard and Randy are glad to see me, but they mostly just gape. I wish they would ask about batteries or pipes or dinosaurs or something. Every time I enter the elevator at the hospital, I want to punch the button that would take me to the Kidney Center and Gayathri. One time I do it, then chicken out and ride back down. She wears a pigeon blood ruby.

I can't stay busy enough. The mondo zucchini bread disappears. One night I pull on the Stevie shirt and call Brian, acting on the spitball theory that if the work crew is healthy, maybe the Spuds will pull through. I try to sound hearty. Brian berates me warmly and asks if I'm ready to come back. I bite my tongue and find more weasel words for staying away. He calls me a candy-ass again, and we both feel better. He says they haven't replaced me. I try to be insulted by that, but I think he means it as a compliment. The bowling team has won three in a row. They've given up on icy undies. Now they're wearing chunky kid's bracelets.

"More practical," I say.

"My wife misses the underwear ritual."

"I'm recording this."

"Perfect. My! Wife! Bernice! Misses! The underwear ritual! And the dolphin suit! With spicy guacamole! You got that?"

I tell him I just want to know how everyone is. He says that Nina, Drow, and Bix are peachy. It sounds as if Nina is radiating contentment. Okay—that's something. I sign off. Log miles on Dog Beach, tune the Studie, deep-clean the kitchen, get rid of some furniture. Wear myself out every day but can't shake the green pills. One night, needing fatigue, I trek back out to Sunset Cliffs. I'm watching the pelicans sweep the dusky horizon when I notice a figure on Sadie's bench. The thick, black hair looks familiar, so I close the distance. Gayathri. She leans forward, looking down as if she's already spotted me and is wondering how to eject. This coincidental meeting is strange—strange enough to seem planned by me. I lose heart and veer away, circling behind. She speaks without looking up.

"How are you, Stan?"

"Does one and one still make eleven?"

"Yes."

I walk around the bench to face her. "Then I'm fine."

She exhales and smiles. Her looking up at me is weird, so I sit on the sandstone. "That's the bench where I met Sadie."

"Really?"

"She was sitting right where you are. Hair blown back, just like yours."

Gayathri looks down again. "I was just visiting Gemma. In Sadie's old place."

Right. Not such a coincidence. She must see that too. I wait.

"Were you going to see Gemma, Stan?"

"No."

"Really?"

I point to the birds. "Had a date with pelicans tonight. How is she?"

I keep my eyes on the horizon, ready to listen. She speaks softly. "The cottage suits her, I think. She adopted an old greyhound. He is happy to lie on the couch next to her all day."

"Name, please."

"Pax."

"Solid. That's a solid name."

"Yes."

I imagine Gemma and Pax on the couch, solving puzzles together. Now we can talk more easily. I stand, order my thoughts, and tell Gayathri that I never did get Gemma's story. Explain that I hope this fact will keep her safe. It's ridiculous to say out loud, but the no-war-stories rule is all I've got. Gayathri looks at me sideways, then jumps up and surprises me with a hug. "I am really sorry I called you Yama. It was cruel."

The transfusion is instant. Her power into me. Her liquid eyes encouraging. It means everything. She steps back, embarrassed, and turns to the pelicans. "These birds seem so wise."

"They're absolutely wise. Do you speak pelican? What're they telling old Stanhope?"

"Stan*hope*? Stan—*hope* is your full name?"

"Well, Sadie said I lost the last part."

Gayathri laughs with something like Sadie's depth. "Well." She walks in a circle, watching the pelicans and me as if consulting one about the other. "I think I'll call you Stanhope."

I'm ridiculously relieved. "Come," she says, sitting and patting the bench. I move to the seat, leaving a stalk buffer. We watch the birds come and go. Because they're on my mind, I tell Gayathri all about Bard and Randy. She insists on the whole story: Their illness. My fear that I made them ill. My fear that they will get a lot worse. She studies her hands—the ruby. "You think I am Anshu. Well, I am, a little. But I am also Gayathri. More scientific—trained in medicine, you know. So here is

what I believe: These sweet boys—what did you call them, the Spuds?—
are children. Children get sick. Sometimes very sick. All the time. They
will recover. Despite this strong belief you have contrived for yourself:
This belief that you are death. This death-ness that you feed and make
stronger. Bard and Randy are just—sick children. I see sick children all
the time. They get well."

"Always?"

"Of course not. *Almost* always. But even I don't think these things turn
out strictly according to immune response and viral evolution. There is
always something intangible to think about. Anshu would insist on that."

She leans back and ponders a string of dark, pearly clouds. "I think your
Spuds will recover—faster, anyway—if you stop believing they will not."

I rub my face and am surprised by stubble. The truth is shameful, but
it's safe to say out loud. "Not sure I can do that."

"Of course you can. You are *Stanhope*."

I stand and step away to hide the surge. Of what? Gratitude. It's all
so unexpected. She has bestowed a title—something greater than Death
Man. I have to honor that. She could be—should be—running for her
life. But she knows better. Knows *I* am better. I hear her stand and move
closer. Want to hold her. Can't face her, or I will. What were we talking
about? The Spuds. "Maybe I should go away until it's over."

"No. Your Spuds need you. You can find your strength together."

I linger stupidly, watching the sea, wanting to say everything—every
childish possibility that courses through my brain: The power of eleven.
The warmth of her presence, even when she's cold and rubbing her
hands. The fear I need to ease, in both of us. The impossibility of that.
The knowledge that all I can project is some sort of blind intensity. The
danger of normalizing that. I should walk away; make it easy for her. But
I can't. "Have you ever worn glasses?"

"I weakened my eyes at school. I wear reading glasses."

Here comes the tractor beam. *Say something, idiot.* "Your—*ring* is—"

"Oh! Anshu gave it to me. He is the only man I wanted to think about."

Past tense. Pelicans wheeling. How long have I been standing here?—
The Spuds! The practical sorceress smoldering before me has made my

duty clear. I leave with her blessing. On the long walk home, I try to calm my feverish mind. Empty out. Fill up with hope for the boys. Hold onto Eva's ring. It's late when I arrive, but there are rumbles next door, so I knock. No news on Ran, but Bard ate something tonight. I hug Halle and Karen without asking. Imagine Randy fighting monsters on the roof. *Kick ass, buddy.*

In the morning, Bard trails silently out to help me fix Halle's garbage disposal. I give him a wrench to hold, but he only lasts a minute. My impressions of sea lions and Kevin, the vigilant ridgeback, work on him, and we catch a flicker of the old Bard. At home, I organize my gear for— what? I don't know. When I check back in the evening, Halle introduces me to her boss, Rick, an unsulky Achilles. He has brought peonies. Why didn't I think of that? But I did think of sailboats, I remember, and bring them in. Bard tries to run to the nearest body of water, but we herd him back to bed. Halle sends a shot of him asleep with the sail over his face.

After lunch the next day, Halle asks if I can go with her to the hospital. The excuse is that we need to take Randy his toy boat, but something else is going on. Halle is joking too much. She's worried. "Stan, can you wear your cape?" No problemo.

He's awake when we arrive but so grave and mannish that I don't know what to say. The Boy Wonder cape doesn't register. "Did you sail your boat?" he asks with attitude. I'm not forgiven for leaving the Spuds in San Diego. The toy helps. Randy pulls it apart but runs out of energy before he can get it back together. As I re-assemble it, I dispense low-key future talk, describing where we'll take the boats, how he might beat Bard in a race. Randy drops off. But as we prepare to leave, he sits up suddenly. "Am I gonna die?"

Halle blanches but catches herself. "'Course not, squirt! What makes you say that?"

"Kid down the hall says he's gonna die. Maybe this is the dying place."

Halle sits hard on the bed. "It's true: sometimes people die in hospitals." She smooths his hair and kisses his forehead. "But usually— almost *all* the time—they get well."

"Oh. I thought I might see Dad."

Halle shoots me an imploring look and makes for the door. Randy's intensity redirects to me. "Dad died. He got—"

I put up a hand. "It's okay, guy. I don't need to know what happened to your dad."

Yes, I do. "He got hit by a truck. We have a picture of his motorcycle. It was, like—*crushed.*"

Tears catch him unawares. Halle zooms back, but I'm closer. Ran throws his arms around me without hesitation, in the straightforward way of children. He pushes his face into my chest and sobs. Halle bends over us. Where are my superpowers?

"Randy, you don't have to die to see your father."

They pull back and look at me skeptically. Time to dig deep. The need is great. "Remember my superpowers?"

Randy nods. I hold his gaze. "Well, I *can* travel in time. I *can* fly. Do you remember what I said about that?"

"You said you have to be quiet."

"What else?"

He wavers. I steady him. "You have to pretend—to be a rock or something."

I dig out Eva's star sapphire ring. Randy sits taller and brightens. He has faced death and was primed for another world. This is the magic he had hoped for. It's just for him. I tell him all about the star sapphire— what it is, where it came from. How Eva first wore it under an impossibly blue sky. We play with the light, winking the star. I let Randy hold the ring, cupping his hands in mine. I'm down to a husky dad whisper. "Eva and our friend Anshu really loved this star. But they both died."

Randy fixes on the rays as I fumble for the narrative. "But—I discovered that I could travel in time. I could fly anywhere to see my two friends. All I have to do is look at the sapphire and clear my head—think of nothing at all. Then, there they are. I try to be empty as long as I can. It's never hard. It's always easy. Always light as a feather. Then, all of a sudden, I'm not empty anymore. I'm full of friend-feeling. My forever friends are with me—and together, we can do anything."

Ran is too thin. He listens hard, with fragile power. He's Anshu, the last time I saw him. *The healing must proceed apace.* Randy's illness has paved the way for his big-boy understanding. I lay a palm on his hot temple. The need is great. "Now, I don't even have to look at the star anymore. Know why?"

He frowns at the gemstone as I push on. "Because I *am* the star. See? It's pretending, but without *trying* to pretend. Once I'm the star sapphire, I can go anywhere in time or space with my friends. Even though Eva and Anshu are gone, they're always with me. They're not inside the star sapphire—they're inside *me*. They help me every day."

Halle stands, watching closely. Randy, looking a full size larger, examines the stone. I don't know how I got here, talking as if I know how to summon all this power. "Now, you keep this sapphire and work on your superpowers. Try to fill up with your dad whenever you can. He'll help."

Randy looks up and hugs me hard. Halle joins in. But I have to finish. "You know how Bard always explains things to you because he's older and knows more stuff?"

Nod. The kid needs to own this. "Well, it's your turn to explain something to Bard. You can tell him about how you can be with your dad by trying hard. But it's one of those funny things where trying hard means *not* trying. All you have to do is be still. And you have to do it a lot. Every day, if you can. Once you're really good at emptying your head of worry or just too much thinking, other things come in. Like your dad. Your mom will help you tell Bard. The three of you can keep this ring in a special place, so it never gets lost. Any of you can use it at any time. Or you can use it together. But the sapphire is just to help you learn. Soon you won't need it."

"What about Rick?"

It takes me a minute to place Rick: Halle's boss. The unsulky Achilles, bringer of peonies. This gives me a pang, but—the need is great. "I think Rick will be your best helper, besides your mom and dad."

Halle pulls a baby wipe from her purse and cleans the boy's face. I stand. "Try to feel like you're about to laugh. Not laughing, but *wanting* to laugh."

That sets the hook. Ran is ready to try immediately. I place the stone on the tray that swings over his bed. Halle and I pull up chairs, and we all focus on the stone. Halle even manages to soften the gauging eye. Ran is fast asleep in seconds. Halle kisses my forehead. She drops the ring in a glass dish, and we leave it on the nightstand. As we walk out, I make sure Halle is okay with everything I said. We're solid. She gets the dad connection. Loves that Randy thought of Rick. She hugs me hard and says that Rick is meeting her at the coffee shop down the hall.

The world is full of elves, gnomes, fairies—little people. We call them children. Their magic is strong. I'm so absorbed with this new Spud connection that I push the Gayathri button in the elevator. *Bing!* Here I am, surprised, at the Kidney Center. I hesitate, but a nurse is waiting with a cart, so I step out of the elevator to give her room. But I'm not ready to talk to anyone—especially Gayathri. I'm shell-shocked, I guess. Randy wore me out. I need recovery time. And water. Lots of water. At the far end of an empty hallway is a micro-lounge with a few chairs, a nice view, and a water cooler. I start for it, then remember the cape. Because of Halle's infernal skill as a seamstress, it will take a few minutes to struggle out of the thing and roll it up—during which time Gayathri might enter the hallway. So I leave the cape on and sprint for the loungelet. There are a couple of intersecting halls, but I can't stop. I keep eyes forward and flash by.

When I reach the little oasis, I gulp water and collapse in a bright purple chair that tragically highlights my canary cape. There's a nice view of Cowles Mountain. What does that remind me of? Oh, yeah—Anshu pointing at Mount Evans from the hospital window in Denver, going on about Gayathri. Man, I hope she doesn't spot me; I wouldn't know what to say. Sure enough, there she is, down by the elevator, pushing a cart my way. She doesn't see me—yet. I could flee, but where? I'm in a little cul-de-sac and can't see a bathroom. I could brazen it out, but I'm not coherent. Would adrenaline pull me through? Better not risk it. I pull the cape over my head and lie still. The cart wheels squeak interminably—way too close. I try meditating and nod off. When I wake, it seems I've been out for hours, but it's still mid-afternoon. Carefully, I undo Halle's perfect buttons, pull off the cape, roll it up, and make for the elevator.

Halle discourages me from seeing Randy for a few days. The kid needs heavy rest. So I pester her for news and hang around too much. Get in the way. Halle and Karen dream up errands for me. I don't pick up on this. Am slow to notice that Rick has replaced me. Gradually, the Spuds improve. They like it when I read to them individually. Bard is old-school. His favorite book is *Mike Mulligan's Steam Shovel*—a favorite of my father's. He's a little old for it and can read it himself, but he loves the illustrations and my Mulligan voice. Randy's go-to is *Dreamers* by Yuyi Morales. We always discover something new in the illustrations. It's the perfect blend of adventure and comfort for a fragile boy. He's a week in the hospital—finally makes it home when he starts putting on weight. He arrives home with a detached air of importance. But he holds onto that sailboat.

Karen stays on and Rick comes by every night. I hit the beaches again. At Dog Beach, a border collie with a blaze like a comet repeatedly drops a frisbee at my feet and backs up expectantly. I finally respond, and we have a good twenty minutes of pitch and catch before she hears a whistle and bolts. The Spuds will live. Not since Eva have I felt so hopeful. Wading in the water reminds me of Admiral Spencer and his order. *Call her.* Aye-aye, sir. But it's tricky. I want to share the good news, but I can't keep dragging Gayathri into my Hitchcock life. I miss her, but that's no excuse for endangering. I need to know she's safe. I don't know what Anshu would say about this. Gayathri would say, "Get over yourself, Stan." *Stanhope.* She calls me Stanhope. Not even Eva did that. Only my mom. No, someone else called me Stanhope: Anshu.

I take another lap along the shore, needing to wear myself out. By the time I reach home, I'm sure I won't call her. There's a party going on next door. I fight the temptation to enter their bubble of joy. This is a family, newly forged. But I congratulate myself so much for leaving them alone that I walk to the bookcase and take out Gayathri's neat script. *One and one make eleven.* She has to know the Spuds are all right. *Lame excuse, Stan.* But I can give her the credit she deserves—tell her that she made a difference. *You're reaching.* I can send a text, but I want to hear her voice. *Now we're back to what Stan wants. Hopeless.*

No. Hopeful. I pick up the phone, heart pounding. I will listen hard for signs of rejection or even annoyance. She has a careful hand, but I have a careful ear.

"Gayathri?

"Yes?"

"The Spuds are all right."

Lub-dub. "That's wonderful, Stanhope."

I draw a blank, but she throws a lifeline. "Thank you for telling me."

Again I can't speak. "Um. Stanhope?"

"Yeah?"

"I miss Anshu."

"Me too."

Eternal deliberation. "Stanhope, do you have a yellow cape?"

Shit. "You saw me working."

"I saw you flying down a hallway."

"That was just—"

She trills. "Then I saw you *hiding*."

Busted. "A cape is good for a lot of things."

"It is especially good for making children feel better."

"Yeah. The Spuds gave it to me—and their mom, Halle."

"So, you earned your cape."

"I just have to wear it when they need me to."

Tick. Tock. She's not chatty, and I sure as hell don't know what to say. "I miss Anshu calling me Gaya."

Is this really happening? I have to know. "May I?"

Another chasm. Then, "Yes. I would like that."

"As long as I'm Stanhope."

"But—you *are!*"

"Well, you'd know."

"What will you do now?"

"I'm going to Dana Point. Thinking of moving there."

"I have never seen it."

I'm as articulate as a turnip. But she always tries. "May I come?"

This is too much: a dream and a nightmare fused. "I think Anshu would worry about that."

"I can take care of myself. A seer once said that I will have a good life if I—"

"Stay away from Mister Death."

"That is not funny."

"Damn right. It's deadly serious."

"I will have a good life if I do what I am afraid to do. I have to risk."

"Mmm. Bad advice."

"It has already worked for me, actually."

My heart is a triphammer again. "I think Anshu wants me to look out for you."

"Stanhope, Anshu was the seer. He was the one who dared me to risk."

Run away, run away! Time to be scary. "Are you afraid of me, Gaya?"

"No."

"Maybe you should be."

"Oh! Damn you for that."

She pauses so long that I wonder if she's crying. But she continues, strong and deliberate. "I cannot be more afraid than you are, Stanhope. *You* cannot run—or *fly*—away."

Gratitude comes in a rush, but my duty is clear. "I don't—require mercy, Nurse Das. You have to look out for yourself. Sometimes you have to be a survivor and that's all. Nothing else is possible."

"We shall see about that."

"I can't—"

"Please help me do what I am afraid to do."

"But I'm the fucking god of death!"

"Stop it. You are just getting even. You know, you really are melodramatic sometimes."

"An exaggetarian."

"What?"

"Eva called me an exaggetarian."

The trill again. "She was right, you know."

Couple days later, Gaya meets me at Blessings Hospital wearing navy shorts and a white blouse. No Shiva. The Champion makes her laugh and shake her head. She chafes me about the cape. As we trundle up the coast, she won't abide talk of my affliction. "Don't feed it," she says. "If this connection even exists, it is a blessing we don't yet understand."

"It's a *Hitchcock*. I'm in a Hitchcock movie."

She laughs. "So—flying with the cape was an outtake? All right—never mind about that. I'm just saying—I work in Blessings Hospital, you know? Hospitals are full of 'curses.' Hitchcocks. I have seen too many people die. But everyone who works there knows you must not feed death. You cannot think of it or speak of it. It will crush you. There are eleven floors in the hospital. When someone dies, we say they moved to the twelfth floor. There is misery every day, but you cannot call it Misery Hospital. You have to name it for compassionate ideas or saints or something. You have to help people find hope and joy."

It's a long, slow drive in the old coupe. We talk about dead friends despite ourselves. She explains every Stan Death away. Eva was just fate and two years before the others. Sadie was elderly, and telling her story gave her permission to go. Pigeon used me to make a point. I wouldn't have known Dennis but for Pigeon. Anshu lived much longer than his doctors expected. Like Sadie, he needed release. He had to give before he could go. This shuts me up. We continue in silence. But Gaya has been wounded too; she has to touch the scar. "I do think of why Anshu talked to you instead of me. I was with him in Denver for weeks, but I began to worry about my patients at Blessings Hospital. Anshu seemed better, so I flew back to San Diego. Then I began to feel as if he was in trouble, so I tried to call. I could not get through."

"He was talking to me."

"Yes. He would never interrupt a conversation."

"That's Anshu."

She rolls her window down a few inches. Keeps her eyes averted as she speaks. "Yes. But, you know, it's all right. Anshu knew I was self-sufficient. He knew *you* needed help. You needed to listen, as always, and he needed to tell you things. Things that he and I had already discussed."

Did I wear Anshu out? Did I take him over the edge? His last words to me may have been his last words to anyone. At least I managed to forward the text to her. I steal a long look at her corkscrew hair whipping in the breeze. "Why didn't Anshu put me in touch with you, Gaya?"

"He was probably planning—"

"He was protecting you."

"Yes, it is possible. He did always try to do that. But he also dared me to take risks. He was Anshu: straight and true and full of contradictions."

"You're more like your brother than you think."

She shakes her head. "Anshu thinks I should ask for help more often. When we were children—"

"No stories."

She shoots me a look of pure exasperation. "Oh, you! You cannot feed this—"

"Hitchcock."

"It's like a puppy, Stanhope. If you name it, you have to keep it."

"And if you talk about your brother in the present tense, he won't be dead."

Ouch. Not funny. It's a vicious version of *you don't look so hot yourself.* I throw up my hands. "I'm sorry—don't know where that came from."

She knows—and lets it go. "I cannot tell you about my life because you *actually* think that somehow this will lead to my—untimely demise."

She ignored my cruelty. *Bless.* "Well, when you put it that way, it sounds batshit."

"*You* say it in a way that sounds sane."

"Do I have to?"

"You do what you like. I will speak freely."

I hold up a Sadie finger. "Careful now. Safety first."

"I do not need your protection!"

"I need to protect."

"Why?"

"Because you're—*precious.*"

Yow—I said it out loud. I look out at the ocean as much as I dare. Gaya is silent for a pulsing mile. Then, "You sound like Anshu."

"Thank you."

She digs into the mondo purse. "Thank you for being Stanhope."

This time I can't let the moment pass. I pull over at a rest area and walk across a lawn toward the sea. When she follows, I turn and step into her embrace.

ANGELS
OF THE FIRST DEGREE
(SUMMER)

I TELL GAYA ABOUT THE DANA POINT CHARACTERS. OUT OF THE BLUE, she volunteers to be my story buffer, intercepting the things I won't allow myself to hear. My no-war-stories strategy still sounds crazy when she talks about it, but I'm so knocked out by her willingness to help that the depth of my insanity sinks in without a flutter.

At Connie's Pilgrim Grill, we grab a table on the deck near Kevin the Rhodesian ridgeback. When the dog sees Gaya, I swear, he gives me a knowing look. When she talks to him in a wise, caring way, he shows her his vigilance with the sea lions. Connie's so chatty with Gaya that I take Kevin for a trot along the boardwalk. It's just what we both need—the sea breeze full of promise. When we return, Connie is delivering lunch. Gaya starts to tell me about Connie, but I hold up my hands. She smiles indulgently, and we talk about Kevin and Connie's verbal leash. Connie bustles by, beaming approval.

Feeling surprisingly shy and formal, I introduce Gaya to *Katy Sue*. The rush of lust I feel when she enters the cabin propels me out the door, where I squat and smile in at her. She beams back, belonging. Duncan isn't around, and I'm not ready to sail the boat alone with precious cargo. *Chickenshit, Stan.* But I can see the negatives too clearly—a growing problem. I start the motor. We putt far enough out to sea that she catches the crystalline freedom. She looks as ready as Duncan to make for the crisp horizon. But when I ask her about it, she says Anshu was the sailor. She's a novice, like me.

"Oh!" she cries, pointing south. A spout. Two spouts. Probably blue whales, from what I've been told. I've seen dolphins with Duncan and Skye, but not these whoppers. They're the first of the season. The wind is out of the northwest, so I hoist the mainsail, then the jib—hardly knowing what I'm doing. Gaya springs into action, laughing, helping in every way, and we feel weightless as we heel over. In perfect minutes, we're within a hundred yards. We spend half an hour in their company, catching a showy breach as we fall back. It's the best sailing I've managed so far. Gaya whoops and hugs me hard. Together we have seen the largest creature that has ever existed on Earth. We talk about it all through the long, tacking return. Now we have a connection beyond sorrow.

We're content, but not tired, so we take the boardwalk down to the beach. Several surfers bob in the waves. In the distance, a dog barks excitedly, running out to a surfboard. She scrambles up, with a butt-boost from a man who also hops aboard. She barks and wags as they paddle out together. The dog moves expertly on the board with the guy, meeting oncoming waves with hops of joy. Sure enough, they catch one, and the dog hangs in like a pro, still woofing. I try translating. "She's saying, 'Look at me!'"

Gaya shakes her head. "She's just laughing because it's so much fun."

We trot to the water for a closer look. Stand together and admire man and dog moving deftly on the board as one. We could watch for hours—but it's not to be. After half an hour, the man hops off and wades to shore. The dog stands in the surf, disbelieving, pleading for more. The guy finally turns and calls. "Caprice!"

Of course—I should've recognized her. Or her person. I wave and tell Gaya only that I met them once before. My moronic flirtation with drowning would be too much information. The guy has to call a few more times, but eventually, Caprice stops lobbying. As she trots toward him, she pulls up and stares intently at me. I clap my hands and she bounds toward us. We get the full-bore, super-soak greeting. It means a lot that Gaya doesn't mind.

This time I get the guy's name: Mark. A good Catholic, he's a volunteer at San Juan Capistrano, the old mission. He has a four-hour shift this afternoon. When I ask where he'll park Caprice, he says he'll probably take her back home, though it's a drive.

Gaya pounces. "Oh!—May we look after her?"

Mark eagerly accepts, telling us that she was a gift from his priest, who found her in an arroyo. I kneel to snap on the leash, and she drools on my arm. "It takes a village."

After giving Caprice a short rest and water at the coffee shop, we walk her along the water. Her doggy grounding buffers the shyness Gaya and I still feel together. We channel our contentment into dharma dog. "Look at you," says Gaya when Caprice touches a nose to her knee. "You are such a one." Such a one! It sings in my head.

Stanhope calls this surfing dog, Caprice, his dharma dog. He will not say why, but it fits her perfectly. She is such a one! She walks easily on lead and always touches us with her nose—it is reassurance, I suppose. Together, we climb steps up a cliff into a steep park with a looping sidewalk that winds upward. Connie appears at the top of the hill with Kevin. She talks and talks to the dog as they come down the sidewalk toward us. This is the verbal leash Stanhope mentioned. Kevin stays close to Connie, listening, even after he sees us. Connie calls out to Caprice, and Kevin trots forward, stiffly. I love the ceremony of dog greetings. Stanhope unclips Caprice and she prances to Kevin. The dogs mouth each other as old friends do. Connie feels like an old friend, too—though we have only just met. She hugs me and laughs, turning to Stanhope. "Gayathri says you're thinking of moving to DP. My tenant needs to move out of my little walk-out basement. Wanna take a look?"

Of course Stanhope wants to look. I am drawn into a funny sort of dream here with him. It seems the more I learn about this man and this place, the more I forget myself. I can imagine being annoyed with Anshu for saying something like that—and for really losing himself in others. Now it is me who needs a talking to. Forgetting myself with Stanhope is comforting—but why? Where is the fear he insisted on conjuring in me? It disappeared when we were driving along the coast in his funny old car. I suppose it's because of Anshu.

Kevin and Caprice lead the way uphill, mirroring each other's movements. Connie's home has an old-fashioned charm, with a tile roof and white stucco walls. An old van is parked in the driveway. Connie's tenant, Cub Crosley, is a wild-looking man—lean and hungry, I would say. He smells musty. He has more hair than Stanhope, but that is not saying a lot. His complexion is dark, which highlights the white stubble on his strong jaw. He often tilts his head forward, and this makes him look like a little boy. His high spirits remind me of Anshu, but his light eyes lack tranquility. He wears surfing shorts, a frayed golf shirt, and sandals. Rather sheepishly, he gathers two beer cans from the armrest of an old couch and balances them on top of an over-full recycling bin.

I try to excuse myself when Connie begins showing Stanhope the apartment, but she insists on including me. Stanhope asks no questions, so I talk to Connie about how things work in the kitchen. By the end of the tour, Connie is explaining a lot of things to me while Stanhope and Cub play with the dogs. When pressed, Stanhope says he will rent the apartment—but he is certainly not discriminating. Yet I can see it will be fine for him. Cub insists we sit on the sagging couch. Really—it's like quicksand! Stanhope and I are thrown together in the middle, and we must peer over our knees. Cub walks to a small, old refrigerator that sits prominently near the door and extracts cans of beer for himself and Stanhope.

We are invited onto a patio, where the chairs are more comfortable. Cub returns to the odd refrigerator for frozen marrow bones, which he formally presents to the dogs. Without any sort of introduction, he takes a violin from an old case and produces a thrilling, wavering tone. It enhances this dream quality that informs everything today. Even the dogs listen—forgetting to gnaw. Connie blesses us all with her Buddha smile. Between jigs and airs, Cub tells us about his band, Cub Crosley and the Shelvadors. They have been playing together for thirty years. They have a lot of engagements coming up in San Diego, so Cub needs to move to the city.

This music has caught me off-guard. It is really captivating. I feel uneasy about Cub—in some respects, he reminds me of brutal men I have known. But his music is enchanting. It opens entire worlds that require exploring. "I'm sorry, but what is a Shelvador?"

Cub points to the appliance. "That old fridge is a Crosley Shelvador. Crosley was the first company to put shelves in a door. So they tried to make a big deal about it. I found that old thing up in Oakland, right after I formed the band. Kept it full of beer for rehearsals. Then I figured, might as well make it part of the show. We put it center stage. Pull beer out of it between numbers. After the show, we invite the audience to come up for suds while we pack up. Sometimes that's my favorite part of the whole night. I've met a lot of people that way—good, bad, and ugly. Ex-wives, and so on."

He fiddles and sings and strides to and fro, nodding his head and posing grandly now and then. His theatrics are hilarious, really. He presents a paradox for me. I should warn Connie against him—but that would not be fair. I don't know either of them fully. I find myself glancing at Stanhope a lot, but he seems to enjoy the spectacle. Cub is like some exotic animal at the zoo. I must learn more. "You did not want to go into the family appliance business?"

Cub squints at the refrigerator. "Oh, Crosley! No relation, to my knowledge. But my knowledge ain't much. Maybe I should look into it. I might be in line for an inheritance."

The thought pleases him so much that he plays a jig that sets our heads bobbing. Cub sits on a tall stool that he must use in performance and talks about what he calls his deedly-deedly music. Still, I'm curious. "Cub is a funny name!"

He takes a long drink and winks at me. "Ain't it? Well, my folks lived up in Hope Valley. One day, when they were out, a bear cub tore open the screen door and messed up the kitchen—ate a pile of peaches and left paw prints on the counters and cupboards. Just after my third birthday, I *also* found myself alone in the kitchen. Similar results. My parents were so impressed that they stopped callin' me Christopher in favor of Cub. The name struck *me* as an improvement, too. What kid doesn't want to be a wild animal? Hell, kids *are* wild animals."

Connie and I laugh. It's not so much that the story is hilarious. It's just that Cub is so unexpected in every way. He is a big surprise. He still seems a little dangerous—I suspect he actually lacks confidence. But he's a master of his fiddle. He stands tall, manifesting prana, knowing that with this instrument he can create new worlds. I have been working hard, worrying about my family, listening to my patients, trying to understand life, thinking that my experience is all. But it is *not* all. I might have been listening to this balmy fellow and his silly stories for most of my life. What kind of person would I then be? It stimulates the imagination—is spiritually invigorating. So I put my misgivings aside. It is not my place to cast a shadow on these relationships. Connie and I put our heads together and laugh. Stanhope looks on with affection, I think. Cub fiddles around our joy.

As we prepare to leave, Stanhope and Cub talk about their living arrangements and realize they might trade flats. Cub is ready to experience Ocean Beach. Stanhope says he will fit in perfectly. Yes, it is true—Cub will not look out of place walking the aisles of Captain Carrot. Connie is thrilled to make these kinds of connections, it seems. She loves to bring people together. She and I cheer when Stanhope says he will let her flat in a few weeks, regardless of whether Cub takes Stan's flat in Ocean Beach. But we all know the trade will occur. They are, neither of them, particular about living arrangements.

As Stanhope and Caprice and I walk back through the neighborhood, Stanhope suggests we try out the swings at a playground. Caprice runs around excitedly, biting our bottoms. I can be silly with this funny man. We're little children—Caprice a puppy—all the way back to the beach.

Caprice's tongue is lolling when she trots back to Mark. At the marina, I watch sea lions while Stanhope checks on something. He returns to say that there is a vacancy at the little marina motel and proposes that I stay the night there, with him paying for the room. Stanhope will stay on *Katy Sue*. As a rationale for staying the night and leaving early tomorrow, he goes on, charmingly, about early-morning adventures he had as a boy. I cannot help chiding him. "So *you* are permitted to tell stories."

He laughs. "Busted!"

"It's all right. We will trade one for one."

I tell him of my girlhood adventures finding and thanking dogs during the Diwali Festival. Dogs are the messengers of Lord Yama and guard the underworld, so it is important to acknowledge their service. Thanking dogs is not such a big part of the festival in India, as it is in Nepal, but I always went out with my uncle Bebo, who is Nepali. We preferred the early, sacred mornings. These are among my strongest childhood memories. I was often too eager and scared the poor things. But they were often too tired to run from me, having been terrorized by the fireworks the night before. While we laugh about this, thanking dear Caprice, I decide that this is the most laughing I have had in a single day for years. How odd that it began with the sad remembrance of Anshu.

I would like to approve Stanhope's plan for staying the night immediately, but make myself think about it. That would be Anshu's advice. We walk to the museum, where elementary-school children run around on the brig. One boy seems to know Stanhope. "Hey, Poop Swabbie!"

"Poop's Mate. I got promoted."

What are they talking about? Stanhope explains that it all started with a conversation about the poop deck weeks ago. With children, of course, you have to be really silly and take everything to the extreme. I laugh on cue, for Stanhope. There is something delightful about a person wanting very much for you to be amused. The dutiful laugh becomes really genuine. I am so *grateful* for that. As we leave the boy, Stanhope clicks his heels and gives a proper upside-down, backward salute. The little fellow responds in kind. They're mates!

I agree that we should stay the night, of course, so the magic can go on. Over a wonderful dinner at Connie's Pilgrim Grill, I tell my new friend about the trip I must make to Denver, for the tidying of Anshu's affairs. Anshu left instructions, but it's all a bit overwhelming. I ask Stanhope a lot of questions about Colorado. I remember particular trails, for example, but am confused regarding geography and logistics. At the neat little hotel, I insist on paying for the room. Stanhope crosses his arms and says that, according to navy regulations, the Poop's Mate always pays. He wins our argument just by making me laugh. I will have to be careful about that. Suddenly the poor man looks as though he might break out in hives, so I dismiss him with a hug. He seems relieved.

We meet at the coffee shop early the next morning. Stanhope introduces me to the impressive Admiral Spencer. I really like this steely, handsome man. As we turn away, he winks at me and gives Stanhope a crisp, "well done, sailor" salute. It's a little embarrassing, but I think I am meant to be flattered. Stanhope and I chatter away like old friends on the drive home, finding excuses for more laughter and unquenchable smiles. As Stanhope says, we have so much to talk about already: Anshu, dogs, whales, Anshu, the *Gita*, dogs, Pigeon, whales, global warming, Anshu, Gemma, dogs, Dennis, Dana Point, Anshu, and whales. Without thinking, I tell him that his shirt is the wrong color for him. Stanhope gives me a look and says, "You don't look so hot yourself." I examine my face in the mirror, but he explains that he learned this come-back from Sadie, who first used it on her mother as a small child. I wish I had known Sadie. But I am good friends with her friend Gemma—and with her friend Stanhope. That is really something.

I slow down as we approach Gaya's car at Blessings Hospital. My face itches. I blurt everything I can think of about Denver—where to eat, where to park (Eva's Yota Force), how long it takes to get to Rocky Mountain National Park, Mount Evans, the Garden of the Gods. Gaya opens her door. I jump out to help with that great, honking purse. But she hops out and flits by with a smile, running on tiptoe like a child. I stand and watch her fumble with keys in the light rain. Step forward, but she pops her car door open and waves goodbye. I climb back into the Studie, but suddenly she's back. I crank down the window, and suddenly she seems shy. She blinks, apparently steeling herself, and leans in. "You come too. To Denver. With me—if you don't mind. I will pay."

It's so much like Eva that I just blink. Gaya mocks my hesitation. "Look at you and your Hitchcock. You do not want to go because of the Hitchcock."

My cotton mouth works mechanically. "I don't—"

"It's funny, Stanhope. Don't you see?"

I stare out at Pigeon's window: Pigeon blood. Hilarious. I want it all to stop.

"You come too."

I shake my head. "Can't take the chance."

"We just took a chance. All is well."

"So far. Which is not very. I don't like the odds."

"I don't like the evens. Don't be so even."

"One and one make—"

"Eleven! You come too."

Resistance is futile. My Borg brain knows this. But I need to keep her safe, even when the gods insist on having things her way. I can't stand up to all this divine power. The truth is, she had me at *Hitchcock*. She slows down at longer words, emphasizing the last syllable. *Hitch-COKE. Stan-HOPE*.

I unfurl Sadie's finger of authority. "No history."

"Not a lot of my history. I may tell you about Anshu."

Suddenly, she's stunning: the raindrops in her hair, the bliss in her expectation. I give her a Halle squint. "Is this how it's gonna be?"

She sobers, betraying a ripple of fear. "No. Sometimes it will be very hard."

Gaya hugs my head and runs to her car. I'm not worthy, yet ache for her. Where's the eject button? I want the other universe. I want to work and plan with Eva again. Organize books. Breathe bouquets and watch football. Oh, yeah. I don't do that anymore. What *do* I do? Listen to people. It kills them.

I can go to Denver without permission. There's no job to work around. But I want to tell someone—negotiate my absence. It should matter that I'll be gone. The Spuds might care, in their little-boy ways. Halle asks me to watch them so she and Rick can play golf. Peachy. After some step-stool darts action, they tell me about their boats. So we stage a regatta on the San Diego River. The boats run aground until we figure out how to launch into the current. Then they nearly get away from us. We have to run like hell down to the beach, dodging obstacles. Sailboats act a lot like prey, so we have to find other things for dogs to chase. The multitasking gets out of hand, and we keep having to start over. Randy wins almost every time, and we talk about that. We shorten Bard's keel, which keeps him from running aground, and modify his sail with paper clips and other found items until the races are competitive. Tweaking the boats is more fun than the actual races. Randy cheers for his brother. Bard returns the favor. They can be blindly competitive, as they are when playing darts or vying for Halle's attention, so this brotherly love is surprising. I feed the cooperation-is-fun vibe, but can't take credit for the result. I think it has to do with a common purpose. The racing took a backseat to making each boat better. Most parents understand these dynamics, but it's new for me.

After cinnamon toast, we lie on the floor with a world atlas until we fall asleep. Eva builds a dream diorama. She laughs as she positions the boys along the river, dogs darting, a Dalmatian pup trying to snatch a boat from Bard. And there's Stan, running interference, shouting daddy wisdom. When Halle arrives, I tell the Spuds I'll be gone for a week or two, but it hardly registers. They have big plans with Rick. I spend the rest of the afternoon not calling Gaya. I'm determined not to take over the trip planning. Denver is her deal. I'm just the interpreter. Best to let her reconnect with me about it—or not.

I have a mailbox surprise: a long letter from Arwen. Both of my sisters have been shy about phoning. At one time, they called a lot, to talk to Eva. After the glasses shattered, it was easier to write. Arwen says

Dad misses the woods. The drives get longer and the walks get shorter. They're planning their big tour to take in the fall colors. Her letter is full of trivia—the roof that's needed, the garden yields, the encroaching neighbors. Ends abruptly, unfulfilled. I break out a pipe. Puff away on the roof, fending off regret. Call Arwen. Her voice is strained. Sure enough, Dad's worse than she's been willing to say. He wouldn't stand for a sternum-splitter, but there are surgical options. Why won't he consider them? They should be okay financially. Arwen cleans houses and lives with Dad, helping him conserve his retirement pay. After Eva, I figured I could live modestly for about four years without working at all. The calculations are quickly done. I tell Arwen I'll send a third of my remaining savings to her and Dad. That should make it easy for him—no excuses for skimping on health needs. Arwen protests, but I jolly her along.

The helping improves my mood, and I launch into fiddly maintenance projects, a la Justin Ellis. Run barefoot out to the Studie to retrieve pipe cleaners and end up fussing with a divot in the windscreen. At least these old cars have beefy glass. The old nightmares of shattering glass spool out automatically: cubes of light exploding out of the hospital, making way for Pigeon. Cubes of light imploding on Eva. Shattering is beautiful. Was it beautiful for them?

In the parking lot, I wave at Halle's Achilles, Rick, who quick marches toward the building. He doesn't see me. Looks grim. What's going on? I'm on the stairs when a van tootles at me. It's Cub and Connie. Connie sticks a new hairdo out the window and hollers goofily. "Yoohoo—poopsie! We tried to call. Cub's got a gig here in the city. We're staying down the street."

Good timing. I give them a tour of my apartment. It's not much, but Cub is easy to please. Yikes—am I ready to move? No, but it's for the best. The sub-lease is settled in no time, but I have to clear it with the landlord, Usher. I call him. He says he doesn't have time to vet a new tenant. I say I'll vouch for Cub, and Usher reluctantly agrees. He'll send over the paperwork. This calls for a celebration, apparently. Cub and Connie are like kids on a field trip to the big city. Cub insists that we go to Inigo's on Coronado

Island for dinner. He'll buy if I drive the Champion. No problemo. Connie sits on the curb and makes a call as Cub and I walk the property.

Connie is bright and girlish as we skirt the bay in my old car. Head swiveling, she chatters away in the front seat, asking about the neighborhood. Their relationship has deepened—she feels proprietary about Cub's new place.

Cub lounges in the back, offering broader commentary. "I can be settled here in an hour. I move around too much to collect anything. And I like people. Gettin' 'em to like me is the trouble. I come and go at odd times. Haunt the neighborhood in daylight hours, when they're just sure I should be out sellin' somethin' for some goddamn monopoly."

Stanhope and I have not spoken since we agreed to travel together to Denver. For my part, I am embarrassed about my forwardness. He is a fascinating puzzle. I must have been giddy when I asked him for help with my work in Denver. I will not have him feel obligated in this way. I will give him a way out, regardless of consequences. Perhaps he will have a new job or something that will keep him here. But how will I manage alone?

Connie calls to invite me to dinner at Inigo's. I suspect Stanhope will be there. I go along to the club by myself, forgetting my good reading glasses and feeling a perfect fool. I am sitting at a booth, reading the menu with my old and ugly black glasses, when Cub, Connie, and Stanhope arrive. There is nothing for it, so I stand, give him a quick hug and say, as efficiently as I can, that I should not have insisted on his being my Colorado guide. "I would love your help, but you should not feel, you know, obligated."

Reverently, Stanhope removes my awful glasses, examines them, and puts them back on my face. "I don't feel, you know, obligated; I feel, you know, blessed."

I sit quickly, relieved. For a long while, I hide behind the menu, trying to regulate my breathing. I suppose I'm as odd as Stanhope. When I put down the menu, Stanhope is watching me calmly. Connie looks eager and pleased. Cub sits upright, with his head forward, his large hands always moving. Everyone seems comfortable with Cub, yet he always explains himself. It sounds as though they're in the middle of a story. "Dad never did—probably couldn't—pull a nine-to-five. He was a carpenter. A handyman. Probably because he was half Washoe, the kids at school never missed a chance to suggest he was shiftless."

Stanhope gives me a desperate look. A war story is coming. He tries to change the subject to Connie's business, then to her and Cub's drive from Dana Point. Connie talks a little about people we know in Dana Point. I try to help. "How is Kevin?"

"He's with Caprice and Mark. If I'm not around, they're all he wants."

But our attempts to turn the conversation fail. We cannot think of how to sidestep this story. Cub is a natural storyteller who wants to tell Connie about his father. I think that, after living upstairs-downstairs for a long time, Connie and Cub were brought together by the possibility of not seeing each other anymore. Their relationship has been wonderful, so far, and now they are ready to reveal their family secrets to each other. Stanhope and I are apparently meant to be witnesses. We cannot really excuse ourselves. Poor Stanhope! He does not want to listen. I try to give him permission with an encouraging smile.

Here comes a war story. I wait for it because Gaya wants me to. Cub pulls back but keeps his chin tucked. "I started to hate my dad, old Jake Crosley, because others did. He was hired by this new housing development up at Hope Valley. As a handyman, mostly, but sometimes he mowed lawns or fetched coffee. Well, they started having beaver trouble. The upper lots were okay, and they sold a lot of those, but the lower lots were getting flooded. Dad was supposed to get the beavers under control, but he was hopeless. Every time his bosses complained, he'd take 'em out and show 'em all the live traps he'd baited. Somehow those busy beaves kept outsmartin' Dad. This went on for months. Everyone in town thought it was hilarious—proof positive that Jake Crosley was useless."

A waitress cruises by and hugs Cub from behind. I like him for coloring in her embrace. Connie is unfazed. We order lunch and Cub tacks on another round. Then the fiddler, the showman, plunges ahead, framing each scene of the story with competent hands. "One night, my friend Lars and I grab a case of beer and head out to spy on the beavers. We set up a blind near one of the traps. Polish off the beer. Not a peep from the critters. But just as we're packin' up, here comes a biggun right into the trap. Chunk! The door closes, neat as nipples. We start down for a closer look, but someone's coming. It's Dad, half in the bag. He stumbles up, sits by the trap with a bottle of Jameson, and *talks* to the beaver for the next hour. Soft and low, like how you might talk to a skittish horse."

We smile as Cub's energy builds. "He asks—asks!—the stinky old rodent to stop buildin' dams around there. *Explains* to him why it's a bad idea. Goes into the consequences of building dams—for the beaver, for himself, for the community, for the world. The beaver just lies quiet and looks at him. He *likes* listenin' to Dad."

Connie and Gaya hold each other and laugh like a couple of school chums. Cub warms to his audience. "Lars and I can hardly stifle ourselves. It's a hoot! But after a while, it's just—sad. The critter goes to sleep. Dad finishes the bottle, stands up, and opens the trap door. The beaver waddles out, in no hurry, like they've done this before. Which they have. Dad and this beaver were just a couple of night-shift workers headin' home at quittin' time. 'G'night, Harold. See you tomorrow.'"

Cub flexes his fingers. "So here's the thing: Drinkin' with beavers is kinda crazy. But it's also kinda cool. Lars is an outlaw sort, and I can see he's changed his mind about Washoe Jake Crosley."

Cub shifts his attention to the beach beyond. "After that, things were easier for me at school. Lars must've told his parents or something. I don't know. I didn't say a word to anybody. But, for whatever reason, people start seein' Dad as a kindly old eccentric. He picks up on this. Becomes a jokester—loves to make people laugh. Challenges people on things, 'cause that's what eccentrics do. Pretty soon, he's too *colorful* to lose his job. A by-God folk hero. *Proud* of his blood. He knew a lot about the wildlife around there—Granny Dubuda had made sure of that. The property owners started askin' him about the trees and animals, and he could usually tell 'em something new. Because he *cared* about the land— every part of it. He became somethin' like a park ranger."

Connie and Gaya settle down but still smile encouragingly. "What happened to the beavers?"

"The people who owned the higher lots decided they liked 'em. They liked the beavers so much the development company had to give four big lots to the critters. Some aspen were destroyed, a'course, but Dad talked the company into coming up with the money to manage that. The animals got their own reserve, and it paid off. Dad gave tours. The remaining lots sold for more money. It was great for the old man. The neighbors saw Dad wasn't lurkin' around in the daytime so he could steal or be lazy. It was just the opposite: he was lookin' out for everyone, including the forest and wildlife. I was proud of him and made some new friends. Dad kept that job until he died."

Connie pats Cub and holds onto his arm. The food arrives, and Cub orders a boilermaker. Connie shoots me a hunted look. She knows what killed Jake Crosley. Brightening, she asks Cub about playing Inigo's twenty years ago. Cub and the Shelvadors rode a wave of local popularity then—opening for all the big acts. The band was poised for stardom when Cub pulled a gun on a promoter and got himself arrested. When the cops searched the van for weapons, they found a well-stocked pharmacy. Cub emerged from jail and rehab to a thundering lack of interest. The band re-established themselves on the West Coast, but the promised national tour was gone. "Nothing had really changed after my jail time. We'd just lost six months or so. But the big boys had had enough of me. Word gets out that you threatened someone in the business, well, the business is through with you."

Cub looks around, checking out the impressive dimensions of Inigo's with a practiced eye. "We're playing here this weekend. First time in fifteen years. We used to pack the place. Hundreds of people, night after night. I know we could've gone big back then."

Impressed with Cub's talent, I'm happy to back him up. "Should've happened."

"What the hell. Life ain't fair."

Connie has acquired a quiet intensity. She leans into Cub and speaks slowly. "That's one of those things that sounds important, Cub, but it's wrong. Life is perfectly fair. *Perfectly.* We just don't see all the causes and effects, that's all. We say life isn't fair because it's hard to insist on fairness. We say it because we're tired of trying."

Cub finishes his drink and blinks at Connie as if seeing her for the first time. Connie sits back and makes her small mouth beautiful. "Sorry. My ex used to go on about that, and I got fed up. I decided he was just trying to make lazy sound important. Life is as fair as you can make it. For *others.* Fairness for others is the only thing that matters. It's the only thing you can control. You can give a tip or a raise or a compliment. Whatever comes *to you* is more random, but that's life."

Cub gives her a rueful grin. "Give till it hurts, huh?"

"No. Give so it *stops* hurting."

Gaya hops up and hugs Connie for her *Gita* wisdom. Cub turns his gob-smacked face to me, wheels turning. He shuts his mouth and turns back to Connie. "Will you marry me?"

Connie laughs. "Ask me when you're sober."

"Stone cold, baby."

"I wish."

Cub's face goes slack again. He turns back to me, and I recoil from the power of his pitch-perfect Van Morrison, singing "Tupelo Honey."

He raises his hand to order another drink, but Connie pulls it down and pours part of her beer into Cub's glass. We toast angels of the first degree.

- X -

WARM IN FUTURE-SEEKING
(FALL)

THINGS GET WEIRDER THE NEXT NIGHT. CONNIE AND CUB PICK ME up in the van and we drive to Inigo's. Connie calls Gaya before I can object. She really ought to leave the over-worked nurse alone. Missing physical work and nervous about Gaya, I throw myself into setting up the instruments, horsing the old fridge across the dance floor by myself. The Shelvadors love me for it. Chet's a chiseled, shy man, proudly Creole, who hides behind big guitars. The drummer, Taz, is a wide, brooding assemblage of tattoos. Wendy's a full-lipped blonde who plays about nine instruments. The set-up is playtime. For an hour, the musicians tweak their instruments and riff, solo and together. Harmonize perfectly and spontaneously. I'm not half the drummer Taz is, but he lets me beat the skins anyway. I'm weak on fills but keep time like an atomic clock. We talk about drummers and Taz's technique for quite a while. The guy is solid: a strong safety—dependable, stepping up regularly to surprise and delight. The drum set is his refuge. We're drum breddas.

Chet sets up with an acoustic guitar, an electric, and a mandolin. Wendy floats here and there, singing questions, checking in with Cub, noodling deftly. I could play with these guys. I think they'd tolerate me for a song or two, anyway. The old fridge is spotlighted center-stage, just behind Cub. Chet and Wendy fill it with mixed bottles of craft brews, telling me about each flavor. While the band finishes setting up, Connie and I order dinner for all. Connie watches the band so eagerly that I give her a hard time about it.

"I never figured you for a groupie."

She extends her arms expressively. "I'm just an old granny who loves to dance."

"With Cub."

She takes my hand and squeezes it. "Is it written all over me?"

I give her an encouraging smile. Gaya appears, magically, as the food arrives. She's a little shy, but Connie hugs her and pulls her into the chair next to me. Chet brings a six-pack to the table, explaining that this particular beer was inspired by Vonnegut. It's called Nice Chime, after Uncle Kurt's Ice Nine substance in *Cat's Cradle*. The brew lives up to its name, contributing a lot to our rowdy, late dinner. Cub and Wendy work out a call-and-response doo-wop tribute.

"I like-a your hair."

"I like-a your guitar."

"Let's go upstairs, where they have a good bar."

They put their heads together. "For a nice time, a Nice Chime, a Niiice Ch-ch-chiiime! Oooooweeeyooooowaaaaa!"

They like the jingle so well that they open the set with it. Then they plunge into "Blue Train." The rhythm section hits a peppery groove. Cub deedles like a madman, shuffling around the fridge, leaning on it, drumming it, kicking it, pouting his little-boy mug under a powder-blue trilby. Gaya gives me a side hug. The place is barely half full—maybe two hundred people—but several couples get right out on the dance floor. Connie drags me out. Dancing is something I never think about and seldom try. I figure if I move my arms a lot, no one will notice that the rest of my body is hardly moving. Connie covers for me with style, swinging her hips and hula gesturing. I try not to think about Gaya watching.

"I just don't care anymore," Connie says when we flop back into our chairs. "I mean, you think you don't care what people think when you're young. Twenty years later, you realize how great you can really be at not giving a damn."

She laughs, pulls on a beer, and looks at Gaya sideways. "What do you think, hon? My last beer?"

"For the night?"

"Forever."

It's hard to know what to say. We nod encouragement. Blissed, Connie tracks Cub as he wheels backward across the stage while the band cooks through "Diggy-Liggy Lo."

Connie is determined to share the joy, pushing us onto the dance floor. Gaya adopts my minimalist approach to dancing but laughs at me anyway. Cub funkifies his fiddle into Sly and the Family Stone's "Thank You (Falettinme Be Mice Elf Again)." Mice Elf! I try to stop grinning like an idiot once in a while, but then I just laugh. Gaya rings her own Sadie bell, which reminds me of the girl in the coral dress. That girl is with us—and her friend in blue, Gemma. The thought of those girls dancing like scrawny chickens on Decatur Street makes me laugh again. The party careens through the night. I haven't had this much fun dancing—or pretending to dance—since the wedding in Estes Park a lifetime ago. Gaya and I are with the band, and we're closing the place down. As the crowd thickens, we slow to catch our breath. The women huddle together—Connie talking earnestly while Gaya holds her hands. Cub announces the last number. "It's been—well, what *has* it been? Epic. But if it's all the same to you, we'll finish with something—hmmm—"

"Epicacious!" I holler.

Where did that come from? Cub laughs. "Yeah. What Stan said."

He holds up a bottle of Dr. Bronner's Peppermint Castile Soap. "It's straight off the label of our favorite soap. I could really use a scrub up with this about now, as Wendy can tell you. But it'll have to wait—for an original composition of ours, inspired by the good doctor's suds: Doctor Bronner's Breakdown! It's—*epicacious*."

Cub coils, ready to strike. Taz keeps brisk time. Wendy and Chet kick it off. "Full truth, our God. Half-truth, our enemy. Hard work, our salvation. Unity, our goal. Free speech, our weapon. All-one, our soul. All-above, above! We all are one!"

The words are right off the soap label—the spiritual ramblings of the good Dr. Bronner. Cub lunges into a cockeyed turkey-in-the-straw, and they all sing. "We all are one! Exceptions eternally? Absolutely none!"

The wobbly thrum crests and builds again, the dance floor jammed with jumping jivers. Each chorus approaches and hits like a tsunami. "Exceptions eternally? Absolutely none!" The song ebbs and slams along for twenty minutes. A hundred times or more, the dancers shout out with the band: "Exceptions eternally? Absolutely none!"

Not a soul in the room knows what we're on about—where all this defiance and joy came from or where it's going. But each full-throated declaration is a release. By the end, as Cub's chuffing whine fades away, we really are all one. One of what? No one cares. The crowd surges to the stage. Wendy opens the Crosley Shelvador and passes out the beer.

The next several days are action-packed. Connie and Gaya continue to confide in each other. Cub and I walk Kevin and sample local brews. Cub comes on strong sometimes, but his success hinges on that, and he's genuinely entertaining, a reliably self-effacing clown. Gaya is wary of him, but he makes her laugh every day. He and I talk of music almost exclusively. My music memory doesn't extend much beyond Natalie Merchant, but Cub is older and teaches me a ton of music history. One day he strums a guitar, sings "A Little Louisiana," and tells me about Jesse Winchester, who is new to me. Cub met him on tour, back in the day. "Helluva songwriter. Helluva dancer, but shy. I lost track of him for a long time, then heard this *monster* CD he finished just before he died. I like that—kick-ass, then kick-off."

Things are mostly peachy, though Eva, Sadie, Dennis, Pigeon, and Anshu invade my dreams. Cub and Connie amp their relationship, playing a couple of love-struck kids, and it's good therapy. They make everything easy, show us how. Despite occasional aloofness, Gaya opens up. I try not to mind her melting away unexpectedly.

We hit Inigo's again on our last evening in San Diego. Connie joins us at a beer-spattered table and asks earnestly if we'll help with something when we come back. "I want to try an intervention."

"What?"

"Cub needs to dry out. I talked to the Shelvadors, and they're with me on this."

"How does an intervention work?"

"I don't know exactly. I'm still looking into it. I'll have a plan ready after your Rocky Mountain trip."

"Why us?"

"Well, the Shelvadors want to help, but Cub knows how to play 'em. They've been partners in crime too long. You guys are fresh and reliable. Cub likes you."

She pats and rubs my arm. "I'll do most of the work. I just need serious backup."

Gaya watches me closely. Does she want me to get her out of this, or is this one of those times when she's determined to face her fear? *When in doubt, go higher.* "You can count on us, Connie."

This wins me stereo hugs. The band takes a break. Cub two-steps up to the table and winks. "Exceptions eternally?"

Connie hooks him around the waist. "Absolutely none."

It's a big diorama night: The cartoon bowling team in the clown-car Studie. Superheroes peering in at zooming bed-mobiles. Pigeon eluding saviors, streaking for the shattered window while Stanhope watches with wrens. Gemma and Sadie shuffling across the lawn at the bungalow, Cinder watching. Caprice scooping a floating tennis ball, Stanhope capsizing in the distance. Kevin at the Pilgrim Grill, locked onto yawping sea lions. Stanhope and Gaya and Connie at the cliffside park with Kevin and Caprice. A bear cub on the counter in a rustic Hope Valley kitchen. Cub's dad singing with beavers. The leaping swirl of Cub Crosley and the Shelvadors. This time I can't tell who the diorama builders are. Two—no, three women.

I'm loading the Champion for the drive to DP when Achilles Rick stumbles out of Halle's place, looking gaunt. I ask about the family. He opens the back of Halle's old Buick wagon and rummages through a tangle of kid debris. "Halle's been real sick. Something like what the boys had. I was ready to take her to the hospital last night, but her fever broke."

I can't speak. I've been playing groupie while the little family was on the brink. Again. Rick picks through knapsacks and action figures and electronic dongles. "Now—you know what she wants?"

He picks a colorful box out of the mess and holds it up with a weak smile. "Animal crackers. She wants goddamn animal crackers."

He waves a hand at the wagon. "I tried to give her a newer car, but she won't have it. This tank is the safest thing she could find for the boys."

Right. The Spuds probably hate the car as much as they hate the car seats. Rick eyes the old Buick with contempt verging on affection. "All she wants is—these damn *animal* crackers."

Achilles tries to go on, but his voice catches. He marches away with the booty, and I sit on the curb for so long that the Spuds come out to see if I'm okay. They get me up and moving, but I'm not okay. I'm leaving and will miss them like crazy—despite my fascination with Gaya and Dana Point. I follow them back to the apartment to say goodbye. I wish I could say everything I feel, but that's all right—they don't need it. They're all thinner; tired but happy.

Cub moves in, and I spend a few nights at my new digs—Connie's basement in Dana Point. It's efficient but hardly tranquil. Footsteps boom at all hours overhead. I always drop what I'm doing to join Connie and Kevin for romps. They play magnificently together, vaporizing my worries. I will love it here—already do. The night before our flight to Denver, Gaya arrives late and joins us for a walk along the boardwalk, catching the Connie-Kevin vibe perfectly. We all walk her back to the little marina hotel, making plans.

Gaya and I catch the redeye to Denver, aiming for the early-morning gratitude vibe. Flying over the western deserts on a clear day is a lesson in humility. Geology, for one thing. For *everything*. One of my old bandmates, Nick, studied geology. He'd take off on drug-fueled rambles about colossal slabs of time and space, heat and pressure. We rolled our bloodshot eyes, but it was more entertaining than we let on. I remember some of the names he used for this part of the world: Basin and Range. San Raphael Swell. The theme of Nick's babble was that the Southwest is being pulled apart, for a variety of debatable reasons. I've never noticed before how obvious this is from the air. Pastel slabs of strata larger than some eastern states are peeling away from torn and twisted mash-ups of domes and gorges. Gaya and I can't get enough of it. Early astronomers suffered from cosmic dismay—a depression triggered by proof of our puny nothingness in the universe. I get that. I've felt it a lot over the last two years. But now it's turned inside out. The humbling blisses. Maybe my escapade with alternating current turned things inside out. Or Anshu did.

Nick, the guitar-picking geologist, figured he'd make his first million by producing text and audio logs of western geology for the major airline routes. He'd include meteorological information for rainy days. What became of that dream? How many people care anymore, to feel so small? Gaya cares. I try to explain to her what I learned about the Southwest. She nods, peering excitedly out the windows. Can't contain herself as she points out a lizard-shaped hogback. A honeymoon thrill hits me broadside.

We take a cab to Park Hill, but Anshu's place looks empty as death. Gaya freezes on the porch, unable to enter. The weather is perfect, so I suggest a walk to the park. We have lunch at the museum and spend hours touring wildlife dioramas. It helps. I try to explain Eva's fascination with the old scenes—the dharma of diorama. Gaya's right there with me. It's an extension of the awe we felt peering out the windows of the airplane. We watch arctic wolves, caribou, polar bears, grizzlies, cranes, wolverines, pronghorns, geese. The Jabba-the-Hutt elephant seal. We hope for their future.

It's still warm, so we walk around the lake in the park, where dogs sport casually on the grass. As we finally walk up Anshu's garden path, Gaya rummages through her loaded purse for keys and instructions. I look for a cricket bat in there. She tries to smile, but it's no use. This is a sad business. The house is Anshu. The red Vespa and Union-Jack Mini Cooper glisten in the garage, the walls of which are covered with maps of the high country. The kitchen is small and efficient. A broom closet has been reorganized for cricket gear. A ready room between the kitchen and garage is neatly lined with outdoor equipment. The rest of the house is as clean and tidy as a hotel. As Gaya expects, we find containers of frozen chai in the freezer. The smell of ginger catches her off-guard and she retreats to the living room. I heat the chai and bring her a cup. "It's a family recipe."

We move to the patio overlooking the private garden. Cumulus towers are assembling on the plains, but the rest of the sky is intensely blue. Below us, lighter blue delphinium overlook grasses with fluttering tassels. The gardener is still on retainer. A hummingbird zips by. "They're still here!" says Gaya with a clap.

She sits, considering. "I have an offer for the house, but I don't know—should I move to Colorado?"

"I was happy here."

The master bedroom is modest, simply decorated with rustic expressions of alpine drama. But Gaya won't use it. She hasn't yet spoken of Anshu in the past tense. I try to leave for a hotel, but she won't hear of it. "Please stay, Stanhope. There are two guest bedrooms downstairs."

We walk the neighborhood. Warm breezes, cottonwoods, peace. Gaya is so sweet and quiet that the honeymoon thrill surges back. I take her to Eva's old pillbox bungalow. Jill, Molly the collie's guardian, lives there now. She's not home, but Molly lies in the shade near the well-tended roses. She spots me immediately and capers to the fence, crooning a wolfish tune. Gaya laughs and kneels for her. Rose fragrance brings Eva back in a rush. As we stroke Molly's wiggling flanks, I tell Gaya about my wife. She asks questions until I've explained the nail filing, the hope for children, the Hubble glasses, the choosing for fragrance. Dogs slow us down a tick, I think, slobbering away anxiety, enabling this kind of exchange. On the way back, Skitch, the retriever, bounds around a corner and deposits a ball at Gaya's feet. She has a strong arm.

Grocery shopping is an intimate affair, sparking debates about the relative merits of cocktail and English cucumbers, and which protein is best. Palisade peaches trigger prancing ecstasies. We buy a whole box.

After watching hummingbirds skirmish into the dusk, we each take a guest bedroom downstairs. Sounds in the night prompt me to investigate. Light seeps from under Gaya's door. Who am I to disturb her? But *she's* the one. *She* disturbs. *Breathe, Stan.* Exceptions eternally? Absolutely none. The light winks out.

We're up early, making lists. Gaya's agenda is simple but large: scatter Anshu's ashes on Mount Evans, dispose of the vehicles and furnishings, and close the house and business sales. We start with the ashes. With a chai jump-start, we're to the top of Mount Evans by mid-morning. I drive the Mini Cooper since I know the road. You can summit two of Colorado's fifty-three 14,000-foot peaks in a car: Pike's Peak and Mt. Evans. The Evans drive would be a breeze if it wasn't for the puckering exposure and lack of guard rails. The windswept verticality is a rush. Mountain goats cluster here and there near the top, their snowy coats glowing against gray-green tundra. Their sloe eyes appraise. We lug the urn from the parking lot to the true summit half a mile away. It's too early for most tourists. We find an open spot, and Gaya recites a passage from the *Rigveda*. "The Sun receive thine eye, the Wind thy *Prana*. Go, as thy merit is, to earth or heaven. Go, if it be thy lot, unto the waters. Go, make thine home in plants with all thy members."

I should know, but have to ask. "What's *prana*?"

"It's the vital principle in everything. You, me, rocks, sky, you know. It came from the sun and connects earth, air, fire, water, and space."

We scatter half the ashes and descend to the parking lot under the watchful eyes of the goats. Shimmery goat kids cavort near the Mini. As we head out, Anshu's 300-pound billy moves onto the road. We give him plenty of room. "That's a load of prana." A few miles down the mountain, we pull over at a trailhead and place the urn in Anshu's cricket bag. We take turns carrying the bag for a couple of miles along a trail that winds through a twisted gallery of bristlecone pines. The distortion resonates, reminds me of what Sadie said about blues on the dobro: *Heaven built out of pain.* We throw handfuls of Anshu at the weirdest-looking trees. The wind picks up, and surreal clouds whiten the needles and cones. Turning back toward the car, we're lighter in every way. Gaya takes my hand as we clamber over granite boulders.

We stop for lunch at the historic lodge. I manage to steer us around the half-mast flags outside, but Gaya sees them on the way out and asks why. I don't want to know. "Does it matter?" She asks others. No one knows why the flags are at half-mast. Maybe these people are like Connie and me and have used up their curiosity about the darkness. *Don't ask, don't tell.* Gaya is about to give up when she gets the answer: another school shooting. This silences her until we're back in the Mini and well down the road. Then we talk about Connie and how she had to stop knowing the news, as most people know it—the news we can do nothing about. How she went on to make her own news—local news. Helpful news.

"Is it so bad to listen to the news?"

"I don't know. Connie just couldn't do it anymore."

Her head swivels to track patches of gold in the aspen. "I understand her choice right now. I think Connie would say I'm full up or something."

"Too much darkness."

"There has always been a lot of it. There used to be more, I think. Not long ago, half of my relatives did not survive childhood. Everyone knows of the Irish Famine, you know, but two or three times as many people died in Bengal in 1943."

Millions starving, many of them children. It's hard to imagine. The best I can do is flash on the old cemeteries Trudy and I explored in Maine. All the tiny graves—times thousands. Gaya turns toward me and tucks her legs, Pigeon-like. "When I was learning Hindi, my grandmother gave me a stack of letters from the old days. The wisdom was striking, you know? Despite the superstition that would sometimes absorb them, there was real compassion and understanding of what it takes to get through hard times. Now, it seems to me that everyone is reluctant to grow up. Diversion is everything. Games or apps or whatnot."

"What about books?"

"Hmm. Books are more likely to have a degree of sophistication. They are more likely to help you think through something. At least, that's what I want to believe."

She rummages through her purse, powers off her phone. Sits back and watches the creek we're tracking. "Perhaps living close to death brings a certain maturity, you know? The ability to take pleasure in— adult things."

I leave it at that. Gaya's right, as far as I know. I hope I don't have to test her hypothesis in real-time anymore. As for the culture, I plead Connie. I don't want to think about how much more sacrifice may be necessary to make us more human again—if that's even possible. Anyway, verticality and quaking aspen shut us up the rest of the way. We're on a winding track through Middle Earth.

Again, Gaya seems reluctant to enter Anshu's house. So we walk again. Stop at a small café. The temperature is dropping, so we opt for warming pozole. She says her mother made something very like it. She begins to chatter, then stops, looking guilty. But I won't deprive her of storytelling now and tell her so. I get a sweet story of her family eating soup and singing songs on rainy days. It was a tradition. We walk through the park and circle the lake again. Gaya goes on about her parents, who died just two years ago. "They told everyone about Anshu's shop. I don't think they even wanted to see it. It could not have been grander than what they imagined."

We both know the shop well. Anshu prided himself on having an unusual variety of precious stones. You can find diamonds cheaper at mall jewelers, but Citizen Jewelers has everything else. Maps of the American West and the world show customers where each gem originated. Our talk of the shop reminds me of Eva's star sapphire. I can't make myself tell Gaya about it. The Spuds are putting it to good use.

Back at Anshu's, the wiry gardener is bent over flowers in the front yard. He tells us that Anshu was particular about the blood-red hollyhocks against the house. "He let me do the whole yard my own way. But he had to have the hollyhocks there."

Gaya lights up. It's something she'd forgotten about Anshu. A new talisman. She pulls the cricket bag out of the trunk and extracts the old bat. "This goes with them!" We plant it at the end of the bright line, at a slight angle—ready to smash the world.

Turning in early, I dream I'm dressed in Marine dress blues. I climb into a truck filled with soldiers, doctors, and nurses. Some are in combat fatigues or scrubs covered with blood. Others are in parade dress or formal wear. As the truck starts to move, I call Gaya and ask her if I should go off to war. The static on the phone is strong, and I can't hear. Finally, she yells, "Jump!" I move to the back, get ready to jump, and there she is, running after us. *She's* the one who jumps. Onto the truck. Everyone makes room, turning outward, trying to protect her. But they're being shot. They're dying.

Was that a scream? I switch on the light. Footsteps up the stairs. I throw on Anshu's red and black silk robe, which Gaya insisted I use, and follow a light to the kitchen. Gaya stands at the table, poring over one of her brother's colorful geologic maps. She looks up, pale, over her glasses. "Isn't it cold?"

I remove a steaming teapot from the stove, make herbal tea, and hold her. She fusses with the lapel of my robe. "Red and black," she says simply—a reference to Anshu. I pour out the tea. She takes hers and sits at the table, blinking at the map of the undulating Southwest. "You can see the tension."

The geologic map is as beautiful as any Pollock. The pulling apart is there. The immensity. But it's not what pulled her out of bed. I wait. Head down, running her hands over the bold blobs of color, she speaks of her brother in the past tense for the first time. "He was watchful. He could take in the whole world with those eyes. So strong—even when his body was frail."

I could say the same of her. But a story is coming. "When we were children, he collected a lot of fireworks and extracted the gunpowder. He was experimenting, you know, as children do. He piled the gunpowder on the floor and tried to light it. It would not burn, so he lay his head down and blew on it. And blew and blew. Suddenly, it flashed, just as he was inhaling, and he breathed in all this hot smoke! He coughed and coughed. We should have taken him to the hospital. But we were too poor for hospitals. It was awful. He coughed through the night. I hardly slept. I can still hear it."

She sighs and sips tea. "I dreamt of that. Of Anshu coughing and coughing, until we were all doing the same and couldn't stop. I ran to him. I thought if I could wash him in the Ganges, he would stop. I pulled and dragged him to the river. But as soon as I lowered him into the water, he became unconscious and slipped out of my arms. He disappeared so fast! I jumped in and swam and called and looked everywhere."

She pulls off her oval glasses. "I will take the house off the market. I can take up Anshu's life, in a way, and use all of his beautiful maps and equipment. The university hospital here will hire me again. I should never have left years ago. My brother and I would have been together all this time. I might have met you and Eva. We could have—"

"Stop."

I stand. "Your life has to be more than an apology for the past, Gaya. Let go of this—so you can take hold of that."

I'm spitballing. It's just something I read. Gaya frowns. I have to come up with something more meaningful. I retreat and lean against a counter. "Losing Eva almost killed me. I couldn't sleep. Just as I started to figure it out, a mondo damn river of alternating current almost killed me. Again, I couldn't sleep. Hell, I *still* have trouble sleeping. But I learned something from all the not sleeping: that the world is never as bleak as it seems at two o'clock in the morning."

I close the distance. "Make all decisions in the light of day."

She blinks and puts the glasses back on. We finish our tea, looking at the map. Like most people, I've never really examined a geologic map. The symbolism—the massive processes—attached to every splash of color strikes us both for the first time. The mutual discovery, the big and smallness, draws us together. This deepening connection is what I sought with Anshu. Whatever else happens, Gaya and I are shoulder-to-shoulder in our soldiering on. I didn't lose Anshu. *We* lost Anshu. And gained the *we*. All that baloney about the inability of men and women to be friends sells everyone short. The possibility of a physical merge can be overwhelming, that's all. The trick is to lose your heads and bodies together. She removes the glasses. We stand and walk softly, like awed children, down the steps. At the bottom, she hugs me, straightens the lapel again, turns away, hesitates, and turns back with soft eyes. "You come too."

I wait for the honeymoon thrill, but it's not happening. How dare I muddle her modest life? I can't even warn her—can't let her know that I still wonder about the Hitchcock. Wonder about us. Wonder about what Anshu wanted. And I haven't been with a woman in two years! Any hesitation would shame her—so that's the answer: keep moving. Be what she needs, every instant. Childishly, robotically, I follow her into her room. It turns out I love to kiss. I'd forgotten about that. Slowing is the key. Softening. Reminds me of Sadie's slow Mo. Molasses. Hold the thought.

"I dreamt of Eva's roses," she says.

Catching the fragrance, I kiss her again. Why did I wait? Because now is better. It's a slow pendulum, arcing from within. The wavering notes of a dobro. The depth of dioramas. The twisting of bristlecone pines. A reaching out. Not urgent, just—inevitable. Now Gaya kisses me on the source wound. On the exit wound. The caring is a release. I step back and look into her small face. "I dreamt we went to war together." She nods and begins again. We begin together. It's beyond mindful—a merge of wisdom and compassion. Source and exit without wounds. Falling in reverse. Our quality together. Eleven.

Stanhope's wounds are red in the morning light. I try to imagine the feeling of being electrocuted, of falling, of trying to recover without proper sleep. I will buy rose oil for his scars. When he wakes, I thank him for being both wild and mindful. The appreciation goes on, and he says something about yab-yum. So I describe the Hindu yab-yum, in which the man is passive and the woman acts out *shakti*—primal cosmic power. I'm shy about trying this, but as we play and sleep and sing, it seems to come of its own accord. I know nothing but strive for patience—tuning the senses, always deferring, until time is nothing. We sleep and eat Palisade peaches and spend the day in bed, making plans. Moving to

Denver seems out of the question now—I don't know why. I will keep the Mini. Stanhope agrees that we should drive it back to the coast.

The next morning, we meet with Zan, a long-time employee of Anshu's who will buy the business. She is an accomplished bicyclist—very healthy and funny. She proudly shows us the merchandise and discusses her plans for expanding the maps and displays that Anshu had constructed. Zan will expand Anshu's collection of fair-trade products, including fashion accessories. She amuses us with stories of Anshu trying awkwardly to date her, then realizing his mistake and trying to set her up with women. "What is it about confirmed singletons that makes them think they have to be matchmakers?" This makes me a little sad because the answer, I think, is that some people make matches for others because they've given up on finding someone for themselves. Stanhope seems to feel this, too. Thinking of Anshu alone sharpens our appreciation of being together.

Every quiet moment, I thank Anshu for this money from his shop and his home. It's a wonderful gift. For the first time in my life, I might look around and consider what else to do or where else to go. With the boon of Stanhope, my listening lover, it's almost too much at once. My heart is really full. The mixture of love and loss and gratitude is almost too much to hold.

The real estate agent has found good buyers—a professional couple ready to start a family. We're happy to throw furniture into the bargain. As we sit at a long table signing the papers, Stanhope says he is haunted by the memory of Anshu and Eva talking and laughing in the driveway. I must excuse myself. We take a long walk afterward.

For two days we organize things for sale, put paperwork in order, walk, and grow closer. This relationship is like a third being that accompanies us everywhere. It's as if we're raising a puppy together or cultivating an exotic plant. It's not always what we want at the moment, but it is what must be. In any event, we cannot leave it alone. We touch, talk, shop, walk, collaborate, and meditate. Through night and day, Stanhope discovers every scrap of what I might be and obliterates all else. We're purposely apart sometimes, but even then, the connection is so substantial that sometimes I think I was wrong to sell the house. We could stay here and see Jill and Molly the Collie every day, and play ball with Skitch. We could curate Anshu's gemstones and other precious things.

But Anshu has made it all too easy. He took care of everything so meticulously that the estate sale is a great success. His cricket club comes by—eight jolly men bearing cricket memorabilia. Now we have real treasures on offer. But the deep feelings that they hold for Anshu—that they share with me respectfully—are more precious. I am finally on the team!

There is still a morning nip in the air when we start running out of things to sell. As I return to the garage, I find Stanhope in a rocking chair with clasped hands, looking pale. He says the coed who bought the Vespa was wearing Eva's favorite sweater. He speaks quietly about the coincidence, saying the girl is "warm in future-seeking." I cry too easily. At the end of the day, we sit in the garden with the hummingbirds, hollyhocks, cricket bat, Eva, and Anshu.

- XI -

The Price of Salvation
(Fall)

THE HONEYMOON THRILL IS MELLOWING TO AN EASY FAMILIARITY. I STILL grin stupidly at Gaya but find that I *can* think of other things once in a while. Now that we're finished with Anshu's affairs, I think of my friends in Colorado—mostly Chuck and Kitty Duran and their deaf daughter, Donna, who had danced with Eva and taken diorama courses with her. The poor kid had been stunned by this Eva hole in her teen life and talked about it mechanically. Trying to help her understand had helped me understand. She's a sharp lip-reader, but you have to speak plainly, directly. It was just what I needed: speech therapy.

She must be eighteen now. She always seemed delicate, but underestimating her is a mistake. Like Eva, she organizes everything and everyone—especially Chuck. Draws animals. Reads Austen, Mary Ann Evans, eco-bulletins. Emotes dryly, in unexpected bursts: "Polar bears are smaller now." Her voice is a puzzle and a comfort. Many teenage girls adopt up-speak—lilting every statement into a question because it draws the validation they need. Others speak from the back of the throat in a froggy, flat voice to disguise feelings. Donna does neither. She speaks off-key, as the deaf do, but without affectation. Could she have learned her easy laugh from Eva—without actually hearing it? Would miming the convulsion free the liberating chime? I hope so.

I love the blessed coolness of the mornings. Stanhope serves yogurt, peaches, and toast while I pour out chai. We feel unburdened, completely free, and talk about a lot of things. Future talk, Stanhope calls it. He wears Anshu's red and black robe. I wear a yellow robe he bought me for sitting in the garden. I keep asking about seeing the bookstore and flower shop, but he always changes the subject. This time, as I sip chai and watch hummingbirds, he brings me his folder on Theo, Sadie's grandson. The drawings have a particularity and sophistication that suggest Theo had known each animal he had sketched—having probably sketched it many times. Stanhope says that the sanctuary where Theo worked is only ninety minutes away, so I suggest we go. I don't think he expects to find a lot of information about Theo there, but it's a beautiful day and we are eager to see the animals.

He tells me funny stories about Chuck, his old partner. These men really should see each other again, and I would like to meet the Durans. Stanhope places the call. After a lot of laughing, he rings off and tells me that Chuck and his family will meet us at the refuge. The unsealed parking lot where we meet them is very hot and dusty. Chuck is just the clown I had imagined, dramatic and kind. I think his silly show is mostly for his daughter, Donna. The deaf girl's mother, Kitty, presents a large loaf of pumpkin bread. Stanhope says, "Bless your baker's heart!" He turns to me and says, "Kitty can't go anywhere without an offering." I love her for that. She is a smiling Parvati—a mother goddess who brings harmony to all.

Donna is guileless. I stop myself from asking about the cause of her deafness. I always want to be a detective so I can apply my training, but sometimes it is not appropriate. The girl hugs Stanhope and wishes aloud for the presence of Eva—with whom she arranged flowers and restored museum dioramas. It is an honest wish. Donna and I are just the same size. She asks direct questions about where I'm from and how I met Stanhope. I think she might offend sometimes by always going straight to the point, but I enjoy it. It is a little unsettling that she talks specifically to me. I will do my best.

We enter a commodious reception tent and watch a video that describes the function of this former ranch: to caretake animals who have been removed from their natural habitat. Nearly all of the creatures were born in captivity—in roadside zoos or at the farms and houses of eccentrics. The predominant species are lions, tigers, and bears. One statistic haunts me: there are more tigers in private homes in Texas than there are tigers left in the wild. Now I fully realize the emotions this day might stir. Stanhope notices my falling behind, and we retreat to the parking lot. Fortunately, we see a girl walking a dog very similar to Caprice. Laying our hands on this beautiful animal makes me feel a lot better. We return to the tent, where Donna watches the video many times while her parents prepare themselves for the sun.

The great size of the sanctuary, at least, is comforting. A large, elevated walkway keeps visitors well above a wide assortment of predators and prey. This arrangement is meant to keep the beasts from feeling stressed and territorial, and it seems to work. Most of the animals rest and move about easily—more relaxed than their zoo counterparts. They seldom glance up at us. Carefully constructed dens and shelters—and the walkway itself—provide shade.

The Durans start the two-mile walk along the walkway while Stanhope and I discuss Theo with the staff. A few workers remember him, though it was many years ago. When we show them Theo's sketches, a middle-aged woman named Haley with a lion tattoo identifies one of the bears as Sam. Then she looks more carefully through the drawings and gives us the names of more animals. Two of them have died, but she will take us to the other three. With the Durans, we continue as Haley explains again what we learned in the video: sanctuaries like this don't breed, trade, or interact with the animals. They are really serious about this. If you drop something from the walkway, it will not be retrieved.

Haley points to a standing black bear. "That's Sam." He looks as though he's smiling, but that's an illusion—he has something in his teeth that he wants to spit out. Nearly all of these animals were born in captivity, but Sam is an exception. Haley says that he kept returning to a campground after being carried off—eventually finding his way back more than one hundred miles. It made him a local television celebrity. The wildlife service received so much mail about Sam that they could not risk the bad publicity that would result from destroying him. So he was offered to the refuge. Haley thinks one of the reasons Sam is popular is because he stands and walks upright more than most bears. "Who knows why?" she says. "Just healthy and curious, I guess."

Still standing, Sam watches us approach. Donna runs to the railing and calls to him, but Haley asks her not to be so demonstrative. Interaction with animals is not banned, but it is meant to be more incidental than direct. Sam seems to know he's in the spotlight. He stands motionless, as if listening. Then he grins again and spits out a twig. He drops to all fours and makes his way toward a small bear who paces between her den and a fence. Haley says this female is new. She is probably used to being in a cage. She may settle down, but it is hard to be certain.

We walk the length of the walkway, with Haley narrating. The Kodiak bears are the size of automobiles. The coyotes play chasing games. The wolves make boredom look magnificent! I was worried about this experience but now feel invigorated. The animals are not where they belong, and they are not doing what they are programmed to do. They are still sadly displaced. But they are better off—they are able to live out their lives in relative ease.

At the end of the walkway, we step down to two large lion enclosures. A young male is isolated in one, so he can become acclimated to the sanctuary without being challenged. A mature lion couple is in the adjacent space. The old male stays near the boundary, looking over this new fellow, but the female lies on a hill in the distance, where she puts her nose into the breezes and watches the horizon. She is fascinating in large part because of her aloofness. She looks as if she is remembering someone. Haley tells us the lioness is Chanda—the cat drawn by Theo.

I have a cousin named Chanda—it means fierce. How does an African animal come to have an Indian name? This kind of juxtaposition is probably normal here. She is an African animal with an Indian name living in the American West. At this moment, at least, she is not fierce, but serene. I would say she embodies the intention of the sanctuary.

Donna is completely absorbed with Chanda. Stanhope gives her Theo's sketch, and she lingers with it as the rest of us descend to a sheltered group of enclosures. Within, there lies a sharp-faced wolf called Thor. He is the son of a wolf that Theo drew. Thor is in isolation, as he is being treated for a paw injury. He watches us closely—feeling vulnerable, I'm sure. Haley explains that his long legs and narrow chest allow him to run efficiently through deep snow. His mate, Grindel, shows off this elegant running. It is not possible to mistake her for a dog. Wolf heads seem enormous to me. Haley explains that this is because we are used to dogs, which have smaller brains.

We climb back up, but something pierces my heart: Donna is really suffering. She lies on a bench, sobbing. Kitty and I run to her and ask caring questions, but her eyes are closed. We communicate via touch. Her despair is distressing, but we center ourselves and try to be patient. The effect is strange: great predators lounge on the ground while primal wails come from this small human on the walkway above. From this vantage point, we can see elephants, lions, tigers, and an ocelot. Suddenly, they are not so at ease. A few move restlessly and look up. After a lot of soothing, Donna stands and holds on to us. Her eyes are open, but she is not reading lips. She watches the lioness—who is still unperturbed—and tries to compose herself for the walk back. She cannot quite accomplish this, poor child. She seems compelled to say something—in her very direct way, of course. "Someone has to—cry for them."

Such a declaration is necessary for Donna, I think. She stumbles, very pale. Kitty and I support her on each side. Kitty marshals her Parvati serenity. "It doesn't—"

Suddenly, Kitty is overcome. I think she wants to say, "It doesn't have to be you," but we all realize in that moment that it *does* have to be—*all* of us. We all should feel the gravity of wild animals deprived of wild lives. Perhaps then sanctuaries like these will become unnecessary, or the world itself will become the greatest kind of sanctuary. Of one heart, we embrace.

Chuck and I walk ahead of the women. He repeats what I already know. Donna has always been focused on two things: English literature and animals. She's too shy to teach but might make a good veterinarian. She reminds me of Theo—what I know of him, anyway. They're both obsessed with injustice. Rage against it.

We stop and wait on the walkway as the women unclench and walk slowly back—broad, sunny Kitty out front; Gaya and Donna trailing, looking like twins from a distance. All three wonder aloud about the day-to-day lives of every type of animal. We hear only snatches. Sometimes they stop to embrace again and gesture and go over Theo's drawings. Contentment catches us unawares, in spite of Donna's hard truth.

At the welcome center, I give copies of Theo's drawings to the staff and Donna. The kid is still shell-shocked and apologizes automatically for her scene. Gaya cups her face. "Never apologize for how you feel."

Chuck knows what to do. He turns his hat around and scoots into the parking lot, arms flapping. "El tora dora, don't spit on the floora, use the cuspidora, that's a-what she's for!" He skips and hops ridiculously, windmilling, smiling toothlessly, whining the tune like a puppy. We applaud. Donna shows more gratitude than amusement, but then Eva's laugh bursts from her, mesmerizing us all. Her father consoles and diverts her as he's done hundreds of times before. Comfort comedy: it always works.

At the refuge, Chuck had asked for my help on a job tomorrow. Surprised, I wasn't sure. Does he really need help, or is he trying to help me as a brother? Never mind. I'll be there.

Gaya is restless in the car—going on about Donna and the pacing bear. It's the in-betweening again, the nightmare shadow. We turn in early, as we always do now, and find comfort—not enough to fix the world, but enough to carry on. What we must concede is soothed by the possible.

In the morning, Kitty and Donna drive off with Gaya. They don't seem to have a destination in mind but are happy to be together. Chuck and I drive to the job site. He wasn't exaggerating the need. This is a load of work—a block-long brick-and-joist box baking in the sun. But we share a boom, and the day goes fast, thanks to Chuck's antics with *norteño*—a kind of Mexican polka. He sings, dances, and teaches me lyrics as we move quick time. I need every bit of it to reframe the work and get beyond Pigeon's exclamation point. After we slay the steaming beast and shower in the basement, Chuck drives toward Denver University. Shit. I protest, but he keeps on in silence. Shit. "I'm not getting out of the truck." Shit.

As we near Navoti Books and Flowers, Chuck finally thinks of something to say. "You got shit for brains if you don't marry that girl."

Eva's Yota Force is with us: a car pulls away, leaving a parking spot out front. Shit. But there's Gaya at the door, beaming like the sun. She's flanked by Kitty and Donna, who wave madly. As I turn inward, something pulls me outward, toward the bracketed joy. While Chuck is still parking, I stumble onto the sidewalk and into Gaya's arms. She grips my lapels in her earnest way. "This is your karma, you know. Yours and Eva's. The shop is really alive."

I can't move, but stillness suits her. "Are you hungry?"

I nod, and she unwraps a slab of Kitty's pumpkin bread. Holds up a water bottle. We sit on the stoop. The Durans and others move eagerly past us, in and out of the store. Now Gaya is part of the eternal picnic on these steps. Small stains on the flagstone speak of all the coffees and scones and upstart dreams Eva and I shared. Hundreds of dioramas spill across the sidewalk: Eva's purple cap, my ancient bicycle, grand gestures, tulip sunrises, cocoa conferences, dogs barking steam. We pick out dozens. Do our best listening.

Eventually, in no hurry, the scenes coalesce, and we move inside. I don't care about any of the changes made but am stupidly thrilled that the name of the business is the same. Anyway, much is as I once remembered. Looks like the owners are not here. Kitty and Donna bustle in for hugs. They still work in the flower department and are eager to introduce us around. Nah—we just want to be. I remember Anshu's satisfaction in being a nameless man on a nameless mountain. There's power in anonymity.

We check it all out, including the loft, which is patrolled by Jimmy, a cocky Jack Russell. Chuck is deep in conversation with a football guy, but Kitty and Donna stick with us, deftly moving potted plants around ladders and sills. Gaya is enchanted by the vintage, illustrated children's books. It's hard to say much, but in the end I'm a bookseller again, recommending titles, buying *Black Elk Speaks* for her. She holds the book with reverence. *Bless.*

Up front, while Gaya samples every rose, I buy a scarlet bouquet. She mashes it in our embrace. The clerk calls it Pasha because there's a naming tradition here. Yes, there is. Remembering the naming feels deeper than Christmas. Bang—here's the timeless, full-spectrum unity I've been aiming for, unawares. I wouldn't have thought it possible, but everything pops. All panes are spotless. All stories begin with names, and I feel the breathing, expanding stories around us. It all makes sense. Now, I can think of window washing without brooding on Pigeon. I can enter a bookstore without looking for Eva. The way is clear.

As we start for the door, I spontaneously climb the marry-me ladder. Donna remembers and beams up at me, with her new friend. Out on the sidewalk, horizontal sunlight highlights sylvan red and gold as we farewell the Durans. After a quick change, I drive Gaya to a rooftop restaurant that showcases alpenglow over the heart of Denver. Her coral blouse reminds me of Sadie. She fiddles with Shiva, shifting from possibility to possibility—how long she sees herself at Blessings, what my work might be. I'm out of particular ideas, but at least now I can imagine some kind of future. It's all about this caring Proteus. I love her attacks of shyness. We consider the massing stars. Trifles we are, and cool with it.

It's still early, so I head out to a creaky, old art deco amusement park where Eva and I once celebrated acquiring the pillbox. Gaya and I play well together. We take rides that whip out over a lake so we can admire, between whoops, squiggly neon reflected in the water. Ancient stucco buildings loom like castles. It's just the foolery we need. So many births and deaths can't go uncelebrated, after all. Throwing baseballs, I win a wristwatch for Gaya, and she pretends to take it seriously. The watch runs backward—must be a joke. I ask the time over and over, and she tells me it's earlier and earlier. She's getting younger, anyway. We scoot hilariously home, spilling popcorn all over the Mini.

In the morning, Molly the collie hoovers up the loose popcorn while we're saying goodbye. Her guardian, Jill, and Gaya close their eyes and push their faces into the roses. Gaya could've built her own diorama here, but didn't. How could I have considered letting her do this alone?

I cannot wait to see Rocky Mountain National Park again! Stanhope drives our Mini through a gorgeous canyon to Estes Park. It's all really liberating. I am so excited that I have to keep telling Stanhope what time it is *not*—according to my carnival watch. As we enter the town, I even laugh at the TEstes Park joke made by a local graffitist. But nature calms me. Elk walk confidently all over the village, aware of their magnificence. Sometimes the bulls are protective of their harems and position themselves aggressively or glare at us. We give them a lot of room. Over lunch at the Stanley Hotel, Stanhope tells me all about his crazy wedding—the clarity of Long's Peak that day and how this band called the Rocking Rudolphs kept everyone dancing all night. I feel a glow in my cheeks as I ask a lot of questions. Stanhope says the saxophone player almost won the limbo contest—while tootling his horn! We laugh and dance and mime.

The old steamer car in the lobby is beautiful. The Stanley Brothers built the hotel to make a point: at the time, only their steam-powered machines could climb the steep grade to Estes Park. Stanhope and I cannot find out why we are not all driving steamer cars today. Some employees say the vehicle was impractical, but others speak of a mysterious internal combustion mafia. In any event, we cannot place any blame on our Union-Jack Mini. It pulls us efficiently up Trail Ridge

Road to more than twelve thousand feet. We make certain the trip takes all afternoon—stopping often for hikes. The colors and enormity are exquisite. Unfortunately, this contentment does not last long. As we reach timberline, brown smoke covers the lower slopes and creeps upward. The Stanley staff had told us that a dozen fires are burning unchecked all over the Rockies. It is sad to think that this is how things are now. We can do nothing, of course, and do not discuss it. Our throats are too raw for speech in any case. We drive on. Stanhope says the haze reminds him of Shiva—of falling and losing Eva. I have visions of Anshu choking—up here, of all places, where he once came to breathe freely.

From a balcony at the high visitor's center, we watch elk move through green tundra and gray granite. Some apparently are lookouts, because they stand at the edges of the herd and make echoing barks. The scene is so restful that we almost forget about the clinging smoke. But a ranger begins a lecture about the susceptibility of bighorn sheep to lung disease, and we must escape. As we descend in the Mini, smoke drifts through the valleys. It is so thick that I find myself trying to limit the sensory experience. I can see Stanhope doing the same. Perhaps a story will help—just a small one.

"My Uncle Bebo likes to talk about how he first saw *Mary Poppins*. He had just come to the US for the first time and was in Denver, studying at the hospital. A kind doctor took him window shopping downtown at Christmas with his family. Bebo loved the crunch of snow under his boots and the robot elves and animals in the shop windows. They all went to the movie theater and saw *Mary Poppins*. The theater had one of those large, curved screens that were popular then."

"Probably the Cooper Theater. People still talk about it."

"Yes. Bebo was completely transported by the experience. He could not believe the imagination that went into this film. Afterward, he stood in a circle with the doctor's family in the parking lot. They held hands and watched snowflakes spin out of the sky."

"Precious."

"Yes. But, you know, *Mary Poppins* really changed Bebo's life. If people could come together and make such a film, then surely anything is possible.

My uncle tried to live his life in that way. He always makes me laugh! We play Poppins a lot."

"The possibilities game."

"Yes."

✳ ✳ ✳

Gaya and I wind through the rugged San Juans into the desert. Slip into a timeless tracking of temple walls. The trip feels too free, too indulgent at first. Here we are, vibrantly alive, as if there has been no body count. But after a few days, contentment wrings out the residual guilt. We acquire some Native American flute music—R. Carlos Nakai, Mary Youngblood—which reminds Gaya of the flutes she heard on the streets of Kolkata. We talk about *Black Elk* and find similar books at a used bookstore in Cortez.

I let the desert wash over me, but Gaya is a detective. She always wants to learn more—studying maps through oval glasses. At Canyon de Chelley, she grills the artists in the parking lot who sell rugs, rock art, and beads. She extracts the whole story of the Navajo emergence from their place of origin and asks about their colorful dress. Because Kokopelli is a flute player—a fertility god carrying seed and song—she buys a fetish of him to ward off the Hitchcock.

We float on our flute soundtrack from Navajo through Hopi country. The views from Walpi, on First Mesa, match the high-minded music. We melt like butter into the landscape. The mood is not wasted: a dark, patient woman walks out to explain the compassion and respect built into Hopi culture. As we walk back, Gaya takes my hand and thanks me for enshrining this deep understanding in Navoti Bookshop.

Sometimes we stop early and linger in a cool hotel room, splash in a pool, play. Love like everything and nothing remains. In Winslow, we stay two nights at La Posada, one of the last old railway hotels. We wander the rich courtyard, the cool hallways and galleries, as if it all might disappear. Gaya is thrilled by towering blue hollyhocks in the garden. Most evenings, we sit outside with Sir Walter and watch the stars pop. I'm self-conscious about smoking my pipe, but Gaya loves it. "It's really evocative—like sandalwood."

Everywhere we go, I try to pull a smile. "Would you like Poppins with that?" "Eighty percent chance of Poppins today," "Exceptions eternally?" and, always, "You don't look so hot yourself." She loves my slang and adopts it immediately. "Stanhope, we're burning daylight, you know." I apologize for lollygagging, and she pounces on the word. She calls me Lollygag almost as often as Stanhope. *Lowly geg.* But the best descriptor is "such a one." It's all I want to be.

I tell her about Mom's dedication to Tolkien's *The Lord of the Rings,* and we find an audio version. She only knows the movies but loves the books instantly. After hours of impeccable narration, I ask her about a stitch in her brow. "I am worried about Pippin and Merry."

She straps on the amusement-park wristwatch every morning and calls out odd times. "It is midnight," she'll say as we slalom sun-drenched corridors. Now we have time for everything. Great slabs of time, everywhere. Ticking along in the Mini, we're sedated by the wondering flute, the endless space. We walk everywhere. Befriend hoodoos. Talk about the tearing, the pulling apart, the lifting and opening. The swirl of strata. I gain some understanding of the geology but can't remember the names of anything. I want the verbs: the movement, the shearing, the cooking, the spilling out. Geologists at the parks and monuments gesticulate and explain. Lost in the flute, we're just happy it all happened— is happening. We pulse through gargantuan splendor.

Some of our discovery is at close quarters. We examine, adopt, and dismiss each other's habits. Gaya always inserts toilet paper rolls to pull from the bottom. Well, I have to correct that. Back and forth we go, until I give in. I flip the roll once in a while, just to keep her on her toes. Twice a day, with great care, she rubs rose oil on my wounds. I have never felt such icy hands. Sometimes I yipe and we joke about it, but her concern is a comfort. Like Eva, Gaya is a punctual meditator. This is good for me. Mornings and sometimes afternoons we sit for twenty to forty minutes. It's a solitary exercise, but it still helps to have a partner. My efforts are feeble for the first few mornings, as Gaya disturbs without trying. Seismically. For one thing, she doesn't sit cross-legged. She kneels. I don't know why I'm charmed by this—maybe it's just the unthinking nonconformity. I steal glances at her as we empty and fill. I think she's a little bothered too, but we get used to it. Contentment—within which the practice takes root—grows from the knowledge that I can still distract this jade idol.

Several afternoons, we're overtaken by smoke. The stinky murk shuts us up. Not wanting to stop, we make good progress. But that's not why we're here. Nothing we try can lighten the mood. Even the transcendent flute music sounds tinny. It can't penetrate the nightmare shadow. Fortunately, as we approach the Grand Canyon, the smoke thins until the air is spotless. Gaya has never seen the canyon and actually trembles as we draw near. She runs giddily toward Grandeur Point, checking the carney wristwatch. "Two minutes to eternity!"

How do you prepare for the Grand Canyon? I wonder if the view might be more staggering if you suddenly materialized on the rim or made the long approach blindfolded. But it's surprising, regardless. You want to focus on the deep or the wide, but vivid panoramas force you to take both together. They crack you open. You look for unity, to avoid being overwhelmed, and you can make some headway there, matching peripheral strata. But eventually, the transcendence enfolds you, steps you down glowing stairways to the silver Colorado.

Stanhope and I walk east, stopping at each overlook. I cannot say anything because I cannot say everything. This place seems to require that much of us. At Yaki Point, we turn west again, walking the intervals and running to views. At Hopi Point, as I lean out to glimpse the river, the dropping sun ignites the landscape. Shadow and color shift before our eyes—at a different rate for each degree of the compass. Now that I understand in a new way, I have to tell Stanhope about it. But when I turn to him, he looks at me with great affection and speaks first.

"Look at you, with your Anshu eyes and jitterbug hair!"

"Oh! It's this place."

"It's *you* in this place."

He is flustering me with love, but I must hold on to my ideas. "This is the eternal return, you know."

"Isn't that always the way?"

I have to laugh and face the breeze to manage my hair. "In school, I was taught about the *eternal return*—an expression of fate, really—the idea that history repeats endlessly. This is useful, at least, as an imaginative exercise—to think of time in monstrously large, repeating units. At university, I learned of a Romanian man, Eliade—who studied in India and loved an Indian princess. He developed a larger idea of eternal return: a return, through ritual and meditation, to the very beginning of myth. It kind of validates the idea of sacred time being circular—or at least the *possibility* of sacred time being circular."

"The dance-of-redundancy dance."

I extend my arms and try to maintain concentration. "I'm not sure I really understood those ideas. But seeing all this today, I thought, *If we place ourselves always at the beginning, we can* defeat *linear time*—which Eliade called the profane."

I gesture wildly in a little dance of ecstasy. "Well, this place—this Grand Canyon—is a *graveyard* of linear time. We *cannot* fathom the time we are seeing here! It does not fit in our heads. So we are left with the sacred. We are *confronted* with it. We must—"

"Walk in a sacred manner."

"Yes! As Black Elk said."

"Renew and renew."

"Yes! Return and return. Eternally."

Gaya and I roll westward, across the expanse. Turn our fine-tuned senses to ocotillo, cholla, hawks, coyotes, ravens. The tectonic stretch elongates time and space. Yet I can't forget that our road trip has to end. I'm Wile E. Coyote in slo-mo, heading for a cliff. Now *there's* a guy who knows death.

Or maybe not, since he never gets it right. He can't stay dead. He gets it over and over again: anvil, flame, bomb, plummet. I can relate. But that's all over. *Please* let it be over.

Dawdling at Lake Mead, we watch a woman quick marching across the parking lot, tracking something with binoculars. We trail after her like children. It's an unwritten rule: find excuses to digress, to wonder. The woman stops and watches, motionless, then turns to us with a smile. "It's a California condor."

We'd noticed the slow wingbeats, but now its bulk is clear. The ornithologist hands us the binoculars. The prehistoric thing hunkers in a vertical sandstone crack. Huge, black, and angular. Pink pinhead thrust forward. Iconic. Inevitable. "He's captive-bred but making it. I hope he keeps moving. No mates for him around here."

She gives us the good news: condors are coming back. This guy is one of more than three hundred—up from a handful. The woman scribbles notes and prattles on like a proud parent. This is her Ph.D., her baby, her freedom, her meaningful work. We ask her to join us for dinner, but she's tethered—she has to chase her charge, with the help of tracking devices, until he's ready to stop for the night, miles away, or at least until he finds something deliciously dead. It's a primal relic until it looks at us. The direct gaze unhinges everything, and I watch myself unfolding. It reminds me of the full-face connections in Theo's animal drawings. The condor looks right at the ornithologist and tracks her when she moves. She smiles proudly. It's as if he's waiting for her. Only when she approaches her car does he swing out over the cliffs. *You come too.*

Stanhope looks so tan and relaxed driving Anshu's little car! Listening to the flute music, watching the Joshua trees on the sunbaked horizon, I feel as relaxed as I've ever felt as an adult. I wish the feeling could last forever. I try to study guidebooks, but it's no use. This is our last day, I suppose. It feels as though I must say what has been left unsaid. I switch off the music and turn to him. "Do you know about *darshan* eyes?"

"No."

"They are the eyes of devotion. Of *bhakti*. Of love. You see it in the beautiful eyes of the gods in Hindu art. When I was a child, I decided that, if I could make proper darshan eyes, if I could develop this sacred sight, I would be *one* with whatever I saw. Whatever I looked at in that way would be irresistible to me. But also the reverse: I would be irresistible to that thing."

"Eyes of the beholder."

"I just thought that whatever I looked at with gratitude and devotion would reciprocate: creation flowing in both directions. It does help to try and see with better eyes, you know, because you cannot separate yourself from what you observe. You *are* what you see. *How* you see."

Stanhope says nothing, so I look at the books again. Suddenly, he pulls onto an overlook, removes my glasses, and kisses me so tenderly that I want to cry.

I have a few more days before going back to work, so we decide to save Stanhope's flat for later and go directly to the marina. There, Duncan tells us that Skye is working for Connie now, at the Pilgrim Grill. We sail around the point and the sea air is delicious. In the evening, we eat our road snacks and play Scrabble in the cabin. Making our cocoon is silly fun. Stanhope says we are children playing in fading light. We know it is nearly time to go home, so we try to make every moment count. We lie awake for a long time, thrilling to the sound and movement of water—listening a little and expecting a lot.

For three days, we explore in all directions. The weather and sea spray are fine. In the evenings, we drift aimlessly and watch the sunset. Stanhope's rich, glowing pipe adds mystery to our contentment. He describes a sailing vision of Anshu's—an aerial view of us zooming along in *Katy Sue*. "We're living Anshu's dream."

We talk about what else to do with the dream. Stanhope says we should send it back in time to Anshu. "Done!" I say. "We should also send it forward to ourselves."

"You sound like Kerouac. I thought your brother was the mystic."

"I have seen the eternal return!"

The sunset is reflected in a constellation of lenticular clouds. They are periwinkle and mauve. First comes a scattering, then unity.

Spouts. Whale spouts in the distance. I point, and Gaya tucks under my arm. She wants me to give up DP and come live with her in San Diego, but something is holding me back. Not just the klaxons of the city—it's a deeper dread. I don't know what to say as we secure *Katy Sue*. I've been avoiding doing anything ashore for fear of losing the honeymoon thrill. But our provisions are meager, and here comes the night, so we thump along the boardwalk toward Connie's Pilgrim Grill. Vegetable aromas greet us at the door, and responsibility closes in. I imagine the schemes and confrontations Connie might have hatched to intervene in Cub's alcoholism. What have we gotten ourselves into?

Skye stands at the front counter in a smock, pale and nervous. She's probably still learning the ropes. She hugs us tenderly. When we ask for Connie, she disappears in the back. Over the next ten minutes, the waiting area near the door fills with a few other couples. I breathe the spices and run my fingers through Gaya's thick curls. Finally, a beefy, well-dressed man emerges and introduces himself as Connie's lawyer. He says the restaurant will close until further notice. When we ask why, he takes a deep breath and states flatly that Connie was killed in a head-on collision two hours ago. "Right out there, on the overpass."

I'm out the door, running. I don't know where. I thread through the parking lot, see that I'm approaching the highway, and veer toward the sea. A distant voice calls. "Stanhope!"

"No!" I shout. Again. Again. Every fourth step. My voice grows softer, but I can't stop saying it. The voice tries again.

"Wait!"

Wait for what? Sanity? No chance. There's the beach. I accelerate into the water—running, walking, "no"-ing, diving. I'm a child again—this time, terrified.

Splashes crescendo behind me. "Please stop."

Please stope. I turn and stand, waves breaking against my back. Stupidly repeat the mantra: "No." Can I say anything else?

Gaya and I watch each other in the gloom, catching our breath. Turns out, I *can* say something else. "You said it wasn't real."

She looks down, gathering her thoughts in her usual way, lowering her voice. "I said you should stop feeding it."

"You were wrong. The Hitchcock is real."

"Do we know that, Stanhope?"

"I do."

"Then, we will live it together."

"No."

"Always no."

"It has to be no. You know that."

A defiant tilt of the head. "I do *not*."

"You were wrong, Gaya."

She splashes me repeatedly as she speaks. "Did you think I was some sort of goddess? Did you think I am always right? Well, here's the news: I am human. I make it up as I go along. Just as you do. Just as *everyone* does."

"You have to do better than me."

"Why?"

"Because this stupid world is for you. Not me."

She splashes me again. "Drama does *not* help."

I submerge. When I resurface, she's a few steps closer. "You were wrong, Gaya."

"I had to try, Stanhope. I had to try to catch you, you know? I'm a nurse. Why would I not help a desperate man believe in the comforting laws of science? Why would I not help a wounded man re-engage?"

"Because his engagement *kills*."

The wind picks up and a wave crests my shoulders. It must be cold, but I can't tell. Gaya shivers but ducks her head as if to show that she will endure. But she emerges looking vulnerable. I need any story but my own. She knows. "Listen to me: I was lost when Anshu left India—so lost,

I tried to love a man who could not love. He only understood power. I did not know such people existed—not really, not in my small world. In the end, I did not want to live. Do you understand? Coming to America, finding Anshu, was my last chance. Now Anshu is gone."

Shit. In spite of all, I love—*must* love. Too bad. It would be easy, otherwise. I could be the Count of Monte Cristo and play God. Stan the bland dispenser of justice and death. But there's this heart; this hell. Is that the price of salvation? I step forward. She holds out her arms. "You think your presence will kill me. Your *absence* will."

She *thinks*. Who knows? The sliver moon is devoured. All I have now is her voice. "Four patients moved to the twelfth floor this summer. I talked to them every day. They touched me and asked for my help. Now they are gone. Now *Connie* is gone."

I'm a cold nothing. "I can't save you."

"We can save each other."

Stop it. Be what she needs. I take another step. She lunges into me and pulls me toward shore as if pulling a jumper from a building ledge. We stand together in waist-deep water as moonlight returns. Who the hell am I? Gaya knows. "Stanhope."

We stagger out and stand shivering on the beach. Pick our way herkily up to the old motel and lurch into the lobby—hypothermic zombies. Gaya tries to smile at the hoteliers, who recognize us. "We fell!" They produce blankets and good cheer. Gaya drags me into a hot shower, and we undress in the steam. Am I hungry? I grunt the last "no." We sleep like the dead.

IF ANYONE CRIES
(FALL)

AT DAWN, WE LINGER AT THE EDGE OF WAKING. I'M BACK AT SQUARE one, trying to get over Connie, trying to get over my stupid self. Turning outward is beyond imagining—but I can be dogged, once pointed in the right direction. The right direction is through Gaya. I trace her collarbone. She's seen the worst of me now: Stan the unmanned. I whisper apologies until she shuts my mouth. She's the way out.

Another long shower, avoiding every thought. The avoiding reminds me to meditate. Gaya hugs me for the idea. We sit for forty minutes, but I can't get anywhere near wanting to laugh. Wanting to forget will have to do. I step onto the balcony to check the misty weather and return to find Gaya sobbing against a wall. I carry her back to bed. Two hours later, after dark roast and grapefruit at the coffee shop, we're feeling almost human—not ready for life, but ready for the next five minutes. Gaya kneads my arm and stares at imperfections. I ask her if Connie knew her time was short.

"Did she know death was coming? She did not say anything directly about it. But her actions ..."

"Such as?"

"Such as putting a proper will in place—recently. Falling in love with a crazy musician. She spoke of those things as if she did not understand her own actions."

She sips and thinks. "And she asked Mark—you know, Caprice's person—if he would take her dog, Kevin, if necessary. So, yes. Now I see that she was making arrangements—perhaps subconsciously. How do you talk about the shadow of death? She couldn't, really."

"Maybe avoiding the news had something to do with it."

"Yes. If I had a short time to live, I would avoid stories of death and destruction."

Right. And the *if* doesn't matter. "Yeah. You need something more. A future."

"Not necessarily even for yourself. Just—Oh! She also said she wasn't making plans. I thought this was because she could not rely on Cub."

As we prepare to leave, Admiral Spencer walks in, bent and pale—almost unrecognizable. He shakes his head. "Connie," he croaks.

Though Gaya hardly knows the man, she jumps up and hugs him fiercely. They hang on for a long while. I take my turn. The admiral is fragile now, shorn of authority. There's a pall in the shop—everyone knows. Death humbles. Impulsively, I invite the admiral to inspect *Katy Sue*. He hardly registers what we're saying, just follows robotically as we march down to the boat. Gaya watches him closely. Anticipating the need, Duncan and Skye meet us there. Even with their expert help, we fumble with small things. As we move slowly out of the harbor, I wonder at how changed the old man is. There's a squall on the horizon that should command his attention, but he hardly looks beyond the gunwales. His sharp lines are folding inward. He jumps when we refer to him by rank. "Spence," he says. I can't do it.

When we're underway, Skye tells us that while Connie kept everyone informed of local happenings, there was never a taint of judgment. She would say, matter-of-factly, that someone was getting divorced, for example, without taking sides. If you asked her what she thought, she'd start with the complimentary and finish with the philosophical. "When Wilma at the machine shop had to have a restraining order against her husband, Connie put the husband in touch with a foreman looking for fishermen to work in Alaska. And she helped him pack. She always knew what to do."

Not knowing what to do, I flounder on, telling everyone about Connie and Cub. The admiral—Spence—listens carefully. The only time he speaks is to ask for more character detail. I see him in sharp relief: his secret, romantic interest in Connie might have faded naturally had she not been brutally taken—with every attendant sorrow of family loss. He shivers. I find a jacket for him below.

Gaya talks quietly about Connie: her bond with the Rhodesian ridgeback, Kevin; their endless walks and conversations. Her adoption of neighbor kids. Her fascination with the swallows that once returned by the thousands. She worked with ornithology groups to lure the birds back after they abandoned Capistrano. It's surprising what Gaya can say about someone she knew for such a short time. She tells us that Connie endured a strict Midwestern upbringing and fell for a clone of her Calvinist father. Dropped out of college to bear children. A bitter divorce propelled her to DP, where she sought only wild creatures and fresh air. She plugged into the community until she personified it—then couldn't leave, even for grandchildren. Kevin the dog and his eager ears seemed ready-made for her. In cahoots they were a chatty shuttle on a loom, winding along the cliffs and beaches, weaving the community together.

We stand close on the foredeck as the wind picks up. Gaya gets to the heart of everything. She shows everyone the swallow necklace Connie gave her. Turning to the admiral, she stops in mid-sentence. The old man stands gaping, frail in his flapping, unzipped jacket. Gaya steps inside it, as if they've known each other forever. Leads him into the cabin. They sit close at the small table, talking tenderly. I ask Duncan to take us home while I make hot chocolate for them. Gaya always acts as if she has all the time in the world, but I know she has to get back to Blessings. A cheer from above drives us to a window, where we watch whales in the distance. "Connie," says the old man.

Topside, I join the future talk. Duncan and Skye tell me about their new venture: custom photovoltaic awnings. They'll start with boat work and branch out from there. Skye's father has some old upholstery machines that can be modified. They give me a card: Solawnia. "So lawn and thanks for all the fish," I stutter—stupidly, as if I can't hear myself. Mom spoon-fed us Douglas Adams, too. Duncan and Skye don't get the reference, but their laughter is genuine. They're dependable that way. If you can stay primed, wanting to laugh, expectation will pull you along like a sail. Love is a billowing spinnaker.

I peek below. The old man is opening up to Gaya as they sip hot chocolate. She takes his hand, asks questions, nods. Mostly she listens. She's the way out.

On dry land, Spence, Gaya, and I meander inland. No more marching. No more duty. I wonder if the old man will recover his military bearing, become the admiral again. Around a corner trot Kevin and Caprice, with Mark. Gaya kneels for the dogs and hides her face in their greeting. "Such consolation!" Consolation. We look for it ever. Kevin looks for it now. He peers around us continually, twisting his ears, listening in every direction for Connie's newsy patter. The truth is that comfort is not so hard to find. Kevin will miss Connie but may be happier overall living with Mark and Caprice. The dharma dog, Caprice, leans into him and grins up at us as if life could not be more perfect. Eventually, she gets the big guy to mouth her half-heartedly. Spence buries his face in Kevin's neck. Walks briskly away, as if trying to catch someone.

As we approach Anshu's Union-Jack Mini, Gaya asks me again if I'll go with her. The asking is a formality but I can't say yes. Connie's death was a sucker punch, just when I was learning to bob and weave. It launched me, spinning, Hubble-like, into deep space. Then, there's who Connie was: everybody's fixer. The healthy way forward for everyone. Finally, there's what the loss signifies. Connie's not just gone, she has been replaced by the Hitchcock, the nightmare shadow. I can't forgive any god for that. Every connection that I value, that helps me hold on, is now suspect. Again. I'm dangerous. Again.

Gaya is my gift for enduring. I'm sure I love her and tell her so. She drops the anvil purse on my foot and hugs fiercely. The artless intensity is all. Goddamn—can I do this? She saved me last night. Again. But I'll wear her out at this rate. As I prepare my excuses, she beats me to the punch, cupping my face. "Take a few days, Stanhope. That's enough, I think. You know?"

I have no idea. Connie's lawyer says it will take months to sort out the real estate. I can stay in the basement apartment for a while. But the place is a dungeon without Connie and Kevin thundering overhead. After two sad nights, I amble down to *Katy Sue*. The boat, too, is empty. No Gaya pointing and asking. I check for calls. It's stupid how long it takes me to get a clue sometimes. I'm on the water aimlessly for three days, inventing drinks and chasing sundogs, before I remember what I should be doing. *Help me, Connie. What's next?* Believing that this death curse is all about me is the express line to insanity. At least that's clear. Turning outward supplies options—and victims, goddamn it. Gaya is Priority One. Just stay away from her, whatever she says. In spite of all. In spite of love. She can't choose life over love, but I can do it for her. She would say life *is* love, and I agree. But she's a scientist. She would have to admit that there are thousands of compatible matches for everyone. In a year or two, Gaya will meet a power-forward MD who will throw my cursedness into sharp relief.

Priority Two is Connie. I'll miss her memorial. Just can't do another one of those. Not now. Connie had a lover, a lawyer, children, grandkids, and dozens of friends who will close ranks. Socializing grief is probably the best way to cope, but I never think of that. I think, *What needs fixing?* When my grandmother died, I jumped up in the middle of the night and polished the hell out of the tea set and flatware she had given us. Eva laughed at all the sparkling silver. Going to Connie's memorial might be a fixing, but the exposure's not worth it. There won't be much future talk there, and I'm dangerous again. I'll be drawn into other lives. Gaya will be there. Forgive me, Connie. I hate knowing you're gone and think of you all the time. But I need separation. The news of your loss was a blow—the drive-by violence of news bulletins that you understood too well. I have to protect myself. The way forward will require strength. Sometimes that means sheltering for a while. So, no memorial. Sometime soon, I'll put your history together and think about what to do next.

Priority Three: the Spuds. I have to believe I'm not a danger to them. Okay, I *want* to believe that. Connie is dead. Maybe the no-war-stories strategy is a bad idea. But the Window Wizards and the Spuds are, or were, okay. I can't check in with Brian and the Wizards again—I have to leave well enough alone. What's well enough? Not this light air. I trim the sails and drift. I'm a fucking madman.

The wind picks up as I turn for home. Dolphins ride the bow wave. I luff the sail to keep them with me. The Spuds would love this. Of course—I have a promise to keep. I pull out the small life vests that I stowed in the cockpit. Would one last adventure with the Spuds be so dangerous, if we stick to future talk? I can't even pretend the idea is not selfish. It's a big chance, but I can't let it go. I need the fix, just to stay away from Gaya. I call Halle and get the latest. She's healthy again. The Spuds are strong. Great. I'm charming and persuasive, telling her that I need to fulfill my promise to the boys. I'll pick them up this afternoon and return them tomorrow night. It takes a village to raise a Spud. School? This is a field trip. They'll have more fun if they're playing hooky. "You and Rick can have a night out." Silence. "I have life vests—their size." That does it.

I grab the mini-vests and hit the road. Traffic is awful, but I still arrive in good time, just after Bard and Randy are out of school. They're trembling with excitement as they try on the vests. I can almost match them. I give Halle nine ways to check up on us, then she helps me install the car seats. Bard rails against that, once again, and I can't blame him. He really is too big for a car seat. But Halle is adamant, and Bard knows he can't blow this adventure. It's hard to make the big-boy argument through tears. While he toughs it out, Halle motions me inside. She gives me a small wooden box that the boys have decorated with stars. Eva's sapphire ring is inside. Halle kisses my forehead, and we're off.

I tell the boys we can hit the drive-up window at a fast-food place, but, as the token adult, I get to edit or veto everyone's order. This triggers protracted negotiations, but in the end, I'm okay with what they're eating. Hope returns. Having these guys around sharpens my decision-making. Maybe daddy wisdom is the key to future think. Randy retains the right to feed the driver chicken blobs by keeping his freshly-washed hands in plain sight at all times. But wheels turn in his swiveling head. Bard schools us about boats. Shit, he knows more than I do. *Katy Sue* is nice, but he's a double-hull man. He sees me trading up.

We bought buckets of alleged food, but it goes fast. Randy leans hard to reach the glove compartment, which he rifles without apology. They take turns pretending to smoke my pipe. "Got a match?"

"I haven't had a match since Superman died."

"Whaat?"

Bard kind of gets it, but Ran is mystified. So we talk about this alternate meaning of match. "You know, like your head and a sack of potatoes."

Bingo. "Gah! Your face and a stupid plate of stupids."

Ran returns to the glove compartment. The kid finds matches like a retriever finds tennis balls. I have to prohibit fire in the cockpit. Chaos builds. When the tobacco tin lid sticks, they apply violence, distributing Sir Walter evenly throughout the Studie. I pull over. We've generated about ten pounds of trash in half an hour. We stick it in the trunk for now. Not much of the tobacco is salvageable. We brush out the spillage— forage for roadside critters. That idea strikes the Spuds as entirely grand. Randy lies on the ground, watching for weasels, playing deaf, until we pretend to leave him. I can't get enough of this stuff. But Bard is fresh out of trivia, and the general excitement catches up to them. They sleep the rest of the way. Good—the best is yet to come.

I drive directly to the marina and scope things out. It's dark and deserted. My pass card to the jetty works fine, but I tell the boys we have to sneak in. We grab our bags and ninja along the boardwalk. The gate hangs out over the water. Randy climbs around it without waiting for Adult Instructions, but Bard freezes. The drop to the water is small, but he's freaked about breaking rules. A red dot blooms on his earnest cheek. Time to head off the hives. "Oh, hey, look at this—here's a card in my pocket that opens this gate."

Bard natters on in an embarrassed way about chickening out, but Randy and I douse it all with future talk. Getting settled in *Katy Sue* is another party. Fort-making requires jumping and screaming. Finally, we're set and settled into Scrabble—Spuds vs. Stan. I almost win, except for the *almost* words—things that look like they should be words, but aren't. "Scropulous," for example. Each team gets three, but only if you make up an inspired definition for each. Anyone can add onto them. I'm proud of "scrop," but Bard comes up with the extension that kicks my ass.

Randy hardly contributes, actually. I forgot about his weak bladder, and *Katy Sue*'s holding tank is maxed. He's ready to pee in the water, but I make a game out of skulking over to check out the dockside loo. It's disappointingly clean and bright, but it's still an adventure for Randy to scamper to it periodically with a flashlight. Too much of an adventure— Bard and I figure he goes about twice as often as he needs to. As the evening wears on, things get out of hand as we bark out the Captain Carrot theme song and sling Scrabble tiles. Just when I think I'll have to play the hard guy and command them to settle down, I remember our secret ring.

"You know how you go to the gym sometimes to have fun?"

They're beyond regular speech. "Yayuss?"

"Well, you can also go to the *gem* to have fun."

Bard gets it immediately. Randy sits up when I produce the box. I pass the ring around, so we all have a good look, then I place it carefully on the table. Now everyone's on good behavior. We're priests in an ancient, mystical society. I dim the lights and shine a flashlight on the stone. "It's like sports. If you practice emptying out, practice wanting to laugh, practice thinking about the sapphire until the sapphire is *inside* you, then you can start to feel that way all the time. No one can make you feel crummy, because you know something they don't know—that you're a sapphire. Nothing can change that. You're precious, all the time. They don't know it, that's all. But you do. And you know that *they're* precious, too. It's all that matters."

We talk about what they might attract—their dad, mostly. A quick hug grounds out the last bit of helter-skelter energy. Then we sit cross-legged, with our backs against the walls. They really try for me. For their father. Randy lasts five minutes this time. Bard steals a glance at me after

Randy slumps sideways. I give him an encouraging nod, and he pushes on to fifteen minutes. I lug them to their nests.

They sleep late—fine by me. The sea lions are the best alarm clocks they've heard, so we hang out topside and watch them. Then everyone is famished, and we drift down to the coffee shop. As we demolish muffins, ridgeback Kevin and dharma dog Caprice come running up with Mark. Kevin is still distracted and alert, but Caprice works on him. How about they all come along on a cruise? Mark has to work but suggests we take the dogs. Now we're cooking. Bard and Kevin commune eye-to-eye, and Randy dances with Caprice. We all walk to a marine supply shop to find doggy life vests. Precious. We even go for the shark fins. Kevin, in blue, is so diverted by the wardrobe and the children that he forgets to look for Connie. Caprice, in red, bites Kevin's fin and pulls him all over the store. We leave the vests on and head back to *Katy Sue*. It's a cartoon parade; we're the stars of the boardwalk.

The dogs swim around the boat as we make ready. Bite The Shark Fin is a big game. I unearth the kid's vests, and they fit perfectly. Skye hollers at us from the jetty—a sight for sore eyes. I scrape the bow along a pier and wave her on. She hops aboard without hesitation, seeing the need. Kevin and Caprice keep jumping in the water but soon realize it's too hard to climb back aboard. Fortunately, their vests have beefy handles. I pick them up like a couple of suitcases and stomp around the foredeck with the shrieking Spuds. The dogs stay aboard as we make way but pace from stem to stern. The wind picks up, and we make six knots. Kevin strikes figurehead poses, but after a couple of close calls, he retreats to the cockpit, where he sits and watches with interest. Caprice, the experienced surfer, crouches on the foredeck, occasionally barking at the mast, just because. Skye and I spill wind and everyone settles down. We join a pod of dolphins heading south. Kids and dogs lunge from side-to-side, pointing and cheering. Fortunately, Kevin is smart enough to stay in the cockpit, and Bard sticks with him. Ran and Caprice are partners in crime, inclined to flirt with disaster, but they check in often.

Skye slips around us, cranking and laughing. She tells the Spuds everything she can think of about sailing. I chime in, referring to their toy boats in sketchy tutorials about propulsion and stability. Bard blathers away, asking and explaining, but Randy's lost in a dream. He peers through the panels of his life vest and alters his world view in every way—lying down and squinting between his feet, mimicking Caprice's moves, gaping up at the mast through his fingers. A teacher at heart.

We cruise on in silence—in reverence—then swing to port, heading for home. As the red-tiled manors of San Clemente heave into view, Skye tells us the town was meticulously planned a hundred years ago. The kids latch onto the idea of designing a community, so we have a good talk about that. Some codes are cool, but how do you figure those out? Should the parks have potties every twenty feet? No, because not everyone has a weak bladder. Should huge houses have all the best views? No, because that would be incredibly scropulous.

As we glide back into the harbor, I find myself looking for Connie at the deserted Pilgrim Grill. Options are narrowing. Victims are piling up. But Skye's laughter keeps us afloat and binds us together. She breaks out ginger cookies and calls us her dream crew. Even Kevin forgets to look beyond the boat. She regales the boys with a final, riveting lesson on how to circumnavigate the globe. We're sorry to see her hustle up the boardwalk.

Halle calls as we're leaving the dogs with Mark at San Juan Capistrano. She sounds tentative. "How're my sailor boys?"

I pull Randy off a flagpole. "Peachy. We're at the mission."

Halle sounds relieved. "Anybody get seasick?"

"Ran was thinking about it. But he's okay."

Concern creeps into her voice as she tries to nail down our arrival time. She's insistent, so I commit to six. Something's up. The need for precision is unlike Halle. Maybe that's Rick's influence. I give the wooden glitter box to Bard for safekeeping and strap the boys into the Champion. They sleep the whole way home. At Ocean Beach, Halle and Rick pounce on us at the door. They hug the Spuds, steer me toward an overstuffed chair, and hand me a beer. Halle tells the boys to put their things away and prepare for a bath. They dutifully wave and trail into their room. Halle closes the door and returns quickly, looking drawn. She and Rick remain on their feet.

"We're just wondering about Cub, next door."

Of course. The elephant in the next room. *Shit, Stan.* I was so focused on the boys and eager to avoid thinking about Connie that I didn't even consider Cub. I tense up. "What's going on?"

Rick exhales and holds up his palms in reassurance. "Nothing, now. Cub's in jail."

I sip the beer, lean forward. I owe them an explanation, but I don't know where to begin. "What happened?"

Rick and Halle exchange looks. Halle's turn. "Last night, we heard someone trying to get in the door."

"Couldn't have been a break-in," says Rick. "He was making too much noise."

Halle continues. "Rick found Cub out there, all drunked up, trying to use his key on our door."

"It was about two in the morning," says Rick. "He was sorry, but then started shouting and crying. Just—*sappy*. I helped him get into his place, then came back to bed. No big deal. We go right back to sleep. Then, pop! Pop, pop, pop! From Cub's place. I run out to our balcony and look around the partition. There's Cub, propped against a railing, firing this huge handgun at lights on the water. Sounds like a cannon. I ask him to stop. He ignores me, so I walk around and beat on his front door. He won't answer.

"Halle called the cops while I kept an eye on him from the balcony. The guy couldn't stand. Looked like he couldn't see. He tried to put the gun down and dropped it. Boom! It goes off. Put a bullet right through Halle's living room and bathroom. Cub had no clue. While he was on his knees looking for the gun, I climbed over to his balcony and grabbed it. He just blinked at me. Then I heard hammer blows. Whack, whack, whack! Here comes Halle through Cub's place with her softball bat. She'd beat the handle off his front door. Scared Cub sober. She made him give her all the guns and ammo he had in the apartment—another wicked handgun and an assault rifle. By then, the cops were there. We told 'em we'd press charges."

Halle collapses on the couch and leans forward, elbows on knees. "The bullet went through Randy's bathroom. He gets up all the time to pee, so he might've been in there. I couldn't get over that. So when the cops came, we told them the whole story. They said Cub has a police record."

"He's done time," says Rick, flatly.

They watch me expectantly. There's no anger that I can see. They just question with their eyes. How could I have put the family in danger? I knew Cub had gone to jail on weapons charges. He told me so himself. It was a long time ago, but so what? I also knew he had just lost the love of his life, and I wasn't there to help. I didn't have time for Cub. I sailed into the sunset. Let Connie down.

There's nothing to do but apologize. I tell Rick and Halle about Connie, but that doesn't excuse Cub putting a bullet through their contentment. I tell them that Cub was a stranger to me a month ago, but that just highlights my carelessness. It's all lame. The only thing that sounds authentic is my promise that it will never happen again. I tell them I'll do everything I can to keep that broken man far away from the Spuds. Rick sits next to Halle and throws a beefy arm across her shoulders. "I don't think the landlord knows yet. The cops came back this morning and picked up the guns. Dug the bullet out of the bathroom wall."

He stands and hands me a new key. "I replaced the door handle."

I check my wallet. $162.11. I shove it at Rick. "Here. For the hardware. And a new bat."

Rick carefully picks out the exact cost of the lock with an appreciative nod. "I think the bat's fine. Man! You should've seen Halle swing. Cub just dropped when he saw her."

Halle blinks and smiles sheepishly while Rick rubs her shoulders. They listen patiently while I tell them all I know. Even after all this, they don't blame me. They're just not built that way. Working as a team, they caper into the bathroom with the Spuds, draw a bath, make jokes, attribute the new hole in the wall to a repair project gone wrong. I slip out and sit on the steps outside. Pull out the phone—looking for comfort, I guess. I've missed four calls from Gaya. I can't listen to her messages and can't delete them. If I hear her voice, I'll run to her like the scared child I am. So I call the landlord, Usher. Sure enough, the police haven't tracked him down yet, so I give him the whole story in a monotone.

Manage his anger as best I can. He says he's on his way. The shoreline dissolves in fading light. I watch the birds, the suburban bustle. What did I want of those little boys? Joy isn't the whole story. I wanted to be a hero: Captain Carrot. Sir Stanhope. Why? It doesn't matter. Close the book. Death Man is no hero. "Hey Jack Kerouac" loops through my tiny brain. I don't know why it helps.

I call the jail, conjure some bluster, and tell them I'm Cub's lawyer. Amazingly, it works. They put Cub on the line. "Stan? You a lawyer?"

I try to stay deliberate. "No. I had to talk to you. Listen: I'm sorry about Connie. But you fucked up. In *my* apartment. You could've killed somebody. Somebody amazing. Do you understand? Several amazing somebodies live next door."

"I'm sorry—"

"You can't come back here. Ever. Understand?"

"Yeah."

I ask him where to put his stuff, and he gives me Chet's number and address. Then he asks me to bail him out. No can do. I can't help Cub yet. When fleshy, tatted Usher arrives, I'm abject. This throws him off. He was looking for a fight. I tell him Cub will go quietly. I'll clear out his possessions. Usher can keep my deposit, and I'll pay for additional repairs. I also need to terminate my lease. How much for all that? At first, Usher hardly knows what to say. I wait for his business instincts to kick in. Without looking at the damage, he says four thousand will do. I write the check. I'm being gouged but am in no position to argue. This has to be sorted out tonight. I give him the key.

Excited talk filters out of the Viking household. They emerge as a unit, looking chipper. The whole family helps me load Cub's stuff into the Champion. This is silly, really, because there's not much. The Crosley fridge must be at a gig somewhere, with all the instruments. But camaraderie is the point. We cavort with the Voldemort Elvises—deciding, in the end, that Cub should have them. In the bedroom, Halle helps me sort through the altar Cub had made of Connie's things. She loves the swallow necklaces. She touches my head tenderly and insists that I come back to say goodbye.

It's late when I return from Chet's, but the Spuds are still tearing around in their rocket PJs. Halle talks as if we'll see each other soon, but the Spuds know what's up. Bard's face is red. He sits suddenly, as if overcome. Randy jumps all over the room and lands face-down on the couch, where he won't budge. Halle bends over him and whispers something. The boy pops up and runs to his room. Halle whispers to Bard and he runs to the master bedroom. Randy returns with the glittery, starry box that contains Eva's ring. He shoves it at me. "Thank you, Stanhope."

My full name—that's a first. I take a knee and accept the ring. Bard comes in with a little velvet box. He opens it theatrically, revealing a diamond ring. "We got a new precious stone," he says.

I look up at Halle. "You're engaged?"

She flushes and watches Rick, who sits in the middle of the couch like the rock he is—like the Buddha. "Well, I guess. Last night. The thing is—"

"It's Dad," blurts Bard.

Halle sits next to Rick and takes the ring from Bard. "The diamond was made from their father's ashes. I didn't even know that was possible. The urn was heavy—in every way, I guess. I kept moving it around. Finally, I put it in the closet. Rick and the boys just took it and had the diamond made."

"It was Rick's *whole* bonus from work," says Randy, bouncing on the couch.

I sit back on my heels. "Why aren't you wearing it?"

Halle blushes as Rick throws a beefy arm across her shoulders. "I don't know. Rick *just* gave it to me. Do you think it's weird?"

Of course it's not weird. What's weird is my loss of strength. I can't Stan. It's too much: the bullet through the bathroom, the letting go, a new dad for the Spuds. I blink at my blurry hands. *If anyone cries—including me—it's time to go.* Bard and Randy slam into my chest.

Usher had said I could stay in my old apartment another night, but I wouldn't do that for anything. Done is done. Another call comes in from Gaya while I find an inconspicuous place to park. The back seat is a comfy bed. At least I'm worn out. I don't even argue with myself about Gaya. Done is done. But at breakfast, I can't stop thinking of her. Surely I can live without her. *But what's the point, Stan? What is the fucking point?* Gaya has a sharp nose that tickles when she jams it into my neck. She has a beauty mark below her navel. She says "you know" all the time, as if I really know. Well, I don't.

I guess it's been a week since Connie died—I have no clue about time and space anymore. I'm sinking. How's the admiral? Do I want to know? How about Cub? He endangered the Spuds—but so did I. I subleased the apartment without vetting. But it's worse than that. If I had gone right out and located Cub after hearing about Connie, I might have managed his mood or weapons. Still, I can't think of him without heat. I'm sorry he lost Connie, but it can't hurt for him to cool his heels in jail. What else? Gemma. I guess she belongs to Gaya now. Maybe I can work remotely, in different ways. Look for Sadie's grandson, Theo. Care for *Katy Sue,* Sir Walter, the Champion, my sisters, and my old man. Carefully. That's all I've got. I drive blearily back to DP, remembering the jokey trip with Gaya. *Thank you for being Stanhope.* I place the phone next to me on the seat and it chirps cheerily away. All those damn messages. Finally, I push buttons.

"Stanhope? Why won't you return my calls? Will I see you at the memorial for Connie?"

"Stanhope. You should have seen how many people came to honor Connie. It was on the brig. Kevin and Caprice were there. And the admiral in fancy dress. I'm sending pictures."

"Stanhope! You make me so angry! You *cannot* decide for me. You think you are being noble. But, you know, your gestures mean nothing. I need you. Just *you.* As you are this moment."

I pull over and scroll through the pictures. A sea of familiar faces. Connie's friends smile for the camera—absently, as if looking for her. Duncan and Skye: red and black. Mark and the dogs, Caprice and Kevin: BFFs. Admiral Spencer in uniform: bereft. The Shelvadors: Cubless. Cub's a hands-on guy, like me. He was out looking for something to fix instead of mourning with friends. He found the wrong things, and now he's in jail.

I could spring Cub—probably should. He's going through what I went through after Eva. I get that. But I can't turn him loose. Can't even think about it. Can't face the dark possibilities—can't even face Gaya. *You think you're being noble.* No. I know I'm being chickenshit. Late in the afternoon, I'm lazing on the water again. I light a pipe. Gaya likes the rich smell. Can I do anything that doesn't remind me of her?

Waiting for sunset, I'm stalked by the phone. I have no idea what to say to anybody. Sure enough, it rings: Professor Justin Ellis. Perfect timing. He's just put down his pipe, I know. He's feeling chatty, so I puff away, taking it all in. Comfort comes in the strangest ways. I have the rolling *Katy Sue*, a silver sunset, a light breeze, no shoes, a comfortable seat, good tobacco, and my dad's voice. He tells me a story I know well— how, after skillfully dropping a tree across his torso, he hollered himself hoarse while we were all watching television. Trudy tried to help. By the time we emerged from our TV trance and found Dad, the dog had assembled a huge pile of sticks by his head. Which were of no use at all. But Justin Ellis never forgot the tokens of concern. He's having the surgery in three months. They need to make sure he's strong enough. I should be there. Maybe I'll bring a stick—start a pile.

As I make ready to return, Cub calls, looking for bail money again. My answer is automatic: "I bailed you out of my apartment." He asks about Connie's memorial, but I say I wasn't there. Cub's in pain. Right. It's a fucking epidemic. I'm ready to throw the phone at the sun but remember Dad and turn it off. Shove it into a duffle. *The weapon is the enemy.* I'm a shit to ignore Gaya, but if I call, she'll make me see sense. I need to be crazy for her sake. Leave her entirely alone. It torques her when I try to think for the both of us. But someone has to get out of this alive. She is protean.

- XIII -

TO THE WORKING SOULS
(WINTER)

A TRAIN RIDE NORTH REMINDS ME OF THE BUS BREDDA DAYS. I COULD'VE taken the Champion, but I need to be freer than that—less ceremonial. I shuffle to various seats and read Jack Kerouac, Mary Ann Evans, the *Gita*. Break out the histories and do what I can: Stanhope the scrivener. It's therapeutic to write about Connie, but my knowledge of her is sketchy. Gaya could fill me in. *Shut up, Stan.* Making sense of the fragments I have is hard, but the effort keeps me sane.

San Francisco is a new city for me, but I see nothing. Catch the first bus to Oakland. Find a place near Berkeley and pick up my old Bus Bredda habits. The hotel's on the seedy side, but clean. I just need a place to flop but there's no flopping. Cold terror penetrates every fledgling dream. The bear comes again, with the swan corpse bouncing against his chest. And a new apocalypse: cars cascading off of overpasses, bodies piling up. When I fall out of bed at 2:00 a.m., no one is there. The Hitchcock is real. But I'm not hermit material. Yet. And I can't end this hell. Why? Eva's future-seeking. The Spuds. Gayathri.

The high points, the meaningful relationships in my life, may all have been mistakes. I can't count on knowing people like that again. Even if I could force myself into ongoing relationships, watching death after death would work me over. It's like what Dad said about dogs: you think each loss will be a little easier, but the opposite is true. Is that how the elderly feel? Or is there a tipping point where you become desensitized? Some old-timers become matter-of-fact about death, fatalistic, like Dad's brother, who joked about the ugliness, the stink, the *inconvenience* of his carcass. Is that a toughening up? Maybe it's the opposite. Maybe you're softened up by loss after loss and ready to go by the time it's your turn. Is that a mercy?

Chuck could riff on a football game for hours. I miss that. Maybe I should get on another work crew. Take comfort in lame jokes, bowling teams, controlled relationships. But that can't last. Eventually, the rules are broken and the stories come. The life-essence stories. The deadly ones. I guess we don't know what stories define us until the end. Maybe that's why I cling to the idea that this random listening and recording is my purpose. Maybe designated listeners are required in our cocksure, social me-me-meing. Maybe there's a shortage of available ears, so the gods have initiated a draft. I'm 1-A. That's the hypothesis anyway. Of course, it's insane. This is my hobby horse, and I'm riding it into the fucking ground. I'll work solo here in Oakland. So I'm more for myself than for others—more survivor than inspirer. So what?

I'm up early, threading south and east through a light drizzle along the waterfront. Hit the Jazz Café at nine. It's in a half-heartedly gentrified neighborhood near the estuary between Lake Merritt and the inner harbor. The place is warm and bright, charged with the mingled aromas of coffee and baking bread. A bona fide '50s-style diner—white and pink, with teal booths and chairs. Lots of fabric on the walls and ceiling for optimal acoustics. Fifties jazz sets the tone: Sarah Vaughan, Chet Baker, Miles Davis, Ella Fitzgerald. Smooth and cool. There are just enough distractions here—just this side of jangly. Hard-core goths mix easily with flocks of weary travelers. I nurse a quiet satisfaction in knowing that the place is paid for. Gemma told me that Theo paid off the note on his mom's business. It makes a difference. The Jazz Café lacks the air of

desperation you find in a lot of mom-and-pops. Waiting to be noticed, I
drum the counter with fingertips and palms. Buddy Rich. The guy could
play the drums.

I'm directed to a small booth as Lena Horne works mindfully
through "Stormy Weather." When I ask my skinny, darting waitress if
I can speak to Della, she says to come back at three, closing time. I'm
ravenous, but the music reminds me to slow down and make the most of
sweet potatoes and eggs. The perpetual-motion waitress looks ready to
bust out laughing most of the time. That beats the drizzle and reminds
me of the meditating Spuds. I sit for a couple hours, writing, drumming,
remembering. Gaya could help with many of the histories: Gemma.
Pigeon. Dennis. Anshu. Connie. Even the admiral, who might be on the
verge. Gaya is everywhere, all the time. Even if I find ways to handle
the Hitchcock and its fallout, I'll be haunted by her—her careful writing,
sketching, adapting. Her "you come too." The raindrops glistening in her
hair. Her "you knowing." Her black eyes. Sharp nose. Am I ready for the
end?

All at once, God help me, I must try and forget Stanhope. I don't know
how to do this. On my day off, I drive to his apartment in Dana Point. His
Champion is there. The doors are open, but I don't know what to look
for. I find one of his fragrant pipes in the glove compartment and put it
in my pocket.

Perhaps he's on *Katy Sue*. At the marina, Duncan, with the beautiful
hair, says the boat has been neglected. He has not seen Stanhope, so I
walk back to the apartment and wait. Without meaning to, I spend the
night in the Mini, sleeping with Stanhope's pipe. An odd dream comes
from this bittersweet aroma: I am the sage Vyasa dictating the *Gita* to
Ganesh, the elephant-headed god chosen to be my scribe. Ganesh has
broken off one of his tusks to use as a pen—because he's so dutiful. I
am pleased he's in my dream. He is the god of wisdom and success and
writing and new beginnings. But suddenly, he flees and I must follow,

breathlessly spinning out my wisdom as we run faster and faster. Others come, animals too, and shout advice to Ganesh. There are thousands of us. I sketch the eyes of the running god and the eyes of everyone chasing. In the end, I draw a vast network of eyes, finding comfort in some and fear in others. I must tell Stanhope of Ganesh, the perfect scribe.

In the morning, a policeman wakes me, but it's all right. He recognizes me from Connie's memorial on the old ship. Everyone knows Connie. When I am not thinking of Stanhope, I think of her. Yet I had known her such a short time! It must be because of our long conversations. A woman in love has a lot to say and two women in love cannot be contained. They overflow and spill into each other. Now I have as much pain as we had love and no one to spill into. I know Stanhope has this pain too. Why can we not comfort each other? How dare he choose this for me! He would say he is saving me from suffering, but he must know that we must face this together. If he will just look into my (darshan!) eyes, we will be restored. I want him to remove my glasses and kiss me again.

All of the newspapers in the coffee shop remind me of Connie. She would laugh about that. I touch her swallow necklace and remember her playing with Kevin. Everything else reminds me of Stanhope—dogs, children, sea lions, pelicans. They cannot say where my wandering lad has gone—my wondering Nachiketa. I must tell Stanhope the Nachiketa story.

But here is a distraction: the shop is offering Christmas treats, though it is still November. My uncle Bebo and I love this Christian holiday. I buy chocolate gingerbread for a friend. As I turn to go, Admiral Spencer waves from a corner table. I join him, and we hold hands. He is not quite the pukka military man anymore. I think, in fact, that he has had a stroke. Some coordination has been lost, and he blinks a lot, as if losing sight. But there is still a magnificence in him. I love his quiet knowing. He tells me that Connie never charged him for food at the Pilgrim Grill, so he gave her many of his ship sketches in return.

"Perhaps we can recover them for you."

He waves a gnarled hand. "They'll find a home."

In a halting voice, he tells me things about Connie that cannot be true. He says she founded a charity for Mexican workers in Texas, for example. I think he must be confusing Connie with his wife. I've seen that happen before. The elderly sometimes lose the ability to separate their losses. Each pain merges with the next, and the grieving becomes kind of amorphous as it grows. Perhaps this helps the pain dissipate. My mother would say such a thing is divine mercy—this loss of the details of loss, as the life force ebbs. In a low, private voice, I explain to Admiral Spencer that I am concerned about his health. He is reluctant to discuss this, but I make him promise to see a physician. When I stand, he regains his courtly manners. I cry too easily.

There is nothing to do but drive back to San Diego. I stop and lollygag at the ocean park where Stanhope and I first embraced in a loving way. I find his old apartment at Ocean Beach and knock on the door, but it looks as though Cub has moved out. There is no furniture visible from the window and no van in the car park. As I turn to go, two little boys run up the walk. This must be the Spuds! Their blonde mother follows with groceries. I help with the children and bags as best I can, trying to explain myself, and Halle surprises me with her warmth. The Spuds run around nervously. They're worried that I have lost Stanhope. We discuss possibilities, but they don't really know. Halle calls him, but there is no answer. The boys tell me to try Captain Carrot. They're upset—throwing themselves on the couch and knocking things over. So I become jolly, as Stanhope would. As I prepare to leave, Halle starts to speak, but stops. She wants to tell me a story, I think. But she considers the children and says nothing. She promises to call when they have more ideas. I am sorry to have added this worry to their lives, but I love how they love Stanhope.

I just have time this evening to see Gemma. When I arrive with my heavy loaf of chocolate gingerbread, she is overjoyed, hugging me tight and blinking a lot. Her white greyhound, Pax, slinks around us like a cat, expressing happiness as much as his shyness will allow. I rub my hands over the silky hound. All at once, I remember running through empty streets early in the morning during Diwali, looking for dogs to caress, overflowing with gratitude. Such joy! It would have been something to find a big white dog like Pax. He is so therapeutic that I must force myself to stop stroking him and sit down.

Christmas decorations peep from corners throughout the cottage. Gemma glows like a Brahmin. "Last night, I dreamt about a white owl. Huge! I was sitting with friends out on the lawn, and this white—*marvel* landed in a juniper tree right *next* to me. I know it was a juniper because I pointed out the owl to the others. I said, 'It's just in that juniper.' What do you think, Gayathri?"

"Auspicious, I suppose. A sign of abundance and good fortune."

"That's just what I thought. I *am* blessed."

I show her my sketches. They're all portraits: Connie, Sadie, Pigeon, Dennis, and several of Anshu. She is too kind, full of compliments. She retrieves Theo's drawings of animals that I have come to know well— copies of the ones that Stanhope carries. She says that my drawings are similar. I see her point. Connie looks so much like the old wolf that it gives me a start.

Gemma makes tea in her aromatic kitchen, touching the piece from Sadie's dobro in its pink frame as she moves about. She does this automatically, as a habit. Pax does not beg but stays by her side. I join them in the warm, sweet-smelling kitchen to slice the chocolate gingerbread. As we settle with our tea, Gemma asks about Stanhope, but I don't know what to say. She asks how we met. Well, it was such an odd meeting! Without referencing the Hitchcock, I tell her of my suspicions about Stanhope and describe how he was so intimidated by the detectives—then, how hard he tried to make our follow-up lunch a success. She laughs and tells me that Stanhope was Robin the Boy Wonder when they met.

I miss Stanhope so much that I must change the subject. I ask Gemma about her husband, Tom. How did they meet? She comes alive. "Sadie and I used to walk through a park to the cotton mill. We would see Tom walking his old sighthound, Juniper. He would always wave, and we'd wave back. Tom was so small that I don't think either of us thought of him as marriage material. Then one day, he was out there supporting the dog's hind legs with a towel around her hips. He just waved, like it was normal. But I wondered about that skinny, old dog. I think she was a saluki mix. Anyway, this went on for about a week. Sometimes she would try to chase squirrels as if she still had four working legs. Well, Tom ran along, helping her chase squirrels. It was ridiculous. I couldn't get those chasing scenes out of my mind. One day, I told Sadie to go on, and I asked Tom about Juniper. We'd had a hound when I was little, but he'd drowned. I'd never had a chance to say goodbye. So I guess I was ready to be charmed by Tom's old bitch. Juniper could walk on her own, but only for about ten feet at a time. Her hips were givin' out. I watched for them every day. Tom and I got to know each other through Juniper. Sometimes I helped pick her up or spelled Tom with the towel. Every time I came, Juniper would make Tom run to me! Lord, they looked so funny running together like that! But I'd never felt so wanted.

"What got to me was the stroller. Tom fixed up an old one for Juniper. She looked at me so proud, sitting up high as they zoomed by! I knew then that Tom was special. No man I knew would think of doing such a thing. They all had so much *dignity*, don't you know? Sadie could see Tom was different too. She had always made jokes about him, but she stopped doing that after Tom rigged up the stroller.

"*Then* we went places! Juniper loved to go fast, her feathers flying. She had beautiful feathers. And things picked up for Tom and me, too. We talked about everything on those walks. Tom told me that Juniper never liked other women coming around. She'd always pretend to be sick when a woman talked to him. But she liked me right away. We were girlfriends. Tom and I would stop once in a while to let Juniper wobble along on the cool grass. Tom would get on his knees and run his hands over her, feeling for where it hurt. Pick her right up when she fell, wrap the scrapes on her toes, and give her medicine. I think he touched her a lot because she could barely hear or see. When I noticed he'd worn holes in the knees of his good pants, I decided I loved him. I waited for him to speak first, but I loved him right then."

Gemma sits back, satisfied. She laughs and points to her arthritic knees. "I told my daughters and granddaughters, look for a man with holy knees! That's a man who can love. A man who can humble himself. A man who might take a knee for *you* someday."

She sighs—deciding whether to continue, I think. She points at an old chest. "Will you pull an old sweater out of there for me, hon?"

The sweater is an old-fashioned, red and black cardigan, with big wooden buttons. I give it to Gemma. She drapes it over her lap and sits on the couch. Pax joins her and rests his head on the sweater. Gemma fondles them both. I take my place by the dog.

"Tom finally did take a knee for me, thank the Lord! But he needed Juniper's help with that, too. We'd spent some months together, the three of us. Tom was never once embarrassed about nursing that dog out in public. Everything Tom and I did had to do with Juniper. She was the everyday something we shared. We took her everywhere—in the stroller or in my mother's car. But Juniper was getting weak, so sometimes we had to leave her sleeping on Tom's porch. I'd put this sweater over her, so she wouldn't get cold. You know, she was just skin and bones.

"When we returned, about twilight one evening, she and the sweater were gone. Well, we looked and looked. We knew she couldn't have gotten far. But she *did* get far. We had to use flashlights. Finally, we found her about fifty yards away, in the woods, on top of this old sweater— still a little warm, but gone to glory. Well, we just—*sobbed.* I could just see her draggin' my sweater off with her. The next morning, I sponged the sweater clean, put it on, and walked back over to Tom's. We buried Juniper together. Then Tom asked me to marry him."

My special friend flutters her eyes and hugs Pax. "Whoever ends up with Pax will *have* to take this sweater. He loves it."

She places her head on my shoulder, and we massage Pax together. I think my dharma dog story might be a comfort. "Now, I have a story for you." She blinks at me gratefully.

"Yudhisthira was a great and humble king. When he was ready to give up his kingdom, he started on a journey across the Himalayas with his family. Right away, they were befriended by a dog, who accompanied them. But, because of their human failings, each of Yudhisthira's beloved relatives fell along the way. Pride or vanity or gluttony or attachment to worldly things made each of them take a wrong step, and down they fell to their deaths. In the end, only the dog remained with the king, keeping him company in his sorrow.

"After many hardships, they reached the top of a high pass. Then the great Indra descended in a golden chariot to take Yudhisthira to heaven. The king asked if his dog companion could come along, but Indra said no. The chariot was only for Yudhisthira.

"The king said, 'How can I abandon my steadfast companion? One who has stayed by my side through all these trials?'

"'You must think of your own happiness,' replied Indra.

"'But my happiness depends on being loyal to my friend, just as she has been loyal to me. So I must refuse your heaven. My heaven will be to rejoice in this friendship.'

"Then Indra smiled and said that was not necessary—that man and dog are welcome in heaven together after all. He told Yudhisthira that this had been the final test. The king showed himself worthy of heaven by being true to his dog friend. The animal is then revealed to be the king's mother, Dharma Devatha—a goddess who exemplifies this sort of loyalty, this sort of right living."

The story reminds me of Caprice because Stanhope always calls her his dharma dog. Gemma and I share the warm doggy feeling with Pax. "Pax loves to ride in my old car. It's our golden chariot!"

Gemma pulls on the sweater, and the three of us walk around the yard, looking out at the cliffs below. She says, "What do you think Stan has in mind, hon? Did you have a fight?"

I really cannot tell Gemma about Stanhope's crazy Hitchcock. So I say, "Oh, a friend died. Stanhope is grieving."

"Any idea where he is?"

I am speechless. Gemma turns, looking holy in her old sweater, and gives me a big grandmother hug. I try to explain. "I did not come to—"

"Shhh. I know."

She adjusts ornaments on a Christmas tree while I calm down. It is a shock to realize how desperately I have needed comfort. I wish Anshu were here. I don't know anything. I don't know whether my choices have been correct or even practical. Should I have stayed with Stanhope, saying goodbye to Blessings Hospital and all of my good friends? No. I am needed at the hospital. People are dying there too; God help us all. Sometimes my training does not protect me. It hurts a lot sometimes when someone moves to the twelfth floor—especially when two or three go at once. At a hospital, the responsibility is shared. Each patient is treated by several nurses, several doctors, several technicians. So why do I try to be fully responsible for Stanhope? Why do I add his pain to my own? Because I cannot untangle our fates. He is in all my thoughts of the future. Surely my work as a nurse helps others more than it hurts me. And what would I be doing if not that? Nursing Stanhope? He would not stand for that. He *is* not standing for it.

Pax lopes through the darkness like a phantom. Gemma watches him carefully. He is her boon from the gods. "It's like a murder mystery," she says. "What's Stan's motive?"

I bend to stroke the gentle greyhound again. "Oh, he's just overwhelmed. He thinks he's protecting me."

She purses her mouth thoughtfully. "What's his comfort? What is he doing right now to feel better?"

"Let me see—he is not sailing. He is not with the children he loves. He thinks he has brought some people bad luck. He wants to make amends, you know."

"Aha! What people?"

Hmm. Cub, perhaps? But there are other possibilities—so many possibilities that it's driving us both crazy. I don't know what to say. Gemma knows. "How about Sadie? He told me he wanted to find Theo for Sadie."

"Yes, but—"

"Theo's mom, Della, has a café in Oakland."

"Oh, I don't know. What are the chances of Stanhope being up there without his car?"

Gemma is well pleased with her sleuthing. "Good!" she says, patting my arm. "The chances are *good*. I dreamt of the Jazz Café twice this week. Someone sent me that dream. I know it."

I am really full of doubt, but will try Oakland, for her sake—and for mine. I have to do something to make myself whole again. I miss Gemma and Pax as soon as I leave them at the door. Suddenly, I have an out-of-body experience, as if I am watching myself from above. I see Gaya walk down the winding path to the street. This God-like point of view seems a trick of place.

There's always walking to be done, Stan. The sun's out. These streets need walking. I stride out through Jack London Square, stopping here and there to read of London's hellacious adventuring. He reminds me of Richard Henry Dana and Jack Kerouac—except that his compassion and insight extended beyond our species. Another Jack-of-all-trades. Another dharma bum. He drank too much, of course. Pirates do. He took hits and lost sailors. Said things that make dainty ears burn. So now we're to scorn him and burn his books. No doubt there's already pressure to rename the square, take the plaques down. But who will read the beautiful pages?

I stop at a bar that Jack made famous, but it's too early for a drink. I walk the wharves, imagine his rough adventuring. "I shall not waste my days in trying to prolong them," he said. "I shall use my time."

Moving west and north, I explore the pocket parks along the water. Track cormorants and gulls and songbirds. In wartime, ships under attack used to chase salvos—always changing course by aiming for the splash of the last near-miss. This baffles the enemy's rangefinders, which keep adjusting for more predictable variables. Chasing splashes makes you hard to hit. So that's the Stan plan: pick out something irrelevant or weirdly tangent, and make for it. Zag away from zigs. Chase a seabird. Try to find Sadie's missing grandson. In the afternoon, I sit in a booth with buxom Della, Sadie's daughter-in-law, flipping through her son's drawings. She devours them, though she must have seen them before. Looks up with big eyes. "Where did you get these?"

"From Gemma."

She shuffles the drawings compulsively. "What can I do for you, Stan?"

Suddenly I know how hard this will be. "I was hoping you had some ideas about where Theo is."

Della stiffens. She's seen too much trouble, and I'm doing a good impression of it. "Why? Who wants him?"

"Uh, Sadie. I mean—Gemma. She told me about him."

Della leans back. "Why do *you* need to know where my boy is?"

I explain that I told Sadie I'd try to help.

"What gives you the right? Sadie is dead. Gemma is no kin to me. Theo is *not* your business."

There's no way to avoid sounding lame. "It's just a promise I made."

A massive, smiley workman in blue overalls steps into the café and approaches the booth. Della stands and hugs him. "Howard, this is Stan. He's asking after Theo."

I jump up so Howard can crush my hand. The big man gives me a look. "What for?"

I try to think of what else to say, but he won't wait. "You a detective?"

"No."

"A policeman?"

"No."

"What is your *job*, man?"

"That's a good question."

Howard seems always in motion, always amused. I covet his overalls. "You think Theo will give you a job?"

"In a way, I guess."

Now they're sure I'm hiding something. Della gives me a tight smile and holds out a hand. "Excuse me, Stan. We have to buy a new countertop."

I take the hand but hold on. "Check in with Gemma if you can. If she says I'm okay, I'm glad to help."

I scrawl my name and number on a paper napkin. Howard looks me over. "You a working man?"

Talking about the bookstore would be too much information, so I try to connect with his overalls. "Window washer. But—I'm ready for something new."

Howard's eyes dart. I know this guy. He's looking for the joke. "Like detective work."

"Sure."

We shake again, but he still needs a laugh. "I'd stick with the windows, man. Good, honest work."

"Right. Except for the good, honest falling."

That'll have to do. Howard gives me a conspiratorial grin and claps me on the shoulder as they file out. They won't check with Gemma.

At Jack London's favorite tavern, I order a beer, then a whiskey to drop into it. Cub's drink, but what the hell. I wonder if Cub is still in jail. For the next half hour, I ponder whether to eat or get drunk. There's nothing on the to-do list. Connie is a tragic headline. Gaya is off-limits. The Spuds are in good hands. I'll probably never see Theo. Who the hell am I, trying to be Super? No hero required. No one cares where Theo is anymore. Not really. Della cares, but not enough to give me the benefit of any doubt. She's afraid I might wreck her hard-won gig—the sweet café. *Saweet.* Gemma cares, but has Pax the greyhound, puzzles, mystery novels, the grandkids, and a long life to reflect on. All I have is a promise to the dead. Della and Howard are telling me to leave well enough alone. What the hell is well enough? I eye the tavern menu and try to get up a dart game. Win at darts and buy a round for my new friends. Lose at piggyback darts, sloppily and repeatedly. Here we go—a pirate's bender.

I wake with a head full of fiberglass. How did I make it back to the hotel? Oh, yeah, the bus driver. Nice guy, but not the happy hippo I was demanding. Sometimes you *need* doo-wop in the small hours. Without thinking, I repeat the walk south that I took yesterday morning. Track birds like a pointer. Grope my way back to the café. The darting waitress provides the same booth, coffee, sweet potatoes, and eggs. This time she calls me Stan—thanks to Della, I guess. She wants me to ask her name, wants me to say almost anything so she can laugh. I don't take the bait. That's how it starts.

I can't go back to Dana Point. The admiral has the shadow on him. Gaya would find me in DP anyway. The Oakland waterfront is strange enough, with its kludges of bleak and trendy, to keep me hanging on.

The salt air is thicker here, touched up with mist and seductively unreal. Nights are oblivion. I hit three or four taverns, playing darts, trying to forget how to listen. It's like trying to forget how to ride a bicycle. The wrong kind of forgetting makes it worse. I try to stick with small talk, but forget. Try to eat more than I drink, but forget. Each forgetting leads to a bigger forgetting. The damn bike wobbles from story to story.

One night I drink dinner and listen to a stick-legged prostitute in a puffy jacket tell stories about her johns—the guys who punish her for not being Mother Mary. The ways they punish her. The ways she gets even— calling a john's family, in one case: the nuclear option. Now she's afraid *he'll* go nuclear—with a Gurkha blade he showed her. Call the wife, get the knife. She won't know until it happens. So I walk her to the bus station and buy her a ticket to Sacramento. Maybe I didn't think it through. We're three sheets to the wind when she rubs cocaine on my gums and kisses me long and slow. She probably expects to be groped, but the lip thrill is plenty. I lose sleep imagining her new life in Sacramento, sucker that I am, but in the morning, she slips out of the hotel as usual. I pretend not to notice. The scared girl in the big coat decided to live or die right here—despite, or because of, the blade.

Mornings are here and now. I try to make sense of tattered plans. Make it to the Jazz Café by eleven, usually—which is something, all stories considered. The wanting-to-laugh waitress installs me in the usual booth and brings me the usual. I tip well, in apology for refusing to engage, refusing to help her release. Cold mist sweeps the streets. Sometimes I see Della, but she ignores me. Maybe I should eat somewhere else. At least Howard slows his bouncy stride and gives me a nod. I hate to ask but wish he would offer me a job. Every night I drink to the working souls—and to the workless fucks who shadow them.

- XIV -

THE TURNING IS OUTWARD
(WINTER)

I'VE BEEN IN SOGGY, RAMSHACKLE OAKLAND MOST OF NOVEMBER. Caffeine sets me up, and alcohol knocks me out. Neither lasts long enough. There's always too much to lose—so much that it feels like nothing. So the cycle starts again, every day. I wander the halls of my funky hotel in the small hours. Try *not* to decide, but forget. Try to be somebody else. My Imaginarium defaults to an endless replay—Gaya running through the rain. I always try to substitute *Katy Sue*. This strategy is flat stupid because I always see Gaya on board, pointing at the horizon or asleep in the rocking cabin. I keep swapping the woman and the boat, knowing it can't work—proof of madness. But the torment is all I have. It's company. Is this how masochism begins? Life is full of impossibilities.

Now I'm in a basement bar, listening to a rough Canadian kid go on about everything strange happening in the world. He's a balding cherub with a sidelong squint and Cupid lips. Says he's a journalism student. "Good luck with that," I say, as if I know all about it. As if I'm some derelict shaman. The reporting profession sounds like a joke to barflies like me. But the kid's unfazed. He goes on as if I'm not profound, as if

I'm not even here. By the time I slam another boilermaker, he's going on about microdosing LSD. "If you're getting visual effects, you've taken too much."

"Then why take it?"

"Hard to explain. It makes me more aware. Confident."

"Hopeful?"

"You know what it is? An objectifier."

"What?"

"You know, we aim for true objectivity, but that's not really possible."

"A microdose makes it possible?"

The kid leans forward and chuckles through stringy hair. "It makes me too objective to believe that. But I know every time I drop that I can correct for major bias."

"Hallelujah, Major. Have another drink."

"The biggest mistake a journalist makes is to knock himself out trying to appear unbiased within a totally fucked up framework."

I try to look as if my brain isn't dissolving away. "You think?"

"Yeah. Well, you know, one party gets caught with its pants down, so we remind everyone that the other party also dropped trou once upon a time."

"He mooned, she mooned."

"Yeah. And we *leave* it at that. Instead of teasing out the aggregate idiocy chalked up on each side. Shit, *everything* is a matter of degree, so let's understand the degrees. The patterns of behavior. But that's too much work. It's easier to pretend, along with everyone else, that both parties are equally corrupt."

"Works for me."

"I rest my case. A microdose helps me see through those guys who are out there waving their dicks and saying it's okay because somebody else once waved a dick."

There's a presence to this pouty boy. I keep buying him drinks. I should encourage him as an older guy ought, offer sage advice, but I'm intimidated. I want what he has—and he gives it to me: a sheet of fifty-milligram gel tabs. He's upgrading to precisely measured microdoses, so

I get the old-school tabs. Windowpane for the window washer who falls and falls. He looks me over, tries not to laugh, and warns me not to take it right away. Right. I missed too much sleep at the Imaginarium anyway.

In the morning, I see that I was just trying to bring the cub reporter down to barstool altitude—make him stupid with alcohol. Clip his objectifying wings. *Pathetic, Stan.* I find the windowpane in a plastic bag wrapped around Eva's ring. The sheet looks like micro-bubble-wrap. More green than blue: the Celtic ray. I cut out a cozy compartment for it in the unused back pages of a book the kid gave me—Huxley's *Doors of Perception.* Like me, he tries to keep like with like. We might be breddas in some universe. He recommended quartering the tabs, so I dismantle a shaving razor and slice carefully. Lying in bed, leafing through Huxley's *Doors,* I let a gelatin pinhead dissolve under my tongue. The book is about the author's experiences with mescaline in 1953. Uncle Aldous was an adventuring genius. The William Blake quote that gave him his title jump-starts my brain: "If the doors of perception were cleansed, everything would appear to man as it is: Infinite. For man has closed himself up, until he sees all things through narrow chinks of his cavern."

At first, I feel nothing. But the walk to the café elongates into a bird safari. Perchers fill every tree; skimmers and soarers embroider the water and sky. Occasionally a hoverer floats with style. So there's a good job for me: tracking birds by their behavior. I'll write a book: *Birds by Verbs.* It's half-written before I even reach the water. Just when I start to wonder if the dose is too large, it rounds off to centeredness. The third eye settles, but with a spark. Peripheries sharpen. This windowpane comes with its own squeegee—and I'm the pro who knows how to use it. I toggle from analysis to synthesis and back again, extracting and merging essentials. Clean every pane. My long-delayed flight plan crystalizes. Future-think spools out. But every few minutes, knowing is breached by nothingness. I don't know if the hollows will fill. Gaya was my ballast. But here I am, awed in front of the streamlined café. For a good minute, until a Bolt zips by, it might be 1951. *The thrifty one for fifty-one.* The absence of the Champion gives me a pang, but it's erased by a rose fragrance at the door.

The waitress is especially kind today, squeezing my shoulder and bopping her candy cane earrings all the way to the usual booth. "Stanhope," she says. How did she know? Today, I'll ask her name.

Gaya looms large in the micro-booth. I can't move. She peers over the oval glasses. Jumps up and hugs in her fierce way. The skinny waitress laughs and laughs, her noun not mattering now that she's all verb. She and Gaya peal out these Sadie-size joy-bells, as if they'd rehearsed. I easily track what would generally be sensory overload—clear blues and pinks, the thick aroma of coffee and bacon, gobs of Gaya's corkscrew hair against my chest, the salty wetness of my shirt. Mel Tormé ambling through "The Nearness of You." I slide into the booth with a click.

It's a square meal—eggs, salmon, sweet potatoes, coffee, and Gaya's ballast. She has a lot to say about the tenacity of her patients, the courtship of Gemma and Tom, the sweater shared by Juniper and Pax, Admiral Spencer's blessed confusion. I listen hard. Don't drum the table once. Gaya had organized her stories for this release, just as I'd organized my stories for Anshu. She had long needed to check in with me, but I was listening to the wrong people. Now she has rescued me again, but speaks with holy gratitude, as if *I'm* the savior. Blessings. She works at Blessings Hospital.

We walk the waterfront, then drive to my hotel. The rush I feel is all Gayathri Das. We're slow as Mo: yab-yum and quick-quick. Teetering wisdom and compassion. Balanced and tipped and balanced. Sometimes I'm her. She is ever me. We make and make elevens. Do I feel remorse for having let down my guard? For having let Gaya back into StanWorld? Not a bit. I couldn't have disguised my relief at seeing her if I'd tried. No self-loathing. Only admiration at her doggedness in tracking me down. It reminds me of the beginning, at the hospital, when she turned the tables on a stalker. Gaya does her homework. Wears her glasses. Finds her Stanhope. Holds him up to the light.

We take her rental car down to the bird bonanza at Lake Merritt. As we walk the path, holding hands, pointing at wonders, she catches me up with her reading. "Do you remember in Colorado when we were talking about how our ancestors were different from us because they lived intimately with death? I looked into that. Researchers say that reminders of mortality actually make people *hard* on one another. If you make a judge think of dying before he sentences someone, his sentence will be harsh."

"What the fuck?"

"This terror of death drives us to try to serve belief systems that will outlive us—a judicial code, a religion, a nation, a cause. That's what this brilliant man named Becker said. Most people try hard to avoid thinking of death. When they cannot escape thinking of it—they are frightened by a medical test result or run into the spouse of a dead friend, for example— they take shelter in something they think is larger than them. Something that will live on. Usually, it is some sort of dogma, a harsh set of rules. So, they condemn the criminal, or the infidel, or the godless communist."

I stop and look out over the lake. Heron. Cormorant. Coot. "And feed the meat grinder of holy war."

"Yes. We try to do good in the world by holding to these beliefs. And we *can* do good with them. But we contaminate them with fear, with terror of death, and create evil."

I see the truth of it, through clouding windowpane. Where's my squeegee? Waving bye-bye to Pigeon. "What does that have to do with the goodness of your suffering grandmother?"

Gaya studies my face, as if she too can't believe we're together again. "All right: here is what I learned. Studies suggest that if you *stop avoiding* thoughts of mortality, but actually meditate on death regularly, the opposite happens. You become *more* compassionate, *more* benevolent. I think we must have been right about my grandmother's kindness having to do with her familiarity with death."

Bean. She says, *must have bean.* Anyway—yes again. I could listen to her go on forever. I enfold her dominant left hand. "If you have to bury a child every year, eventually you're not so big on holy slaughter."

"Yes. But only if you are able to really grieve. It is still possible to be heartless and selfish about each particular death—someone suddenly being out of the way of your ambition, or a dying child leaving fewer mouths to feed. On the other hand, if you sustain compassion through every misfortune, you come to think about mortality in general terms.

You see that the belief system within which you seek refuge is just a human construct. Eventually, I think you find yourself needing to be something more than just a good Hindu or Christian or patriot."

Hmm. Able to grieve. What about the nightmare shadow? Is that a grieving? Or just the emptiness of ego? I can't get my mind around it. I sit on a bench facing the water and fish out my pipe—safety, at the ready. "So, if I'm not actually *causing* death—if I'm just *witnessing* it for some cosmically incomprehensible reason—the Hitchcock is good for me."

"Good for *us*. Perhaps. There may be long-term benefits to death rehearsals. I'm sorry it hurts so much."

I fill and light the pipe. Gaya rests her head on my shoulder. Yes, death rehearsals hurt, but this tousle-haired objectifier is absolute compensation. She jams her nose into my neck, and I want it there forever. When she looks up, her face is grave. "I will find a good death meditation for us."

Oh, goody. "For *us*."

She rubs her full lips on my neck and sits up. Ducks explode off the lake. "I said that sometimes it will be hard for us."

"For *us*."

She won't take the bait. She won't fight with me anymore about being together or apart. She doesn't ask me to explain my absence. All she says is, "I was expecting to find you broken if I found you at all, but you are still Stanhope. I am so relieved!"

"You should've seen me yesterday."

Pipe smoke slides lazily out over the water. The last bit of windowpane clarity takes hold. Ouch. I can't deny the truth. Preoccupied with my own hero-need, I couldn't see Gaya's everyday heroics. Like the dharma dog, Caprice, Gaya saved me in the surf at Dana Point. While I was in Oakland, drinking and trying to un-be, she was learning to cope, studying our subject, holding the hands of those facing mortal terror—and, in her spare time, tracking me like a bloodhound. Well, there you go—I'm not even the hero of my own fucking Odyssey.

Gaya is sleepy. I walk her back to the hotel and tuck her in. She needs a study break—a dozen study breaks. While she dozes, I run into the misty street, looking for something. A drink. No, that will have to wait. Something else. There it is: a florist about to close. No hollyhocks, of course. Just small roses with a big bouquet. That'll do. I trot around with the flowers until I find a cozy bistro, where I make a reservation. Then a funky art theater appears in the murk, advertising a rare showing of *The Philadelphia Story*. Thanks, Mom. The time to make up your mind about people is never.

She wakes when I return. The flowers pull a fresh smile. When I suggest a drink before dinner, she stops at a market for a couple of ginger kombuchas. New to me, but I like it. We find a bench on the wharf and have a little non-cocktail party. No Hitchcock allowed. The pelicans show off, stealing from homeless people and dumpsters via diversions and cheeky familiarity. Grifters.

At dinner, I try to order wine, but Gaya countermands. She's so full of inspired alternatives that I just smile and nod. I wouldn't refuse her anything. I can't stop imagining her alone, searching for me for weeks. The waiter brings bubbly water with a splash of apple cider vinegar. She's never seen *The Philadelphia Story* and laughs all through it. Only some of it is the witty dialog. We twine our limbs in the dark like randy teens. I see relief in her every gesture. She must have thought I might reject her. As if I could turn away from those tractor-beam, darshan eyes.

I have this idea that, at the beginning of a relationship, one person loves more than the other. The one who's more loved must then choose between power and love. I loved more, at first—and she *didn't* choose power. At Sunset Cliffs, after consulting with the pelicans, she leaned into my greater love. We traded roles after Connie died, mostly because I needed someone to blame. Now I lean into *her* greater love. Because I can't help it. Because it's my turn. But I didn't expect all this Technicolor payback while watching a black-and-white film. The certainty rushes to my head. Pours out of me. We settle into each other's orbit. As the credits roll, we kiss and kiss. She gives me those glistening eyes. Quotes the movie: "Put me in your pocket." As we near the square, the hooker in the big coat steps into the light and bestows a shy smile. The night is devoid of knives.

✳ ✳ ✳

In the morning, I treat Stanhope's wounds. While he showers, I joke about the shabbiness of the hotel room. It is not so bad really, but the rug is nearly transparent. I have so much to talk to Stanhope about, I hardly know where to begin. I center on gratitude and find myself paging through Aldous Huxley's *The Doors of Perception*. My odd and lovely friend returns to bed and tells me that he received the book from a Canadian journalist who microdoses LSD. He shows me the LSD tablets he was given—trying to give me a shock, I suppose. It *is* worrying, of course. He speaks of taking microdoses together someday, but that seems a diversion. It's not something I want to think about right now.

Late in the morning, at the Jazz Café, I finally tell him the Nachiketa story. "Nachiketa provokes his father by reminding him that he should behave more generously. Out of anger, the father sends his son to Yama, Lord of Death. But the boy must wait three days, fasting, for the god's return. When Yama returns, he is ashamed of having kept his guest, Nachiketa, waiting. Poor treatment of a guest is an insult to the gods because guests are meant to be *treated* as gods. So Yama grants the boy three wishes—one for each day of fasting.

"Nachiketa asks for peace for his family. Then he asks for knowledge of the fire sacrifice. And Yama grants these boons. But for his final wish, the boy asks for complete knowledge of what comes after death. Yama refuses. He says this is only for the gods to know. He offers the boy any worldly wealth imaginable if the boy will only change his wish. But Nachiketa insists on having this knowledge. Material things are transient. How can he ask for anything less than the deepest understanding of death from the god of death himself?"

"Go big or go home."

"Yes. Yama is still reluctant to teach this great lesson but is secretly pleased with Nachiketa's eagerness for truth. Over time, he patiently explains many things. The heart of the teaching—the fuck, as you say— is that the all-encompassing soul, Atma, is immortal. Atma serves as a kind of charioteer, guiding the horses of the senses through the shifting landscape of desire. After death, the grasping body is gone, but Atma remains. The goal of the wise is to know the soul, Atma, whose expression is *Om*."

"And if the wise fail?"

"They are not released from desire. They are caught in the cycle of rebirths."

"Did Nachiketa make it?"

"Yes."

"And how am I like this excitable boy?"

This makes me laugh because Stanhope really *looks* like an excitable boy. I can hardly contain my love as I take his wondering head in my hands. "You keep asking questions. You will not settle for anything but the deepest truth. Like Nachiketa, you listen and wait and listen."

Gaya is describing herself. *She* is Nachiketa. The skinny waitress chitters gleefully across the room, enabling me somehow. "Gaya, I might have stayed here for years, pickling my liver, if you hadn't tracked me down."

"I don't believe it. The road is hard, you know? You needed rest."

Yow. She looks at me and sees Sir Stanhope. I can't untangle that now. It would be a spiritual felony to harsh her radiance. She'll learn the truth soon enough. Until then, I have to play the part. The realization hits like a silver-screen smackeroo. Am I ready for my close-up? Seeing myself amped through Gaya is surreal and a little scary. The rush I felt in the movie theater surges back with attitude. Muscles bulge in my shirt.

Gaya is needed at Blessings, of course. We take a final walk with the birds at Lake Merritt. I talk about going back to DP to reconnect with the admiral, who's losing his grip on life, but she'll have none of that. She asks me, again, to stay with her in San Diego. She'd never spell it out, but it's clear that she needs a little domestic help and a lot of unconditional love. Me too.

"Also, we must accomplish our intervention for Cub."

"Cub's in jail, Gaya."

"I posted his bond."

"What?"

"He asked me to post his bond, so I posted his bond."

Of course. Cub called Gaya, who always keeps the faith. "He will soon have a long engagement at Inigo's. If he can fulfill it, he will pay us back."

I am not worthy. It's time to drop the superhero routine. Time for truth. With deliberation, I tell her all about my careless sublease, Cub's drunken shots, the bullet through the walls. Cub hadn't told her the whole story, of course. She stops and looks out over the lake. Retreats to a bench. "I met your Spuds, you know. They're just as I imagined. Just as you saw them with your loving eyes."

"How are they?"

"They are completely wonderful, Stanhope. Worried about you."

I join her on the bench. She takes my hand and swings her legs. "We have to be careful. We put the children in danger." She rubs her cheek on my forearm. "But we also kept them from danger."

We. "Back and forth across the razor's edge."

I can't believe how easy it is to let go of Oakland. Two days ago, I was ready to crash and burn here, in exaggetarian slo-mo. Now I can't pack fast enough. Walking back to the hotel, I wave stupidly to my street friends. Gaya talks me out of a farewell drink at London's tavern. Again she offers kombucha compensation. Our last stop is the Jazz Café, where we buy boxed lunches. The skinny waitress helps us at the counter wearing snowflake earrings. I want to thank her—for what? Facilitating our reconnection? Amping our gratitude? She makes it easy by uncorking her big laugh and hugging us both together. I finally remember to ask her name. "Eva," she says.

Gaya darts to the door, rifling through her purse. I catch up but can't think of a thing to say. As we drive to the airport, Gaya tells me that Connie and Wendy had worked out a plan for intervention and treatment for Cub. Okay. I keep trying to forget Cub, but this is my chance to come through for him and Connie. Maybe I'll have a new temp job: life coach for a hosed-up friend. On-the-job training will have to do. Gaya lays out the plan: we'll go to Cub's show at Inigo's on New Year's Eve—opening night. It's a good way to show our support. Our appearance should be a pleasant surprise. We won't spring anything on him until the next morning, when he's hungover and inclined to listen.

"We'll meet at Chet and Cub's house before the show to rehearse the intervention."

"Whoa. What *is* that? Do we need a cattle prod?"

"Don't be so Stan. We will only read letters to Cub, describing the problems we're having with his addiction. There will be a psychologist at the rehearsal and at the intervention, coaching us."

"Cub can be violent."

"Yes. But there are no more guns, we know that. And I think he will listen when we tell him that this is Connie's wish. We even have a letter from Connie. She gave it to Wendy just before she died. Wendy will read it. Cub will listen to Connie's words."

Of course. Connie knew. Deep down, she knew. We sit in silence for a few minutes, feeling her presence. I push on reluctantly. "Okay, we read Cub our letters. Then what?"

"We take him to a detox center."

"What if he refuses?"

"Then we have to leave him alone. We cannot force him."

"What if he takes a swing at somebody?"

"Gemma told me that Stanhope is a superhero."

"Great. I'm the heavy? I'm never the heavy."

She strokes my head playfully. "But—you have male pattern *boldness!* Besides, there are six of us. And, you know, Connie's words will be enough."

Conversation falls away, and I watch her. She's working on something big. I touch her occasionally, and she responds. She's seriously troubled, but her trouble isn't with me for a change. She's not ready to talk about it.

On the plane back to San Diego, sipping tea, I compose my letter to Cub, telling him about Halle and the Spuds—especially Randy, who might have stopped a bullet. Man!—Our pint-size Captain Carrot might have proved mortal. He was brave in the hospital: *Am I gonna die?* Yeah, Ran. We're all gonna die.

I really should consider Cub's point of view. Connie would insist. All the funny stuff comes bubbling up. "Remember Cub's story about his dad drinking with the beavers?" This scores a trill. We go on about Cub and his dad and the beavers for most of the flight. Trying to perpetuate the mood, I tack on another story I picked up from Cub about his mother's dedication to columbines. Every year, she passed out columbine seeds to her neighbors. Cub claims that Hope Valley is still full of blue columbines, thanks to her. The world remembers us in unexpected ways.

The main feature of Gaya's little apartment is its proximity to Blessings Hospital. Nearly everything about the place speaks of her work—or of Anshu. She hasn't figured out what to do with her brother's tent, sleeping bag, and other outdoor gear. They lie in a corner like forgotten toys. A slow slide show of her family and friends ticks along in a digital picture frame: Anshu, mostly—also Connie, the admiral, Kevin, and—oops, there's Stanhope, looking like an abandoned marionette. But only when he's alone.

We'll cocoon through December, then follow through with Cub's intervention. Gaya has to work twelve-hour days in the run-up to Christmas, so I jump into the role of support drone. In the morning, I feed her my chunky cinnamon toast and fill a box with lunch items— mostly fruit, nuts, and boiled eggs. Then we walk to the hospital together. I envy her lunch-bucket life—her difference-making day after day. In the evenings, she fills me in on the middle-aged guy who's starting to skip dialysis treatments regularly, the young woman who detests her fistula, the kids learning the odds. We talk about the imminent death legislation Pidge was pushing. There's not much hope. Sometimes I find her in the kitchen in the small hours, just as in Denver. But now there are no maps—just her laptop, which requires frowning. I do what I can. Tea and neck massage. Sometimes I can talk her into sketching, but she works listlessly and won't show me anything. When I walk her to work, she talks compulsively about Gemma, Connie, Cub, the admiral, her patients.

Time to mix things up. I drape lights around the squat cedar outside our door and add wooden ornaments. Plop a showy poinsettia onto the dining table. It all helps. Late in the month, when Gaya's enthusiasm wanes again, I upgrade my short-order meals and queue a load of *Star Trek*. She's a fan, fortunately, and the stories draw us in. *Voyager*'s "Survival Instinct" is a deft distillation of Becker's *The Denial of Death*. Gaya pulls the book out, and we talk into the night. These diversions squelch the shop talk, but she's still pensive overall. Sometimes she doesn't track the *Trek*.

Twice, she comes home to say she has taken Cub to lunch. "He needs to talk about Connie." Of course he does. I can't make myself call him. Gaya invites him over, and I'm relieved when he can't come. We have a quiet Christmas, allowing ourselves one gift apiece. Gaya's to me is a hardback of Somerset Maugham's *The Razor's Edge*, one of her Uncle Bebo's favorite books. My gift to her is a recorder, with which she noodles immediately. We walk the park, read aloud, fiddle with music, and talk, telling ourselves how great it all is. And it *is* great. But something is missing. I can't get over my pathetic November. Gayathri speaks entirely of the past and worries about everyone. She'll feel better when we put Connie's plan in motion for Cub.

Early New Year's Eve, we meet the Shelvadors at Chet and Cub's duplex. The place is neat, despite being crammed with at least a dozen of Chet's stringed instruments—immaculate Gibson twelve-strings, battle-scarred Strats, banjos, mandolins. Chet's a craftsman. You can see it in his hands. In the curation.

Cub and the drummer, Taz, are at the club. Taz's job is not to keep Cub sober—that would be impossible—just to keep him fiddle-ready and out of jail. The psychologist, Roger, arrives: a wiry Errol Flynn. He's low-key; calls himself a facilitator. Chet tells Roger that Cub has been worse since Connie's death: roaring every night, woozy and snoozy every day. Roger asks about other drugs, but nobody knows for sure. The psychologist has us read our letters aloud. Wendy's single-spaced two-pager alludes to an intense affair with Cub in the glory days that was derailed by his stinkin' thinkin'. We applaud her courage. Gaya's letter strikes the right balance. She ladles out love and respect while revealing Connie's confession that she would have accepted any of Cub's marriage proposals if he'd been sober for one of them. Chet quotes great musicians on the evils of the bottle. Wendy reads for Taz—a eulogy for performances blown because everyone was too gassed. I go last.

Roger has a few suggestions. Wendy should speak directly to Cub and take less of the blame. I have the opposite problem. My letter should express more emotional support. Figures. Cub endangered the Spuds. *Let it go, Stan. You placed him in the apartment.* Wendy concludes our rehearsal with Connie's letter:

Dear Heart,

You're the goddamnedest musician most of us have ever seen. And a great entertainer. But you're hiding in a bottle. The world can't hear you. Truth be known, it looks like you prefer it that way. Torching your dreams has become a comfortable habit, Cub. The thing is, I can't watch any more. I lived too long with a man who was afraid of success. I can't do it again.

I made you a cake for your birthday, Cub. Didn't know that, did you? You *drank* your birthday. For two days. I hardly saw you. I had to take the cake to the grill—where you never come anymore. Maybe the birthday doesn't matter. What matters is that you have a different excuse for drinking every day, for missing out on things—me especially. Who knows how much time we've got? I want you to have lots of birthdays. But I don't see it. You're wasting away in a bottle.

For the first time in my life, I'm having a hard time imagining a future. That's a hollow feeling, Cub. I wish we could talk about it. Night after night, I watch the possibility slip away. I'm asking you now, upon my great love, to climb out and get right with the world. Then come to me. Honestly, Cub, if you can do this, the sky's the limit. I can't wait to see you again.

Love forever, Connie

That should do it. Still, we need to do this right. Wendy and I revise our letters on Chet's ancient computer and read them out again. Roger pronounces them tolerable. He lays out the guidelines: truth, compassion, no drama, no matching, no improvising. No matching means we shouldn't match Cub's emotions, especially if he's aggressive. No improvising means that it's better to repeat a basic message than to get into anything we haven't thought through.

Connie would love the playful camaraderie as we help Chet and Wendy load instruments in Chet's pickup. As we watch the musicians drive away, Roger shyly asks to go to the club with Gaya and me. He's a music lover and a stranger to Cub, so his presence won't arouse suspicion. Not wanting to arrive too early, we walk to a nearby cantina and dawdle over tamales. Roger's earthy wisdom puts us at ease. It turns out he plays the sax. With a rakish grin, he tries us on. "Van Morrison *is* a saxophone."

Gaya laughs. "What?"

"The guy is a sax. Even when he's not playing one, he sounds like one. Look at how he sings—tongue forward, noodling and scatting and growling. He's a saxophone, man."

The band is well into the first set when we arrive. Cub looks great in a black trilby with red trim, tearing through JJ Cale's "Clyde." The original version perked along in a laid-back groove, but Cub's take is manic, with weird bridges and improv. Every note is bent. The song's pick-and-grin innocence is warped into psychedelia. Cub's strong voice binds it all together. Roger digs the chunking groove, but it doesn't stop him from making a diagnosis on the fly. "Cub's drunk, but he's got something else going on. Coke, probably."

No doubt. Taz gives us an apologetic head shake and shrug. There's nothing to do but enjoy the show. Fortunately, most of the music is up-tempo. Cub makes sure a guy at the mixing board is tweaking appropriately, then jumps and stomps like a rock god half his age. No one can sit still. Gaya and I start dancing with each other and end up dancing with everybody, including Roger. Cub and the Shelvadors play a lot of covers. Each sounds like the best possible version of the song. "Drunken Sailor Hornpipe," Led Zeppelin's "Kashmir," Bob Dylan's "Hurricane,"

Nirvana's "Smells Like Teen Spirit," Natalie MacMaster's "Fiddle & Bow"—you name it. Chet steps up and sings Jesse Winchester's "A Little Louisiana," then Doug Kershaw's "Louisiana Man." The band plays Celtic and Cajun chestnuts mostly, but no genre goes unmolested. They thrust and parry between songs.

"What's the difference between a fiddle and a violin, Cub?"

"You're buyin'—it's a fiddle. You're sellin'—it's a violin."

Cub has six other answers to the question, and they work them all in. When they're ready for another break, Cub surprises everyone with Yeats.

> When I play on my fiddle in Dooney,
> Folk dance like a wave of the sea;
> My cousin is priest in Kilvarnet,
> My brother in Mocharabuiee.
>
> I passed my brother and cousin:
> They read in their books of prayer;
> I read in my book of songs
> I bought at the Sligo fair.
>
> When we come at the end of time
> To Peter sitting in state,
> He will smile on three old spirits,
> But call me first through the gate;
>
> For the good are always the merry,
> Save by an evil chance,
> And the merry love the fiddle,
> And the merry love to dance:
>
> And when the folk there spy me,
> They will all come up to me,
> With 'Here is the fiddler of Dooney!'
> And dance like a wave of the sea.

The place is boiling when the band takes a break. Cub waves to us, looks like he's making his way to our table but never makes it. The Shelvadors make it. Taz tries to explain about the coke, but no one blames him. Wendy says Cub can outfox anybody when it comes to controlled substances.

After ten minutes, Cub lurches back onstage and drives the show relentlessly. Often he jumps right into the next number without a pause. We all get a workout. Eventually, Gaya begs off dancing and the old familiar stitch creeps onto her brow. Two hours in, while Cub replaces a string, Taz waves me over and hands me the drumsticks. "Cub wants you on this one."

Cub winks. I squint back at Taz. "Can I *play* this song?"

The drummer stands to leave, clapping me on the shoulder. "Oh, yeah."

I nervously take the stool as Cub tunes the fiddle. He crouches, weirding a long whine. Gives me an evil grin and jumps into "Dr. Bronner's Breakdown."

It takes me a few seconds to figure it out, but the song is not hard. I stay heavy on the bass and slide into a heartbeat lub-dub. Cub gives a big nod of approval, and Wendy riffs off the new beat on piano. Everyone in the place—everyone on Coronado Island, probably—is drawn in.

"Exceptions eternally? Absolutely none!"

Deedle-dee-do, deedle-deedle-deedle do! Cub wobbles his trilby and galumphs through the Shelvadors, making eye contact with each of us. I know he's on jet fuel, but his eyes are clear. Something new shines in them: tranquility. He reminds me of someone I know well. Someone whose body is just as fluid. Someone who beams like the sun. Anshu.

Driving a rocking house is what it's all about. Here we are, giving and receiving like hell. Wendy and Chet and Cub and I exchange "wow" looks. Years ago, I had similar experiences, but this one's the best. I'd always assumed reaching this high was all about turning within. Watching Cub work the crowd, I know, as Eva knew, the turning is outward.

THE GREAT MOTIONS
OF LOVE
(WINTER)

THE FINAL CRESCENDO REVERBERATES. WENDY COUNTS OUT THE LAST seconds to midnight, and the place goes crazy. Cub motions me out front. Looks me in the eye again, and we all bow together. He's making amends, wants forgiveness. Piece of cake. Happy New Year.

As Taz returns and settles in, Cub quaffs another boilermaker. Glares into the rafters. "What's the most beautiful thing in the world?"

Crude answers are offered up. Cub stares everyone down, but his answer is barely audible. "A woman in love," he says flatly, with a catch in his voice that surprises everyone. On the organ, Wendy floats the opening chords of "Tupelo Honey."

Cub switches to acoustic guitar. Chet wanders tastefully through the melody on electric. Taz sits back and closes his eyes. Wendy sustains the churchy vibe.

"Connie. Short for Connemara. Her father loved the west of Ireland— almost as much as I loved his daughter."

Cub pulls on a beer. "There's a chain-link meanness about the country these days. That's what Connie said, and I believe her. An indifference to pain. Even an eagerness, in some, to punish the poor. This troubled her."

Cub strums thoughtfully as the crowd gets restless. "Yeah—I know. I can be mean too." He looks our way. "And jack-assily careless!"

Cub bows with arms spread and looks as humble as I've ever seen him. "Guilty as charged. I am—*sorry* as I can be for all the trouble I've caused. But tonight, I'm channeling my sweet Connemara. 'Cause she can't be here. She can't be anywhere."

Cub sits on the high stool and strums thoughtfully. "She taught me all about consequences."

Wendy laughs. "Connie-quences!"

"Ha! Yes, chillun, let us consider the *Connie-quences* of our actions."

The band sinks deep into the melody. "One time she said to me, 'Some people think you have to go through *hate* to get to love. If they love John Lennon, they're ready to hate Paul McCartney!—Well, why not love 'em both? They loved each other.'

"I moved into a neighborhood one time, and some of the wives started givin' me the evil eye. We'd hardly said 'boo' to each other, but they decided they knew all about me. So I finally started askin' 'em, 'Who we hating today, ladies?' You know? It's on the to-do list. Every day."

The band plays expertly with the song for a few minutes as Cub noodles with the guitar. But he has more channeling to do. "I get quality time with close friends a few hours a week—if I'm lucky. Most of the time, I'm sellin' a stranger a song or introducin' the van to a mechanic or meetin' a promoter. Everyday stuff. Connie called these *ricochet* relationships. She had a good time every day because she was *great* at ricochet relationships."

He straightens up and takes in the room as if just remembering where he is. He holds up the beer. "To angels of the first degree."

Everyone drinks with Cub. The band steps neatly into "Tupelo Honey." You wouldn't know that minutes earlier they'd been jumping around like over-stimulated lab animals. Cub alternates lines and verses with Wendy, who sings with reverence. Chet joins in with a sweet tenor.

The song goes on for a long while, in no hurry. We're all out on the dance floor, shuffling reverently. Gaya presses her face into my chest and whispers memories of Connie. It's the memorial I missed—the one we all needed still. In due and diligent course, the melody fades to nothing— no, everything—and we stand blinking at each other. Then applaud like thunder. Cub seems embarrassed by perfection. The Shelvadors embrace Cub and each other, bowing. Wendy pops open the Crosley Shelvador, but there's no beer stampede.

At nine New Year's morning, Gaya and I pick up Taz, Wendy, and Roger in the Champion. We're supposed to read out our letters again, but it doesn't seem necessary. We know it cold. And after last night, it looks like Cub will meet us halfway. Still, Roger reminds us of the rules and rereads Connie's letter.

Chet meets us at the door of his neat apartment, looking relaxed in an open shirt. He's a craft beer man but seldom drinks more than one a night. This morning, he provides great coffee, bagels, and cold cuts while we wait for Cub to crawl out of bed. I bring in a case of kombucha, thinking it might help wean Cub off of the hard stuff. We fool around with guitars, music lore, recipes, and lyrics until after ten. Then Chet checks on Cub. A minute later, he pops his head out the bedroom door and motions to Roger. The two are in Cub's room for a few minutes when their ominous murmurings get to Wendy. She shoots Gaya a look and pushes into the room. Here come the klaxons.

Taz and Gaya and I follow Wendy in. Chet's on the phone, giving details of the deceased. Cub lies flat on his back, a colorful quilt pulled up to his chin as if he'd been tucked in. Except for the pallor, he could be sleeping. Happy New Year.

The room is spare. Cub had lined up the Voldemort Elvises across the top of a chest of drawers. It's jarring to be reminded of the Spuds in this death room. I set the bobbleheads bobbing, amping the absurdity. Wendy slams her phone onto the bed and wails. Gaya moves to console, but the big blonde can't slow for it. She paces, sobbing. "I was fine with Connie. I loved her. But she's gone. Why couldn't Cub see what might be? Why couldn't he see *me*?"

She raises the pitch. "Why couldn't he stop!? Why couldn't he choose *life!?*"

Gaya practically tackles Wendy, and they rock together. Roger kneels next to the bed and places his fingers on Cub's neck. He looks at me as I approach. "OxyContin," he says, nodding to a bottle on the nightstand. "He was probably trying to come down after the coke."

He stands and looks down at the corpse. "Hypoxia. Opiates and alcohol depress breathing. The breath can just stop. Then it's organ failure, coma, death."

I can't look away from the waxy, untroubled face. "What about suicide?"

Roger shakes his head. "I don't think so. There are pills left in the bottle. He's probably been on the opiates for a few weeks, based on what Chet said. He was so jacked last night; he probably took extra so he could sleep."

Cub never heard Connie's last words to him. We should've intervened a week or two ago. Too bad I had all that moping to do in Oakland. Oh, shit: the klaxons. Deafening now, as they always become. Sucking my breath away. I step outside, but there's no escaping. All I can do is pace the backyard with my hands over my ears. This is a listening I cannot do. It's a problem. A nightmare shadow. *Breathe, Stan.*

EMTs are in charge when I step back in. I guide Gaya to the living room couch. Hold her sorrowing head as she rummages in the purse. "I saw it," she says. "I saw this coming."

Over the next couple of days, we spill to the police. Everything we can think of about Cub. We all get together a few times, debriefing each other. Roger shifts deftly into bereavement counseling. Wendy says Cub has a plot in a nearby cemetery. "We gave it to him years ago. Kind of a joke. But we also hoped it would scare him straight."

"Too subtle for an alcoholic," says Roger.

We all embrace regularly. I lay out my take on Cub's death: It wasn't planned or perfect, but he made a good end. As good as he could pull off, anyway. He gave a stellar performance—probably his best show. Paid tribute to Connie. Cooked all night with Wendy and the Shelvadors.

Recorded it all for posterity. Suggested an epitaph for himself with "The Fiddler of Dooney." Apologized. Drank a farewell toast with hundreds of fans. Unburdened his soul. Rode out on a following sea of love.

I'm probably handling Cub's death better than I handled Connie's because I'm being forced to socialize the grief. Our intervention squad didn't save Cub, but it looks like we'll save each other. Wendy receives comfort from beefy Taz—a long-awaited opportunity for him, no doubt. She frets about what to do with the intervention letters. It doesn't seem right to ignore them. We agree to bury them with Cub. I ask for copies, for the history. "There is no history," said Emerson. "Only biography."

Stanhope and I take refuge in strict home and work schedules. I am fretful, even so. Connie's death was difficult because it was a surprise. Cub's death was difficult because it was *not* a surprise. I was expecting it. The dread had risen on our return from Oakland. Will it subside now that Cub is deceased? I expect to feel better but cannot. I am apprehensive about everything.

Gaya and I arrive early for Cub's funeral at a suburban Catholic church. The place is already packed with middle-aged music fans and their children. Right on time, a tall, dark girl steps up to the pulpit wearing one of Cub's trilbies. We're surprised to learn that Cub has a young adult daughter, Silk. She lives in Hope Valley with her conspicuously absent mother.

Silk looks exactly like her father as she scans the room defiantly. "I bet everyone in this room had a legitimate beef with Dad. And a whole lot of other people, too. It's just like him to skip out on a stack of unpaid bills. He hurt Mom and me as much as he hurt anybody, I guess. But— when he wasn't around, which was most of the time, he still soothed me. We'd play his music, and it's amazing how much that helped. The *one* time he was around for a long stretch—I think it was four months—he taught me guitar. Now I play in a band. That helps me forgive Dad. It even makes me grateful for him—and I never thought I'd say that."

She has her father's flair for the dramatic. "We all know that Cub didn't have much." She walks to a box and pulls out a tall stack of hats. "But he did have these. *Twenty-two* trilbies! No one would recognize him on stage without one of these dorky hats! Now that I think about it, the Cub I really loved—the one who taught me to love music, the one who laughed a lot—I always remember in a trilby. I've kept a few, but I'll put the rest out here on the table. You're welcome to 'em."

She descends the stage and arranges the hats on a table. "Come on up, don't be shy! I'll fetch my guitar while you look 'em over."

People gradually trickle forward and examine the hats. After a dozen or so have been taken, there's a lull. Gaya surprises both of us by hopping up to pick out a vintage red and black number. She still looks drawn but shows some spirit by tossing it to me. "For traveling." It takes me a few minutes to identify the emotion this stirs. *Pride.* I'm proud of Gaya, Silk, the Shelvadors, Cub, everyone in the room.

Silk returns to the podium with a guitar. "I heard Cub's last show was one for the ages. I'm sorry I wasn't there. But I've got the recordings. Don't know if they'll make much money, but they will make a lot of people happy. I'll make sure of that."

She strums Bob Dylan's "Knockin' on Heaven's Door," asking the audience to help with the chorus. Nearly everyone in the audience is seriously into music, and we make the rafters ring. Before leaving, Silk invites others to come up and speak. There's an awkward pause. Wendy's not up to speechmaking but talks earnestly to Taz. I figure I can buy them some time. I jump to my feet and walk to the pulpit. Look out on a sea of nonconformists.

"What Silk said about being hurt by Cub reminded me of an old story. When the Greeks set out to attack Troy, they got lost. Ended up in Mysia, which was ruled by King Telephus. In the ensuing battle—because there *has* to be a battle—King Telephus was speared by the Greek hero Achilles. When the wound wouldn't heal, Telephus went to the oracle at Delphi and asked for advice. 'He that wounded shall heal,' was the answer. So the injured man went back to Achilles and asked for help. Achilles scraped bits of his spear tip onto the wound. It worked. The gash that might have killed Telephus healed miraculously.

"So—the wounder is the healer. That's why there's always hope. It's never too late for anybody. If you can express beauty, you can heal—can compensate for the damage you've done—even after death. Whatever you might say about Cub, you can't deny that he was dialed into beauty. He channeled it every day of his life."

Chet and Taz and Wendy and Silk lead cheers. Taz saunters to the pulpit and says that things were looking up for Cub just before Connie died. He was changing and might have made it all the way to clean and sober. The big man speaks quietly, keeping his eyes on Wendy, who radiates approval. He takes a deep breath and gets into Cub's microphone phobia period, after he was electrocuted. Everyone loves it. By the end, his voice is booming. Wendy meets him in the aisle, and they leave together.

After the benediction, we walk out to the small cemetery. Chet, Taz, Wendy, and I are pallbearers. As we gather around the plot, a big guy appears at the edge of the crowd. He looks familiar, yet out of place.

I've heard the burial prayer a few times, I guess, but I'm a better listener now. It's a straightforward petition for the soul's admission to "Paradise, his true country." I pantomime knock, knock, knockin' for Silk's amusement. After the graveside ceremony, she seeks us out and jokes about the trilby. She's thrilled that Wendy has asked her to join the Shelvadors. It's a tough business, but everyone thinks the band can make it without Cub.

As Gaya and I make for the gate, the familiar-looking big man approaches and extends a hand. I'm wary, but Gaya grasps it. "Detective Morris. Nice to see you."

He nods. "Call me Ben."

"Did you know Cub?"

"Met him last month. In jail. Guy was a mess."

He stands back and looks around. "Good turnout. I couldn't hope for half of this crowd at my funeral. But I don't have much stage presence. I'm just trying to keep the word *hapless* out of my obituary."

Gaya smiles. I can't. Ben zeroes in on my weakness—probably can't help himself. "Now, a guy who subleases his apartment to a *mess*—a guy who hangs out with everyone who's fixin' to *die*—"

I nod. "Yeah. *Hapless* is the word."

Ben chuckles and shakes his head. Gaya looks uneasy. Here it comes.

"Detective Nichols called me after he talked with Cub in his cell. Your name came up, Stan."

"I thought it might."

Ben waits politely. I might like the guy if he wasn't so good at his job. Gaya fills the gap. "He cannot say why, Ben. We don't know."

He looks down, adopting a familiar aw-shucks pose. "I knew a guy, Billy Mills, who lost *four* friends and family members in one summer. Course, he lived in a rough neighborhood."

Ben smiles ruefully. "And *he* was one of the main reasons it was rough."

I don't know what to say. Gaya steps forward, ready to defend. Ben turns to her and speaks with gravity. "Billy had a girlfriend too. Sweetest kid I ever met."

Gaya looks ready to duke it out with the big man. I have to intervene. "Wish we could help you, Ben."

Detective Morris pulls cards out and gives one to each of us. "All right. Anytime you want to talk."

He holds out the hand again. As I grasp it, I have to ask what happened to Billy Mills. Ben points to the far end of the cemetery. "Billy's over there, resting easy. He never could get over making things hard for everybody, including himself."

❄ ❄ ❄

This is my karma. In the beginning, I chose to be suspicious. I called the police on Stanhope. Now the detectives are watching him. They are watching *us*. We cannot simply grieve. We must worry also about being considered dangerous. Often I find myself thinking of how essential we felt in the world, how hopeful, when we stood on the cliff at the Hopi village of Walpi, looking out over the desert. We had the same feeling while flying over huge hogbacks and when admiring the dioramas at the museum in Denver. I don't know how to recapture that spirit. We crave a deep sort of constancy, but always we must adjust to an ever-changing world.

At home, I try to sleep while Stanhope takes a long walk in the park. Gemma calls. This is my salvation—at least, for the moment. We have a jolly old talk. She tells me a funny story about one of her great-grandchildren. The girl was helping Gemma cook. When Gemma asked if she wanted to take a break, the girl nodded. So they walked to the living room and sat down. But the child was restless and watched Gemma carefully. Gemma asked, "Do you know what a break is, honey?" The girl said, "No. But I think it has chocolate on it."

When Stanhope returns, I tell him the story. Of course, we cannot speak of chocolate without eating chocolate. So we walk to a shop, holding hands. Precious, Anshu would say.

We spend most of Saturday in the park. A young sheepdog bounds up, barking and running around us. An Asian woman fast-walks to us, her long hair streaming, and calls the dog—Chester. "He's looking for your dog. Everyone should have a dog!"

Stanhope and I kneel for Chester. "He has a point."

I pull Chester's tail playfully, and he chases me. He's a bearded collie, only six months old. The woman is Keiko, a professional dog walker. "I've been doing this for seventeen years! Can't believe it's been that long."

"Congratulations. A real profession."

"I'm just so grateful! Ten years ago, I was in a car accident. It wasn't that big a deal, but I guess I had a brain injury. I couldn't speak for months."

"Were you in hospital?"

"Are you kidding? No insurance. It was so weird! I was just out there, walking around, trying to figure things out. I couldn't even understand anybody. My language skills were gone. I was trained as an anthropologist, so I thought that language was the essence of intelligence. Wrong! Now I had complex thoughts all the time that had nothing to do with language."

Chester won't allow me to stop playing with him, so I must multi-task. "My God! How did you cope?"

Keiko feints at Chester and laughs. "Well, I expected to freak out, but it never happened. It was like the freak-out response was unplugged too. Maybe I'd been around dogs so much that I was dog-like about it. If a dog loses a leg or something, she doesn't miss a beat. Some of my clients are happy tri-paweds. It was like that for me. The whole experience was kind of fascinating. At first, I thought, *Am I seriously brain-damaged?* But then I watched all these elaborate thoughts come and go. So I decided I hadn't changed much. I just couldn't communicate normally."

I find myself looking at Blessings Hospital—my edifice, so to speak. My reason for being. "And you never saw a doctor?"

Keiko pulls a tennis ball from a bag and throws it. "Nope. Just figured it out every day. Friends helped me with a few things, but it's amazing how much you can communicate with facial expressions and gestures. Dogs taught me that, too. At the time, I was also working as a paralegal. There was no way I could do *that* anymore. But the dog walking was perfect. The dogs understood me better than anybody. More referrals came in, and I just nodded and smiled. Goofing with dogs just filled my life, organically. I didn't even have to decide anything. It just happened."

"How did your language skills come back?"

"Gradually. Over several months. But it didn't change anything, really. I had my vocation. My *avocation*. I'm just so grateful!"

This is food for thought. So often, I forget how much life experience is beyond the purview of my institutional care-giving. In any case, Keiko's joy reminds us of Gemma, so it seems a perfect coincidence when Gemma calls again. She extends a charming invitation for Sunday brunch. I will bring a big bottle of chai.

The magic of the cottage kicks in as soon as I pull the Mini up to the curb. In my mind's eye, once again, I see us walking up the winding footpath. Pax is even cooler than I'd imagined—a serene dharma dog. While Gaya dotes on him, Gemma pulls me into the fragrant kitchen. "Stan, I told you to forget Theo for a while." She points toward the living room. "Do you *know* how hard that girl works?"

"I'm learning."

"Well, be a good student. Pay *attention*. *She* is your purpose now. Theo will come later. Do you understand?"

"Yes, ma'am."

Gaya's chai is a big hit. Gratitude lifts all boats, and the chatter begins. The prevailing topic is how Gemma knew that Gaya would find me in the Jazz Café. "Sadie sent me a dream!"

Eventually, children noisily arrive, and we head for the door. Gemma and Gaya embrace, blinking eye-to-eye, then we're out. I'm out of body again. Here comes Stanhope and Gaya, floating out of the little cottage and down the walkway. Every light in the cottage is on, and it reverberates with laughter.

The reconnection with Gemma is a tonic. Gaya is still more apprehensive than usual, but lighter at last. On the way home, she explains Gemma's dream about a white owl landing on a juniper while Gemma sits among a circle of friends. "I think the dream has to do with expansion. Remember Tom's old dog who died? The old sighthound who brought Gemma and Tom together? Her name was Juniper."

That night, Gaya sleeps ten hours straight. We have a good week. Her appetite improves, and we sign up for dance lessons—Gaya is done with my waist-up dancing. But Friday afternoon, she calls from work and tells me in a small voice that Gemma has died. "Her granddaughter can meet us at the cottage tonight."

I have fresh minestrone from Captain Carrot ready when Gaya arrives home. She eats little and talks less. We have a long shower, remembering everyone. Gaya recites all the gifts Gemma brought her and the other nurses at Blessings: lavender from her garden, fresh almond bread, crocheted dishtowels—she brought offerings everywhere, just like Kitty Duran.

We drive to the old cottage in the Studie this time. The tracking shot spools out and freezes in a diorama. Sadie and Gemma are the curators. Sadie and Gemma, who ran with a teenage gaggle and resisted being anybody's fuss. Who wanted to live screwball-comedy lives with adventure and music. Well, there was comedy, as when they danced like scrawny chickens or played with Cinder in the backyard. There was adventure, as when they snuck into the Gatto on Decatur Street or moved to California on a shoestring. And there was music, lots of it, from Mo's old dobro, Theo's original songs, the laughter of children.

Dariana welcomes Stanhope and me in a striking dress of royal blue. Pax does not greet us at the door but lies motionless on the couch, nose in his sweater. He does not move as we stroke him. In the kitchen, she rubs the framed metal resonator from Sadie's dobro. For this family, the artifact is a sort of gentile mezuzah. We take our tea to the living room and sit with Pax between us. Dariana sits opposite. She has her grandmother's lopsided smile.

"Gremma and I had a thing, a routine, where I would call every night at seven. Last night, there was no answer. As I drove over, I could hear Pax howling a block away. Then I saw the ambulance. I followed the howling to the backyard. There were four EMTs. One woman was holding Pax. Another was working the phones. And two guys were packing up Gremma Gemma—so *reverently*.

"Well, Pax couldn't stop howling—it was okay, he just had to do it. Those first responders were kind and patient with us. After they took the body, I tried my best with Pax. He finally stopped his caterwaul late last night. But he won't leave this old sweater."

Considering the history of the sweater—Juniper's death, Tom's dotage and proposal, Gemma's contentment with her peaceful companion—I understand Pax's attachment. I kneel in front of the couch and place my head on his. Stanhope rubs my back and speaks with Dariana. "Will you stay here?"

She nods. "We'll keep the cottage in the family."

"Pax?"

"Pax belongs here."

Of course. I want to speak but cannot. All we can do is console Dariana and walk to the door. Pax picks up his head and watches us. He points his nose to the ceiling but cannot make a sound. I feel exactly the same way.

On the day of the funeral, I rise early. The winter morning is damp and quiet. I am very silent, but Stanhope is quickly by my side. We walk the park adjacent to the hospital, through grassy slopes and waxy rhododendrons. The breezes from the sea are delicious. We watch a determined Labrador retriever pull a sleepy person from tree to tree. I must say what's on my mind. "I knew about Cub."

"I know."

"And I knew about—Gemma."

"You know who's going to die."

"Yes."

"Okay. Who's next?"

"Admiral Spencer."

"My guess too."

I have to stop walking. "I cannot think of anything else. I cannot serve my patients. I *cannot* live a pukka life."

Stanhope draws me to him. "I know."

"It has happened before, with my patients. And my parents. I think it is a premonition that comes with too much death."

"What do you want to do?"

"I don't know. I want to go away but don't want to leave Blessings Hospital. I have responsibilities."

Stanhope places a warm hand on my cheek. I try to collect myself and speak clearly. "I'm avoiding something. I cannot leave until I know whether I am running from this or toward that."

Gaya points out Dariana in the middle of swaying robes. Her Baptist gospel choir manifests the loss of Gemma with hushed hymns and ecstatic calls to glory. The ratcheting power of it all is stunning. A wide, animated woman starts the choir crooning softly. We tremble as it builds, then move and shout with hundreds of mourners. Many sing along with the choir. The first song, "Grateful," by Pastor Hezekiah Walker, is perfect for Gemma.

Eulogies are given between songs. Gemma's oldest child, a stocky man in an impeccable suit, talks about how Gemma put a silver dollar in his lunch box every day. "Usually, I'd spend it, but sometimes I'd save for a baseball glove or just make towers of silver. Every day I considered all the trade-offs—and managed my money. Eventually, it was no big deal to make a profession of it."

The choir jumps into "Take Me to the King," by Kirk Franklin. Dariana steps out of the choir and up to the podium, beaming. "I went to the Humane Society with Gremma Gemma to find her a companion. Every dog was up on hind legs, asking to be adopted. It's hard because you love them all, you know. But Gremma went right to her spirit dog. She knew him immediately. His name was Whizzer, but she called him Pax before we left the building. She made that old racing hound so happy that he actually got something called happy tail. That's right— *happy* tail. It's an injury that dogs get from too much wagging. She made him—*too happy!*"

Laughter and shouts. Dariana stays at the podium and sings lead for the first verse of "People Get Ready," by Curtis Mayfield. Gemma's daughter, a large woman in black crepe, steps up. "Mom wanted to go to one of those murder mystery dinners for her birthday. Well, she figured out whodunit right away, but she wouldn't say so. She let everyone else speculate and stretched the fun out as long as she could. On the way home, she says, 'I knew that doctor would figure it out. Wasn't he nice to talk to!'"

Everyone laughs. Dariana shakes her head and smirks. "She looks at me over her glasses and says, 'Dariana, I believe that doctor has *the news!*'" As she turns to leave, the organist hits evocative chords. The choir hums and builds into "Oh, Happy Day," by Edwin Hawkins. After the song, Gaya squeezes my arm nervously and pops up, to my surprise. She trots to the podium with a notepad and bends the microphone down.

"When Sadie died—"

A man shouts, "Sadie Coulter!" to applause.

Gaya laughs. "When her oldest friend, Sadie Coulter, died, Gemma and I talked a lot. She gave me this quote from Rilke: 'I do not wish to say that one should love death, but one should love life so magnanimously, so without calculating and selecting, that love of death—the turned-away side of life—is continually and involuntarily included. Which actually happens invariably in the great motions of love, which are impetuous and illimitable.'"

A woman shouts, "The great *motions* of love!"

The choir returns to "Oh, Happy Day." Gaya runs back and sits quickly. She looks thin. She's eaten haphazardly since Oakland. Except for the brief recovery after she spoke to Gemma, she's been running on adrenaline. The joy in this moment is real, but it's just as exhausting as the last few weeks of loss. Gaya is crashing, but she wouldn't leave now. I just have to run interference for another half-hour and get her home.

The morning is cool. Rain freshened things up while we were inside. Dariana and Pax wait at the gravesite as a hundred of us troop to meet them. Gaya tightens her grip on me and stops when she sees Pax. Someone has tailored Gemma's old red and black sweater—Juniper's sweater—for the dog. He sits beside the open grave. Seems to look without seeing. Tries to howl, but can't.

Here comes Detective Ben Morris, smooth as cream. "We've gotta stop meeting like this, man."

"I guess you need to talk to me."

Uncertainty flickers across Ben's broad face. He holds both hands out to Gaya in consolation. She takes them gratefully. He steps back and scans the crowd. "Pax is my guy. He's just who I need to talk to."

Together, we watch Gemma's casket descend into the ground next to Sadie. Pax looks skyward and tries again. Nothing.

Shiva Could Not See
(Winter)

Stanhope and I arrive back home in the middle afternoon. I cannot eat. We meditate, but not very successfully. The mood is damp. Rain comes and swells within us. We go to bed early, but I have a disturbing dream about being alone in a crowd. I must think about this. Stanhope comes into the kitchen while I'm filling the teapot. He opens a window and breathes deeply. The rain will not stop. "You should eat something," he says.

I try to respond, but I cannot. Stanhope opens the refrigerator. "How about Stanhope's Pumpkin Surprise?"

I have to hug him for this. "Later."

"Massage?"

I put the teapot on the stove. "Have some cardamom tea."

We sit quietly at the table. I suppose I must tell Stanhope what I have been thinking for weeks now, as dreadful as it is. I don't know quite where to begin, so I start with something suggested by my dream. "In that book of yours, *The Doors of Perception*, Aldous Huxley talks about how alone we are in all circumstances, even when making love. We cannot dissolve one into the other as we wish. He says we are 'island universes.' We *know* this. But I don't want to know. I want to pretend."

Stanhope's hands and arms are always so warm that I find myself rubbing my hands on them. "The merge is never complete."

He blinks, looking very wise. "Not physically, in the moment. It can be *spiritually*, in the moment. And it can be physically, in the future."

This seems important, so I walk with the idea and settle on the couch. "Think of all the living things that gaze into the sky and—like Pax—they cannot even howl."

Stanhope brings the tea and we sit close. "*Weltschmerz*."

"Yes. World sorrow. I feel it keenly sometimes, despite the wisdom, despite the expansive ideas that I learned from Anshu and from the *Gita*."

"You're not a goddess, remember? I love your uncertainty."

I touch Stanhope's earnest face. "This terror of death tops everything. We wish so fervently to live forever that we manifest evil."

Stanhope does not like thinking about this—or he does not like *me* thinking about it. He stands and walks about. When he stops, his face is comical. "Did your mom keep your underwear in the refrigerator?"

"What?"

"You know, on hot days. Did your mom keep your undies on ice?"

I roll on my back and have a good laugh. What is he talking about? He explains that one of his Window Wizard friends, Nina, had a mother who did this with her underwear. So of course, the Wizards bowling team decided to freeze their underwear for good luck. So absurd! He says this made them a better team. I'm grateful for this release but try to give these Wizards their due. "You were a team of superheroes."

He strikes a pose.

"And you rode together in your Champion. You were the Champions!"

"The Chumpettes."

"The Avengers."

"The Averages."

"You are such a one."

"*You* are. We make such an *eleven*."

Stanhope dives onto the couch. He has nearly jollied me out of what I must say. But—help me, Shiva!—I must say it. I busy myself with making more tea. "There is no getting used to so much loss, you know."

"You can still save yourself."

This is the moment. I kneel and speak carefully. "Stanhope. *You* must save yourself."

He squints comically, but I hold up a hand. "This Hitchcock does not belong to you. It belongs to me."

Stanhope exaggerates his squint, trying to keep things light, but I am going the other direction. I must cover my mouth. He reacts to this in a caring way, but I am determined to drive home the point. "I knew Anshu best, you know. And Gemma. And Connie. Also, Dennis and Pigeon. Cub and Admiral Spencer, we knew to the same degree. *I* am Yama. Not you."

"We don't know the admiral's in trouble."

"I think it is not so bad to be Yama. He is an expression of dharma. He was just the first person who died, so he has to help all who come after him. He has a lot of grace."

I am suddenly very tired, so I curl up on the couch with my head in Stanhope's lap. I take his hand in both of mine. "Once, Gemma even introduced me to Sadie. I never saw her again, but she was in Gemma's stories. So you see, we both knew the people who died. And here is something else: I told you that four of my patients died over the summer. That happens, and I can usually cope, but I allowed myself to become really close to them. I forgot how to protect myself and others. Someday, I will describe them to you."

I need to rout this idea—exterminate it. But I can't show alarm. All I can do is stroke Gaya's curls and think. Once again, I was so absorbed in *my* relationships, *my* strange fate, that I couldn't see the shadow sapping her spirit. She might be right about owning the Hitchcock, but I can't say so. At least, not now. It would be twisting the knife. I won't concede an inch. Eventually, she leaves it alone. We meditate, then doze on the couch until morning light silvers the window shades. Gaya stands and kisses my neck. "I have to dress for work. Will you make toast?"

She would never consider staying home, so I don't suggest it. She grabs the mondo purse and disappears into the bathroom. I dress distractedly, shuffle out to the kitchen, pop bread into the impatient toaster. Hold the lever down. I'll fix it today. Gaya trails out as I place cinnamon toast and fruit and chai on the table. We eat in silence. She smiles and touches me a lot. I want to say everything but settle for nothing. She pulls a small handbag from the mothership purse and apologizes distractedly, as if to the purse. "I'm a little tired today."

The hand-in-hand walk through the park to the hospital opens us up. It's a Poppins morning, breezy and fresh. I want to apologize for not protecting her, for thinking it was my problem alone. But I can't get around to it. Pointing at birds, saying their verbs, is enough for now. Gaya's yellow jacket contrasts with the soft landscape. She's tentative, though very affectionate, cupping my face in her hands as she says goodbye. Still, I can't speak.

I tidy the apartment, read the histories, look for Gaya's sketches. Fix the hell out of the toaster. Walk the hell out of the park. Wonder about the Spuds. Wish for a dog. The mondo purse on the kitchen table seems out of place. That's why Gaya seemed unsure this morning: she didn't have her bulwark. I don't remember seeing her without it before. A purse that big makes a small woman look tiny. But it's solid backup. Who knows what's in there? A phaser? A cricket bat? I can't let her face the world without it. I peek inside. There's Stanhope's Pumpkin Surprise, in a glass bowl. She needs her lunch, at least. I'll take it to her—make sure she eats. Maybe I'll say what needs to be said. I shoulder the uber-bag. It will make her smile.

I doubt anyone at Blessings Hospital knows about Gaya and me. Gaya's not the type to go on about her boyfriend. Who knows? Maybe she'd be the type to go on about her boyfriend if the boyfriend wasn't shortish and baldish—a window washer, forgodsake. A tallish, hairish doctor would be easier to talk about. *Shake it off, Stan.* The nurses at the Kidney Center do a double take. They recognize the purse. One or two remember me as the stalker from months ago. I can see them trying to puzzle out the connection. When I ask about Gaya, they say she's on leave.

"But she came to work this morning."

"Special circumstances. Should we hold her purse for her?"

"That's okay. She left it with me."

They exchange "Yeah, right!" looks. Will call security as soon as I'm gone. I think about asking to talk to a supervisor or something, but I know they won't tell me what's really happening. Back at the apartment, Gaya's Mini is missing. The keys are not on the hook by the door. She must have come back while I was at the hospital. Must have even avoided walking back through the park. Something's going on. Was she fired? Not likely. She's too needed. She's "on leave." Instantly. Must be something serious. I punch Gaya's number, and her mondo purse rings. How far would she go without phone or purse? But it's just like her to casually leave things that almost everyone would consider necessary. Better than tipping off Stanhope, whom she is determined to save. She's back to essentials: wallet and keys. Her sketchbook is in the car.

She went to work distracted and found herself suspended, so she made the leap she'd been considering. I wander the apartment, looking for clues. Open every zipper in Gaya's purse and dump the contents of each compartment on the floor. Flash drives, store coupons, gift cards, glasses, a couple of plastic dinosaurs, a jar of roasted almonds, hair tools, mints, the carnival wristwatch, a bag filled with receipts, a bag filled with business cards, the phone, dog treats, five emery boards (*Eva!*), a phone charger, tampons, a puzzle book, a mini-*Gita*, Thoreau's *Walden*, a map of Middle Earth, an old-fashioned letter—opened—and a partridge in a pear tree. You name it. It'll take days to figure out. It's odd. The apartment, the Mini, are kept neat and tidy. But this luggable is a portable junk drawer. It's Anshu's cricket bag. Gaya and her brother grew up believing that they had to keep bags of tricks with them at all times. For comfort. For safety. For fending off world sorrow.

I keep thinking of *Katy Sue*. It's another way of thinking of Gaya. Can I take her purse with me to Dana Point? Then I really would be stealing, in the eyes of the law. Staying put, in Gaya's apartment, might also be illegal, technically. I curse the considerations of rights and property that spill from torn intimacy. She might come back, so I stay. Sort and re-sort the contents of the purse. The receipts are from a standard assortment of local businesses—no pattern that I can see. The business cards are equally unhelpful. The snail-mail letter is from Gaya's Uncle Bebo in Vancouver. I think she'll be okay with my reading it. Bebo calls her *Chamdi* and asks a lot of questions about her health. Eventually, he gets around to his own health, which is failing. Asks for advice in finding a nurse to help him out. He's too kind to ask directly but plainly hopes that Gaya will help. He provides contact info. Signs himself *Tapori*.

Gaya would show me the letter, explain the nicknames. Is she on her way to Vancouver? I call Uncle Bebo. His liquid voice is a comfort (*Anshu!*). I can't tell him Gaya is gone, so lamely ask what gift she might like. He says nothing about seeing her or talking with her recently. Suggests a puppy. Okay—she's probably still here. But she might as well be on Venus. I hate the distance between us. Time to back off. I breathe, try to meditate alone.

Without trying, with no malice, Gaya is feeding me the pain I dished out so casually. When I bailed, I distracted myself with travel and drugs and jazz and birds. How is she distracting herself? Where did she go? I wander the park aimlessly. Here comes Keiko, the dog walker, striding purposefully, hair flowing, halting to play with Chester at regular intervals. Keiko takes what comes. She asks about Gaya and I stupidly spill. *Whoa there, big fella.* I stop myself, mid-sentence. But Keiko bestows a musing smile. "I just read this great quote from Lao-Tsu. 'Rejoice in the way things are. When you realize nothing is lacking, the whole world belongs to you.'"

I see the truth of it. We watch Chester, the young-old sheepdog, sport around bushes and trees. For a few minutes, gratitude is my ballast. But it can't last. The idea that nothing is lacking is not supportable. Something is seriously lacking. The goddamn lack is in everything. Keiko gets it. She surprises me with a hug. Holds up a small fist in solidarity as she walks away.

As soon as I step back into the apartment, I see it. I had left the repaired toaster on the kitchen table—must have looked at it twenty times since I returned from the hospital. But there, in one of the slots, rests an envelope with my name on it.

> My dearest lollygagger,
> Everyone talks to Stanhope, and now it is my turn. I am sorry I cannot give you the future talk you love. The future is a blank, and I have to face it alone. I sought you out because I did not understand. Now it is I who must leave. I love you very much.
> Something is happening at the hospital—I may have made a mistake. I should find out about it soon. There is nothing to do but wait. I can no longer do my job properly—all this loss is a great distraction.
> I must be quiet and decide about my career—disengage and see what happens, or what does not happen. I want to understand everything about us. Perhaps we are not eleven, just two. Isn't that always the way?
> You are ever in my thoughts! Gaya

Gaya is only doing what I tried to do, but I can't even consider the possibility of letting her go. Why? She's in trouble, for one thing. She left too much unsaid. Does she sense another death? Mine? Her own? I have to know. She needs her bulwark, her Stanhope, in ways she doesn't understand. My rejection of her leaving is total.

The deep friendship I was hoping for with Anshu came through Gaya. Men and women *must* be friends, or it's all a charade. So what if she's dangerous? So what if I am? We will live dangerously. We judged first so we could love later. A few times in my life, I've found myself in the talons of egotists who betrayed my confidence—who exaggerated and publicized every weakness I dared reveal. I know Gaya has been in those clutches too. But together we experienced the opposite: warm, equal union. Eleven. That's worth fighting for. I will use my time. I will find what is lacking.

❄ ❄ ❄

This morning, after Stanhope's sweet farewell, I'm met at the door of Blessings Hospital by an administrator. He says I'm on paid leave while they investigate Harvey Gray's overdose. Prosecutors are considering making a criminal case. Suddenly, I find breathing difficult, but try to listen carefully as a lawyer tells me what I must not do. Mostly, I must not speak about this case. They will want me to make a statement eventually and recommend that I hire a lawyer. I don't know about that. Where might I go to be alone and think? I walk the long way home, through unfamiliar neighborhoods, and work on my breath. What will I say to Stanhope? I have no idea how Harvey Gray overdosed. Perhaps I did it by accident—I don't know. It fits a pattern, anyway: I become too involved, then my help turns to harm. I cannot believe I laughed at Stanhope's paranoia.

I should leave now. I have been considering it. Am I strong enough? I must be, for Stanhope. I need his comfort and advice, but the talk would go on and on. He would try to help, and it would become hard to leave. At the apartment, my purse is gone. Stanhope has taken it to the hospital, I'm sure. This is my opportunity—I must leave now. I have my wallet and the Mini and my sketchbook. I have to be quick. Writing a note for Stanhope takes a long time because my hands are shaking. The aroma of one of his pipes calms my nerves. I put it in my pocket.

Where shall I go? One of the doctors told me about a wildlife sanctuary not far away, in Parnassus. Yes—I seriously need a sanctuary. Not a place to be lazy, just a place to work differently. Stanhope talks about working with his hands and keeping his mind to himself. This is what I need. I will work hard in the service of animals. It will keep my mind off of Stanhope, the investigation, and all our lost friends.

Now I cannot drive safely and must stop at a convenience store. I sit in the parking lot and try to calm myself. In my jacket pocket is the rose oil that I use every morning on Stanhope's wounds. If I had only remembered this morning to rub the oil into his scars, all might be well. In the other pocket is Stanhope's fragrant pipe. Why do I need such comfort? As I buy tissues and an apple, laborers in filthy clothes come and go, buying terrible food to eat in their trucks. What does Stanhope call them? Lunch-bucket men. But these poor fellows don't even have lunch buckets. They have no one to prepare good food for them, as Stanhope does for me. The poverty shows on their faces. My Stanhope lunch is in the purse I left at home. He was bringing it to me. Well—I cannot keep indulging in this way, so I buy a newspaper and find a puzzle, which reminds me of Gemma. Recovery is my only goal at this moment. Time does not matter, so I have a small meditation. Then I work the puzzle, eat the apple, and watch the men in ragged clothes look for comfort.

The slow drive to Parnassus sharpens my awareness. The sanctuary itself is restful to ear and eye. There is no one at the reception kiosk. I should have made an appointment, but waiting is all right. A big roar makes me jump, but then I love the roaring. It fills me with wonder and gives me confidence. Now I imagine a future again—just a small one. It is presumptuous to assume I will fit in, but surely an organization in the service of animals always needs help. One of the things I like about being a nurse is that you can never really misrepresent yourself. If you don't know something, you must say so. You cannot pretend to know something or guess at what might be correct in a situation. Lives depend not only on the knowledge and awareness of medical professionals but also on the professionals being honest about what they *don't* know. I think the same must be true at a wildlife sanctuary.

Irene is so welcoming that I'm sure I have made the right choice. She looks familiar to me and I to her. Soon we work it out—she is Dennis Murphy's sister. Dennis was another patient who died—the partner of Pigeon. We thought he would live with an expanded criteria kidney. We have become adept at that kind of thing. But sometimes it does not work, and everyone becomes discouraged again. I try to apologize, but Irene will not indulge that. She takes the time to say how much she loved her brother, but she won't speak again of his loss. That's for my sake, probably, but I think she cannot really think of it anyway. She's too busy to be burdened continually with sadness. And she obviously loves this work. As I fill out the volunteer application, she tells me about some of her favorite animals. Jupiter, the grizzly, loves apples. Greta, the tiger, likes to show her belly. Hector, the young mountain lion, stalks everything. I can start right away.

Anshu would love the air up here. And the beautiful oaks. The woods are open and airy. There are lions, tigers, and bears of all varieties, with some domestic animals as well. The dogs, cats, donkeys, and goats are a wonderful surprise. In town, I find a place to stay in an old hotel that has been converted to apartments. This is all very easy. I love my little dharma job already. Thanks to Anshu, I needn't worry about money. All I have to do is keep my mind within the sanctuary. Before I can think about whether I should have a friend, I have a friend. Irene is my next-door neighbor. She seems proud that we know each other through Dennis. Certainly, Stanhope's trick of avoiding talk of the past works in her case. Irene is always in the present, making jokes. "All of the animals had a hard time, one way or another, but don't let any of them give you a sob story. Nobody's ribs are showing. They do all right for themselves." If she is surprised or upset, she says, "Jeez-o-Pete." It always makes me laugh.

I'm happy to start in the kitchen, making food for all the animals, wild and domestic, and sometimes for people. It's simple and a big change for me. My chai is very popular. And I love learning about all the beasts. Most are healthy, but some limp or have bald patches from mistreatment. Bianca, a young white tiger with hip dysplasia, is a favorite. White tigers are artificially produced by inbreeding, solely to make a profit. They are often as unhealthy as they are beautiful.

The amount of food required for the predators is a shock. Most of it comes from large grocery stores. We pick it up almost daily, and sometimes, I drive the truck. I also do clerical work. Mostly I hide in the kitchen, preparing food—bloody protein mixtures for the big cats and peanut butter and jelly sandwiches for the bears. Everyone likes the really large animals—the Kodiaks and male cats. But I like Hazel, a small black bear with nice manners. She waits her turn at the feedings. I suppose you could say that she is forced to do that. But she seems more refined anyway. She really makes an effort socially. She walks around with every one of the other bears. The big fellows respect her.

No contact with the wild animals is allowed. We can get close to them during feedings and exchange looks—even darshan looks, I think. But we cannot touch them. I don't know about my cohorts, but I feel closer to the farm animals because I can touch them. Every mammal craves touch, I think. I've often been able to provide comfort in my profession by holding someone's hand. Now they say we should not do that. But the habit is hard to break, especially with old patients. And I miss holding Stanhope's hand. I compensate by rubbing the heads of Fred and Ginger, the donkeys. They follow everyone around—especially me because I spoil them. I love their relationship. They are always together, always touching.

I sketch a lot and work hard so that I'm exhausted when I go to bed. Lemon and honey with ginger—chai in the mornings—keeps me going. I manage to avoid thinking about the hospital investigation, but I think a lot about my patients. If I made a mistake, I need to find another profession.

I feel as though I am falling again, through an empty sky. No one can see or hear me—not even me. I know this lightless place. I died in just this way, a long time ago, for Mahir. We lived in the same neighborhood. He was four years older than me, but I saw the child in him. He was always pushing his thick hair off his forehead. I loved the human futility of this back-and-forth. Mahir grew to be a cold, tall man, like his father. They used their stature. They would stand straight, with their heads back, and ask a high price for everything. But I loved the little boy who fought with his widow's peak all day. I could still see the boy, way up there, behind the demanding eyes. The boy was gentle with me, and the man remembered how to be gentle—until the end.

Mahir was learning the spice business from his father. I would go with them, sometimes, to talk to the farmers. I loved the rich colors and aromas. The father, Saan, encouraged this. He would speak with me as Mahir's equal, as if we would be partners in the business. Every time Mahir suggested something, Saan would ask my opinion. I loved imagining my future with Mahir, our success together. I loved a lot then. I was trying to see and be seen in darshan ways. I wished to be loved by

Mahir but also wished to be loved by the world. I tried to see everything with love. And it was working. Love was coming to me—from my family and the farmers and their animals and Mahir. Eventually, it even came from a very proud man—Saan. Everyone was afraid of Saan, but he was kind to me. I was changing the world.

We talked every day about the future of the business. Saan said that it might take time, but we would all become rich. We were going to have a fleet of trucks to reach more lucrative markets. Mahir was going to modify some software to analyze the logistics and find new places to sell. Honestly, I was seduced by this. Spices are rich, beautiful, fragrant, and delicious, after all. Our work seemed a lot like my brother's gemstone business. My family had never had money. We were relying more and more on what Anshu was sending. Real financial relief seemed possible.

I thought I should balance this materialism with some spiritual feeling, so I would sit and look at sacred art—paintings of Shiva, Shakti, Lakshmi, Krishna, Parvati, and other gods. Their beautiful eyes were a comfort. The gods never close their eyes because they must watch out for the world. When Parvati playfully put her hands over Shiva's eyes, the world was plunged into darkness. Eyes are essential for the gods and for devotees who live among the blessings of the world. Darshan is sacred seeing—seeing things as they are and may be. I was thinking a lot about sacred sight when I worked with Mahir and his father. I tried to make my eyes as beautiful as the eyes of gods and goddesses—beautifully full of devotion. I would practice Hatha yoga and finish in kneeling meditation, among the sacred eyes of the gods.

Saan saw something else in my eyes. When I was in the office, on the computer, I would find him standing close. When we were all at the market, Saan would find errands for Mahir to do. I could not object because I had to show respect for this older man. I thought about talking to Mahir about it, but he worshipped his father, and I could not risk changing their relationship. I looked at my beautiful gods and decided I should be like water and flow around obstacles. So I tried to adjust. I avoided being alone with Saan and started spending more time with my family. I looked into various schools. Mahir hated the idea of my going to school. All he could think of was the money we might make, and I had become integral in his planning. I was useful to them. I had set up the books efficiently, so they could see how to manage expenses.

When Saan started touching me, I tried to work hard and ignore him. When that didn't work, I stayed home, considering what to do. I dreaded talking to Mahir about it. I tried to think of something else he could do if he had a falling out with his father. He had a fine singing voice, but artists have a difficult time making money. I spent more time researching opportunities for Mahir than I spent researching schools for myself. I realized I might have to leave the relationship for Mahir's sake. I worried so much that I could not eat. In the end, I made myself really ill. Mahir was charming during my illness. He brought me his mother's saag curry and talked to me through my window at night. He even sang a Sandhaya Rani lullaby we had both loved as children. It's about a girl who becomes fascinated by stars, imagining them as pearls falling from a necklace.

After my recovery, I went to the office, but something had changed. Mahir and Saan stared down at me in silence. Mahir was pale and shaken. I forced myself to stay but collapsed into a chair. When I insisted on an explanation, Saan walked out. Such a coward! In tears, Mahir explained that Saan said I had been trying to seduce him with my eyes. That was a shock. Saan had accused me before I could accuse him. I hardly knew how to respond. I told Mahir what had really happened, but it was too late. He knew I was telling the truth, but he could not let himself believe it. He could not sever the tie with his father. He loved me, but he loved his father's business more.

I tried to make Mahir see the truth, for his own sake. We talked about *darshana* and its power. But it was all too late. He asked me lots of questions, shaking his head like a disappointed teacher. Soon, he was pacing and making accusations. I could see he was working himself into a temper so he could do something. What would he do? Would he turn me out? Would he confront his father? But he had thought of a third possibility. "He touches you sometimes. Is it so terrible?"

It took me a moment to fully understand this. "Yes. It can only become worse."

"You should not have made him think he could have you."

I felt myself falling, like a star from the necklace of stars in my favorite lullaby. How could there be such a vast emptiness? It was like the world disappearing when Shiva lost his sight. I tried to think of whom I could talk to. No one. I could not distress my family. I was ashamed of not rejecting the advances more forcefully. Mahir paced in a circle around me. "Is it not something you can endure for a short while, Gayathri? For me? For us?"

I had thought he might abandon me for his ambition, but this was worse. He wanted me to *prostitute* myself for his ambition. How could he love me and ask this? He must not love me. I sat still, trying to breathe deeply, but my strength was gone. I was still falling through a starless night. "Please don't ask."

He glared at me with contempt. I remained still, trying to bring the energy down so he could think—so he could unlearn all this *maya* and set himself on a new path. I slid from the chair to my knees and extended my hand. "Meditate with me." But he kept pacing. I closed my eyes. I could hear Mahir's heavy footsteps but immersed myself in *pranayama*. I gained control through breathing and soon found comfort once again in the lullaby. Then the melody melted away and a refuge came—celestial peace. *Samādhi.*

I awoke in the hospital with my jaw wired closed. Mahir had rushed me there, full of remorse. Though I was in a lot of pain, everything was now clear. Mahir and Saan came to the hospital often, but I would not see them. Watching the quiet and caring professionals who attended me, I realized I could be a good nurse. And I knew who would pay for my education. Anshu and my father would insist.

Not having to speak was a relief. I became an excellent listener. For long afterward, I could not kneel. I felt too vulnerable. And I could not close my eyes. I expected pain in the darkness—the pain I felt when Mahir struck me. I felt the world was falling away because Shiva could not see. I became hyper-vigilant. I watched everything—and saw too much. I even developed insomnia. Every day, I felt worthless. I had believed in Mahir so entirely that I could not *dis*believe him when he set my value at naught. The rewiring of my brain—the softening of my eyes—was a protracted process. At least I had schoolwork to concentrate on. After two dark years, Anshu sent a message asking why I was not meditating. I don't know how he knew. Once I allowed myself to really think about why, the reason was clear. My kneeling meditation had been violated by Mahir's blow. Understanding this filled me with resolve. Those men had robbed me of my refuge, my *Samādhi*. Right away, I re-started my practice and began to regain the feeling of blessed integration.

Remembering all this, I realize I have been neglecting my practice again. Once more, it has to do with the belief that I am not worthy. Correcting this is my only hope. I no longer have Stanhope, but I have a sacred stillness. I will kneel every day, close my eyes, and trust the darkness.

Sub Specie Aeternitatis
(Spring)

I THOUGHT GAYA'S PURSE WOULD LEAD ME TO HER, BUT I'M NOT GETTING anywhere. Walking the park and sitting with the sapphire keep me sane. I can't watch *Trek* or anything else alone, so dive deep into Becker, the Jacks, pilgrim Dana, and a Julie Andrews memoir. It's damned Poppins of Gaya to have the memoir. Eva also read the book on restless nights, I recall, and now I know why: it's about finding your way home.

The lack drains everything. People try their small talk on me, and I'm grateful, but I can't engage. Pidge's words echo in my head: *I might be cut in half. I can't just talk about the weather.* For several days, I try to track word of Gaya through social media. It seems promising at first, but finally turns opaque, betraying everyone. Even docs and nurses and other caregivers seem to end up pouring out disdain. I have to swear off the me-me-maelstrom. I remember Bus Bredda: *Screens become screams. Too flat.* I'm out of commission until I stumble upon a retro CD shop and find Jesse Winchester, the songwriter Cub liked. The heartfelt songs draw out the venom, allowing me to mourn everyone—especially Cub.

Every day, I see Keiko and her dogs. Soon she'll ask again about what is lacking, so I ask about *her* life, *her* work. She says she uses some dogs for hospice therapy and invites me along. I can see the good of it. It might even be my work—but I can't do it now. I have to make a leap toward life, toward Gaya.

Gaya's phone rang a lot at first, but I couldn't make myself answer it. Most of the calls were from the hospital, where I'm not trusted. I've come up with a dozen schemes to get information from her friends there, but I can't make myself go near the place. Soon they'll come here because they can't reach her by phone. Until then, I can't risk being taken out of action.

After the first week, the incoming calls drop by half. Now I'm reduced to trying to puzzle out the repeating numbers that come in each day. Most aren't in her phone. The ones that I can trace are meaningless—political offices, charities. This inefficient winnowing goes on and on. Finally, one incoming number syncs with one of the business cards: Detective Ben Morris. Of course—he's on the case. It wasn't me he wanted to talk to at Gemma's funeral, it was Gaya. This rattles around in my brain for a couple hours. I can't access most of the features on Gaya's phone because I don't have the password. I'm not much of a geek. Who am I to invade her privacy anyway? I need help. But I can't talk to the hospital, can't talk to the neighbors, and Keiko's power is all on the spiritual side. I only have one potential ally. I take a deep breath and touch the last incoming number.

"Morris."

"We've got to stop meeting like this."

"Stan! On Gayathri Das's phone."

"Got me there."

"Is she available?"

"No."

"Hapless, man."

"Tell me about it."

"What can I do for you?"

"Help me find her."

"Tell me she's not running from someone."

"I'm not Billy Mills, Ben."

He says he's heading out to a spring football practice at San Diego State. Asks me to meet him there. The big man is easy to spot at the top of the bleachers, waving in the sun. He wears a black and red SDSU AZTECS sweatshirt. His eyes linger on the mondo purse tucked under my arm. He knows it's Gaya's. It's hard to know how to grill each other, so we watch practice for a while. He pulls two beers out of a cooler and hands me one. I hand him Gaya's phone. "Can you get into it?"

"How long's she been gone?"

"Two weeks."

"You should've come to me sooner."

"You might find a way to throw me in jail. Then I'm no use to Gayathri."

He gives me a knowing look and pockets the phone. We watch the action for a while. Ben is vocal, proprietary about the team. "Jule, come on! Hands of stone! Knees up, Speedy!"

I sit tight, sipping beer. Anything I say might hurt Gaya. Finally Ben says, absently, "I get a lot of good information at cemeteries. All that eternal rest makes people open up."

"No doubt."

"But sometimes you have to back off. People are in distress."

"Thanks for giving Gayathri a break. Gemma was a good friend."

Ben opens another beer and gives me his full attention. "You okay?"

I check for stubble—sure enough. "Yeah."

"I lost my wife too, Stan. Couple years ago."

"Sorry."

He looks at me strangely. "*Sub specie aeternitatis.*"

Now he's speaking in tongues. I draw a blank. Ben smiles. "'Under the aspect of eternity.' Spinoza. My wife used to say that whenever I was confused, which was about every day. She taught philosophy. I think it's supposed to mean that it helps to take a big step back and look at things from the heavenly bleachers. Where you can't see the numbers on the players or the color of the uniforms or even the game clock. A point of view beyond time and space. I've never made it all the way up to those seats. But sometimes I try. For Beth's sake."

The idea reminds me of the out-of-body experiences I had at Sadie and Gemma's cottage. How Gaya and I felt looking down on the Great Basin, in front of the dioramas at the museum, at the Grand Canyon. "I think I understand."

Ben nods. Turns back to the field and yells some more. After a nifty interception, he points proudly. "That's my son, Rafer."

The kid is something special. A long strider with a huge wingspan. A few plays later, Ben gives me a sour look. "I know you're not Billy Mills, Stan. And I have all kinds of good feelings about Gayathri. But I have to talk to her because an investigation has been ordered. A patient was overdosed. You and I both know that Gayathri has been around a lot of bad news."

He pulls on the beer and looks at me steadily. "Now you say she's missing. I don't know what to do about you two, Stan."

"Do nothing."

"Not possible."

The practice winds up, and Ben leads me onto the field. Rafer, Ben's Adonis son, stands by himself, helmet on. Now I remember—he's the autistic player I read about at the Pilgrim Grill, when I first met Connie. The kid is textbook safety: strong *and* free. He's on the autistic spectrum, supposedly unable to relate, but has become a lynchpin for a *team*. He is connected. Essential. Two teammates caper up to him, crab-like, and he pulls the helmet off to boom out a laugh.

Ben asks if I have any other clues for finding Gaya. I give him the purse. He says he'll call me. All the way home, I try to think of something I might say to Ben to take the heat off Gaya. I have to talk to her, but Ben will get to her first. The guy is good at his job.

Sure enough, Ben calls a couple days later, early. "She's at the wildlife sanctuary up in Parnassus."

Right. Animal therapy. "How did you find her?"

"The old-fashioned way. I talked to her friends at the hospital."

Not rocket science. You just have to be someone other than Stanhope Ellis. "You going up?"

"I'll see you there tomorrow."

"Thanks, man."

"Stop by the office and pick up Gayathri's damn suitcase."

I make it to the refuge mid-morning. Daydream about Eva and Gaya as I walk to the reception kiosk, until a lion's roar nails me to the ground. The sound is surreal. A woman waves from a hilltop and trots down. "Stan! How are you?"

Who is this person? Dennis Murphy's sister, carrying a bucket. "Irene! You look great."

She's lost twenty pounds and stopped coloring her hair. It's short now—gray, with chestnut-brown remnants. Her movements are quick and sure. She drops the bucket and surprises me with a hug. "I've been here for nine months now. I'll be a keeper soon. After Dennis died, there was nothing to keep me in the city anymore."

She gives me that sweet smile and claps her hands. "This is the work I've been looking for, Stan. Making peanut butter and jelly sandwiches for bears! I'll probably drop dead mixing the food someday, and that'll be fine. They can chop me up on the spot and feed me to the big cats."

Irene says Gaya has the day off. They're neighbors. I ask about Lester, her old Weimaraner, and his buddy, Popeye, the cat. "They're with Gayathri today. They love it up here a'course."

The old motel converted to apartments is easy to find in the heart of town. Gaya's Mini is not in the parking lot. I walk upstairs and knock on the door anyway. No answer. Try the door. It's open. Gaya is not big on security, and it's probably not needed anyway. The place is a standard '80s motel suite—a few rustic rooms and a kitchenette. I'll see to the Studie while I wait for Gaya. It's been shuddering for a while. I drive it around back and open the hood. Just what I thought—a ragged motor mount. I have a hunk of scrap metal and rubber that should do the trick. I run up to Gaya's bathroom and put on my old bibs. The repair takes a while because I have to jack up the engine to take pressure off the mount. Just as I finish, I hear Gaya return, so I walk back up to her place. The door is standing open. I lie on the sofa with my legs hanging over the armrest.

"Stanhope?—Stanhope!"

Gaya runs out of the bathroom carrying a roll of toilet paper. Throws it at my head. "It pulls from the *bottom!*"

"You always do it wrong."

She looks healthy and amused, wearing an open flannel shirt over a golf shirt and shorts. "You're the one."

"No. I'm *such* a one."

We blink at each other. I turn and sit up.

She points. "You have holy knees."

I rub my protruding kneecaps and gape. "I was about to say, 'You don't look so hot yourself,' but—you look great."

She takes a step back. "Oh! It's the animals."

I stand and smile. "It's *you.*"

She turns away. "Stop it. I want you to have a happy life."

"Then never leave me again."

"I am not safe to be around."

"No one believes that."

She busies herself with tidying. "You should talk to Detective Morris."

"I have. He's on your side."

She turns back and steps into my arms. We sync for long minutes. She has something in her shirt pocket: the pipe I've been missing. Gaya has had me with her all this time. *Put me in your pocket.* I want to joke about it, but realize I can't. It's her secret. The knowing is enough. We collapse on the couch. She picks at my ragged overalls. "You're always fixing something."

"We're fixers, you and me. Like Mary Poppins. Like Connie."

She kneels and lays an icy hand on my forehead. "Yes."

"But there's no fixing death. There's only—"

"Accommodation. Yes."

She applies another cold palm. "I thought I was saving you. I wanted to save you. But really—I hoped you would find me."

"I always will."

"God help us!"

We pick up Lester the Weimaraner from next door—acknowledging Popeye the cat, who shows off her pinball moves—and walk all over town. Gaya finds a voice message on her phone from Halle. Calls her back, elated, and they talk like old friends. I feel like a callous idiot when Gaya describes finding me in Oakland. I was trying to forget all that. But it's good to hear those two connect.

Encouraged by the mood, I ask about the investigation. "I am not supposed to talk about it, but—I need help. Harvey Gray, an artist who had just been diagnosed with renal cancer, nearly died from an overdose of opiates. He was in a coma for hours, but, fortunately, regained consciousness. No one knows how all those drugs came into his bloodstream. We were just about to move him to oncology, so there may have been some confusion. But even if different nurses administered his pills one after the other, it wouldn't have amounted to so much.

"I helped Harvey with messages and things. He's a brilliant visual artist. An expressionist. A gallery owner brought some paintings to his room and compared Harvey to Jack Yeats. I was always busy, but once in a while, I would hold Harvey's hand, and we would talk. The paintings are haunting, but also *exhilarating*, you know? Bold, colorful animals and people blending into each other and into deep backgrounds. He says he painted some of them on LSD. He kept trying to give me one. I think they are worth a lot.

"We could find no explanation for Harvey's overdose. Then we started hearing from his sister Emily in England. She called and wrote every day, threatening everyone. She claimed criminal negligence. That launched an investigation. Soon I will return for testimony."

I tell Gaya about Detective Morris. "He'll be here tomorrow."

"Can he not wait for my testimony?"

"Ben is on your side, Gaya. He was there when we met, remember?"

Gaya smiles sheepishly. In the morning, we walk to the sanctuary. "I like the roaring."

There's a good spirit about the place—rolling terrain, clean air. The animals have healthy coats. They're segregated by species but show interest in others. There's no elevated walkway, as at the Colorado sanctuary, but the animals don't seem stressed by being stared at. This sanctuary uses a double fence system, and visitors can pay to enter one of the fences for feedings. Stress among the animals is soon conditioned away, as they associate humans with being fed. The keepers and volunteers all speak and act in relaxed ways. A steady stream of volunteers and donors keep things going. *Eudaimonia.*

The next day, Detective Ben Morris shows up in his SDSU gear with eight boxes of pizza. We distribute them among the crew. Ben slips into easy jokes. "That roar went right through me, man. My whole life passed before my eyes. Damn near put me to sleep."

After lunch, Gaya leads Ben around the refuge. "You must watch a lion's tail. If it is twitching, you might be on the menu."

We veer from the big cats and Ben gets to the point. "I had a lot to talk to you about, Ms. Das, but I received a call on the drive up here that changes everything."

"What?"

"We heard back from Harvey's sister, Emily, in England. I thought she was one of those people who's always out for blood. I see people like that all the time. But I was wrong about her. Emily forwarded a message she found on her computer from Harvey. It was from an address she didn't know, so it took her a while to find it in her spam folder."

Gaya glances away from the lions. "I sometimes loaned Harvey my phone. He must have deleted the message after sending it. What did it say?"

Ben stops and holds up his phone. "It's a suicide note."

Gaya turns away and leans on a fencepost. I take up the slack. "He wanted to quit before getting fired."

Ben squints at the big cats. "That's right. Skip the pain."

"What now?"

Ben turns to Gaya, who watches the cats. "That *might* be the end of the investigation. But it's not my call. We'll see. Somebody could make the case that *you* wrote that message, to cover up a murder."

Gaya shrinks. "Oh."

"But I don't think anyone will do that. Harvey's sister, Emily, won't do it because she's satisfied that Harvey wrote the note. Me? I'm suffering from a serious case of no curiosity in the matter. Take a look."

He hands his phone to Gaya, and we read it together.

> Angels appear as needed, I'm bound to say. For weeks I have been comforted by Gayathri, a small miracle from Kolkata. She takes my temperature, doles out pills, and jabs me mercilessly. She admires my daubs and scribbles. Sometimes she takes my hand and we talk about the creative process. She's a rare listener. It brings Portia to mind: "The quality of mercy is not strained. It droppeth as the gentle rain from heaven."
>
> I won't die in that odious oncology ward, Em. I will die here, now, with Portia. I've given my pounds of flesh. Devious bugger that I am, I've been stashing pills in my easel for months now. Goodbye, sis. We had such fun!

Trembling, Gaya excuses herself and walks quickly downhill, toward the kitchen. Something tells me to leave her alone. Ben and I walk the long way around the lion enclosure, watching two females trot across their territory. We're missing the feeding, but there are advantages to that. The animals, no longer focused on food, watch us carefully and lazily play. The fences and buildings are well-maintained. I can help with that. Possibilities multiply in the bright sun and lavender breezes.

I touch Ben's shoulder. "Thanks for believing Gayathri."

"Sometimes the truth just sits there, winking at you. She was the truth in the case. It was a lot easier to go after *you*."

We meander back. Ben is relieved to be off the clock and talks about his scholarly wife. "Beth was hyper-conscientious. I mean, sometimes it was ridiculous. If we were out hiking, miles from nowhere, and she saw a single strand of rusty, old barbed wire across the trail—half-buried in the dirt for a hundred years—she wouldn't cross it. When she made professor, the dean was on sabbatical, so he couldn't sign off on the promotion. She felt like an impostor for months, until the guy got back. One night, the whole bed is shaking like a train is going by. It's Beth—freaking out about being called a full professor in print for the first time."

The listening soothes. As we approach the kitchen, one of the donkeys saunters toward it from the rear. We track the lionesses in the distance, absorbed in their certainty. "Living with that woman was an education. I could never be so rules-conscious as she was. She was a steady reminder that there are lines that shouldn't be crossed—even when they're hard to see."

Ben points to the big cats. "*Lions* that shouldn't be crossed!"

As we enter the lunchroom, Detective Morris is razzed about the pizza by some of the crew. As the banter thickens, I make my way back to the kitchen. Sure enough, Gaya sits at a table by the back door, drinking her ginger brew and eating a peanut butter and jelly sandwich. The top half of the door is open.

Gaya blinks hard and tries to smile but won't look at me. "I have to eat. I don't know what else to do."

"Sometimes, peanut butter and jelly is just the thing."

"For bears, it is always the thing."

She chews and blinks and stares into the middle distance. "I don't know about Harvey. I think I allowed myself to get too close. He might have died because of that."

"I understand he'll die soon enough."

"That does not matter. I should not have had anything to do with him going sooner."

"Harvey has already lived longer *because* of you."

She's not listening. "I don't know how to hold myself apart."

"Good."

The donkey arrives, taking full advantage of the open door top. Gaya wipes her hands, gulps tea, frowns at him. "That's Fred."

I walk to the table. "You think you violated the Prime Directive."

"Oh, *Star Trek*. Maybe it's something like that. Non-interference is best. I cannot help someone without interfering, I think."

Fred fixates on the last apple in a bowl on the table. I hold it up. "Okay?"

Gaya finally glances at me. "You need to find another one or cut it in half. Ginger is coming."

"Are you sure?"

She nods. "Those two are almost always together. Once in a while, they avoid each other for an hour or two. One time they stayed apart for a whole day. Fred followed Ham the dog around and Ginger stayed with the goats."

As if on cue, Ginger appears next to Fred. Suddenly, Gaya stands and rushes the donkeys. Presses her face into their knobby heads and sobs.

"I cannot escape."

"Please don't."

Her small body shudders. I step forward and embrace them all. She turns and shelters against my chest. I call on my superpowers but can't come up with anything that might really help. Why are the generous so alone? I wish I could still believe the burden was all mine. But I have to say something. "If Yama is here, it's the gracious, teaching Yama. And it's not just you. It's the two of us together. Like Fred and Ginger."

It's not enough. But touch helps. *Listening* helps. Gaya unpacks her despair, her resentment of this familiarity with death—the loss of naiveté, the loss of every innocent wish. The weight of bleak anticipation. The roller-coaster vertigo. The waste of Harvey the artist. The diminishment of watching one after another fall silent as the grave. I do my best listening. I ask and ask, until she tells me about a man named Mahir, and his father, who brutalized this trusting girl. For a blind instant, I imagine hunting them down and erasing any possibility of their hurting anyone again. But that would just feed hate, which insists on the worst of all possible ends. There can be no direct solving, but there's multiplying: one and one and eleven and so on. Here's Supertanker Stan, receiving all the pain, taking it away. An hour passes before we remember the apple.

Ben's voice booms through the lunchroom next door as we walk out with Fred and Ginger. The burros trot ahead as crows harry them from above. I tell Gaya that I've been thinking about a new crow category for the *Birds by Verbs* book: Wheedlers. Loiterers, maybe. Crows, jays, magpies—these birds are too smart, with too much time on their hands. They look and act like hoodlums, but study after study proves them squawking brainiacs—streetwise Einsteins. No wonder the insistent *caw* seems to demand an answer. Beyond the aerobatics, the tool-using, tobogganing, and general showing off, there's real wisdom. Social sophistication. I tell Gaya that once, Eva and I found ourselves watching dozens of weirdly silent crows roosting together. Then we saw one gnarly, old guy tottering on the ground beneath them. He was dying. We'd stumbled into a death watch. Crows die too, and the death of a relative, a sage, shuts them up. I'll never forget all those wise guys with nothing to say. Gaya's eyes brighten. She wonders aloud about bird intelligence and playfulness. Finds reasons to smile, which is all I want.

Seeing Ben off is hard. He lingers, spinning stories of his wife. He's naturally hilarious, but his isolation is clear and sobering. I find myself hoping that his resonance with these animals might amount to something. Fred and Ginger follow us out to his car, adding ceremony to the leave-taking. Ben calls them beauties and promises to return. Writes a check to the sanctuary. I extend a palm. "Don't cross any lions."

My hand disappears in his. He nods. "Sub specie aeternitatis."

Gaya laughs. "What!?"

I start to explain but am silenced by a lion's roar. Gaya laughs and gestures, making clear that this is all she needs to hear. Ben steps closer, beaming, and is rewarded with a hug. As he drives away, Gaya pats my chest. "A detective and a philosopher. I wonder what they talked about?"

"Everything. Just like us."

"Yes. I am the detective."

"You think?"

Gaya takes some short shifts and sleeps hard for the next two days. We walk for miles. Four messages from Blessings Hospital trickle in. The investigation has been terminated. Her job is waiting. The news triggers longer walks and bouts of sketching. Gaya wants to return to nursing, wants to stay in Parnassus, wants to care for her uncle in Vancouver. All *I* want is her. She still has my pipe—probably in that purse of hers. We have plans to make but talk only of animals. I stay busy fixing things. The employees and volunteers are wonders. Most started in traditional careers that were blighted by competition and greed. The stories are fascinating, but I try to focus on future talk. The one exception: Sadie's grandson Theo. A few of the old-timers remember him.

A huge wind generator dominates the sunrise corner of the ranch. It needs maintenance, so I volunteer to scale the thing. It's just the job for a crow's nester like me. I get it done with the help of a manual, special tools, and a blistering set of curses. It pays off. Gaya looks as proud as she might be of any power-forward MD. Day by day, we feel valued here. It's easy to imagine staying on. Disagreements occur, but nobody gets their hackles up. The work filters out egos and control freaks. Everything is for the animals, and workarounds are the order of every day. The old hands are chatty and helpful; the newbies trail along in silence. Children and grandchildren come and go. The kids know what's happening here: curation.

Irene is joyful and attentive to Gaya and me. It pleases her that she knew us individually, before we met. Often we eat together, and she's always presenting something from her beloved blender. She loves our love, and we love her middle-aged blooming. I have to admit that her transformation is probably not the sea change it first seemed. My blind assumptions exaggerated her growth. *The time to make up your mind about people, Mom, is never.* We work out schedules for sharing Lester and Popeye, who gain confidence from the extra attention. Popeye is always ready for ball-on-the-stairs. Lester is too leggy to be a competitor, but gamely bounds up and down the steps, never once getting the ball. Popeye celebrates her victories by hurling herself into Lester's bed.

Irene's bluff manner reminds me of Connie. She has an easy work patter. All the animals are "children" or "boyfriend" or "girlfriend." Gaya is "Sweetness." One day she tells me that a tiger is coming out from Colorado in a swap.

"For what?"

"A predator to be named later!"

Turns out there's a complication for us there. Gaya tells me that Donna Duran, Chuck's daughter, is her primary contact at the Colorado sanctuary. I should have guessed the kid would end up working there. She's thrilled to have found Gaya again and determined to accompany the tiger out west for a reunion. Gaya is flattered but also intimidated. She's already spread thin, looking after old patients, the animals, Uncle Bebo, me. The sketching sessions become more private and prolonged. She tells Donna that she may not be at the refuge much longer.

Family duty eventually tips the scales toward Vancouver. We talk it out. The Harvey scare was a sign that Gaya is becoming too involved with patients. She needs a longer break from professional nursing. We could both go on forever at the sanctuary, but Bebo needs her. Nursing her favorite uncle would require a loving variety of professional care—the kind she's best at now. This brings my own family duties to mind. In a few months, with or without Gaya, I'll make my way to Maine for Dad's surgery. I promised, after all, and Gaya insists I follow through. Why else are we here?

We decide to slip quietly away. Donna seems drawn to us, but we're not ready to chance the connection. We tell ourselves we'll circle back when we have a better understanding of our work. Or when Yama is finished with us—if ever. Gaya transfers the Colorado coordination to others. Then she calls Blessings and gives notice. When we tell Irene, she nails me from across the room with a sandwich. "Jeez-o-Pete!" But she bounces back. "You just keep in touch. I'll tell you all about what's going on with Fred and Ginger and Hazel and Jupiter. Bianca is having hip surgery soon. We might get an elephant, you know. And your friend Donna is coming out. She'll be my roommate, poor soul. Lester and Popeye will love that. Just need to find her a good set of wheels."

"Stanhope, let's give her the Mini."

Right. The Union Jack Mini will stoke Donna's Anglo-lit fetish. It's a lame substitute for the connection she craves, but it will do for now. When we tell Irene about Donna's compulsive reading of Austen and Evans, she brightens and points to a sagging bookshelf. "That kid needs a good bodice-ripper."

- XVIII -

THE SILENCE IN SONG
(SPRING, SUMMER)

WE STAY IN PARNASSUS FOR ANOTHER WEEK, WORKING LONG, LINGERING hours while paring down our belongings and making plans. For the first time since Oakland, Gaya is fully engaged. She talks about Uncle Bebo and Donna and asks me about my family. Mornings are golden. Jupiter, the griz, shimmers in the light. The lion roars roll out like Buddhist koans. Bianca and Greta, the tigers, paw each other and doze. The donkeys, Fred and Ginger, follow me job to job. Hazel, the black bear, does laps with her buds. Hector, the mountain lion, slinks and freezes and slinks. Gaya and Irene run a jolly kitchen, scooping out buckets of peanut butter and jelly.

Our last night, I find a Ruby Rocket concert on the Internet. There's my old bandmate, Ruby Watson, and her female cohorts, pealing out tasty riffs. The band cooks so seriously that I can't stop watching. Gaya, Irene, Lester, and Popeye join me on the couch with popcorn. The women razz me about Ruby, but I don't care. Soon we're dancing ridiculously— Irene showing me how to move my feet—while the critters tidy up the popcorn. Sure enough, after more than an hour of soulful reeling and rocking, a redhead slows, sits at a piano, and begins Pink Floyd's "The Great Gig in the Sky."

Dark and intense, Ruby swings her guitar onto her back and steps to the microphone. As the song builds, she's as inspired as I remember—better, in fact, as her voice has a new timbre. This time the song doesn't use her up. She burns brighter, in fact, as she wails. Just when it can't be more other-worldly, a natty bass player joins in. Her falsetto compliments Ruby's throaty contralto perfectly. They face each other and trade interpretations of the melody like dueling guitarists. But there's no competition. Love is the driver. Shifting tempo faultlessly together, they kill it and bring down the house. Hug joyfully and interact with the audience. The song is meant to be about death, and was nearly the death of Ruby, long ago. Now she feeds on it. Probably with the help of this friend, she found the beating heart of the song and unlocked its secret—that it's about life.

The lions roar magnificently on our last morning. As we load Stanhope's Studebaker, we find a bra under the seat. It is not mine. We decide that it belongs to Window Wizard Bix's girlfriend—I think her name is Erin. My listening lover says he is pleased with this artifact—pleased that his Champion harbors a little story of passion.

We still have room in the backseat for Irene, Lester, and Popeye. We take them to the refuge. Stanhope gives Irene a folder of paperwork for the Mini and explains how to transfer the car to Donna. At the kitchen, we make coffee and sit on the veranda to watch the restless lions. Irene sighs and waves an arm. "I wish Dennis and Pigeon could have seen all this."

I embrace her from behind. "They see it."

Clearing out Stanhope's apartment in Dana Point is nothing—someone has boxed up his few possessions. At the marina, we walk along the boardwalk to *Katy Sue*, where we picnic and feed Skye's stale ginger cookies to snow-white gulls. Stanhope describes his sailing escapade with the Spuds and the dogs, making me feel almost as if I were there.

We cast off and repeat our old routine: a lazy cruise all the way to sunset. Stanhope smokes a pipe, and I breathe in the aroma. He says his father's pipe smoke always made the family feel safe. I take up that feeling, as if I am part of that family. We toast Anshu and everyone we have lost. We wish elephants on Irene, Donna, and the sanctuary.

On the boardwalk, we run into our sailor friends, Duncan and Skye. Skye is full of local news—as though she was mentored by Connie. "Wilma down at the machine shop is trying to buy Connie's grill. Her husband up in Alaska gave her a big divorce settlement."

Duncan tells us that the admiral is in a home on the coast. "We see him a lot, but he doesn't always remember us." They invite us to go along with them this afternoon to see the admiral. In the meantime, we walk to Mission San Juan Capistrano. Mark, the surfer, Caprice's person, is working in the gift shop. He confirms what Connie had alluded to: swallows don't flock to Capistrano anymore. We should not expect to see many. "We did a lot of work to lure them back—put up artificial nests, mostly. It helped, but I don't think we'll have irruptions of swallows here again."

"Are they dying out?"

"Birds are in decline all over the world. But I don't think it's that so much as that the swallows are dispersed. A handful still nest in and around the mission, but that's not what brings people here. We still have the history—the legend of Father O'Sullivan giving the swallows a place to stay. That story is still an attraction. The spectacle is history, but you can see swallows all over California in the spring. I see nests under bridges every day."

We spend hours at the mission. It is quite large: archways bounding green courtyards, a cemetery, a magnificent church ruin, a chapel, and great bells forged centuries ago. I lose Stanhope but find myself unwilling to leave a courtyard garden full of intense colors—bougainvillea, hibiscus, bird of paradise. Stanhope finds me, as always, and we luncheon by deep red hollyhocks as tall as Anshu. Now and then, swallows appear. Stanhope says that *darting* is their verb: nimble, pivoting, shooting like streamers. They are jewels of the sky, I think. There are not many—just enough for today. In honor of Connie, I buy a swallow figurine and a dozen swallow necklaces. I can be generous, thanks to Anshu!

We rendezvous with Duncan and Skye and drive in the rain along the coast to see Admiral Spencer. These two are quieter now, and more pragmatic. They talk a lot, mostly with each other, about the costs and logistics of manufacturing and distribution. The solar awnings business is really absorbing them. Stanhope gives me a worried look—I think he wonders if their sailing dream will be postponed forever. As if in response, the storm suddenly builds, the wind rocks Stanhope's ancient car, and waves crest the guardrails. Stanhope pulls into an overlook to wait out the storm. We discuss the sea level increase we can expect in our lifetimes because we cannot think of anything else. This is very depressing, but Skye comes to the rescue, showing us the admiral's detailed sketches of graceful warships. He might have made a living as an artist. Duncan says his talent came with a disdain for authority that alarmed his parents. So he was pressured into enlisting. In the Gulf of Tonkin, he discovered that he had a genius for organization and could be cool under pressure. Who would appreciate those talents as much as the navy?

In twenty minutes, the worst is over, and we continue driving—a little sadder, it seems. Admiral Spencer is sitting up, sketching, when we arrive. Yes—he has been in decline. His eyes are hollow. He puts the drawing down and reaches for me—remembering our talk on the boat after Connie died, I'm sure. This is an honor, to be singled out by a strong man in time of need, but I have to remind myself to be strong—to be cheerful, warm, and encouraging. The old gentleman stares at Stanhope, trying to place him, I think. Stanhope gives him a crisp salute and the admiral responds in kind, relieved to see one of his sailors.

Skye hugs him and shows off his drawing. The work is skilled, but the composition is weak. He once drew sleek ships that seemed ready to steam right off of the page. Now his subjects are the window, its sill, and the parking lot beneath. Yet the Pacific Ocean, in clearing weather, is visible from where he sits. Duncan says that Admiral Spencer's son paid extra for this room, so his father could watch the sea. But the great expanse, the stage upon which the admiral's life played out, is falling away. I imagine him being excited about drawing a ship but being unable to remember properly. He clearly glimpses the water sometimes but cannot hold the scene—he can no longer see big ships slicing through the waves. So he sketches what is small and near.

Perhaps I can help with this problem. I find Connie's swallow figurine in my purse and place it on the nightstand. The admiral's eyes kindle. This is something of speed and movement that will stay within his field of view. It might fuel the memory of a ship—or the memory of a woman called Connemara who loved swallows and creatures of the sea. I leave him with this distraction and retreat to the hallway, trying to compose myself.

Gaya requires holding when she returns. The admiral was never talkative; now he won't try. The rest of our visit passes in one-sided silence. But that's okay. Gaya has given him Connie's swallow, and I can outline his history—nothing comprehensive, just shadows and light, maritime weather, art in wartime. Admiral Spencer studies his swallow, but as we prepare to leave, Spence looks up, beams like the sun, and gives a big, childish wave.

Back at *Katy Sue*, we tell Duncan and Skye of our plans. I hand them an envelope and a set of keys. "*Katy Sue* won't take you round the world, but she has some bright days ahead. Maybe she'll lead to bigger things."

They protest, but we're adamant. Skye flings her arms around Duncan and gives a Celtic yip. They want to gush, but we wave off the embarrassment. As a diversion, Gaya gives Skye one of Connie's swallow necklaces. It's good to see them laughing again. Our last glimpse is of Duncan fussing with Skye's jitterbug hair.

It's a quiet drive to San Diego. Letting go of *Katy Sue* was letting go of Dennis and Pigeon. Letting go of the Mini was letting go of Anshu. All okay. It limbers our future. Gaya tells me more about her Uncle Bebo in Vancouver. She can't talk about him without smiling. He calls himself *Tapori*—vagabond—because he was the first to leave Kolkata and has seen much of the world. He calls Gaya *Chamdi*—brave one—because he recognized her courage even when she was small. Great: a man I need to meet in a city I haven't seen.

It's late afternoon as we wend toward Old Town. I turn impulsively off the highway and drive to the batting cage where Halle and I connected. The kid at the office hands me a big cup of tokens. Perfecto—a little exercise before dinner. Gaya bounces excitedly as we walk to an empty cage. I give her Halle's gauging eye. "Can you hit?"

"I was a good cricketer."

Of course she was. "This is different."

I demonstrate. Like Halle, Gaya loves my easy outs to the shortstop. I give her a sober look. "See? Plant your feet. Square your shoulders. Eye on the ball. Step into it."

She takes the bat, laughing. I knew she'd like this. She might even have a knack for it, though she resembles Halle not at all. She misses hugely, then bears down. Dribbles out a couple of grounders. Spins entirely around on another miss. "I've gained a little weight, you see. Too much peanut butter and jelly."

"Good. You were too thin."

She looks at me as if I need a whack, but speaks uncertainly. "I'm pregnant, you know."

No, I don't know. I mean, I knew it was a possibility—just never allowed myself to consider it. Didn't think Gaya, the gods, our foggy future, would tolerate such foolishness. I seize up. Gaya looks terrified. "It wasn't until I went up to Parnassus—"

My reaction is a surprise to us both. I grab the cup of tokens and throw them high in the air. "Doubloons—for dangerous living."

Gaya laughs. Drops the bat and protects her head from falling coins. We wrestle giddily. Remembering Halle, remembering Kerouac's mother, I kneel.

"Oh! Your holy knees."

Whatever. Everyone is present and accounted for. "Gaya, will you marry me? I have no prospects. Not much hair. And there's the Yama thing. But—I'll do anything for you."

She's cool. Looks me over. "Hmm. I think I might, you know."

The Hitchcock overwhelms. Gaya pulls my worried head to her micro-belly. "The opposite of death is not life, Stanhope. It's birth."

I lay hands on her stomach, willing genius. Her hands are frigid on my head. She speaks outward, to the world. "I think the only way to balance all this death is to have a lot of births. Not just this physical birth that we look forward to, but a hundred spiritual births—*rebirths*—every day. Or a thousand, you know."

I know. Holy shit, she *is* a goddess. She kneels and looks me in the face. "I liked what you said at the apartment about spiritual merge in the moment and physical merge in the future. You were talking about a child, I think. *Our* child. After extraordinary loss, we have gained everything."

I pick up the bat and gather doubloons. Feed the machine. Plant five pitches in deep left. Now confident, channeling Halle, Gaya does the same. We take turns, every connection a release, until the kid asks us to leave. I drop a ten in his cup. After a Captain Carrot meal, complete with prancing ecstasies, Gaya suggests we sleep in the backseat again, so we find a quiet beach corner. She's a *shakti* tigress, then instantly asleep. I dream of a swan beating enormous wings above a grinning Sam the Bear.

In the morning, we clear out Gaya's apartment and hit Dog Beach. Eventually, we settle on a bench under a tree for meditation. I do a better job of it than usual—emerge wanting to laugh. Find myself tracking a gaggle of joy in the distance. It's not Halle's Viking family, but it could be. Dad drops to his knees, roughing up two kids and a puppy. Thinking of Halle and her ring reminds me of Eva's sapphire. I pull it out, watch it wink in the sunlight: birth and rebirth. Gaya stirs next to me, stretching, beaming like the sun. I wave the ring at her. "Eva's sapphire might work for the wedding. I'll get something else if—"

She slams into me. "Don't you dare!"

DEH. *Don't you deh.* She holds up the ring. "It's a star sapphire!"

STAH. *Stah safiyah.* I take her hands. "We bought it from Anshu."

She blinks. "You worried so about your Spuds."

"You worried about Pippin and Merry."

We are worthy. Gaya laughs. "'I will take the ring, though I do not know the way.'"

Precious uncertainty. Children darting. Dogs loping into the waves. Diamonds winking on the sea. Sadie's bell ringing out: *eudaimonia.* We take it out for a spin, to Sadie and Gemma's cottage. There we find a shy girl doing her homework on the couch with Pax. She asks about Gaya's ring, and Gaya responds warmly. They talk for some time about rings and meanings. Then Gaya pulls out one of Connie's swallow necklaces and asks the girl to give it to her Aunt Dariana. The girl responds with such reverence that Gaya gives her a swallow necklace of her very own. Pax is gracious with us but dotes on the child. As we leave, I get the telescopic, out-of-Stan sensation I always feel here. Does Gaya feel it too? She blinks at me dreamily and asks if I have more photos of Eva.

We spend most of the afternoon at the hospital. I'm given the eye again when we walk in, but Gaya is out front about our relationship. She introduces me as her fiancé. Shows off the ring and goes on surprisingly about my histories, my bookselling, my scaling the wind generator, and the heroism in window washing. That brightens the mood. Stan was a stalker. Stan*hope* is Daddy Wisdom.

Gaya has made arrangements to meet with a baby doc, so I leave her and walk back to the Studie. Pick up *The Doors of Perception* and head for the park. After losing myself in birds and verbs for a while, I settle on a bench with Uncle Aldous Huxley. Here comes Keiko, the dog walker. This time she has a massive, old German shepherd with radar-dish ears. He watches me intently, looks intimidating, but proves to be half-blind and mellow as they come. We're companions for the next hour. Keiko asks about Gaya, and I find myself telling her the whole story, asking for advice. She shrugs and smiles. "Simplicity, patience, compassion."

Gaya asks me to go to Oncology with her to see Harvey Gray. Harvey's room is a gallery—paintings propped on chairs, leaning against walls, covering the TV. Textured blues and reds, mostly—brights on darks. Mammals stripped to the soul. The patient looks much the same: his healthy shock of salt-and-pepper hair contrasting with translucent skin, toothpick limbs. The chapped lips are full. A leggy woman with the same mouth stands next to the bed. She gives way as Harvey reaches for his Portia. Gaya takes Harvey's hand in both of hers while the woman takes a fidgety turn around the room. When Gaya smiles up at her, she reaches out to each of us.

"I'm Emily, Harvey's sister from Bristol. I'm *so* sorry about being a nuisance. I was just—terrified."

She keeps moving, examining the paintings. "I should have been here, really. But I'm here now, at last, for the duration."

Gaya smiles encouragement and checks Harvey's monitors. Emily fusses with his sheets. "I was working like a fool, distracting myself with stress—a healthy strategy, I'm sure."

I can relate. I like this giraffe of a woman. Harvey waves a weary arm. "Em—just need a moment with Gayathri. She's leaving, you know."

He smiles at the irony. Emily steers me to the door. "We'll find tea, shall we?"

We wander shyly to an empty cafeteria and take our cups to a wobbly table. As I shim the leg, Emily tells me she's an engineer for a shipping company. "It seems important most of the time. Now it seems nothing at all."

"I've never seen anything like Harvey's paintings."

"Aren't they stunning?"

"Arresting, I guess. That's the word. Were they really—"

"Done on psychedelics? Yes. Harvey does go on about that. He likes to shock people. It's all so dramatic—like his paintings."

I hold up the Huxley book I still carry. She narrows her eyes and laughs heartily. "Dear old Hux! We both read that one. While we were tripping our blessed souls out, as I recall—vividly."

"You like to shock too."

She flashes an evil grin. "It runs in the family."

"How do things look for Harvey?"

She leans back and sighs. "They'll try some dreadful things that might allow him to draw breath. But it's not living."

Simplicity, patience, compassion. I open Huxley to page LSD. Pull out the translucent windowpane and wave it. "This might help."

Her look of surprise is comical. "Is that what I think it is?"

"It's whatever you two can imagine."

She laughs again. "Of course! Like Hux."

"That's right. LSD helped Aldous Huxley die."

Emily looks around guiltily, but there are no witnesses. She stares at me for a long minute. Shakes off her natural theatrics. "How much—"

I wave a hand. "A gift to me, a gift to you."

Wanting something to say, I tell her about my supplier, the Canadian journalist. Objectifying, he called it. She blows out her cheeks. "You are a dear."

"Things should go where they belong."

I hand her the gel tabs. "Fifty milligrams each. You can find your sweet spot."

She drops the bag in her purse and grins. I give her a hard squint. "No one in the medical profession can know about this."

"Quite right."

As we re-enter Harvey's room, Gaya holds up an inspired slab of inter-dimensionality. Figures emerge from the painting: a chestnut foal lying quietly, ringed by maned humans. There's a rough delicacy to the young horse. The humans are eight wise, windblown mares. Black, with darshan eyes. The bodies overlap and blur together, unshackling desire. Dissolving it. Harvey waves a hand, speaking quietly. "Horses are often dulled, you know—overworked, ignored, isolated. They won't lie down unless there's something like a herd. But we let them stand alone. They can't dream properly."

The painting is a gift of dreams. A release from vigilance. Harvey eyes it wistfully, as a loving father. "I planned a whole series of equine phantasmagoria. Healing, you know. *Day*-mares. Some ideas are in my sketchbook."

His future talk is for others: *Here's the raw material for moving forward.* Gaya sets the painting against a wall and kneels on a chair, eyes bright. "I think this art is not just arresting—it is *renewing*."

A spiritual reboot. Harvey nods. "I do try to find—a *dawn* in each instant."

Gaya nods as if reassuring the world. "Yes. The eternal return."

Harvey waves dismissively. "Take it."

Gaya shakes her head. "We couldn't."

"Take it, for God's sake! Who else should have it?"

Emily steadies her brother. "We'll keep it for you, dear."

Harvey settles back. Cocks an eye at me. "My kingdom for a bloody horse."

I wish we could laugh. Emily points at the canvas. "Nine, actually."

Gaya curates—sets the canvas on a chair and moves other pieces around. Takes Harvey's hand again. Emily beams at us. It's as if we've all known each other since the tripping days. A nurse appears, dispensing hyperbolic art appreciation while checking monitors. We wait her out. As she leaves, she asks Gaya a question about another patient. They walk together down the hall, talking. Emily theatrically peers out after them, closes the door, and waggles the bag of windowpane with a pirate grin.

"Harvey, Stanhope brought us these brilliant dimples!"

Harvey holds up a scrawny fist. "Moksha."

They talk excitedly, like children raiding the liquor cabinet. Emily allows Harvey to fondle the stuff before she stashes it back in her purse, shushing her brother. When Gaya returns, Emily insists that the two of them go for a walk. She needs to apologize directly, no doubt. When they're gone, Harvey gives me a bemused look.

"You're worthy! I was worried about that."

"Me too."

As I consider Harvey's work, a klaxon dopplers through the building from the street. I jump up to pace, hands over ears. Harvey looks on with the face of an angel. "Awful, isn't it?"

Breathing is a chore. "It's this—nightmare shadow."

Harvey honors the reveal. "Not *nightmare*. Just shadow. Perspective. A touch of beyond—the silence in song. I live for it."

It recalls the quality of mercy: flat calm. Placid as the thin Rasta I glimpse as we leave the hospital—his white-fringed face framed in the windshield of an old Plymouth turning into the parking lot. He smiles *through* me and waves. Bus Bredda looks fragile but fearless. Creation stepper, he.

We're spent by the time we meet Captain America Bix and his frizzy-haired, alabaster girlfriend, Erin. Bix and I have anticipated each other in our Wizards bowling shirts. Craft brews take the edge off. Erin tells funny stories about Norway and Denmark. She and Bix are as excited about our trip to Vancouver as we are. Their chatter devolves into touchy, dreamy speculations of what it might take to emigrate to Canada. By dessert, it's twenty years on; Bix is a tenured professor, Erin manages a horse and travel empire, and they're debating which school will matriculate their genius offspring. Future talk. These two don't have much personal history to trouble them. They're free to think of history in the largest sense. They're always well enough and don't have to leave it alone. I see them hooking up with Skye and Duncan on the far side of the world.

Watching Bix and Erin twine their fingers and visions, I remember Anshu, framed in Colorado blue, talking about *self-fulfilling* being the only true prophesy. Thank you for that, my Friend. There *is* no future when we don't talk about it. Indigenous peoples keep reminding us that we have to dream the world into being, but we don't listen. We don't dream—at least, not big enough. Yet! (Pidge's hopeful word.) The future that we occasionally get around to imagining is stupidly apocalyptic. "Poor curation," Eva would say. "Let's build dioramas that reimagine sanctuary and evolution. That model hope and power."

Bix brings me up to speed on the Wizards. Drow spends so much time with Nina's boy that Mom is getting jealous. Sport is their thing—USC and SDSU football just now. Brian leverages deals on season tickets, and the families go to games together. Bix has no interest in these things and misses our history talks. But it's okay—he runs a lot. Erin took my place on the bowling team and brings his lunch every day.

He veers back to history. "I'm reading about the Buffalo Soldiers. They were famous for two things: loyalty and taking care of their animals. Desertion was a problem back then, but not with those guys. General Pershing served with them and talked 'em up so much that they called him Black Jack."

I had no idea. Pausing for effect, I drop the keys to the Studie in front of Bix. "Here's your mount, horse soldier. Your Champion."

Bix shakes his head, laughing. "Living history! Too much, man."

Erin hugs Gaya. Remembering the fugitive bra, I'm tempted to make a joke about the backseat, but who am I to talk about that? A fist bump seals the deal. "Just take us to our hotel."

It's a jolly ride—Bix driving, Erin teasing him in three languages, Gaya and I digging the back seat views. At the hotel, I show Bix the parts cache in the trunk. Gaya gives a swallow necklace to Erin, telling her about Connie and Capistrano. Then—we're free.

When I rise, Stanhope is already kneeling, meditating against fluttering curtains. I join him. The morning is perfectly Poppins—breezy with sun showers.

Gaya and I pour ourselves into an ocean of glass. To be a supertanker of stories, I need to empty out like this every day—to make room for incoming. It's in the job description.

I motion for Stanhope to stay kneeling while I rub rose oil into his wounds. After this, I drop Cub's plumed hat onto his head. "Hope is the thing with feathers!"

I love a studious woman who can quote Emily Dickinson. A risk-taking woman who is expecting: expecting hope in a husband, expecting a place in the world for her child, expecting to laugh. Cub said a woman in love is the most beautiful thing in the world. Maybe that's because of her expectation—the seeing and willing of promise. It's a billowing spinnaker.

Stanhope and I walk two blocks to the train station, traveling light for a trip of unknown duration. I have more to discuss with him, more to show him in my sketchbook. Isn't that always the way? Having a lot to talk about makes me happy, even when the subjects are difficult. Some of my information will surprise my listening lover, but I am not afraid of how he will respond. I have seen him go off the rails, and he may do so again, but his love abides. I will go off the rails myself, as needed.

As Gaya and I approach the station, a border collie turns our way, straining in her harness to greet me. The woman she pulls is curious—does the dog, Astra, know me? I kneel and rub the overworked ears. There's the comet blaze. It's the collie I met on Dog Beach a year ago, after I learned the Spuds would live. The dog who insisted that I play frisbee with her. I explain this, and the women laugh together.

Recognition is everything, I think—seeking and finding through darshan eyes. "It's a good sign, Stanhope: Astra recognizing you."

Astra chuffs and nips my nose. She boards the train car adjacent to ours, and this thrills Gaya. Carrying cups of chai, we move from seat to seat like children. Gaya tucks under my arm and studies a map, breathing ginger contentment. Maybe gratitude is swallow-like: if you don't expect irruptions and stay aware, you get the onesie-twosies all day long. *Click-clack*. The flickering sun reminds me of the too-much/not enough strobe—the art-echo neon in Ocean Beach and the toolbox dive. I watch Gaya and her jade Shiva.

Astra is in the next car! I must force myself to wait for a visit. Stanhope pulls out the histories he has written and reads new passages. Being read to on a moving train is really wonderful—especially if the narrative has to do with beloved friends. It reminds me of Ganesh the scribe, who listened well and wrote out the epic *Mahabharata*, including the *Gita*, in one sitting. I tell Stanhope about Ganesh, to inspire him and ease the pain.

Gaya's belief that I might record meaningful history, as Ganesh did, is solid comfort. She shifts to my side and pulls out her sketches—

the ones I wasn't allowed to see. Each page is a portrait of a person we knew, merged with an animal familiar. The effect is haunting. The first sketch—a horse—is her best work so far.

This sketch is rather crude, but it will have to do. I try to explain it to Stanhope. "Harvey, the expressionist painter, is a horse because he remembered every horse left alone or overworked or unable to dream."

Gaya sketches left-handed, of course. I take the hand and speak to her art. "He soothed them on canvas."

"Yes. Admiral Spencer is an osprey with sharp eyes."

"The artist who went to war and loved the sea."

I keep turning pages for Stanhope. "Gemma is Pax the greyhound— greeting and gifting, you know. Always grateful."

"Gemma made a good end. Pax is getting there."

"They will always be together. Cub is Sam, the upright bear in Colorado. Such clumsy power!" I turn another page. "Connie is a wolf—a teacher and social savant. She was the beating heart of the community."

"Poor Connie. She couldn't save the swallows or Cub—or even herself."

"She saved *everyone*. Everything changed when Connie died."

"Yeah. Kevin's probably learning to surf."

"A big dog like him! He probably has to crouch a lot."

Imagining Kevin on a surfboard keeps us humming for miles. Gaya turns the next page slowly. There's Pigeon, with the eye of the tiger. *I always try too hard.* Pidge and I shared dreams for a while—might have swapped lives in an alternate universe.

The tiger sketch is my favorite. I have to hug Stanhope.

I can finally tell someone—Gaya. "Pigeon's jump was the bravest thing I've ever seen."

"He gave a lot of people hope."

I point to the gilded Pacific. "Saweet!" The world remembers us in unexpected ways.

"Dennis is a cougar—quick and loyal. Maintaining things. Understanding what is necessary. Anshu is a mountain goat."

"Of course."

"Strong and gentle." I find myself rubbing the beautiful eyes.

Gaya turns the page to Sadie. This one's even better than Harvey the horse.

"I thought a lot about Sadie. She is the lioness we saw in Colorado. Self-possessed. Remembering someone, I think."

We talk about Sadie and Gemma. Speculate about where Theo might be. Gaya touches her micro-belly.

"We have other things to do in the coming year."

"Yes, we do. I can see the search for Theo becoming theatrical. Like Diogenes's search for an honest man."

I warm my hands on Stanhope's hot head. "*You* are theatrical. The job might be something like that, but in the end, we are looking for a real person. Someone Shiva-like, who may already be renewing the world." I turn to the last page.

Yow. I have to stand and walk the length of the train. *Click-clack. Click-clack.* Of course Gaya sketched Eva. She does what she's afraid to do. The histories wouldn't be complete without the curator. Eva is a raven.

This is the sticky bit. Stanhope comes back to me. I take a deep breath as he settles into his seat. "I met Eva, Stanhope. Anshu introduced us long ago. She showed me the sapphire. I did not remember until you gave it to me. That is why I asked for the photographs. Then I was sure. But I did *not* know how to tell you! I thought I should remember more of her, so I worked on the sketch for a long time. A raven is magic, you know. A messenger from beyond."

I smooth Gaya's unsmoothable hair. *Click-clack. Rebirth.* Here comes the proto-diorama: Eva in the garden, on the ladder. A raven in the roses. Fragrance. Pinwheels. A bounding dog. Swallows darting. Precision. Lenses broken. Reverence. In the distance, a foal rising, faltering. Rising again. The weather eye ascends. We trundle through endless dioramas, built by those who teach us how to die.

I touch Stanhope's dreaming face. "The faces in my sketchbook seem to radiate power. We did not know most of these people for long. Connie and Cub would say we had ricochet relationships with them. Even your life with Eva was not nearly long enough. But this connective tissue keeps us going, you know."

I know. Proteus in the whispering world. We shuffle pages—mix and match faces. Harvey and Bix would have hit it off. Eva and Gemma. Cub and Sadie. Admiral Spencer and Dennis. *Blood relatives.* Shadows deepen and merge. Gaya beams and removes her oval glasses.

"Anshu would have loved Connie."

"And Halle."

I ask the question I wanted to ask Anshu long ago. Gaya says she absolutely believes in reincarnation—the Hindu paradox that, though we will live many lives, we must try *not* to. The goal is to finally get it right—to skip another slog through this vale of tears; to live on in spirit.

"Anshu never talked about it. He said we should forget this linear, profane time."

It's the time-poetry Anshu spun after Eva died. Gaya holds up the jade Shiva.

"Shall I tell you about Shiva and Yama?"

"Please."

"A wise man prayed to Shiva to help him have a son. Shiva granted this, but he warned that the boy, Markandeya, would live only sixteen years. Markandeya grows to be wise, like his father, and becomes a devotee of Shiva. This devotion, together with a mantra given to the boy by Lord Brahma, prevents the servants of death from taking Markandeya at sixteen. Finally, Yama, the god of death himself, comes to take the boy. But Markandeya holds tight to a symbol of Shiva. When Yama violates the symbol, Shiva emerges from it and kicks the death god, killing him."

"Bam!"

"Yes. Shiva is the conqueror of death."

"What happened to the boy?"

"The holy Markandeya was granted eternal life. He is forever sixteen because Shiva is also the conqueror of time."

"What a guy."

"But Shiva had to revive Yama. The world was filling with people. Death is a necessary part of life."

"Exceptions eternally?"

Stanhope wants to lighten the mood, but I must be serious. "Absolutely none."

Gaya is not smiling. She takes my hand and runs her lips along the bleached hair of my forearm. *Butterscotch.* Suddenly, she rummages through her purse and pulls out the watch we won at the amusement park.

I hold the watch out to Stanhope. "It is not running at all."

I take the carnival watch. Gaya places a palm on the window, as if to stop the world.

Suddenly the outside world feels empty again. I find myself thinking out loud. "Shiva conquers time."

This one's easy. I drop the watch back in her purse. "So do we. It's one of my superpowers."

I cannot help laughing as I think of Stanhope running down the hospital hallway in his beautiful cape—the cape he earned, that was lovingly made for him.

On we roll. Outbound. Out of our own centers. Making and remaking our beds. Saving ourselves and each other. *Click-clacking* toward our final

scenes: Titian tableaus, clown-car pageants, proud gestures. We can't
know what they will be, but we can imagine. We can watch for potential
ends. Feel potentiality itself. Listen. We can be sketchers and scriveners,
rocking together in future, forward movement, believing the visions that
fuse on the horizon.

The only way to be a superhero, I think, is to be super human—which
means feeling uncertain. "I think sometimes we are strongest when we
are weak. Then we *must* connect with one another."

I'll buy that. A rose fragrance catches me amidships. A woman
who looks like Keiko glides down the aisle, toddler in tow. The child's
porcelain face teeters on the verge of possibility, and I want to laugh.
Remembering a ready smile, a sweet swing, I float a possibility. "Anshu is
a good name for a boy."

I must shield my eyes—of course! "It means sunlight, you know."

Solar power flickers through the train. We're slowing. *Precious.* But—
what's that? A Union-Jack Mini tracks us on a frontage road. Is it Donna? I
can still hear her keening at the sanctuary in Colorado. How many Union-
Jack Minis are there on the West Coast? The car darts forward. Is Donna
an accident waiting to happen? *Breathe. Let it go.* Gaya picks up on my
distress. The stitch in her brow returns, and her eyes dart across the sky.
But I remember another sweet swing. "Halle is a good name for a girl."

Stanhope was worried for an instant but seems to be recovering. I
can reassure him, I think. "I was thinking of Sadie."

Harvey's horse painting drops into my clear consciousness—a resting
foal. Fresh, free from desire, swaddled in expectation. It rises, dark limbs
moving through a coral sunrise: maiden, mother, crone. *Click-clack.*
Rebirth. Gaya. "Solid. There's a story in it."

Here comes Astra the collie! "Yes."

THE BEGINNING

Afterword

THANK YOU FOR SEEING *MORTAL WEATHER* THROUGH TO THE END. I hope and believe the work is uplifting overall, but if you are having thoughts of suicide, please seek help. John Green and others have described suicide as a permanent solution to a temporary problem. Everywhere and always, there are undreamed of benefits in seeing your life through to the best possible end.

I believe the world is dying from a lack of imagination. Bigotry, for example, is driven by the inability or unwillingness to imagine the lives of others. Imagination is its own reward, providing the essential foundation for living and dying well. Imagination plus love equals true compassion, which can and must be the salvation of the world. So please stick around. We will need every wise head and warm heart in the end. The kicker is that habitual compassion is the express line to flourishing joy or good spirit: *eudaimonia!*

KPMc

Acknowledgements

MANY THANKS TO THOSE WHO HABITUALLY FIND THE BEST IN OTHERS: Nancy Allen, Mike Anson & Jan Faulkner, Tom & Marilyn Auer, Jane Austen, Annie Banannie, Aimee White Beazley, Lori Ball, Michelle McCarthy Beck & Roger Beck, Dr. Ernest Becker, Dr. Mark Berkson, George Blevins, Roscoe Bosco, Diana Branum, Jody & Vicki Brown, Jackson Browne, Rae Bryant, John Burbidge & Bruce Robertson, Tyler Buttrill, Liz Caile, Dollie McFall Carnahan, Jessica Taylor Cass, Ethan & Justin Cass, George & Judy Cass, Bruce Cockburn, Alice Covergirl & Hazel, Dean Dinair & Kathleen Rubenstein, David Dinner, Rob & Carol Doak, Ralph Waldo Emerson, Mary Ann Evans, Lawrence Ferlinghetti, Jasper T. Fetchmeister, Deborah, Larry, Joseph, Jon, & Mary Findley, Ben Fountain, Dr. Dell Foutz, Dr. Viktor Frankl, Sarah Fuchs, Erik Gabbey, Delphine Gatehouse, Peter, Lesley, & Molly Gray, Ruth, Marvin, & Elwood Gregory, Moxie Grinface, Vince Guaraldi, Sheila Hackbarth, Edward & Paula Hamlin, William Hawkins, Thor Heyerdahl, Tom & Janet Hicks, Claudia Hinz, Anna Hoag, Mary Hopwood, Mark, Sue, & Sam Hoyle, David Hughes, Lauren Humphries-Brooks, Aldous Huxley, Stig & Inger Johansson, Charles R. Johnson, Dr. Jim Johnson, Hamish & Julia Johnston & Annie, Neal Katz, Bill Kellogg Senior & Junior, Erin Keogh, Ken Kesey, Bob Kirgan, Wendy, Steve, Ryan, & Matt Knudson, Kaki Kohnke, Diana Krall, Hilary Lane, Bill Leamons, John Leventhal, Kelli Leverson,

Barry Lopez, Gordy Low, Marty Lynch, Dane McCarthy, Dorothy Ruth Swinberg McCarthy, Jack & Dane McCarthy, Harry & Carole McCarthy, Patricia Elizabeth Porter McCarthy, Chuck & Vicki McCoy, Robert McFall, Helen McGill, Sarah McLachlan, Mike & Terri Maize, Kathleen & Tom Majors, Andre Mallinger, Monty Marina, W. Somerset Maugham, Natalie Merchant, Roger Mifflin, Dale Miller, Christopher Morley, Van Morrison, Sid & Linda Morton, Hey Nani Nani (and a hot cha cha), Tom & Denise Neu, Frank Nowell, Dr. Julie Parsons, Terry Person, Dawn W. Petersen, Aimee Piacentino, Ruthann Piacentino, Sherloc Piglord, Zephyr "Pinky" Pinkerton, Bill & Holly Poehnert, Pokey Porter, Elvira Bianca & Ralph Edwin Porter, Katarina Prenda, J. B. Priestley, Professors Ig, Met, and Sed, Bridgit & Jesse at Quiethouse Editing, Bonnie Raitt, Teri Rider, Sharron, Jim, Dorie, & Paul Riesberg, Dr. Jack Roadifer, Chelsea Robinson, Rick & Karen Russell, Ran Diego & Pilar Russell, Tracy Sage, Dr. Reginald Saner, Dr. Jaina Sanga, Charlie Schneider, Dude Sideleaper, Sharyn Skeeter, Zeke The Sneak, Osito Spiritdog, Teri Snyder, Ricky & Lucy Ricardo Strouse, Brandon & Kyle Strouse, Henry David Thoreau, Oscar Tennispro, Bill Tippit, Mylor Treneer, Susan Treneer, Pat Wagner, Jess Walter, Dominic Wakeford, Claud Wheatley, Pete & Gerli Willets, Jolee Wingerson, Jessie Winchester, Oprah Winfrey, Reece Witherspoon, David Woghan, Linda Wolpert, Jack Yeats, William Butler Yeats, and Drs. Joanne & Robert Young.

Last but hardly least, many thanks to 99Designs, Afro Celt Sound System, Aspen Summer Words, B&B De Zak, Barbed Wire Books, Barnes & Noble, The Beat Book Shop, Berrydin Books, Betty's Books, Between the Covers, Black & Read, Blue Owl Books, The Book Cellar, Bookshop.org, The Bookworm, Boulder Public Library, The Book Lounge, Capitol Hill Books, Capsule Reviews of Original Work, City Lights Booksellers & Publishers, Colorado Mesa University, Copperfield's Books, Denver Public Library, Dickens Alley, Down Under Books, The Elliot Bay Book Company, The End, The English Bookshop, Explore Booksellers, Firehouse Books, Gilpin County Library, Goodreads, Inkberry Books,

Innisfree Poetry Bookstore, Juniper Books, Kauai Writer's Conference, Lighthouse Bookstore, Little Horse Books, Owl And Pyramid, Libro, Louisville Public Library, Lafayette Public Library, Loveland Public Library, Longmont Public Library, Maria's Bookshop, Molokai Public Library, Nederland Public Library, Ocean Beach Library, The Old Sage Bookshop, Old Town Bookstore, Page & Blackmore Booksellers, Paonia Books, Picton Public Library, Powell's Books, The Queen's Health System, Quiethouse Editing, Red Letter Secondhand Books, Reedsy, Run for Cover Bookstore, Seabreeze Cafe, The Science Fiction Bookstore, Shorey's Books, Stage House Books & Prints, Story, Talk Story Bookstore, The Tattered Cover Book Store, Trident Booksellers, The Tunnel Inn, The University of Colorado Hospital, The University of Denver, The Used Book Emporium, Waterstones, West Side Books, Whampus Books, Whileaway Bookshop, Whitcoulls, The Womb Bookstore, and every health care organization, bookstore, book club, bookworm, and library on Earth.

Dear Americans: Please stop hating anyone about anything. Just stop. We are not victims or rulers. We are partners in democracy. Our future depends equally on great unity and great diversity.

Let's talk!

Dear Reader,

I hope you enjoyed *Mortal Weather*. I would love to hear what you liked or disliked about the story.

Also, please do me a considerable favor: review the novel on Amazon and Goodreads. You have the power to influence others to share your journey through the books you read. In fact, most readers pick their next book because of a review or on the advice of a friend. So, please share!

Please follow me on social media and sign up for updates so you know when my next books will be available. Yes, there are more! I will be releasing chapters of my upcoming books on substack, so be sure to subscribe.

Thanks again for spending your valuable time with the colorful characters of *Mortal Weather*. Let's connect again soon.

KPMc

www.kpmccarthy18.com
18kpmc@gmail.com
facebook.com/KPMcMW/
instagram.com/mortalweatherguy/
kpmccarthy.substack.com

About the Author

AMONG OTHER THINGS, KEVIN PATRICK "CAPTAIN COHERENCE" McCarthy has been a geothermal geologist, technical writer, and screenwriter. For six years, he ran a critique service and published a quarterly review: Capsule Review of Original Work (CROW).

His published work includes two nonfiction books, about 35 poems, and more than 40 essays. It has been featured by many orgs and pubs, including Bridport, New Millennium, *Common Ground, Writers Resist, The Chicago Tribune, The Mountain Gazette*, and *The Bloomsbury Review*. "Porterhouse Jive" won a Vonnegut parody contest in 2007. *Spirit Rocks* won a Silver REMI Award for dramatic screenplay at the 2008 Houston International Film Festival. *Mortal Weather* was a semifinalist in the 2020 University of New Orleans Press Lab competition. "Enough Sky," the epigraph for *Mortal Weather*, was Commended by The Poetry Society (UK) in 2014.

Kevin is a fourth-generation Coloradan who explores the world with wife, Tricia, and dog, Nani.

PHOTO CREDIT: BONITA HENSLEY

Printed in the USA
CPSIA information can be obtained
at www.ICGtesting.com
JSHW020210161023
R13019500002B/R130195PG50194JSX00002B/1